PRAISE FOR IRVINE WELSH

On *Trainspotting*

The language in *Trainspotting* is . . . exhilarating once you get the hang of it, and finally poetic in its complications. . . . Literary in the best sense, using language at every level to tell a story." —Jane Mendelsohn, *New Republic*

"Blisteringly funny. . . . Don't abandon everything for the movie. It's worth making the effort with *Trainspotting* not merely because relatively few writers have rummaged through this particular enclave of British youth culture, but because even fewer have dug there so deeply."—*New York Times Book Review*

On *The Acid House*

"Irvine Welsh is the real thing—a marvelous admixture of nihilism and heartbreak, pinpoint realism (especially in dialect and tone) and almost archetypal universality." —David Foster Wallace

"Welsh gives free range to his dangerously fertile imagination. . . . The constant [in the stories] is Mr. Welsh's sure-handed, incendiary use of language. . . . Poetic and enigmatic." —*New York Times Book Review*

On *Marabou Stork Nightmares*

"For anyone who gets high on language, [*Marabou Stork Nightmares*] is a fantastic trip . . . a real tour de force." —Madison Smartt Bell, *Spin*

"Extremely funny . . . as clever as Alasdair Gray, as elegant as Jeff Torrington, as passionate as James Kelman, Welsh has got it all." —Tibor Fischer

"A powerful investigation of a life gone bad, written in a demanding and insistent prose that gives no quarter." —*New York Times Book Review*

"*Glue* is a great example of why Welsh caused such a fuss in the first place—and, on its own terms, as thrilling and ambitious a book as Welsh has written."
—Dennis Cooper, *Los Angeles Weekly*

"Welsh is at his best here. *Glue* is epic in scope and daring in form."
—*Time Out New York*

On *Porno*

"Damn it if Welsh can't write the hell out of anything! A gleefully perverted farce."
—Ken Foster, *San Francisco Chronicle*

"Welsh's characters are a pack of solipsistic misfits, screw-ups and scammers, forever in pursuit of daft projects and concocting improbable rackets, the intricacies of which Welsh weaves together to hilarious effect."
—Lara Miller, *Salon*

"Brawling, bonking and Scots brogue aside, there's room for some solid satire—of gentrification, globalization, and the hypocrisy of Britain's Labour Government."—*The New Yorker*

On *The Bedroom Secrets of the Master Chefs*

"What begins as a narrative-switching character study quickly veers into Chuck Palahniuk territory. . . . Hilarious insight into everything from foodie culture to the dark side of *Star Trek* conventions."
—*Philadelphia Weekly*

"A family saga, a revenge fantasy, a *Twilight Zone*–esque parable, and, most importantly, a very fun read. . . . A modern-day *Picture of Dorian Gray*. . . . A wonderfully imaginative story full of family and sex and food."—Gilbert Cruz, *Entertainment Weekly*

"Tart sentences and bleak atmospherics. And the Jekyll-and-Hyde routine keeps the pages turning, even as it puts a fresh slant on that time-honored phrase, the Significant Other."
—James Marcus, *Los Angeles Times Book Review*

If You Liked School, You'll Love Work . . .

IRVINE WELSH

W. W. NORTON & COMPANY

New York • London

For Max Davis

Copyright © 2007 Irvine Welsh

Printed in the United States of America

First published in Great Britain in 2007 by Jonathan Cape
Random House, 20 Vauxhall Bridge Road, London SW1V 2SA

For information about permission to reproduce selections from this book,
write to Permissions, W. W. Norton & Company, Inc., 500 Fifth Avenue,
New York, NY 10110

Manufacturing by Courier Westford
Production manager: Devon Zahn

Library of Congress Cataloging-in-Publication Data

Welsh, Irvine.
If you liked school, you'll love work— / Irvine Welsh. — 1st American ed.
p. cm.
ISBN 978-0-393-33077-9 (pbk.)
I. Title.
PR6073.E47135 2007
823'.914—dc22   2007014665

W. W. Norton & Company, Inc., 500 Fifth Avenue,
New York, N.Y. 10110
www.wwnorton.com

W. W. Norton & Company Ltd., Castle House, 75/76 Wells Street,
London W1T 3QT

1 2 3 4 5 6 7 8 9 0

CONTENTS

Rattlesnakes

The air conditioner on the silver Dodge Durango had fucked up earlier: the filter and cooler malfunctioning. Instead of sweet, chilled air, it had inexplicably started blowing hot desert dust into the vehicle. It streaked their sweaty faces and hands, merging with the previous layers they'd kicked up during their weekend of intoxicated dancing madness. Throats, dehydrated by drug and desert, dried out even more, as tearless eyeballs burned. They had been forced to switch it off.

It had been a long trek out from the Burning Man festival, and a treacherous drive across these back desert roads. Now they were lost in this dust storm. Eugene's spine was starting to hurt; his large linebackers frame uncomfortable in the seat. The dirt on his wet and slimy hands was turning to mud on the wheel and it was getting hotter all the time. His big chest rose and fell as his lungs struggled to fill up with the warm, dead air.

This damn Dodge of Scott's! 40,567 miles on the clock and the fucking air con doesn't even work!

As the storm continued to kick up, the sky growing murkier by the second, Eugene was feeling the sense of his own stupidity snapping at him like a rabid dog. The short cut hadn't materialized and as far as he could make out there were no fellow travelers around of any description. Eugene studied his pasty, wan reflection in the mirror, his filthy hair scraped back in a ponytail, the sweat from it now running down his big forehead in rivulets of mud. Picking up an old white towel by his side, he wiped it, glad he couldn't see his eyes under his shades. Fatigued beyond tiredness, Eugene pressed on as demons danced slowly in his peripheral vision. A bolt of lightning crackled in the phosphorous sky in front of him. He was unfit to drive; he was unfit for *anything*, he considered ruefully. The drugs and the sleep deprivation had taken him into a mildly psychotic status quo, which was now even starting to bore him. He was praying for clarity soon, both in the wild environment outside and in his troubled mind.

One thought was burning him: Scott and Madeline should be awake to take their turns at the wheel. But he knew they were on a different trajectory to him, and so he'd been stuck with the driving. Rancorous bile rose in Eugene's gut as he pushed on. Thunder quaked and rumbled in his ears on top of a tinnitus bass line that he feared would stay with him forever.

This goddamn mess.

And Madeline. Asleep on the passenger seat next to him, his eyes straying onto her long, bare legs; tan augmented by surprisingly arousing streaks of muck, making her look dirty, real dirty, suggesting a mud-wrestling slut dried out and he could see those legs right up to the cutoff denim shorts . . . running towards him on some plowed-up field . . . her long, curling blond-brown hair cascading onto her shoulders, heavy with desert dust . . . dirty . . . filthy . . . running towards him . . .

It was hot.

It was goddamned hot.

Eugene glanced down at his groin, and swelling was already very much in evidence through his camouflage shorts. The storm had made visibility poor and he could really do without the further distraction. However, the rational side of his brain was shutting down and his eyes kept turning to the easy swell of Madeline's breasts through her brown cotton tank top.

This goddamn cock-teasing bitch has been stringing me, and for all I know, Scott, along for days. Those lingering, enticing gazes. Then, when you get too close, she just freezes over.

After the festival they had elected to drive out to the desert for a yagé experience, looking to try out the contraband a Peruvian shaman had sold them. It had been Madeline who had spotted the tent of the Temple of the Mystic Light and insisted they attended the shamanic healing ceremony presented by one Luis Caesar Dominquez, self-styled Peruvian mystic. Madeline and Scott were more impressed by the slide show and lecture than Eugene, who had some good hits of X burning a hole in his pocket, and resented missing this German techno act he'd wanted to catch.

When it was over, Madeline thrust a pamphlet into his hand. — It says that Mr Dominquez trained for years with the Kallahuayas shamans of the northeast Lake Titicaca region, the Amautas of the islands of the Andes, and the Q'ero Elders of the Cusco region, who they reckon are last remaining descendants of the Incas!

Eugene shook his head as they stood outside the tent, watching the people file by. — I'm clueless about that kinda shit, he confessed. — Kallahuayas? Q'ero Elders? Means jack to me, he shrugged.

Madeline was unmoved. Eugene once had a sense that she found his open, straight-down-the-line, proud-to-be-a-dumbass act somewhat endearing. He resolved in future to be more circumspect in his ignorance. He recalled that old adage: it is better to remain silent and let people think you are an idiot, than to open your mouth and confirm this impression.

Scott was happy to pitch in. Eugene had almost forgotten how he read and preached all this New Age bullshit. He'd known him long enough to just tune him out when he started with that stuff. — It means he's the Bill Gates of fucked-up

5

shit, Scott grew animated. — It means he's one of the top teachers who share ancient and hidden knowledge to awaken the latent healing abilities in everyone who's ready. His eyes widened, big and spooky. This time Eugene listened with intent because he saw how much this crap was impressing Madeline. — It's all based on an ancient Andean prophecy that is part of the Inca legend of the Pachacuti – a time when the world is turned upside down and a new consciousness emerges.

— I'll bet the dude can get a hold of some good shit, Eugene conceded.

And that was when they'd approached Luis Caesar Dominquez, and the shaman had taken them back into his tent and discreetly sold them the yagé. Madeline and Scott were instantly smitten. To Eugene, under the ethnic garments, Dominquez looked as mystical as a vote-seeking politician, or a real-estate salesman.

But they had the yagé.

The setting was perfect; it had been a clear, cool night and they'd constructed a fire in the red soil and pitched up the big, easily erectable, family-sized tent they'd shared at the festival. Scott and Madeline had gotten very excited, and as they looked expectantly at the cups, they seemed high already. Almost in spite of himself, Eugene couldn't help pissing on their parade.

— That Dominquez guy is just a glorified drug dealer. He's got access to that shit and knows how to harvest and prepare it into the elixir. And he goes around with that lame slide show calling it enlightenment. Fuck, man! I should've done that the time I got busted for dealing coke in that shithouse on Haight; just given the judge a power-point presentation and talked about energy and go-getting, he laughed, exposing his big, capped teeth, replaced at cost after a college football training accident a few years ago. — That's if this shit *is* yagé, he added, then forced another smile as he saw Madeline looking grimly at him.

Inside each capful was a reddish-brown concoction. Scott took some first, with the others following suit. It tasted bitter and salty. They all drank a second cupful, as recommended by the shaman Dominquez, who had told them that it should produce an experience lasting three or four hours. Then, if so desired, they could drink some more.

The nausea seemed to hit Scott first. He staggered to his feet and moved over to a line of big rocks where he started barfing up. Eugene was just about to shout 'pussy' at him, when he was overcome by a sickening, queasy sensation, which seemed to start in the balls of his feet. Soon he, and then Madeline, were staggering toward the pile of rocks as they threw up small quantities of intensely caustic liquid, in short, wrenching spasms.

The shaman had warned them about this vomiting effect, but it certainly wasn't pleasant. The liquid had tasted far fouler coming back up than it had on the way down, and was so bad that they were all feverishly shuddering for a few seconds.

Then the effects started to take a hold of them. Scott and Madeline began to space out, giggling and euphoric. But Eugene was disappointed. He'd been expecting a really heavy trip and in the event it was all pretty mild. He took another cup. Then another. He didn't feel bad, but it was obvious that for Scott and Madeline it was the mind-blowing high of a lifetime. Eugene looked around the barren desert, and tried to see what they were seeing. He felt like a ragged urchin pressed against the window of a great, opulent house where a raging, decadent party was taking place. He upped his consumption to six cups of the elixir and felt his heartbeat race, but the big doors of the mansion house stayed fastened shut. Why was he excluded? Eugene had done big hallucinogenic acid trips with Scott and even, recently, Madeline. He knew that both were seasoned acid-heads. But they had their set of keys. Where were his?

7

As he sat wondering what to do next, Eugene heard Scott reciting something to an open-mouthed Madeline as the pair of them sat side by side, looking into the sky, — 'When the Eagle once again flies with the Condor, a lasting peace will reign in the Americas and will spread throughout the world to unite humanity.' These words are from the Andean shamans who believe we're living in the Pachacuti; a time when we must go within and know ourselves more deeply, to heal our emotional wounds of the past, and use the power of that healing to help others in their healing.

— That is sooo awesome, Madeline gasped. She pointed upward. — Lookit that sky . . .

While they were taking off onto another astral plane, all Eugene had done was to shit: loads and loads of it, deposited with the puke behind the closest big boulders in the rock-strewn terrain. He'd listened for a while to Scott going on about the internal purging actions of the drug, and then simply lain down in the tent for the best sleep of his life. Meanwhile, Scott and Madeline hallucinated, partied and talked till dawn. Something in Eugene had resisted the trip, and that concerned him. He recalled Dominquez saying in his lecture, though, that the drug often got you where you needed it. Eugene conceded that his body, with all the charlie and booze he'd indulged in recently, was crying out for a cleansing. Since splitting up with Lana, he'd taken up residence in several North Beach neighborhood bars, his psychosis drawing in on him, the walls of those temples of liberation shrinking to become prison cells. His jailers were the other drinkers and their obsessions. They would crowd his head with their stupid advice. He needed to get out of town for a bit, and Burning Man seemed to fit the bill.

It had been Scott's idea. Madeline had come along, in her usual pushy way, Eugene thought, although he had very much

8

welcomed it. He had tentatively lined her up as a possible replacement for Lana.

Eugene and Scott, old college buddies, had met Madeline last Halloween. They were drinking in Vesuvio's Bar when she came in with three girlfriends. All of them were dressed as Storm from the *X-Men*; skintight black catsuits, big boots and platinum-blond wigs. At first all the girls looked identical. It was a while before Eugene recognized one as Candy, a student and an ex-co-worker in a North Beach tavern he once bartended in.

They all chatted sociably, drinking some more before heading off to join the packed throngs of revelers on Castro. Eugene had found himself talking a lot to Madeline, but in the crowd they had all gotten separated from each other. As the night wore on, the carnival mood on the streets had then turned sour. One man was fatally stabbed as a small mob of Mexican youths rampaged through the crowd. They had taken exception to what they perceived as the hijacking of the ancient Day of the Dead ceremony by the city's gay community. Paranoia hung heavily in the air. There was a lot of jostling and screaming and Eugene, who was on a nasty coke come-down anyway, had been happy to call it a night and head home. That night he thought of that hot chick – they were all hot in that Storm get-up but the one he'd talked to – and wondered if he'd see her again and hoped that she'd gotten home okay with all the trouble of that night.

Eugene needn't have concerned himself. After this, he seemed to keep running into Madeline. The next day he saw her in Washington Square Park, practicing t'ai chi on her own. He'd been sitting reading a newspaper. She waved at him and it took a while for Eugene to connect that she was one of the Storm girls at the bar the previous evening. After a bit she came over and they went for a coffee, discussing the previous night's events with concern. Then he saw her again a couple of days after, in the City Lights bookstore. They went for a drink, which quickly became several; trawling some neighborhood bars they both knew, ending up in a place on Grant. Despite Madeline being quite new to town (she'd told him she'd come in from Cleveland at the end of last summer), they had a few mutual haunts and wondered how it was that they hadn't run into each other before. They planned to go for some sushi, but somehow ended up at a dive bar on Broadway, sandwiched between strip clubs and sex shops that buzzed with neon. Eugene was impressed that Madeline was totally at ease there, even though she was the only woman present who wasn't obviously touting for business. They'd talked about sex then, but in an abstract way, as he was at the time too depressed about the Lana situation to make a move.

They started hanging out a lot together: Madeline, Eugene, and Scott. Even at the time, he thought it was weird the way she fussed over them like they were fags, bought them little presents and cards on their birthdays and the like. When Scott had mentioned the Burning Man trip to Eugene, she'd interjected, — Count me in! with such bushy-tailed zeal that it would have been an injurious snub not to do just that.

And while Eugene was rapt in his anticipation, Scott appeared downcast. He liked to engineer what he called 'buddy time'. A frat-boy thing, Eugene supposed.

The developing relationship with Madeline was mystifying to him, though. Eugene was twenty-six and had never been friends with a chick he hadn't banged. He wondered whether she was a dyke, but then she would casually go and bring up some guy she'd once fucked. He knew everything about her and nothing at the same time. In those North Beach bars Madeline would sometimes look at him so tenderly; it unequivocally told Eugene that she harbored fervid passions for him. She was still shy of twenty, and he wondered how much experience she'd really had with guys. One time they'd kissed drunkenly, but not particularly passionately, with Eugene holding back, still wondering about Lana. But when his former girlfriend's ghost receded, Eugene's feelings for Madeline grew exponentially. Sometimes he could sense that she wanted him, perhaps so desperately that if she let herself go, she'd fall totally, unreservedly in love and give herself completely to him. Be his. In his power. To be neglected. Hurt. And he wanted to tell her: I'm not that kind of guy. I don't know what sort of shit you heard about me and Lana, but I'm not that kind of guy!

But it was only sometimes that she looked at him like that. On other occasions the look of loathing she vented at him could glaciate his blood.

So Madeline confused Eugene. He'd never met a girl like her before. That was because, despite his wastrel behavior and occasional bohemian affectations, his big, strong, athletic build and his overt sporting sensibilities did not encourage vacillation in girls, who tended to be obviously attracted or completely repelled from the off. But Madeline was different; a constant enigma to him.

Eugene only tried to get beyond first base once after that. A drunken pass. He'd attempted to kiss her again, this time more urgently, at a party. In a dirty kitchen that shrunk with the beer and cocaine until they were in each other's faces, a field of intensity insulating them from the rest of the festivities. It had seemed the right time. But Madeline pushed an implacable, upturned hand onto his big chest and said: — One thing, Eugene: you and I will never, ever fuck.

He'd woken up the next morning, despondent in his crushing hangover. The phone went. It was Madeline. Before he could apologise, she beat him to the punch. — I'm so sorry about last night, Gene. I was kind of loaded. I guess I said a lot of things I didn't mean.

— Fine, but I —

— Look, I gotta go and sleep it off. Call you later, babe, and she hung up.

And this short message was enough to erase Eugene's despair and to offer him fresh hope.

Mostly, though, when they were alone together, which meant without Scott, they'd talked about Lana. Invariably Madeline brought this up. It was as if she knew that it crushed Eugene's libido around her. She would listen intently, eager eyes widening, studying his every reaction. And Eugene had to concede: Madeline sure was a good listener. Even if he began to suspect it was all purely to educate herself, then that quality had been welcome. Because the others, even Scott, just seemed to talk about *them*. They expected him to forget that he'd given up a promising football career to party with Lana, and then she'd fucking ditched him. And their bullshit advice: they could stick it up their asses.

It was good that somebody could listen.

But now he wanted more. Driving down that dusty desert road, in the storm, the body of the silver Dodge Durango slapped insistently by the winds outside, him choking slowly on the hot, dead, air inside, no turnoffs in sight that would signal civilization, even in the form of a weather-beaten outpost of a gas station. All Eugene could think of was: he wanted more from Madeline.

And as he fought his own soporific comedown she was slumbering deeply, as if oblivious to the storm outside. And he could ascertain by the heavy snoring coming from the back that Scott had also tripped over to dormancy.

In his fevered mind's eye, she was running towards him, streaked in mud. She was trying to swerve past him like a surging quarterback would, but he'd be building up his momentum in his strongside role and like Willie McGinest he'd bring her down as a lion would a weak gazelle, them both crashing into that filthy dirt . . .

It was as if his hand made the decision for him, rubbing against the tip of his cock and sending pulsating jolts of electricity into his belly and groin. Eugene felt his body stiffen and his eyes bulge under those Ray-Bans as his breathing became more irregular. One arm locked on the wheel while the other did the business; fabulously obscene images of Madeline popped and sizzled in his fried brain, augmenting the peaceful, innocent reality of her dozing by his side.

Ahead, the horizon, brought closer by the hazy heat, flickered intermittently through swirls of red and black dust. The road was only just visible. Madeline was facing him, her knees brought up to her chest. If only she had turned the other way, Eugene thought, he could watch her ass and jerk off without the possibility of her opening her eyes and instantly seeing him. But there was little chance of detection, he calculated in insect coldness, as she would be too disorientated, sleeping through her yagé comedown, to grasp what he was up to straight off, and in any case, he was doing it through his shorts . . .

but the bulge . . .

damn that fuckin bitch . . .

a cock-teaser even in her sleep . . . but now we're getting down and dirty in this mud, baby, oh yeah, real down and dir—

Suddenly Eugene heard a snap followed by a long screech and his free hand shot from his groin to the wheel, which felt like it was being wrenched from his grip as the vehicle jerked to the left, then, as he tried to compensate, violently to the right. Madeline sprang into consciousness as she flew across his lap. She might have felt Eugene's erection had it not instantly subsided. It was Eugene who was like a man falling on his own shotgun, ejaculating a shattering bolt of fear into his chest.

Time stretched out in slow motion. Eugene experienced first an irritation, then a frustration, that everything was spinning away from him, beyond his control. Then they tumbled over and back, in a twisting, fairground ride, which preceded an almighty, bone-shuddering crash, followed by them coming to rest in the most beautiful peace Eugene had ever known.

It didn't last long. He heard a desperate screeching coming from Madeline, but the noises in his own head made it too discordant for him to focus on her anguish. His eyes remained closed as Madeline fell silent, save for a heavy, gulping rhythmic breathing. Then Scott's voice, coming from the back; weary, almost bored in its concern: — Dude, what the fuck . . . you trashed my fucking vehicle, man . . . He hesitated. — Like, are you guys okay . . . ?

— I'm bleeding . . . I'm bleeding! Madeline screamed.

Eugene opened his eyes. Madeline was still crushed into the front seat next to him. He looked her over, then cast his gaze down his own body. There was a gash on his arm, just below the bicep, with red-black blood ebbing from it. — It's okay, man, he turned to her, — that's my blood on you. I've cut my fucking arm. Look. He held it up to her.

Madeline was relieved, then guilt and concern surged in her as she looked at his wound and grimaced. — My Gad! What happened?

— That fucking dust storm, Eugene shook his head, — I couldn't see a goddamn thing. You okay, Scott?

— Yeah . . . I guess so, he heard Scott behind him, — but my fucking car, man, he moaned.

Eugene looked over at Scott. He seemed fine, just a bit bemused. It appeared that the Dodge had come to rest at an angle. It didn't look too bad. The windshield and the windows hadn't even shattered. But suddenly, a dull clunk of fear thumped in Eugene's chest, and he fretted about the dramatic but real possibility of an explosion from a leak in the gas tank: about being incinerated alive. He tried to open the door beside him. It gave an inch, then stuck in the earth. In panic, he turned to Madeline. — We'd better get out of here. Try your door!

Noting his urgent tension, Madeline didn't hesitate, grabbing for the handle and pushing the door open. Eugene watched her scrambling out the car, looking like a strange bird emerging from a cracked egg, awkward and gawky. Like all the sex appeal had been shorn from her. Or perhaps it was just his own libido vanishing, he considered, as he hastily climbed out after her. Scott followed, falling out of the rear of the vehicle onto the sand and shale, looking back nervously as he scrambled to his feet.

The warm wind was driving hard, whipping dust and grit into their eyes. Eugene wrapped the towel around his arm. They checked the car as best they could. Eventually satisfied then that there was no gas-tank leakage and the vehicle, though at an angle, was stable, Scott shimmied under the car. — The axle's gone. Snapped clean in two, he sulkily informed them.

They got back into the Dodge, slamming the door shut and locking the blowing sand out.

There was a silence for a while, as they sat at the uncomfortable angle, stealing despondent glances at each other. Madeline's eyes suddenly lit in inspiration and she suggested that they checked their cellphones. Scott admitted in embarrassment that he'd lost his. Eugene's had run down and he couldn't charge it up. Madeline tried hers, but was unable to get a signal. — What kind of network are you with? Scott accused.

— T-Mobile. She looked defensively at him. — And what about the one you lost? What network is that?

There was more silence. Then Scott passed the small first-aid kit over from the back, and Madeline helped Eugene clean and dress his wound. Fortunately the cut was less deep than it had seemed.

Eugene attempted to work out their location. He had earlier given up on the map – the reverb from the drugs aftermath and his fatigue had made the lines and symbols and colors one big head-fucking mess. He had an autistic younger brother, Danny, who did these incomprehensible drawings. Now Danny's art made more sense than the gazetteer he was compelled to revisit. Instead of taking the Interstate 80 across the Sierra Nevada, they'd gone north out of Black Rock City onto the 395 and then started to hit some of the back roads to get into the Nevada desert in order to do the yagé. He estimated that they were now probably about two hundred miles northeast of Vegas. — If the axle's gone, I guess we're gonna have to stay here until help comes or the storm blows over and we can phone or look for somebody, he ventured.

Scott shook his head in the negative. — I wanted to go to fucking Vegas, man . . .

Eugene looked at Madeline, who remained impassive, then turned back to Scott. — Don't think it's gonna happen, bro.

— And I had somebody coming to paint my apartment, Madeline said, sweeping her road-heavy locks back from her face. — I needed to get things sorted out.

Scott's big dark eyes fell searchingly over Eugene. Shaking his head, he asked petulantly, — How the hell did you manage to crash?

Sucking in a deep breath, Eugene struggled to force the words through his tightening jaw. — It's kind of called fatigue, man, he sneered. — If you recall the idea was that we'd fucking *share* the driving duties, remember that one? His sarcastic voice rose. — But I guess that poor old Eugene here had to do the lot cause you guys were still out of it. I do nat believe that you have got the fucking audacity to complain! Asshole! Eugene snapped, and then was out of the car, slamming the door behind him. Scott glanced at Madeline, who smiled tensely. Her grin vanished as a sound came from behind them. It was Eugene. He opened up the back of the Dodge and pulled out the tent.

As he struggled with the steel and fibreglass poles in the strong winds, Eugene hoped that it would stay up, and he was secretly relieved when Scott and Madeline appeared by his side, even if their coming to his aid meant that his quiet martyrdom would be harder to sustain. They worked in silence, assembling the frame and laying down the flysheet, then pulling over and securing the tent. They took the sleeping bags and some clothes in from the Dodge. As they finished constructing their camp, the storm began to subside.

— I wonder how long we're gonna be out here? Scott asked. Then he quickly added, although he was aware that Eugene's behavior had shown this not to be judicious, — I'm sorry, but I gotta say it, buddy: I'm really pissed about the fucking vehicle. I got it for the band. I told my old man that it was my goddamn livelihood and he fronted me the twenty grand. It's eating at me. I have to say it. I have to speak about it.

Eugene gave his old college buddy a measuring look. He saw a thin, wiry guy with a crew cut and girl's hands. Scott had never done any kind of work in his life. Worse, thought Eugene in some bitterness, he probably never would. He was just sitting around, ass plonked on the stools of various North Beach bars, telling the diminishing number of bodies who cared to listen about the various bands he was planning to get together, while he waited on that trust fund kicking in. Swallowing down his anger, Eugene realized there was nothing

to be gained by blowing up at Scott now. Besides, he was tired.
— Sorry, dude. I'll sort things out. Tommy at the garage in Potrero Hill will be able to fix this.

— So now we just, like, wait here?

Eugene sat cross-legged, looked around the parameters of the orange tent. — Look, man, I thought this was for the best, he yawned, feeling his body start to relax again, the way it had after the yagé. — I'm pretty pooped. I gotta get some sleep. Somebody will come by. This is America, he smiled, — you're never more than a mile from somebody trying to sell you something.

Scott and Madeline quickly looked at each other, a flash-bulb consensus that this was the best course of action. They began to bed down in their respective sleeping bags. Yep, somebody would come by, Eugene thought. Kick back. Rest. Relax. Repair. Get strong. It sounded so good.

The old 1982 blue Chevy pickup truck had been the first thing that Alejandro had bought when he came to America. It had cost him two hundred dollars, most of it borrowed from his sister Carmelita. It was a rusted wreck, but he had talent as a mechanic, and had lovingly resurrected the vehicle. He knew that a truck could always earn you extra money.

Now it was holding up well, the engine ticking over nicely as they cruised down a back road through the desert, Alejandro and his younger brother Noe, who sat in the passenger seat, silently completing a crossword-puzzle book.

When he contemplated their flight from home, Alejandro couldn't think of Phoenix, although they had now lived there for almost three years. That city was only Carmelita's home; the place she'd dragged them to.

Not that he held his native town in any higher regard. It was an old fishing village, south of Guaymas on the Pacific

Coast. It had survived, and indeed, for such a poor part of Sonora, could even have been said to have thrived, as a transport hub. It was close to Highway 15 and was also a stop on the coastal train route. The main town centre, an ugly 1970s series of poorly maintained low-rise buildings, sat uncomfortably next to an old village that had grown up around a small harbor, which held fewer brown-rusted boats every year.

They were simple people, Alejandro thought in a cold rancor; fools who had fished for years when there was nothing left to fish. Some of them in the village seemed to have barely noted their slide from poverty into destitution. They believed the fish would come back. Then, when they started starving, they moved north, then across to America.

The place Carmelita had taken them to.

The town had nothing going for it. On the highway you would see luxury air-conditioned coaches full of wealthy *norteamericanos* bypassing it, heading for the foothills of the Sierra Madre occidentals and historic Alamos with its beautiful Spanish colonial architecture. Those tourists would never come near his home town.

On leaving school, Alejandro sweated at menial work in a garage and its attached shop. It was owned by a wealthy, aggressive, fast-talking *chilango*, named Ordaz, who had promised that he would train him as a mechanic. Eighteen months later, Alejandro was still stacking shelves in the shop, and cleaning the garage and washing cars. He had yet to hold a spanner in his hand.

Alejandro had confronted Ordaz about this. His slick city-boy boss had simply laughed in his face. When Alejandro grew vexed, his employer's expression took on a sinister hue and he told the youth to gather up his stuff and leave.

So there was nothing to keep them where they were, save their mother's grave in the old cemetery at the base of the hills above the town, and the local prison, some 150 kilometres away, which held their disgraced father.

It had been Carmelita who had sent for them after she herself had obtained a job through a friend who was working in Phoenix. She was offered employment by a wealthy family following the professionally prepared CV she had sent them, and the smiling photograph, Alejandro recalled with distaste.

She had found them a place to live and got Alejandro some gardening and landscaping work and also enrolled Noe at a local school. Now they all cleaned up after the *guero*. Did his gardens. Watered his lawns. Looked after his spoiled children. Served his food.

And she did more than that, the filthy whore . . .

Alejandro seemed invisible to his employers. That was unless something went wrong; then he would instantly feel the eyes of accusation upon him. One woman went as far as to blame him for the theft of an artifact that she was subsequently found to have mislaid. No apology was issued to him, despite the police being called and aggressively questioning him. But mostly they ignored him as he watered and tended their gardens in order to stop the desert reclaiming them, under a hot and merciless sun.

What did these people respect? Those gringos? When you saw them on the television, they always said it was hard work, but they let their women lie around by the pool all day. Sent their children to school and more school and trips and vacations. They themselves spent all their time on planes and in hotels and in cars. Where was the work?

They respected nothing but money, Alejandro had considered. Money and the gun. After the Chevy, his second major purchase had been a Smith & Wesson .38 revolver. When he had it in his pocket, he felt stronger. More worthy of respect. It changed him; his face, his walk, but in such a subtle way.

Because now they seemed to see him. Even if he was feared

rather than respected, he sensed that he was no longer invisible to them.

Alejandro drove through the storm in his old Chevy pickup truck, irked at his teenage brother trying to work out those pointless puzzles by his side.

Noe was weak, Alejandro considered. He was becoming a *norteamericano*. Would he end up a cowardly murderer like their father? Perhaps not. There was a certain niceness about the kid. But Alejandro recalled that it was his mother who had said that about their father, when he'd once asked her what she had seen in his papa. He was the sweetest man, his mother told him. But Alejandro had seen how alcohol could debase and corrupt that decency and charm. Felt it in himself. When he'd gotten drunk, punched, then hit with the pool cue, and then attempted to strangle, the *hombre* in the bar who had insulted him. He looked at Noe again. Was it not his father who had taught Alejandro the old saying: *La puerca más flaca es la primera que rompe el chiquero.*

The weakest ones are the first to rebel.

He could see his idiot father now, his pained face and sad, shifty eyes, the glint of his bald pate behind the glass screens of the prison. Despite Carmelita's promptings, Alejandro had only gone to see him once; to abuse and curse this pathetic, wretched creature, to witness him cowering in his gray prison issue tunic, his shiny rat's eyes filling with tears.

And then there was Carmelita. Let her have children of her own to boss and baby. He, Alejandro Rodriquez, had had enough.

Alejandro again regarded his puny little brother, who looked at him in such a strange way since they'd taken the bitch's money, the money she had gotten from whoring herself to the wealthy gringo.

Her nonsense. Her delusion that she and this rich, married

norteamericano were in love. When, then, would he move his wife and children out of the house she stayed in? When would they walk hand in hand down a street? When would their sad, furtive, animal trysts be replaced by something less deceitful? When would she share his bed at night?

The job she had gotten Alejandro doing the rich man's garden. The gratitude he was meant to feel for having his brains fry in the heat every day. Then, that day last week when the *norteamericano* was supposed to be at work and Alejandro had walked in on them in his sister's room. The blood from her bad time that he'd seen in her discarded panties, which lay on the floor by the bed; it hadn't stopped their depraved lust.

We have done her a favor in taking her stinking whore's bounty. Now we shall see how much the cynical norteamericano *really loves her!*

Eugene was thinking about Madeline. A sequence of images, between thought and dream, started to play through his head. They seemed to gain a three-dimensional clarity he would never have thought possible. Then he heard a rustling sound, and he could see it through his closed eyes. Madeline was unselfconsciously naked in the tent, ready to climb back into her sleeping bag after getting up to pee outside. Yes, he could *see* her, even through the membrane of his eyelids. But Eugene needed to get closer still to her opaque figure, as her nakedness would contain surprises, secrets, like every girl's did. You always thought you'd be able to envision them perfectly with their clothes off – curves, flesh tones, proportions – but they always held mystery. The nipples, the color, the moles, the texture and extent of the pubic hair: they were always different to what you imagined. Like Lana, whom he'd masturbated about so many times at Long Beach Poly before he got her naked in their high-school grad year; his mind becoming a data bank of intricately constructed pornographic narratives in which she starred, or co-starred, with him. The first time that he saw her nude in his bedroom at his parents' house he almost felt like asking her in his shock: What have you done to your tits? But Madeline; he had always seen her in a certain way. Perhaps if he just opened his eyes now . . . they would meet with hers, and then . . . no. She wouldn't be there, surely: not like that. She was in her sleeping bag. Far better to sustain the delicious virtual reality of it in his substance-enhanced head-space.

But.

But now she was crouching over him, almost touching him. Eugene felt his breath draw into his lungs and his heart pound. Then it happened. Her hand slipped down into his bag and touched his leg. Then it was caressing his thigh in slow, twisting movements. Her fingers seemed so cool and his cock stiffened. He should open his eyes. It *was* her. She was really doing this to him. Open them.

No.

Keep this going a little bit longer because his cock was so hard and . . .

. . . and her cool finger was tweaking its head . . .

. . . and . . .

AAAAGGGHHHHH!

A terrible jab.

She'd stabbed him.

Eugene was up and he was screaming, — WHAT THE FUCK, MAN!

It wasn't Madeline. It was a rattlesnake: a long, green, twisting rattlesnake. It was sliding across his stomach, out of his sleeping bag, onto the plastic floor of the tent.

Scott and Madeline were immediately woken up by his cry. — Damn! What is it! Madeline hissed as Scott blinked into a furtive consciousness.

Eugene pointed at the slithering creature as it headed across the groundsheet. — A rattlesnake . . . a rattlesnake bit my cack!

Scott groped around, laying his hand on the torch by his back. As he clicked it on and directed the beam, they watched the snake moving away from them. — Looks like a Mojave rattler, Scott ventured, — those dark stripes on his head . . .

Grasping his heavy-heeled brown shoe, his features cut in a vengeful tenacity, Eugene started to climb out of his sleeping bag. — Sonofabitch . . .

— Don't kill it! Scott shouted.

— What!

— You never heard of conservation, man?

— Conservation? What the fuck! You expect me to *conserve* some fucker that just bit my fucking dick!?

— Listen, man, you'd better sit down . . . these guys are pretty damn toxic.

At those words, Eugene felt shaky for the first time, sinking back onto the floor, pulling the bag to him. The rattlesnake slithered underneath the tent flap, into the freedom of the desert. Eugene touched his crotch. Although his genitals were as flaccid as they had ever been, he could feel his pulse in them, pounding on his fingertips. — Oh my God . . . it bit me . . . my goddamn pecker . . .

— Don't lie down, Scott shouted, — keep your heart *above* the wound!

Eugene quickly pulled himself up, resting on his elbows. He took heavy, ragged breaths.

— Where did it bite? Scott asked again, as Madeline stared at Eugene.

— My privates . . . Eugene said more modestly, — a rattlesnake! Damn!

— For God's sake, Eugene, Scott gasped, — those things are

fucking dangerous!

— I fucking *know that*, Scatt, it bit my damn pecker. Eugene went onto his knees, letting the bag fall around him, and pulled down his shorts. There were two red puncture marks an inch from the tip of his penis. — What am I gonna do! he squealed, in a sudden panic.

— If only that shaman were here . . . Scott mused, looking around the tent for inspiration.

— Fuck the shaman! Eugene cursed.

Madeline shook her head. — He's only saying because these people have healing knowledge, Gene.

Eugene grimaced. — Well, he ain't here, he said mournfully.

— I couldn't tell for sure what type of snake it was, Scott pursed his lips, getting out of his bag, rising in his green boxer shorts as he stepped toward Eugene, — but I'm sure it was a Mojave green; these sons of bitches are one of the most venomous snakes around. Their toxin attacks the nervous system, not just the tissue . . . that poison's gotta come out!

— How the fuck can we . . . ? Eugene gasped in horror.

Scott edged closer, eyes trained on Eugene's cock. — We gotta open up the area around the wound. You make two criss-cross incisions over each hole with a knife, to draw out the bad blood, he explained, and he reached across for the large, multipurpose Swiss Army knife in his bag.

Madeline was trying to get a signal on her cellphone. In the storm the device seemed a useless and dead artifact, technology rendered impotent and void by nature's whims: complacent men against indifferent gods. — This is supposed to be fucking America, she hissed in frustration.

Eugene looked agog at the glinting blade in Scott's hand. — This is Boy Scout bullshit! His voice went high and fey. — That sorta crap's probably been discredited for years! Nobody's slicing up *my* fucking dick!

— It's just four goddamn little nicks, Gene! We ain't got time to pussy about here! Scott wailed.

For the first time, Eugene realized that he could actually die; that his life could end out here in the stony, unforgiving desert, in such sad, unlucky circumstances. He thought of the footballing career he chucked away to party with Lana, following her around clubs as she 'networked' for the purposes of her own advancement. The bitch would hear of his demise as she accepted an Academy Award with a fake tear and a halting choke in her throat. Trembling under the terror and exasperation of it, Eugene gasped, — Okay . . . okay . . . I'll do it, he said, steeling himself as Scott handed him the knife. Then he looked at his cock in his hand, the two angry red holes, and the blade of the knife. Something ugly rose in his gut and he thought he was going to pass out. — You . . . you do it, his tones hushed as he handed the knife back to Scott and lay down balancing on his elbows to keep his torso raised, looking upwards at the orange roof of the tent.

Eugene gritted his teeth as Scott took his penis in his hand. Winced as his friend made the first cut. Though he had to hold him firmly to get purchase, the sensitive skin of Eugene's penis yielded easily to the blade. Droplets of blood spotted up in a line along the incision. It only started to flow when Scott made the second, crisscrossing cut. — Maddy, throw me over that towel!

Madeline quickly complied and Eugene screamed as he looked down and saw the dark red blood quickly absorbing into the white towel. — WHAA . . . YOU'RE FUCKING CASTRATING ME, MAN!

— If you don't stay still, I goddamn will!

Scott quickly crisscrossed the second wound, urging Eugene to hold the towel against himself as the blood flowed out. — It's done, he said, then looked at his friend, — but we ain't finished yet. Somebody's gonna have to suck the poison out.

Eugene instinctively glanced toward Madeline. His expression was hopeful and pleading.

She gaped at his bleeding cock in the towel. It was large and fat. She'd always thought of him as smaller in that way for some reason, even though he was a big guy. Maybe it was swollen with the snakebite. — Don't even think about it, she snapped. — That bloody mess . . . that is so gross!

Eugene felt utterly wretched. He now fancied he could feel the deadly venom of the snake, winding its way through his veins and arteries, meandering with slow menace toward his heart. He looked at her in apoplexy. — You goddamn selfish bitch, he half begged, half threatened.

Madeline lurched forward a little in the bag she kept wrapped round her, even though she was still wearing her brown tank top. With her free hand she swept her tumbling hair back from her face. — I ain't gonna suck your cack. It's dripping with blood! You could have herpes or Aids or any shit. No way, she said, her frosty finality taking Eugene back to that party.

— I'm probably fucking dying, man . . . it's fucking medicinal, it's first fucking aid, Eugene pleaded.

— I'll do it. Fuck it, Scott said.

Eugene regarded his friend with sudden trepidation. There was something about Scott, crouching there in those green boxer shorts. There had *always* been something about him: from way back in college. His girl's eyes. His lady hands. Scott had had few close friends at UCLA and after they'd graduated he'd followed Eugene up to San Francisco on the basis that it was a 'cool spot'. Moved close to him in North Beach. And he'd never really seemed that interested in pussy. The kid was just plain weird. — Keep away from me, man . . . Eugene said, raising his hands, — I want her to do it, he pointed at Madeline

27

who again shook her head.

— For God's sake, Eugene, you might get seriously ill. Scott took another step forward.

Eugene upturned his palms. — Back off! Just keep away from me you goddamn faggot!

— Whaaat! Scott protested in disbelief. — You let me cut holes in it with a knife, but you won't let me get the fucking poison out! He pointed to Madeline. — She ain't gonna suck your cock, Eugene! he roared.

— You're darned right I ain't . . . Madeline said, looking at Eugene's bloody penis with horror. He expected her to suck on *that*, and have every sniggering dude and frat boy back in the neighborhood make a face as she walked into a bar? No way.

— You selfish freakin – I'm fuckin dying! Eugene cried. — You're murdering me!

Madeline looked at Scott, then at Eugene. — Listen, you asshole, Scotty's offered to suck it out. You're murdering yourself with your own fuckin homophobic bullshit. You think when we get back to San Francisco that he'll be in every bar on Castro boasting about sucking a bit of poison out of your miserable limp dick?

Eugene let this sink in, and looked at Scott, who shrugged. And so he gave a sad, tired nod as his friend knelt down and once again took his cock tentatively in his hand. He looked down at his old college buddy. Eugene had never seen eyes so faggish as the ones in the head that gazed sadly up at him. My God, he thought. It all makes sense now. He nodded and looked back up at the roof of the tent. Madeline watched in fascination, as Scott's mouth sucked below the bloodied, swollen tip of Eugene's cock.

The storm had taken them by surprise. It had seemed appropriate, the anger of gods scorning them in this terrible flight from Carmelita's vengeance. They had just wanted to get away, though they had no real notion of where they were going. The younger brother, Noe, the more circumspect of the two, regarded Alejandro, five years his senior, stern as he drove ahead through the dust.

Taking from your own was so bad, Noe fretfully considered. Carmelita would never forgive them. God would never forgive them. They had ended it; all those years of their big sister's protection and love. It had been America. They had been promised a better life here, but it had changed Alejandro. Hardened his heart. Noe thought of how Carmelita had taken them to church in Ciudad Obregón every Sunday, always making sure that they were neat and tidy. Insisted that they attended school and even visited their father in prison as they prayed for his soul, and put flowers on their mother's grave.

He looked at Alejandro's square jaw, his heavy features in which those sunken eyes were set. Killer's eyes, Carmelita had once said, after Alejandro had beaten a young man to a pulp in a bar, over some petty argument. The eyes of their father.

Yet it was Carmelita who always made excuses for Alejandro. It had been he who had found their mother, back in their home town in southern Sonora, bending at the kitchen, breathing heavily, pain etched on her face as she smoked a cigarette. A pot of rice and one of fava beans had cooked down on the stove and the house stank of burning food. And then Alejandro had seen the blood in her lap, and on the big knife that lay on the table. He'd started to cry and asked her what had happened, even though he knew, and in demented rage, he quickly searched the house for his father. He was certain the knife had been wielded by the old man's drunken hand, his breath stinking of tequila and the cheap perfume of whores.

But the old man had fled.

Their mother had begged Alejandro not to call a doctor or the police, said that it looked worse than it was, protecting her treacherous husband even as her own life blood oozed out across her lap. Then she keeled over and fell heavily onto the tiled floor. Alejandro screamed and ran for help. It was too late; their mother was dead before they could get her to the hospital.

Sure enough, the police found their father a few hours later, and he instantly cried out his confession. They had argued and she had pushed him to his limit and he had blindly struck at her with the knife, his mind muddled with drink. When he saw the blood, he'd crossed himself and wandered for a while, eventually ending up back on the seedy Boulevard Morelia at the dingy *Casa de Huéspedes* he frequented, and in the arms of his favorite whore. She was a big, meaty woman named Gina, and the police officers found him sobbing and singing an *alabados*, a poignant hymn of praise on the suffering of the Virgin Mary, as she cradled him like a baby.

Then their big sister Carmelita had tried to become their mother. She took the boys to America and worked so hard to give them a better life. Noe remembered passing the old harbor for the last time, the mottled cloudy sky, the squawking of the birds and then driving across the desert roads over the yellow rock and tumbleweed-strewn terrain toward the highway. All the time Carmelita singing, and telling her excited little brothers about how good their new life in America would be.

And this was how they had repaid her!

A sister who had so recently seemed a browbeating harridan was slowly being recast as a madonna figure in Noe's penitent soul. He looked over at Alejandro's tight mouth again, his big gold-ringed fingers on the wheel of the Chevy.

It is him, the bullying oaf! He has done this to me. Taken me from my school, from my friends. Poisoned my soul. He's just like our shitbag of a father!

Alejandro turned at that point, catching his scrawny younger sibling's angry gaze. — What is wrong? he snapped.

— Nothing, Noe said meekly, kittenlike under the harsh stare of his older brother.

— Do not look at me like that, he spat and contemplated Noe again, his cold black eyes murderous.

A bolt of fear struck Noe square in the chest and he turned away to the side window. It felt cooler on his cheek, reminding him of the times when their father would borrow his brother's old car and drive the family down to the beach at Miramar, by Guaymas, along the Pacific Coast of Mexico. He recalled the distinctive shapes of the towering denuded mountains, which surrounded the bay. The time he cut his feet paddling in the water on the shells from the delicious oysters native to the area. How he and Alejandro would beg for change when the anglers from all over the world would converge on Guaymas to participate in the tournaments and pursue the fish catch in the Sea of Cortes.

Now, looking gloomily out through the settling dust at the slowly visible horizon, broken only by big rocks, he contemplated his now saintly sister again. What had they done to her? The money. Her savings. All her hard work. Her chance of a better life: they had ruined it.

There was something ahead. The dust was clearing and a peculiar-looking object, giving off a luminous orange glow, was visible by the side of the road. Alejandro stopped the car and the brothers got out, each disappointed that on closer inspection the entity that had excited them was something as banal as a tent. Beside it was a 4x4 vehicle, which had almost turned over on its side, having run into a steep sudden rise of dirt, sand and shale, trapped by some rocks and banked up from the road. Alejandro pulled his .38 revolver from his inside pocket, and transferred it to the external pouch of his leather jacket. Noe went to speak in protest then thought against it. To his knowledge, Alejandro had never shot anybody before, but with a lunatic rage and desperation propelling him through this strange land, both sensed that he was destined to do so, and probably quite soon. Noe just hoped and prayed that it would not be him.

The settling sky brought out a red sun, which shimmered in front of them. In the growing light they could vaguely ascertain smudged figures in silhouette from inside the tent. Noe touched Alejandro's arm, in a spirit of affirmation rather than any attempt at restraint, but in the event, it was brushed aside. Alejandro confidently opened the tent flap.

Instantly greeted by that smell he knew so well, the meaty, sour scent of spilt blood in the heat, Alejandro could scarcely believe his eyes as he surveyed the scene before him. One gringo was on his knees, performing fellatio on another, as a pretty girl looked on. They were a truly disgusting people, Alejandro thought with rancor. The penis of the man was covered in blood. The girl, she had a bloody towel in her lap. The animal had obviously fucked her in her stinking pussy when she was at her dirty time of month and the other gringo pig was sucking him clean! He wondered, in a bitter rage, if those were the sordid games his sister was participating in right now, the sissy boyfriend of her wealthy lover licking her foul menstrual blood from his dick as she watched on eagerly like the whore she had become. Now the cock-sucking *norteamericano* pig turned and spat a mouthful of bloody saliva onto the ground.

Inside their own tent!

The Americans turned in shock to see the Mexican brothers.

— Two faggots and a dirty leetal lady, Alejandro said evenly,

32

his features creasing up in malice.

— This is . . . a rattlesnake bit me . . . Eugene stuttered, then shouted in outrage, — Get the fuck out of here!

Alejandro's face tightened further and he took a step into the tent. — Hey, seesay boy, you no talk to us like that, see, and he pulled out the gun and aimed it at Eugene's cock and Scott's mouth. — I blow your leemp deek off and thee teeth from thee head of your faggot friend too, he scowled.

Scott and Eugene froze, looking in open-mouthed vacancy at the barrel of the pistol.

Madeline swallowed hard, then crouched backwards, feeling the wall of the tent behind her. — What . . . what do you want?

Alejandro looked her up and down. A faint, mordant grin of contempt crossed his mouth. Then he turned to the others. — Feenish, he spat.

Scott looked up, Eugene's cock, dripping with blood, still in his hand. — What . . . we weren't –

— Leesen to thees, Alejandro commanded, gun trained on them, — you feenish sucking hees deek, and you suck it right. Suck it like a leel gorl would suck your deek, he smiled coldly.

— But – Scott protested.

— FEENEESH! Alejandro roared, as Noe nodded frantic-ally, imploring them to acquiesce with his brother's demand.

— Do as he says, for Gad's sake! Madeline begged.

As a terrified Scott started to obey, Alejandro regarded Eugene. — And you; you weel enjoy eet. I wahn see you come in hees face like he ees your beetch.

Suddenly Scott started to gag on Eugene's cock. It looked horrible and it tasted foul, the metallic blood so strong; he began to wonder if it was the snake's poison in his mouth, going down his gullet and into his stomach. He thought he'd spat out most of the venom but he couldn't be sure.

And then there was Eugene's dirty blood. He thought of his old college friend's behavior at UCLA and then in San Francisco. By taking that shit into his system he was sleeping with every campus slut, every drunken waitress or bartender, every poxy whore on Sunset or the Tenderloin that his buddy's filthy dick had ever been inside. And this meant, by extension, he'd taken in every diseased cock that had breached all those germ-incubating pussies. The odds against him not contracting something seemed so overwhelmingly vast. He could now hear Eugene's boasts of those whores he'd enjoyed on their trip to Vegas last month, and he could, in his mind's eye, envision their harsh, painted faces as well as the complacent, arrogant smirk of every John who had brothel-crawled across the globe from Tijuana to Thailand on expense accounts. Scott's ears rang with the phantom clinks of Vegas slot machines and stoical chants of stern-faced croupiers as they flagged up impossible odds against the avoidance of fatal infection, as his mouth struggled around that sweaty, bloody cock.

But he had to go on. Because a bullet from this range in your face offered worse odds still. Worse odds than just about anything.

That gun; they had a *gun* pointing at them! These men were psychopaths. The crazy eyes on that sonofabitch with the revolver, it was like looking into hell. In a bitter fear, Scott decided that he was destined to die hopelessly, his skull blown apart by some wetback assassin's bullet before he could liberate his trust fund. His money. The legacy bequeathed to him. Everything Pops had worked for. The old man: all he had ever expected Scott to do in life was to simply stay alive long enough to collect. And he couldn't even do that one damned thing. There would be no band, no success, nothing to impress his father. He would perish out here in the desert and his last memory in his short life would be of Eugene's goddamn bloodied cock in his mouth. The horrible injustice of it all hit home, and Scott started to sob. Then he heard Eugene protesting, — I can't do this. I can't come. I can't even get hard! I don't like him. I don't like boys . . .

Alejandro laughed loudly and thumped his chest in disbelief. — He no like boys! You hear that, my leel brother? He turned to Noe. — He has a faggot sucking his deek and he no like boys! He shook his head in disgust. — You steek it in thee leel gorl on her bad time. You are animals!

Eugene protested, — Look, man, I told you I got a snakebite and –

— Shut up weeth your fucking mouth! Alejandro roared, eyes blazing. — *Estás como los frijoles, al primer hervor se arrugan!*

They hastily complied as Alejandro turned to Madeline, and grabbed her roughly by the arm.

— Alejandro, please . . . Noe pleaded.

— Be silent, leetal brother, he commanded in a low hiss, pulling Madeline over to Scott and Eugene. — Take off your top and your brassiere, hc whispered at her in soft threat.

— You really think I'd – Madeline started in defiance then faltered, as she looked at Alejandro for a second, then again at the .38 in his hand. In one quick motion, she pulled off her tank top. Noe, now half in the tent, saw the St Christopher's around her neck, hanging on her chest bone above her breasts and was moved to cross himself and say a silent prayer. He then drew a breath as Madeline removed her bra.

Alejandro thought of them all; the lazy wives and daughters of the rich men. How, as they lay by their pools, in their bikinis, sipping their drinks, they never, ever saw him as he sweated in their gardens. And he wanted them to see him. Wanted them to take off their tops. Free those big breasts they had pumped with silicone. *Now* he could make them.

— You see her teets, seesay boy? Alejandro turned to Eugene who had his head to the side. He'd bowed it at first, but that had only forced him to regard Scott. — Look at her, seesay boy, Alejandro urged, waving the pistol, — look at those fine teets, so feerm. She want you, seesay boy, she want you so much . . . so much . . .

Alejandro gasped, and a horrified Noe realized that his brother had dropped his trousers and was masturbating himself with his free hand.

Noe took a step back out of the tent, trembling as he held the flap open. Madeline closed her eyes and Scott sucked, fearfully swallowing that dark blood. Alejandro continued jerking himself off, filling the tent with his commentary. — She want you just like the leel faggot want you, seesay boy, so wheetch one you choose? Wheetch one, seesay boy? You, beetch, he spat at Madeline, — you touch those teets! Make your neepels hard!

Madeline began caressing herself, first in stiff fear, then attempting to divert her thoughts to Scott, in an effort to black out everything else. She was trying to think about whether or not she was in love with him. Those soft, dark eyes, so full of sadness, yet hope. He was a beautiful boy and they'd had a great experience together on the yagé, and she'd seen something inside him, his soul, and knew there was more to him than the fearful trust-fund kid trying to avoid and appease a distant father and an alcoholic mother.

She thought of how she should have phoned her own folks. They liked to talk to her at least once a week. She knew they worried about her. What would they think if they knew she was here, now? Madeline considered the path, so apparently mundane, that had taken her to this terrible place. Just over six months ago she was working in Walgreen's and living at home with her parents in the Cleveland suburb she grew up in. She hated it, and had particularly detested her high school. Most of all, she despised her surname: Madeline Frostdyke.

Or Frigid Lesbian, as the nastier kids had called her at school.

In San Francisco she could be Madeline Frost. Sometimes, when her feminist spirit was ascendant, she would take on her mother's maiden name, Kennaway.

When the insults started, Madeline reacted by trying not to draw attention to herself, but that was exactly what she ended up doing. By letting her conservative mother dress her, Madeline Frostdyke, in her fifties-style outfits and her big glasses, became one of the most obvious geeks in her school. And she'd have stayed that way, trying too hard to be anonymous, but then puberty hit her hard, and left her with curves that her shapeless, dowdy clothes couldn't quite conceal and drives that a decent, God-fearing suburban American household couldn't contain. However, save for a couple of encounters hastily engineered largely in order to gain rudimentary carnal experience, she was determined that Cleveland, so cruel to Madeline Frostdyke, was not going to get the best of Madeline Frost.

Jackie Kennaway, a diligent law student at the Jesuit University of San Francisco, was surprised when a vivacious, stunning-looking young girl turned up on her doorstep. She was even more taken aback as she realized it was her formerly awkward young cousin, Madeline.

And so the girl from Cleveland moved into the spare room that Madeline's aunt had absent-mindedly mentioned was available in Jackie's apartment in San Francisco. Madeline initially expressed a desire to follow her cousin into the university, in her case to do business studies, but it soon became apparent she wouldn't be joining Jackie on campus. Instead, Madeline took to San Francisco's social life like a bear to bacon, making friends with some of her studious relative's more outgoing acquaintances.

Through one of them, Candy, she had met Eugene. Unbeknown to him, he'd instantly reminded her of Kevin Dailey, the boyfriend of her horrible nemesis Sara Nichols, who gleefully orchestrated many school-bullying campaigns against her. Sara had been quick to enlist Kevin in the offhand dismissal of Madeline. Now she realized that Sara had noted first what the rest of the high-school divas would eventually recognize: Madeline Frostdyke was a looker, and a possible rival, whose confidence needed to be kept low.

Sara had made sure that cool, sporty, conventionally handsome Kevin never took an interest in Madeline. But *this* version of Kevin Dailey wanted her so badly. That was the thrill of it all. But it was just a game, because it was really Scott, moody, doe-eyed Scott, that she wanted to be with.

And that had brought her out to the desert and this nightmare.

So now there was just this tent and the podgy Mexican youth's rasping voice: — Suck hard, leetal faggot. Look at the leel gorl, seesay boy, look at the show she put on for us with those beeg fine teetays . . . maybe you should suck on them, huh, seesay boy? Huh? Like you fuck that dirty pussy, huh?

Dirty pussy? What the fuck was that fat, twisted, spic asshole talking about? Eugene wondered, as he stared at Madeline's breasts. They were good tits, no getting away from it. Full, firm, but real, with one observably bigger than the other. The way she looked with her eyes closed. Trying to concentrate: to not be powerless and humiliated. And he understood it. He thought of his own sad, solitary experience in the pornography industry. He had been trying to make some extra money as a student at UCLA, and he and Lana were in a decidedly 'off' phase of their ongoing on-off relationship. His buddy Jerry did it, so why not him? He was cut, as he worked out, and he was hung. It seemed a good way to make money: fucking hot chicks. He remembered as a kid having a bit part in a couple of scenes from *The Other Sister*, filmed, like so many Hollywood movies, at his high school. Eugene had even entertained the dumb-ass notion that somebody might just take notice of him and he'd make mainstream Hollywood before Lana.

When he went up to that house in the Valley for the audition, there were three other guys in the frame, or trying to get in the frame. He didn't know any of them. A fat man in a dark blue suit, no tie, had greeted them. The only thing he could remember about the other dudes was that one of them wore a White Stripes T-shirt. They all waited in a room with soft drinks and magazines. Eugene was told he'd be last. During the wait he grew increasingly edgy. The first two guys had both shuffled through the door with an arrogant gait only to exit in silent, hunched-shouldered humiliation. After the second one departed, Eugene and the White Stripes guy looked at each other in some trepidation. Then White Stripes went next, leaving Eugene alone. And he was in there for ages. When he came out White Stripes was wearing a shit-eating grin, with the fat guy slapping him on the back. The pornographer's parting words were: — Remember, work on those abs! Then he summoned in Eugene, to whom White Stripes gave a euphoric wink on the way out.

In the other room, a naked girl, long straight black hair, plenty of makeup, pendulous fake breasts, orange suntan, reclined on a sofa. Behind the camera was a train-wreck of a guy with a Texan accent who smelt strongly of alcohol. The guy shook his hand, introducing himself as Ray. The girl didn't speak, but cracked an ugly, predatory smile at him when the fat man said: — And this beautiful young lady is Monique.

Eugene went across to her and kissed her chastely; in the confident manner he'd seen porn performers execute upon meeting new partners.

— Right, son, let's see what you got, the fat man said urgently.

With an engine full of lust, Eugene eagerly stripped. This Monique chick was hot. But the trouble was that his dick somehow wasn't receiving the message his brain was sending it. He knew he had to forget the camera, the others around him, and just focus on Monique. Her tight ass. Her shaved pussy. Her big red lips. Her heavy, silicone tits.

But there was nothing happening. Nothing at all. Monique's whorish ministrations and exaltations were wasted as her features slowly froze in a mask of boredom. Soon Eugene was forced to quit, leaving as humiliated as the first two guys. The fat guy had said, — Don't worry, son, there's very few bucks that can just party in front of the camera on demand. I get some real studs come waltzing in here all best-in-show; 90 per cent of them skulk out like beaten mutts.

And now, when the chips were down, once more his hard-on would fail him. But this time it might cost him his life. The camera, the goddamn camera. Now the camera was the barrel of a gun and the pitch-black eyes of the killer holding it. Eugene looked at Madeline again. She was so beautiful, and he would die without knowing her. With her eyes closed, she attained this tragic but heroic nobility. Her tits were so gorgeous. If only *she* was sucking his cock . . . those lips of hers, working skillfully on him, now taking him right to the back of her throat, but her somehow just standing there, virtuous and serene . . .

Madeline . . . Madeline . . .

Yes. It was her. It WAS her. His cock stiffened up.

Oh fuck, Madeline . . .

Suddenly, Eugene felt an explosion rising from within him as spasms shook his shivering body. He was climaxing like never before. Then, through his euphoria, he suddenly remembered the golden rule of porn: the audience needs to see the 'facial', and this deadly audience probably more than any other. Eugene quickly pulled out, splattering Scott's face and bloodied lips with cum, horrified as he spangled in ecstasy. — Oh my Gad . . . he moaned, then whispered at Scott, — I'm sorry, buddy . . . I . . .

Alejandro ejaculated almost simultaneously, his jism shooting across Madeline's leg. Then he put his dick away, pulling up his briefs and trousers, fastening and zipping himself in a few casual, perfunctory movements. He handed the gun to Noe who physically shrank from it. Eugene and Scott glanced at each other. — Take it, Alejandro commanded, and the boy slowly moved toward the gun and took it in his trembling hands. — Point it at them, he urged. The boy obeyed, the gun shaking almost uncontrollably in his grip. Scott looked away, his bottom lip seeming to mimic the rhythm of the pistol. — Keep them covered, Alejandro said cheerfully, slapping his terrified brother across the back. — Feel its power, he urged, — be a man. If one of them even speaks, shoot them. Then his eyes fell upon Madeline's cellphone, which lay by her bag on the groundsheet. — I theenk I take thees, he smiled, picking it up.

Madeline had opened her eyes and crossed her arms over her breasts. — Please leave it. We need it to phone for help, she begged. — We're stuck out here. We won't say anything about this!

Noe, the gun still shaking in his hand, looked in a hopeful pleading endorsement at Alejandro, who steadfastly ignored him, instead glaring at Madeline, who fell silent. Then his hard gaze fell on Scott and Eugene. — You should tell this beetch to shut her fucking mouth or she will get you all keeled, he smiled. — Now I need your other phones. You, he pointed at Scott, — where are they?

— I-I didn't br-ing mine, Gene's is back here. He pointed behind them.

Dumb-ass pussy, Eugene thought.

Alejandro regarded him with an almost piteous expression. — You did not breeng your phone?

— No, Scott stammered again, — I l-lost it. Check the bag if you like . . .

— I believe you. I theenk you are too scared to try to deceive us. Throw the other phone to me.

Scott lobbed Eugene's cell over to Alejandro, who crouched down and picked it up. He played around with both phones for a while. — You know, if I were you, as soon as we are gone, I would contact the po-leece, he mused.

— Please . . . Noe, still trembling as he pointed the gun, pleaded to his brother, — we should go now!

Alejandro raised a hand to silence him.

As a sniveling, hyperventilating Scott wiped some sperm from his face and started to retch blood up, Eugene lay back against the wall of the tent, his heart pounding. Looking up, he could see only Alejandro's ice-cold stare closing in on them. — But now there will be no contact with the poleece, the Mexican sang breezily, — because now, we shoot you.

Madeline turned to Eugene in appeal, her face long and white with abject terror. And he knew then that he really loved her; would do almost anything for her. But he wouldn't take a bullet for her. Eugene wanted her to get it first, then Scott. Because he saw the way that crazy guy was with her and he didn't want to leave her out here alone with him. His hand went into his pocket, as he fingered the handle of the knife. He would probably only get this one slim chance, and that was if he was very, very lucky. Otherwise they were stone dead by the side of a desert road with buzzards picking at them.

— Please . . . Madeline begged Alejandro, suddenly falling to her knees. — I did nothing wrong, she begged.

Alejandro looked at this woman, and saw the dangling cross hanging round her neck. Like the one his mother wore. He thought of his father once again, that animal who had shown no mercy. — Hey . . . relax. He held up her phone and started snapping them with the camera. — If you are good, the only shooting is with the camera on thees phone, he almost whispered, and his hand reached out and gently touched the side of her face. Eugene glanced at the petrified Noe, and was about to lunge when Alejandro suddenly turned toward him, his eyes murderous again. — Go and assume thee position again, faggots, or you get thee bullet!

Madeline gave them a perilous, yearning stare and Eugene, in bitter despondency, nodded at Scott and they had to go through the indignity of the ritual once again. Every snap taken by Alejandro seemed to last minutes, his leering, mocking commentary now a warped parody of a fashion photographer. Eugene shut his eyes, and he could hear the bigger Mexican saying, — Now if you tell anyone about thees, all your friends and family will have those nice peectures sent to them! These will look good in thee family album, two seesay boys and the gorl with the teetays!

And he only knew it was over when he felt the cool, still air on his cock replace the wet heat from Scott's mouth. Only then could Eugene hear the footsteps of the departing brothers receding and he opened his eyes. In the gray twilight he was aware of an echoing retching sound, like nothing his ears had been privy to before. It seemed as if a malign spirit was smirking in celebration of a particularly vile debasement it had engineered. He thought that it was Scott or even Madeline vomiting, but their vacant gazes and an insidious scorch he was suddenly aware of, told him the source came from somewhere inside of himself. Eugene turned to the canvas, those big arms holding him up as the bile poured from his guts, a nervous laughter punctuating every strength-sapping heave. Outside, he could hear the engine of the Chevy starting up and chugging away into the fading desert light.

If You Liked School,
You'll Love Work . . .

I.

TREES

The ex-missus came round the old gel's house with the kid. To try and make a bleedin point. Using her as a farking weapon against me. Funny how people change over the years. Looking across the table at Trees, that desperate stare, them sort of jerky movements, with her holding her hands that way she did, like they was trophies on exhibition; I was gutted just how little I actually felt. This was the woman I'd kipped with every bleedin night, barring accidents (usually happy ones as it happens), for sixteen farking years. Mad, but I suppose that I wanted to feel *something*, anything, just to tell me that it all wasn't a total farking waste of time.

Just as worrying was that I saw me own sheer bleedin indifference mirrored in her vacant gape. She had her hair cut short and dyed it her old brown, but it was just a little bit too rich and deep in colour and to my mind just drew attention to the fact that her looks were going. The sort of haircut where the Skirt-in-Question announces to the world: 'I've given up the ghost of being young and officially turned into my old mum.'

I dunno if it's cause she can see the disdain in my eyes, but she's looking at me like I'm worn goods n all. Me! Still a 32-inch waist, although, granted, you got a bit of a blubbery overhang them days. I got to thinking that there must have been some point we had stopped being human, being real, to each other. Now we just went through this pantomime, which, being fair, I don't think exactly sat well with her either. It ain't much

47

fun when you communicate as the least flattering version of yourself. Whenever we got together, which, thank God, wasn't often, we just reminded ourselves of what a pair of cunts we'd become to each other. Exchanging glances, all we could see was failure and humiliation and we'd never see anything else. Apart, we could put each other up on a bit of a pedestal; remember the good times, the love even, but together? Forget it.

I can't wait to get home, and that sure ain't here no more. Nah, it's the Canaries for me: all-year-round sun and holiday skirt gagging on it. You can stick England up your fucking arse.

Looking round my old mum's house now, it saddens me how little she's got to show for her life. A bit of furniture, the telly and a few bleeding knick-knacks on the mantelpiece, that's her lot. Represents the last of that generation who kept their noses clean, dutifully lined up to fight in some daft farking war, and listened like nodding dogs to the Queen slavering shit every Christmas. Of course, just like their forefathers, they were royally shafted. Since World War I they been waiting for them homes fit for heroes to emerge. So where are they? Don't see any on this poxy estate.

Yeah, I might do a bit of decorating for the old gel next time I'm over for an extended stay. A lick of paint. Some wall-paper. Brighten things up a little.

I look again at Trees. Certain things need a bit more than a superficial renovation to make them palatable.

Mum, God bless her, has taken Emily into the kitchen. Like the old gel, the poor little cow ain't daft; she knows we're having a confab about her, but off they go. So now Motherfucker Teresa here's lowering her voice and saying, — I'm at my wits' end, Michael. She won't do a bloody thing; no homework, nothing around the house to help me out . . . the school's been doing their nut . . .

— Yeah, I believe that to be the case, I agree, sort of absent-mindedly.

She looks at me and shakes her head. — And what do I get from you? Bleedin platitudes, she scoffs at me, — same old bleedin platitudes.

That's a new word she's learned: platitudes. Posh word for a Hardwick. Don't wanna be giving the likes of that crowd a bleedin education, it only breeds dissatisfaction. They'll all be happier tarmacking drives.

— Look, if you want me to come along to a meeting at the school, just give us a little bit of notice. It ain't easy when I'm running a bar hundreds of miles away . . .

I see something nasty flash into her eyes and realise that I've made my first big mistake. True to form, she pounces. — Oh, poor Mickey, must be such a hard life, running a bar on a baking hot island! She shakes her head. — Platitudes.

And the narky cow draws first blood. Our boy has to settle back onto the ropes, stay calm, keep ducking and diving.

The dodgy springs from this old chair are digging into my back. Should replace the old gel's suite. Not that she ever uses this one. This was the old man's chair. A dump like this, and what was the old fellah's party piece? That Tony Bennett song: 'The Good Life'. Loved that one he did. He didn't have much of a good life here, neither did I as it happens, when I was stuck with that narky mare. Springs in my back and I'm getting grief from this cow. — C'mon, Trees, this ain't gonna solve nuffink . . .

— . . . while I'm working in that lab five days a week and trying to bring up *our* daughter!

I can see she's pretty tensed up. Probably choking on a snout. Her weakness, that is, and I ain't got no sympathy for them who can't stand above their addictions. Knows better than to light up in my old mum's house, though.

49

Teresa Hardwick's making all the running, trying to land the big punch, but Michael Baker is still nippy on his feet.

I blow out some air making a farting noise through my lips. I stop when I remember that was one of the things I did that got her goat. We all ave em. Hers that did my head in? Too bleedin numerous to mention. But one would certainly be the way she makes that mouth of hers go like a cat's arsehole, as she's doing now. — I appreciate that you ain't got it easy, I'm telling her, doing my diplomatic bit, — but that bar's my livelihood. I ain't coming back here to sit around doing nuffink. At least this way I can make some money to send back over, I say, and maybe it comes out just a little bit too smug.

Stinging jab from Baker! Hardwick felt that one!

Of course she steams in like a Millwall mob with the numbers on its side. —Yeah, you're all abaht sacrifices, ain'tcha, Mickey?

Strong counter from Hardwick. She tries to land another big right, but Baker's on his bicycle.

— Look, I ain't gonna sit here trading insults with you across no room. You know what'll happen, I appeal, — we'll both start raising our voices. It makes it just like before, and it don't do me no good, don't do you no good and it certainly don't do Em no good. And I got to respect me mum's house.

— Good at that, ain'tcha, she hisses like a bleedin witch, — respecting houses.

Oh! That was a low blow from Hardwick!

There's a long silence, with her just looking at me, judging me. This is a lot of bleedin use, this winding back the clock like it was yesterday. Some people ain't got what it takes to move on. Character deficiency, one might say. I get up and stretch, managing to stifle a yawn. She hated it when I yawned when she was jawing. Have to get used to it these days. I clock the old picture of my dad on the mantelpiece. Funny, but nowadays that tash would make him look well dodgy. — I'm going back tomorrow, I tell her. — Keep me posted.

Good stuff from Baker there, who was obviously winded but kept dancing his way out of trouble.

Trees takes the hint and stands up and I notice a new roll of fat under her chin. Always was a bit too fond of crisps: ever since our courting days. The Hardwick family, though, they were all proper scum. Reared on junk food, they was. Her mum thought that gourmet cooking was putting a load of fish fingers under the grill instead of in the frying pan. 'I always grill my food,' the pompous old trout used to remark. So I suppose Trees didn't do too badly, coming from a house like that. My old man had their number, right enough. Well dodgy, that crowd, he told me when I first brought her home. Don't like the idea of Em hanging about there. Not exactly the place, to put it diplomatically, that you'll learn anything worthwhile. Alright if you want thieving and fortune-telling as your specialist *Mastermind* subjects. The Hardwick gene — never that far from the surface in Trees — comes crashing out as she says in a low hiss, — That's right, you just do what you always do when the going gets rough: run away and leave everybody else to clear up the mess after ya, and she goes all bleedin stiff like somebody's rammed a steel rod up her jacksie, then heads through to get Em.

Another low blow and the referee has disqualified Hardwick! The winnah, and still undisputed champion is . . . Mikeeee Bay-kah!

I feel like shouting back at her: it's a mess of your own farking creation, gel, cause it's only since she's been alone with you that all the bleedin problems have started, but I bite my tongue and I'm thinking about that plane home. That's Trees though; not content with being the architect of her own demise, she's determined to drag everybody else down. Count me out of that little game, some of us got a bleedin life, thank you very much! As old Winston once said: 'Although prepared for martyrdom, I prefer that it be postponed.'

It's all over!

2.

CYNTH

Farking weather: sunshine paradise all year round they say. Pull the other one! This freak storm only went and washed all the notice from the board outside the pub, after I'd taken ages chalking it up, Worthington's Cup; Chelsea v Man U. I spent bleedin yonks getting that Chels crest just right.

My mood ain't helped by Margarita, our cleaner, who only goes and comes in an hour late. I tap my watch n tell her: — You havin a laugh or what?

She starts rabbiting on; something about her husband and son and a farking car crash and this mad storm. I empathise, take her outside and point at the runny noticeboard. — Tell me abaht it.

This little old English pub, the Herefordshire Bull, in sunny old Corralejo, is my power base; well, mine and my partner Rodj's, to be strict about things. It's a no-frills house of ill repute of the sort you might actually find back home: two small bars, a public and a lounge, each containing a big screen, and a jukebox (the lounge) and a dartboard (the public). On the other side of the bar, the expat cowboys we inherited when we bought it from a retired farmer five years ago. A right little den of iniquity. But it ain't a bad life, truth be told. I like to think that we, the English, well, some of us any roads, have brought a little calmness and serenity to this island.

A couple of Jap geezers are my first customers tonight. Don't see many of them in Corralejo, though there's a nice little bordello full of South American beauties round the corner, getting a fair old rep by all accounts. Bit expensive though, and I never did see the point in paying for something that's easily obtainable for free if you ain't the picky sort. One Jap puts some John Lennon on the jukebox. I nod over towards them and sidle up to Cynthia, who's washing some glasses and give her a subtle pat on the bum, whispering: — *Sro kreep on praying rose mind graymes too-geh-eh-thah* . . .

I love Cynth's fat.

She gives my arse a saucy little squeeze back and winks at me. I've only gone and . . .

Oh well, destination planet sleaze.

Thought it would be busier tonight cause they're both big expat teams, but there surprisingly ain't many Chelsea nor Man U around. A couple of Geordie lads come in and start giving it the big one about soft southerners but I ain't rising to no bait. Lairy northern cunts. The main thing is that Cynth's here and I'm looking at her big, heavy buttocks and those pendulous breasts and I'm thinking, 'This is a woman whose basic structure can no longer contain her sexuality.' Tits and arse expanding all over the fucking shop. Jawline still defined, skin on the face still tight. Every farking pint, every slice of pizza, it only goes straight to the gut, tits and arse. That's why I like to see her indulge: in fact I bleedin well encourage it!

— Have another beer, babe, I say to her.

— Not on duty, Michael. You trying to get me drunk? She giggles. Good fun is Cynth, and that's a quality you appreciate in skirt. Course, there's some who're that way inclined till they get what they like to term 'commitment', then turn straight into narky old mares. That's the stage when they start to see your role as a psychological punchbag, taking the blows cause they can't hit back out at a life that's disappointed them. You become a everythingologist in the bar game. Walton, Guildford, Romford, Streatham, I done em all.

— Take another slice of that pizza then, gel, I suggest, pointing to the congealed mass of dough in our hot tank.

— Nah, I can't, can I, cause I'm getting so bleedin fat, she protests.

— No you ain't, don't talk nonsense, anorexic you are, I tell her, — that's your problem. Read all about you binge-and-purge sorts.

— That's bulimia, she says, touching her gut.

— That might be the case, but it's the same thing, innit, birds worrying too much abaht nosh, I grin, cause I like a bit of meat on a gel. The way that weight of hers wobbles and shifts as she moves; I really love to watch her serving, especially when she stretches a little to reach up to the optics to fill a glass. I've seen me on the other side of that bar ordering a Scotch I don't even want just to cop an eyeful of that. Most of all, I suppose I like the way I can change her, love watching her spread out after a week's indulgence, all instigated by yours truly.

Them supermodels might look great in clothes, but let's face it: you wouldn't wanna fuck one of em. Feel like one of them Indian geezers lyin on a bleedin bed of nails.

Rodger ain't exactly shrouding himself in glory at the moment. Bertie only went and caught him with his fingers in the till, metaphorically speaking. Actually, they were in Marcia's snapper, behind the bar n all, the dirty fucker. Course, Bertie starts sounding off to me about mates and a mate's missus and how you don't go there. 'You do not cross that farking line, Mickey,' was how he put it. I don't see no fucking line, but I ain't gonna tell him that.

Of course, if I had a missus myself, then I might think differently. That ain't ever gonna happen though: once bitten, twice shy, is what I always say. Right now, though, it's give us anuvah, muvah, that one don't bleedin well play in Chateau Mickey. Cause the truth is, the only way you'll get skirt of any quality is to nick the attached but disaffected ones. And they usually ain't up for jumping ship till they've checked out that there's quality goods on offer elsewhere. Then there's your stepping-stone skirt; can't work up the bottle to leave their geezer without a patsy like you around to share the flak. Course, once he's gone, you soon get your marching orders or she becomes so crazy you have to give her the elbow, and you're left high and dry like a daft cunt and a rep somewhere between a sleaze-bag and a muppet. Basic human nature, and if you ain't worked that one out after five years in the licencing trade, then you never will.

After all, I had a go at that Marcia slag myself the other night. Bit thin for my tastes, but there's something about a skinny bird pushing forty. If they ain't let themselves go by then, they got to have one big vice. I've found through experi-ence that it's inevitably shagging. A skinny tart pushing forty is usually a dirty slag: pretty game for anything once you get past the first hurdle. It's that first fence that's often the problem. Giving it the old cock-teaser malarkey again, Marce was. Cut to the chase and grabbed her outside the toilets. She only went and slapped my bleedin chops, hitting me with the old inno-cent routine before scarpering. Told her it was a fair cop, that I must have misread the signs. Jack Daniel's'll do that for you. Every farking time.

Rodj seems to be making an impression though, the cunt. A sleazeball of the highest order is my business partner, with that gelled hair and a permanently laughing face, even when he's pissed off. There's definitely some good shagging in old Marce, I'll wager, so I can't exactly blame Rodj for trying to get some in. Mind you, married to poor old Bertie, God love him, she's got to be desperate for it, I'd be surprised if that wasn't the case. Have to say though, looks like old Rodj is now in pole position, even if he ain't good at closing deals.

This island's full of fucking junkies! Two cunts sitting in the corner of the bar, staring at the farking walls. Sorry, but did I leave London for a reason? My bleedin mistake. Mind you, the quality of football in the so-called Premiership would have every cunt on gear. The game's shit, too fucking tactical, all the flair geezers stifled by five across the middle. Playing percentages and charging muppets forty nicker for the privilege, and mugs like me for the satellite equipment and packages. Then you got them commentators and pundits; the telly company tell them to talk up every farking game, so you got them cunts having a farking orgasm while we're at home falling asleep on the flaming couch or in the boozer begging the barmaid to turn the cunting jukebox up. So another Scotch goes down and my face glows and I realise that I've only gone and got arseholed again!

Any roads, Cynthia and I have been getting it on. Unshaggable till you down a couple of Scotches, then she fairly sets up the horn in you. Birds will make a cunt of you all the time. Not that I'm cynical; a cheerful sort by nature really, but I only make the observation.

Cynth and me didn't half cane it the night before I went back to me mum's in Walton: a big session on the red wine. I think I got right up between her there and then, I believe that to be the case, but I was too farkin rat-arsed to remember much about it. So I wakes up feeling horny, as in fucking Alpine, and gets my fingers moving south of the border. Gor blimey, it was like trying to work with a block of sandpaper. Funny though, the things you learn with a bit of experience. As a young buck I would have taken that as a sign that she don't fancy me and said something defensive like: What's up with you, you farking frigid lezzer, you fucking peculiar or something?

Experience though. Now you know that as she's been canning the vino, she's just a bit dehydrated. So I brought her a big glass of water. — Get that down ya, gel, I told her.

— You're so sweet, Michael, she said.

Didn't dare tell her I was just watering the flaming garden, did I?

Phase 2 involved getting her up and moving around, let the metabolism kick in. With a tourist bird I'd've suggested a bracing walk along the seafront or the beach before taking her back and nailing her, but that weren't an option with Cynth, as discretion was of the essence. She's still a married woman, after all, even if her relationship with that golf wanker is tenuous to say the least. So I offered to make some tucker, scrambled eggs on toast.

Sure enough, a bit of sweet talk over the table, some fresh orange juice and another big glass of water and the next time me hand went downstairs it was like sticking it under a running tap.

I brought her off that way, then slipped the old how's your father in for a bit more Sunday sport. There's plenty to cushion you when you're on top of her, and I love sticking my finger in her belly button and going: 'Ow's my Pilsbury Dough gel then?' And as I give her one, I get a hold of that big, fat wobbly arse and those flabby love handles and, of course, those floppy great tits. It's bleedin wonderful, but there's no way that I'd let Cynth go on top. She suggested it after a bit and I sort of skirted round the idea. I mean, who'd want all that beef on top of em? If I want buried alive I'll go round some East End boozers bad-mouthing the Kray twins, thank you very much.

Excellent fuck, Cynth, but she went a bit funny afterwards with all this 'hold me, Michael' stuff. Birds are like nosh-ups, have a big one and you're satiated. Don't wanna go near one again for a bit, do ya? Basic psychology, but something skirt never get. She went a bit frosty, and I was trying to get some bleedin kip in for the next morning's flight to Gatwick, so we ends up rowin. She only tears off into the night, but, well, for me it's mission accomplished, innit. I reckoned that with a seeing-to like that she was well bound to be back. Sure as night follows day.

And I wasn't wrong. True what they say about absence making the heart grow fonder, and the ravine wider. There's no mention of the previous argy-bargy and she's all over me like a cheap suit tonight, asking me about bleeding Walton-on-Thames. — Great town, I tell her. — Whenever I leave I always keep a little bit of Walton in me. What about you?

— I'm from Faversham, she says, — you know that . . .

— Well then, I say, how'd you like a little bit of Walton in you?

She punches me in the chest but she's looking around making sure the coast is clear and she whispers, — Your place at midnight?

— I shall be waiting, I say in my best MC tones.

Fair play to Cynth; she don't keep me too long, once I turf em all out and lock up. She double-backs and I hear a familiar knock on the door from the back staircase. I let her in, then we're on the couch ripping each other's clothes off like teenagers and all that flab's flying all over the place, and I'm on her in a sweaty hump and she's off like an alarm clock n all.

Jesus fack almighty!

The next day at least the bleedin rains have eased off a bit but the weekend hangovers have kicked in ever so bad. Cynth couldn't stay, told her old man she was playing cards with her mates and cleared off early. I don't lie around in bed too long.

I'm up and strolling through town to pick up some nice fish, fresh off the boat, then phoning Trees-the-ex back in Walton-on-Thames. Before you can say Jimmy Pursey the dopey cow only goes and tells me that she thinks it would be a good idea to send our Emily over for some of the school holidays, which translates as 'I'm knocking off some geezer and I want her out from under my bleedin feet'.

Thanks a farking bundle, you filthy old trout.

Puts me in a right shit frame of mind, that does. Still, you got to keep thinking: calmness and serenity. So I gets in the motor and takes a trip down to the Kraut side of the island using the FV1 coastal route and bypassing that farking dump Puerto del Rosario. As you get onto the FV20 and head south to Gran Tarajal it could be a different world. It's the best-looking bit of the island by far, and the portion which the old Squareheads have thoughtfully commandeered for themselves. Makes you wonder who won the farking war. I park up outside a boozer I occasionally use and poke my head round the door but it's dead. There's this waitress who works in a restaurant I like down here, but it don't look like she's in today. No worries: they've a nice bit of grilled lemon sole on.

A bit of tucker sets me up and when I get back for the evening shift Rodj is already in, and Cynth ain't far behind.
— How's it goin with Marce? I ask him discreetly.
— Nuffink's going on, he shakes his head angrily, which means it most certainly is. No need for the cunt to get all bleedin narky; it ain't as if they've exactly been discreet about the whole thing!

I clock a couple of dodgy-looking geezers standing at the bar. One's a big burly fucker with a crew cut, wearing light-reflective glasses. The other's a weaselly little cunt with shifty eyes and greasy hair, slicked back. He's dripping with tom; two earrings, at least two gold chains round his neck, bracelets on his wrist and sovereign rings on nearly every finger. Farking little tart. But it wasn't so much how they looked as what they were saying that got me interested. You got to watch putting your nose in but I got intrigued and found out that by hiding behind the gingham curtain which drapes at the side of the small public bar, pretending to be looking at the books, I can hear every bleedin word they say. Meantime, the cunts think I'm in the back shop! So here I am, fiddling away, but getting a proper earful.

— . . . but there's a few around here she's going to have to sack if she's gonna go all the way to the top. Baggage and such. I mean, I ain't naming no names but that gel's got star potential and I'd be loath to have it undermined through some dodgy associations . . . it sounds like the weaselly cunt with the gold is saying.

— You're thinking of Graham, I take it? the big cropped-haired bastard says. His voice is gravelly, like a villain on *The Bill.*

The other cunt has a high, nasal, snidey tone: — Like I said, I ain't naming no names, but if the cap fits . . .

— You got to save her from herself, Trev.

— Well, we're gonna have to sit down togevah, just the two of us over a nice meal, bottle of wine, and have a serious little chat . . .

— Serious chat . . .

— A serious chat about her future, cause I'd hate to see her blow it. But what *she* needs is a little discipline, a firm hand. Otherwise she's gonna throw it all away.

— Cruel to be kind, Trev.

— Exactly, Chris. Tough love I believe is what they call it nowadays. And if that Graham was to just somehow disappear it would make my job a great deal easier.

There's a silence as the big brick-shithouse geezer goes,

— Disappear . . . let's be clear about this, Trev. Disappear from her life or disappear for good?

The other cunt's voice goes low. I think he says, —Whatever it takes.

— If he did vanish off the scene, she'd be very upset.

— In the short term, Chris, in the short term. But she'd get over it. Course, she'd need a shoulder to cry on.

Then Cynth comes through and shouts something, whipping the curtain away, dozy farking cow, which is so farking mortifying as them geezers see me standing up from behind the bar. They look daggers at me giving me that 'how much have you heard' thing, but I just keep staring at the ledger in my hand, worrying that my cheeks are flushing. — Yes, my lovely? I say as distractedly as I can.

— We need some San Miguels and Coronas up here right now.

— Where's Rodj? I ask, as if I don't know.

— He nipped out for a moment.

A wooing, no doubt, the cahnt. — Bleedin hell, gel, can't it wait? I'm engrossed in those books. Totally engrossed, I turn to the geezers at the bar. — Got to do everything around here, I shake my head and smile, and the big cunt gives me a tight grin back, but the weaselly geezer's eyes are all black pools.

I drop the books and head downstairs, cursing that fat, stupid blundering cow.

Farking villains. Never did like the cunts, even back home. Don't get me wrong, I've pulled a few strokes myself now and again, but I don't get off on all that gangster bollocks. Most of those cunts are just fucking bullies and you're the mug who's got to listen to their bullshit and laugh in all the right places. Wouldn't be so bad if it wasn't so farking boring most of the time. Yeah, some of these geezers *are* genuinely witty, but most of them's peddling the same farking shit you've heard a million times before.

Eventually, the cunts drink up and leave. The greasy little fucker with the gold gives me a long, slow, hard nod and I'm paranoid all bleedin day, in me own farking place.

At night it's a better atmosphere in the pub and I lock Vince, Bert and myself in for a card school. Funny to think that by keeping Bert here right now, I'm probably assisting Rodj in his quest to nail his missus. Mixed feelings about that one. Vince is a decent sort, from Manchester, or near there. Rents out properties here on the island. Dodgy as, never seems to do anything, always away on little trips, but generally has a horsechoker of a wad in his pocket. Bertie runs a sporting-goods shop but if you ask me it's been bought with funny money. He's a shifty little git, and every time some new face comes in the boozer he seems to get a bit antsy.

Vince and I are winding Bertie up. — You mean to say that you've never had a homosexual experience in your life before? I ask him.

— Course I haven't, Bertie says, all offended.

I'm shaking my head, looking at the dross I've got in my hand. — How old are you, you've got to bleedin thirty-seven and you've never had a gay experience?

He looks to Vince who smiles and shrugs, which freaks old Bert right out. — Of course not . . . you're bleedin tapped, he goes, then he turns to Vince again. — Have you?

Vince looks at him with his big hooded eyes. — Of course I have, he says in that Manc voice, — I mean, you got to try everything once, aven't ya?

Poor Bertie almost chokes on his beer. He puts the glass onto the table, looking at Vince all sorta weird. — But . . . I can't believe I'm hearing this . . . he says and turns to me. — What about you?

— I'm thirty-nine for fuck sakes, I tell him, — I mean, we ain't *all* led sheltered lives.

— I ain't led no sheltered life . . . he protests, his voice going all high.

— Yeah, sure, Vince shakes his head.

— Well, no, he starts, all hesitant, — cause there was once . . .

And we're all ears as he only goes and describes this encounter with a bentshot at some bleedin queer bar down in Clapham. Well, Vince and I just let him finish and then shout together: — WE'RE ONLY FARKING JOKING, YOU FARKING GREAT BIG POOF!

Outed! Always knew he was bleedin suspect. I point at him and shout, — File under arse behnnndit!

Bertie begs Vince and I to say nothing, insisting that he was just a bit freaked at our so-called disclosures and making it all up so as to fit in, which knowing Bert is quite possibly true. We're having none of it though, the dirty bleedin arse bandit. But the geezer's pretty distressed so the only thing to do is tell him we'll keep shtum about the whole thing.

Of course, it's only all around the bar the next night, innit. Somebody obviously kissed and told but mum's the word on that one.

Thing is, it fair sets old Bertie off on the warpath with Vince and I as main suspects. Marcia's only gone and heard all about it and kicked off about Aids, putting poor old Bert on an indefinite no nooky ban. Not that she gave him that much in the first place, by all accounts, or rather by Rodj's account. Now Bertie's gathering evidence for his appeal. But this one ain't going to go to Stewards, not if I can help it.

After closing time he only goes and comes round to mine with a bit of attitude on him. — One of you two has been blabbing about the other night! It's all round the bar, Marcia's heard all about it!

— Bollocks. I ain't said nothing to Marcia. Who told her then?

— One of the geezers at the bar, Bertie says, open-gobbed.

— Who?

— I dunno, do I? he whines. — She won't say.

— Well, that covers a multitude, don't it? I shake my head. —Why won't she say? I ask. Thing is, with geezers like Bertie, it don't really matter how pissed off they are, you just keep asking the questions and you soon draw their sting.

— I dunno, do I? he repeats like a flaming parrot, all flustered.

I shake my head. — Sounds suspect to me, mate.

— What? What sounds suspect?

I feel like saying, 'You, you fucking dodgy little arse bandit, you sound farking suspect,' but I explain it to him. Bertie, God love him, he ain't the sharpest needle in your old mum's embroidery kit. — If my missus had told me that she'd heard that I was an iron, I'd want to know who'd told her. I wouldn't be happy hearing that it was just pub talk. I'd be asking myself: who stands to gain from her thinking that you're bottled beer?

You could quite literally see the coin drop. — Was Marce on with Rodj the other day? he gasps.

— I believe that to be the case.

Then he headed off, eyeballs bulging out like a Jack Russell's bollocks. As if he was planning to do some serious damage. Not that he's the sort, really, but there's no telling what some geezers will do over skirt. Crimes of passion n ah'll. Think ancient Rome; Caesar, Mark Antony and Cleopatra. And it ain't just big empires what's been brought to their knees by minge; some tidy little businesses in the licensing trade have gone right down the flaming Swanee when the guvnor and or his missus have been caught on the wrong side of the duvet. See, I'd mentioned Bert's little secret to Rodj earlier, knowing full well that, in turn, he'd be compelled to tell Marcia. So my hope now is that Rodj does a runner and

Bert's *sine die*, leaving the field clear for yours truly to fire into Marce.

I'm sitting back feeling pleased with meself, when me mobile sings out, signalling a text coming in. It's Trees-the-ex. Her message reads:

> Bell me on the landline
> between 4 and 6. Urgent.

Tight-arsed cow. I have a shower, make myself a sandwich of cheese, tomato, lettuce and mayo, then pick up the blower and dial, getting a funny farking tone. Forgot to knock off the zero on her number after 0044. I try again and get her voicemail. — Neither Teresa nor Emily are in at the moment. Please leave your number and we'll try to get back to you.

I leave a message. — Trees, it's Mickey. You wanted me to call between 4 and 6, from your text. You said it was urgent, so I called right away. Do you want to get back –

— Michael, she says and you know that the cow was sitting there all the time letting me farking rabbit on like that. — How are you?

— Busy, I tell her. — What's up? Is Em okay?

— Oh, well, I ain't gonna be popular, am I. Thing is, Em's been playing up so I'm sending her over to you for a bit.

It might be hot here but ain't nobody told my blood that right now. The farking cow. — What do you mean? You said *some* orf the holidays. I got a flaming bar to run, I can't –

— You can't make time for your own daughter. Fine. I'll tell her.

She's loving all this, the farking cow. I take a deep breath. — You say she's coming for a bit. What is a bit?

— Dunno. She's flying out tomorrow on the 8.15 from Gatwick, gets in at 12.30.

—You can't do this without bleedin well sortin it with me, that is bang out of order. I got things to do!

— N I ain't?

That bleedin cow is in her farking element. She knows that I can't knock Em back. — You know what I mean . . . I need notice, you can't just hit me with a fait accompli like that. C'mon, Trees, give us a break –

— Nah, you give *me* a break, Mickey, she whines, that adenoidal tone squeaking down the blower, like a proper Hardwick. Forgot just how much it does your crust in. Patience of a saint I must have, putting up with that all them years. — She wants to see ya. She's been a proper narky little cow and I ain't havin her sitting around talkin the hump with me and Richie . . .

Surprise, surprise. — So this is what all this is abaht, you and some farking trouser –

— I've said my piece, she says, all cool, but she can't keep the smugness out of her voice. — Be there at the airport to meet your daughter.

— Trees . . . I'm pleading now, — Terry . . .

Then she only goes and puts the farking blower down on me!

I dial her number again but it's only the flamin voicemail, — Neither Teresa nor Emily . . .

— Farking cow, I spit and head downstairs to the bar. Knockout blow to Hardwick, Baker left KO'd on the canvas. It don't bare thinking about. I pour myself a double Scotch. Cynth's in and she's watching me. — Bit early, isn't it?

— Been a funny old morning, I tell her, heading down to the cellar, leaving her standing there, hands on hips like a big, shapely vase. It's always nice and cool down here, just the place to go when you wanna charge the old calmness and serenity batteries. Suddenly, I hear a rustling sound and I see a big furry

67

rat; long-haired cunt, marching across the floor. He vanishes behind a stack of beer on pallets. I pick up the brush. Then I hear the tinkle on the mobile: another flaming text message coming in. Bleedin hell, it's only from Seph, this farking hairy little Greek gel I was nailing last summer. Telling me that she's only here on Friday for two weeks. How farking complicated can life get?

Old Roland seems to have scarpered. So down here in the cellar I'm taking stock of my life. It's all here in the barrels and the stacked pallets of bottles: piss. My assets all converted into a supply of alcohol to sell for profit. Disinhibition, good times and hope; that's what I peddle. How many birds have I nailed through them over-imbibing that most glorious of drugs? Too many to count.

I shake off my thoughts and get upstairs. Cynth comes over and sidles up to me. I know by her look what she's got on her mind and she opens her mouth to confirm that I ain't wrong. — When we gonna see each other then?

— Tonight round mine. Eleven forty-five, I say, but it comes out all wrong, as I ain't making much eye contact, I'm warily checking the bar for strangers.

Nothing will alienate skirt quicker than your distraction. You gotta at least provide the illusion of the old undivided. — Anything wrong? she asks.

— Nah . . . well, yeah, I come clean. My gut's still blistering from that phone call with Trees, even if Seph's text just proved that you just have to tough out the bad till the good comes round the corner, which it always does. Didn't take very long in this case. I should be chuffed, but there are practical affairs to put right. — The ex is only sending the bleedin kid over tomorrow, ain't she. I mean, what am I gonna do with a young teenage gel here? I look around the boozer, then nod upstairs. — You know the flat, it's tiny.

Cynth rolls down her bottom lip. — You got a spare room.

— Yeah, but it ain't got no bed and it's got all my gear in it.

— I've got a fold-down bed; you can have that. When I come up to yours later we'll go through your stuff and sort it out, she cheerfully volunteers. — How old is she?

Good sort, Cynth. I'm looking at those stiff red lips of hers and she's got me all ears now. — Thirteen. Going through the narky little cow stage by all accounts.

— And she's gonna be here most of the school holidays?

— The ex ain't said but I believe that to be the case, yes.

Cynth seems to think about that one. She never had no kids but I think she always wanted them. No luck with the geezers though; told me once that her first fellah was a cunt, a proper tightwad, who didn't want no breadsnapper around. Number 2's been shooting blanks for years and is now any roads settled into a golfing life. She seems too bleedin keen on the idea of Em being here though. But it don't half get ya thinking; if these two hit it off, it gives me a bit of time to be indulging in some extra-curricular activity with a certain young lady from Greece.

Interesting gel, young Seph. We met the other winter when she was over here. To be honest, a bird with a tash don't do nuffink for me, but after a few Jack Daniel's she could have been farking Taliban for all I cared. Bottled her up a few times last summer, then again in November over there when Chels was at Olympiakos in the Champions League. Made some of the geezers pretty green that day, swanning round Athens with a young thing like that on me arm, tash or no bleedin tash. Lovely long black hair; all the way down to her arse. Even them big Nana Mouskouri glasses couldn't keep the old fellah down. In fact, you get to a certain age and that thing starts to appeal. That's what happens when you've watched too many stag vids and seen too many facials.

I might suggest a waxing.

— Penny for em? Cynth asks, and I'm looking at that great expanse of doughy gut between the bottom of her top and the top of her shorts. Plenty of the old cellulite in the mix, but it's funny how it don't look half as bad on tanned skin.

I pinch a fold of belly lightly between forefinger and thumb. — I do believe that you are losing weight, gel, I tell her.

She puts her hands on her hips and does a little swivel, giving herself the once-over in the bar mirror. — You really think so?

— I believe that to be the case.

— It ain't what the scales say, she goes, spinning round and looking at that fat arse. Rodj sees this from the bar of the public, raises his brow and gets back over to pulling pints for two old geezers that've come in with their wives. Looks very guilty n all. I'm wondering whether he and Bert have had words.

— Bathroom scales, I scoff. — Always bleedin farked, ain't they. Can't rely on em, can ya, I tell her, taking a slice of pizza from the glass display case and sticking it into the microwave. — You need fattening up, you do.

— You're so sweet, Mikey. You know, when I was with Ben I was never good enough for him. He always used to moan about my weight . . . and Thomas, he doesn't even see me as a woman . . .

I move over and pin her against the bar. — Some geezers don't know when they're on a good thing. I tug down the zip of her shorts and slip my hands in and start touching her bush lightly.

— Michael . . .

— You're a naughty gel. No knickers, I say, thinking, bleedin hell, no prizes for guessing what she was after all along!

— Stop, Michael, somebody might come, she gasps as I pull

70

up her top to expose those big tits, flopping away without a bleedin bra in sight.

— I believe that to be the case, I murmur, as she pulls the top back down before Rodj comes round.

3.

EM

Waiting around at the airport the next day, I feel well farked. Fucking armies of holidaymakers; old cahnts in the mood for winter sun for the old bones, sly-looking husbands ready to team up with like minds and bodyswerve their miserable fat cows and screaming kids, and young uns and some not so young on the hunt for a good drink and a rattling opportunity.

After cleaning out my gaff the other night, Cynth and I nailed another couple of bottles of red and then did some tequila slammers. Farking suicide mission. Any roads, I humped her a couple of times then cooked up some steak, onions, mushrooms and McCain's oven chips, the low-fat ones.

Got up the next day still drunk and left a decidedly sheepish Rodj running the show. — Gonna be a recurrent theme, mate, I tell him. — I'll have to be leanin on ya a bit. All hands on deck.

— Yeah, well, I know you wanna spend time with Em. Don't worry about it, he says.

— You, sir, are a gentleman and a scholar.

Poor Rodj. Don't think he's even had the satisfaction of properly nailing Marce but he's certainly got someone on the warpath! Apparently Bert's been spotted in various boozers making threats about a certain party! Smarmy git though he might well be, what the likes of Rodj forget is the adage about the construction of omelettes requiring certain eggs getting well smashed. And when things start getting cracked, that's when his sort start getting nervy.

On the way to the airport I bell Seph. She's a goer but a bit of a loose cannon and you got to watch her. Her old man is the chief of police on this small island, which is only a short hop from Piraeus, the old port of Athens. 'My father is the chief of police for thee whole island!' she boasts all the time. Wouldn't mess with her over there cause the old man sounds like a proper cunt; the sort who's probably fitted up more geezers than C&A's.

She's on my turf now though, or soon will be. Hopefully I'll be on her turf soon n all. Normally I enjoy a bit of rug-munching (a gentleman's sport long before the old bulldykes muscled their way into the picture) but she's got a flaming Axminster down there. Thought I'd come face to face with Dr Livingstone at one point, before necessity compelled me to come up for air.

I'm waiting at the arrivals gate and then Em sees me and her face lights up for a second before she remembers she's a teenager and I'm her old man and she just gives me an awkward pat on the shoulder instead of a hug. And it hurts, cause I wanted to wrap my arms round her and say 'How's my little gel then' but I ain't said that to her, ain't had that sort of thing with her for bleedin years and I know that I've missed so much, so bleedin much, and I'll never have it again.

Gor blimey if there ain't bloody tears welling up in my eyes so I pull down the shades from the top of my head and point to the exit.

— Good flight? I ask, managing to keep my voice even.

— A plane's a plane, she shrugs back, not even noticing that her old man's all choked up.

— Yeah. You ain't wrong.

So we get to the car and I start rabbiting on, shit really, just trying to fill in time. How's school and all that bleedin malarkey.

— I hate school, she says as she sits with her knees up, picking at the skin round her fingers.

— Don't be like that, I tell her. — My old man, your grandad, he used to say to me, 'If you like school you'll love work then live happily ever after.'

She don't say nothing to that, just sort of rolls her eyes.

I try to explain: — What I mean is that it's your start in life, so you gotta go in with the right attitude. You get out what you put in, don'tcha?

She just shrugs and don't say nothing. And I suppose she's right to be a sceptic n all. The stuff about the old man, he said nothing of the kind, I just made that up. Churchillian-style motivational speech, that sort of thing. Reality was, the old boy didn't give a monkey's about what I got up to at school. Yeah, she's right, school was a load of bleedin bollocks. My teachers were all sneaky, poncey fuckers, every one of them. Well, except that Miss Johns in English; the way she'd bend over you to correct your work and them tits in that tight top and that hair cascading down in your face and the bleedin perfume ... farkin well shouldn't have been allowed. No wonder I grew up not bein able to keep my hands off skirt; damaged I was, well and truly bleedin damaged by the educational system! Should get a farking claim in! Good solicitor, that's what I need, a decent brief, like the geezer wot sprung us all and got the compensation when the Old Bill, bless em, made another farking cock-up.

Thing was, though, the likes of Miss Johns was different. Encouraged you, didn't they. Didn't think they had all the questions and answers, honesty lies.

— Mum told me that you got put in jail for fighting at a football match once, when I was a baby, she says.

What the fuck is that dopey old slag saying to the gel?

This rookie scraper has evidently been trained in the Hardwick school of low blows.

— I got arrested because I was near to where it was all going off and the Old Bill was grabbing anybody, but I never got put in no jail, well, remand, yeah, but I wasn't convicted. The case was dropped; I got compensation cause they was proved to be in the wrong. That's how I got this place, and that's how you and mum got the house, I tell her, and that's as about as much as I want to say on that subject and I move sharply on. — So how's things with ya then, you got a boyfriend at that school?

I'm only joking, pulling her leg, but she turns to me all seriously and says, — I don't really like the boys at school. It may be because I'm still too young, or maybe because they're too immature, but I think I've got a bit of virginity left in me yet.

Shit . . . that hurt . . .

Farkin hell, I feel like I'm about ten years old and I've been told off by my big sister. Then she suddenly looks at me all weird. — You used to see other women. Before you left me and Mum.

I feel my face going all cold and tingly. That way you do when there's a few of you in a boozer and a big mob of tasty-looking geezers comes in. You're fronting it but your bottle's well shaky. Nobody's saying nothing but you're just waiting for it to kick off and for some cunt to ram a flaming glass in your face. What's farking well going on here? — Who told you that? I ask, as if I don't bleedin well know.

— It's true but, ain't it? she says, sounding like somebody else. That flaming Hardwick gene.

Well on the ropes here. Think calmness and serenity. Use the experience, keep ducking and diving.

— Look, one thing you're gonna realise in life is that there's more than one reason why people do things. Sometimes there's a lot of them. It takes more than one person to change things, like in a relationship.

She seems to think about this, then she goes, — These women, when you were lying in bed with them, then her voice goes harsher, — shagging them, did you ever think about me and Mum at home?

I ain't havin this. I slow down and pull up by the side of the road. I draw a big breath. — Look, I'm your dad and we're gonna be staying together for a bit. You got to give me some respect; I respect you, you respect me.

I don't believe it! Mickey Baker is throwing in the towel! His corner are saying that their boy has taken enough punishment!

— Whatever, she says, now all distracted, like her mind's on sumfink else. She opens up a magazine she's been carrying. It's one of them celebrity gossip shit-sheets that kids and thick cunts read. The so-called celebs are mostly Luton reserves level; there's some fat munter who once had a hit record and is now bloating for England and ramming Colombia's harvest up her hooter since her fella scarpered with a fitter bird. I worry about Em's choice of reading: the sort of thing a Hardwick might read. More interesting to her, evidently, than her old fellah, whom she ain't spent any proper time with in months.

I'm fuming cause I don't know this kid at all. She's been poisoned against me, by parties who shall remain nameless, and I've got my work cut out here. This ain't my little gel. This is a weird kid whom I don't recognise; all tall and skinny and dressed funny and comin out with all sorts of daft stuff.

— That's what they call the Red Mountain, I point out the window, — Montana Colorada. Past them you got the Dunas de Corralejo, which has a wealth of coastal vegetation that is totally unique to this part of the world, I explain

76

with enthusiasm. I'm thinking that they must teach them shit like that at school: the environment n all that for fack sakes.

She ain't giving a toss.

— All volcanic, this is, I hear my voice tailing off in an apology as I look over to the Isle of Lobos. There seems to be some clouds over there, hope they ain't headed this way. — We can take a trip over there, I suggest, — in a glass-bottomed boat. Fancy that, do ya?

— Yeah, she says, briefly looking up from her mag as we head up General Franco Avenue.

She ain't flaming interested, but what can you do? We drive home and I take her down to the Herefordshire and intro her to Cynth, Rodj and the likes. She takes her stuff upstairs to the flat, and when she comes down a bit later, she's got a book in her hand. That puts me in a more cheerful frame of mind. Better than reading those junk mags.

Now Cynth's goin all strange and saying to Em, — When I was young I really liked smoothing out silver paper. You know, different-coloured sort of metallic paper. Kids probably don't do that any more, she says looking at Em who's now reading her book, Philip K. Dick. Funny, I always liked science fiction when I was her age. Arthur C. Clarke. Brian Aldiss; 'The Failed Men'. Skinny geezers wot buried themselves in fields for years. Intelligent sorts, kind of lizard-like with big heads, but who'd just given up. Couldn't be arsed no more. So they dug themselves into the dirt in their millions and hibernated, till some cunt came along and ploughed them all up. But they still just lay there in their muck, not giving a monkey's. That shat me right up as a kid. Cause you gotta be bothered.

Yeah, there was loads of them geezers, Harry Harrison, the one what wrote about Mars and Isaac Asimov, the robot geezer. And that chap what wrote about all them plants taking over. Yeah, sci-fi: mad for it I was. Then I stopped. Dunno why.

Well, skirt, I suppose; in a contest between the imagination and the hormones, there was only gonna be one winner.

— Did you do that when you were a kid, Michael, smooth out silver paper? Cynth's rabbiting on.

— Yeah, I tell her. Smooth out silver paper. What the fuck is she on about?

Cynth made the effort, I'll give her that, but Em ain't responding to none of my jokes, she just sits with a long face all day. All night she's buried in that book as I'm playing arrows with Vince and Rodj. — What about that last night? Vince goes.

— What? I say, looking at Rodj, half expecting to hear something about him and Bert!

— Geezer shot dead. He throws down the paper in front of me.

My Spanish ain't great shakes but I can make out that a British holidaymaker was shot dead outside the Duke of York pub over in Lanzarote. A parky little chill comes over me and for some reason I think back to them two geezers what was in the boozer the other night. A funny pair, right enough. Proper shit me up, they did: that cunt going on about people vanishing. They didn't do a very good job of making anybody disappear, by all accounts. Police found him right there in the house. I'm trying to remember what it was they called the geezer they was jawing about.

I look over at Em, still reading old Philip K. Dick. Some mind, that geezer. *Blade Runner, Minority Report, Star Wars*, the brains behind all that shit, he was. Nice work if you can get it. Too bad he's dead now, so he won't have seen any dosh for it all. Life can be unfair, but mind you, you dunno how much the cunt was worth alive.

Rodj's been on the treble eighteen for centuries, after looking like he was gonna take me to the cleaners. Bottle always goes: couldn't bleedin well check out in the farking supermarket. If Marce wants a length from that department, she could be waiting a long time, especially with old Bert doing his nut. An ominous silence on that topic.

I hit the fourteen and finish up all nifty on the double twenty. — Bastard, Rodj curses and then looks at Em and Cynth. — Pardon my French, ladies, he adds. They both look unimpressed, as well they might.

— This geezer wot was gunned down, what do they say about him? I ask.

— Businessman on holiday, Vince goes.

Businessman. Every cunt's a farking businessman nowadays. Covers a bleedin multitude, that one. — What sort of business was he in?

Rodj shrugs and pours himself a large snifter from the bar. He glances to me and I find myself nodding back in agreement without thinking what I'm doing. Sure enough, I've a glass of Scotch you could float the HMS *Belfast* in. — They didn't say, Vince shrugs.

Nah, they wouldn't bleedin say. So, in reality, we know nothing.

Later that night Seph bells and tells me she's over in Lanzarote. I inform Cynth that I've business over there and ask her to look after Em tomorrow. They ain't best pleased, nor is Rodj, but shit happens and I ain't up for explaining things.

4.

SEPH

I decided that it was about time that I went to visit my old mate Pete Worth at the Cumbria Arms, over in Lanzarote. It was a bright Saturday morning and I got into the motor ready to head down to the ferry, change islands and drive up to the nice little bar in the old town harbour at Puerto del Carmen, where I'd arranged to meet Seph. I was anticipating a carefree, seamless little jaunt.

Didn't work out like that though.

I'm passing the garage, and I look over and I see a sight that makes my arsehole clench like a bookie's fist. It's them two geezers, the ones what was in yesterday and they're only talking to Emily and Cynth . . .

I stop the car and get out sharpish. As I stride across the forecourt, the geezers get into their own motor and head off without seeing me. Emily and Cynth clock me soon enough, though. — I thought you'd gone, Cynth says.

— Nah . . . only running late, innit. I look over my shoulder. — What did them geezers you was talking to want?

— Trying to chat her up, Em laughs.

Cynth goes all that silly little girl way, like some old boilers tend to whenever there's a fresh slab of beef around. That old routine ain't fooling nobody. — No they wasn't, and she even touches her flaming hair, — they was just asking about the bar, that's all.

I do not like the smell of this, and I ain't talking about

Cynth's knickers neither, though by her posture I detect a fair amount of spillage in that department. — What do you mean, asking about the bar?

— Well, they were in the other night for a drink . . . Cynth says, her eyes going wide.

— Yeah, yeah, I remember . . .

— . . . and they were just saying how nice a pub the Herefordshire Bull was, made them feel right at home. They was asking about how long it had been up and running, that's all, she says, looking all guilty, like she's been caught telling tales out of school.

I grab a handful of Cynth's fleshy arm. Pulling her away from Em, I lower my voice, — Asking about the guvnor, was they? I dig my other thumb into my chest.

— No . . . she says, then admits, — well, just if it's an Englishman what runs it and where you come from . . . They was just making conversation, that's all, and then she shrugs my grip off and starts rubbing her arm, looking at me like I'm some sort of beast.

Questions and answers, honesty lies. Cool it, Mickey son. Think what Roger Moore or Kenneth More or Bobby Moore would do in this situ. Think composure under pressure. Calmness and serenity.

— Sorry, darlin, I'm a bit uptight at the mo, I apologise, stepping into her with a peck on the cheek, leaving my face up close to hers.

She's staring back at me like she don't have a clue. Cynth ain't no mug, but like most skirt, thinking outside the box ain't exactly her forte.

I see that Em's distracted, looking at stuff in the garage-shop window. — Listen, Cynth, if those geezers come sniffing around you, or Em or the bar, I want you to bell me on the mobile straight away, capeesh?

Cynth takes a step back. — They wasn't the law, was they?

— Worse than that, darlin, I lower my voice, — HM Customs and Excise, I believe, I touch my nose and wink. — Keep shtum abaht this one gel, alright?

— Of course . . . she says, then looks worried. — . . . There's nothing wrong, is there?

— Nothing we can't sort out, I say, looking across at Em by the shop. I leap over to the kiosk and order three big chocolate ice-cream cones. — There ya go, I say, dishing them out. Takes me back to the summer jaunts me, Em and Trees had down in Hastings. Good times. Em don't look too chuffed though. Cynth blows out her cheeks and says, — We just had one . . .

I'm reasoning that Cynth needs to keep that calorie count up. Getting extra fat is one thing, but *sustaining* it is a problem. If she falls below one thousand five hundred a day, it'll start dropping off. Loads of snacks with high sugar content does the trick, along with convenience food loaded with additives; that and plenty of booze. — Can't have too much of a good thing, I tell her. — If we hadn't had that stuff around in the Second World War, the Yanks might never have come in and we might all be poncing around in jackboots right now. Come to think of it though . . . I wink at Cynth. — Right, I look over to the car, — I'd best scarper. My old mate Worthy, he can't abide lack of punctuality. Reckons it shows disrespect, and I'll tell ya wot, I wag my finger in lecturing mode, — he ain't wrong.

Cynth looks at me all that pleading way and she goes, — When will you be back?

— A few hours, gels, worse bleedin luck. No rest for the wicked, I shout at Em. — Bye, princess!

Then I'm in the motor and that ice cream gets slung out the window as soon as I'm out of sight. Chunking up in skirt is fine; I reckon lots of us geezers are closet chubby-chasers. It ain't an option for me though; no decent minge wants porky trouser. I get down to the harbour and I'm ramping the motor onto the ferry. Never really liked Lanzarote; too commercialised. Mind you, Fuerty's getting that way n all, and Worthy, to give him his due, fairly rakes it in at the Cumbria. He can stuff it though, it's the QOL issue, innit.

When I get to the bar Seph's sitting at a table outside, writing postcards, a white bag at her feet. Looks as lonely as a virgin on Valentine's Day. She's wearing shades under a big straw hat with a scarf tied round it. That's a fetching little aqua-coloured dress, plenty of flesh on show, and her hair's tied with a blue ribbon in one ponytail, one of those jobs what hangs to the side. That'll have to go when I nail her: I wanna see that stuff farking flying all over them pillas.

Course, when she sees me she starts playing it all stand-offish; kiss on each cheek, Euro-style. I was hoping for a big embrace and a tongues job from the off. The chaste approach don't impress me none. Right load of old bollocks that one: you don't come all this way if you don't want a bleedin good rattling at the end of it.

The good news is that the tash has gone! She's been doin a bit of waxing, or zappin with the laser, by the looks of things.

I sit down and she starts tellin me about the aggravation she's getting from her old man, this police geezer. Seems he wants her to go to college somewhere, and she's thinking about England. Asking me what part's the best.

Maybe it's all down to recent personal experiences with certain parties who shall remain nameless, but I suppose I ain't painting that much of an enticing picture. I tell her that the North's grim, the Midlands are dull, and the countryside's boring: full of farking inbred mutant toffs, and London's chock-a-block with scum and ponces these days.

83

— I was thinking about Brighton, Sussex University, she says, and I'm hoping that long vodka I've set up for her will thaw her out a bit. Worked before, and you gotta stick to tried and tested methods. What was it that the great man said: 'It has been said that democracy is the worst form of government except all the others that have been tried.'

Got to come in on the B-word though. Even *my* liberalism's got its limits. — Nah, you don't wanna go to flaming Brighton, do ya. Full of bleedin arse bandits, innit, I explain, and that gets me wondering if she's into the Greek love, her being Greek and all that. Ain't my thing, that kinda dirt; I'm not sayin I ain't stuck it in some manky holes in my time, but they've all been front uns. — The best part of England to go to now is Wales, I venture, — it's all sort of unspoiled, Aber . . . whatever the fark they call it, by the sea n all that. Good university town, I am led to understand. Prestigious, some might say.

She lifts her shades over her head and her big dark eyes blink in the sun. — Wales is good?

Good? What is farking good? I find myself squelching through a swamp of moral relativism every day, as the geezer on the Discovery Channel said the other night. I shouted at the screen: 'Tell me about it, mate, it's called the licensing trade.' — Yeah, but the only problem with Wales is that there's too many Welsh. They don't count themselves as English down there, and neither do we as it happens, although they still come under England.

She shakes her head, and delves into that white leather bag of hers for a packet of fags. — I would want to be close to London.

I can see the point. Seen enough sheep in Greece, I suppose.

A very civilised people, the Greeks. Homer. Aristotle. Socrates. Plato. Just some of the names who'd walk into the starting line-up of any country's Grey Matter First Eleven. But your classics ain't exactly what's on my mind just right now. — So, eh, what do ya want to do? I ask, knowing full well the answer. It's a long way to come from Greece and they got enough beaches there.

Suddenly there's a big light in her eyes and a smile across her face. — I have come to tell you that I have fallen in love, she says.

I look at her and in spite of everything, all the farking aggravation it's gonna cause me, I can't help but feel a little warm glow, nestling in the gut. — Well, you're young, but I understand . . . I tell her, and grab her hand.

She shakes it all sort of funny and says, — It is good that you understand these things, after what has gone between us.

I'm thinking: the older the fiddle, the better the tune right enough, but I elect to keep shtum as it's an emotional time for her. She's still young. Proper idealistic n all. Though I suppose I'm the same. Numerical years: it don't matter a fark. If that's the way you are, you never lose it.

Her little face glows and she says, — His name is Costas and he comes from Athens. He is an actor and . . .

And I can't hear nothing all of a sudden.

And she goes on and on about this flaming bubble and squeak geezer, waving this packet of Marlboro Lites in my face as she talks, but I can't hear the rest. I'm thinking, what the fuck is she doing over here then . . .

But all I can do is look at the turkey ducks, them birds that just lie out on the ground around the harbour. Fuck knows what they are, I ain't seen them anywhere else. They just sit there on the tarmac, like they was all gonna lay eggs. All together, a proper little mob of them. They got turkey-like faces and necks and fat bodies but they got ducks' bills and webbed feet.

Weird-looking cunts, but they ain't no bother to nobody, just like them old boys who sit and talk on the benches, or the tourists under the patios of the harbour bars. Yeah, the old town here is quite picturesque. The rest? Too shit to even discuss.

The turkey ducks.

It's me who's the right bleeding turkey now though. Turkey ducked. Or maybe not. — So, what brings you here? Don't tell me that you came all this way just to share this news, excellent as it is, with your old buddy Mickey? I say, reasoning that she probably wants a good old-fashioned seeing-to before she ties the knot with this bubble thespian. Last days of freedom n all: perfectly understandable.

— I am here with Costas. He is filming here and over where you stay in Fuerteventura. He plays an Italian policeman from Interpol in a movie they are shooting.

You cunt! A wasted afternoon, by the sound of things. Farking films. They're always shooting farking movies here. In theory at least, they got the weather all year round. It's Worthy's boast that *Moonraker* was shot in his flaming backyard. Well, at least them bits on the moon was.

But right now I'm feeling like one of them Failed Men, only don't farking bother ploughing me up. Cause there ain't gonna be no nailing taking place this afternoon, not with this pace of drinking any roads. — Same again, señorita! I shout at the waitress.

So as I slide back into a mire of despondency, she starts recounting the tale. — I met Costas back on the island where my father, who is chief of police, was able to advise him on how to play this detective.

All I can do is smile through my disappointment and nod like a fucking muppet as the drinks slide down.

After the tale, she gives me one of them looks and says,

— You are a good man, Michael, loyal and faithful. What was it your friend said back in Athens? 'He shines like a diamond fountain.'

— Diamond geezer, I correct her. — That was Billy Guthrie, bless him, I say, and I'm starting to feel the drink, so I clink glasses. — Diamond fountain of love, gel, that's me.

Reminds me that I must call Bill, see how he is. He wasn't well for a bit. Packed in the drink, then lost a bollock in a freak paintballing accident. So much for harmless sport. Don't know what the fuck he was up to, mind you, surely some abuse of the old equipment going on there. That's what being off the booze does for ya.

Not that we'd know much about that here. Seph's looking well trolleyed. She can't decide whether or not she wants a cigarette. She takes one out from her packet, then puts it back in. — You would have been a good man to marry, but in men of your age the seed is likely to be spent, my father says, she kindly informs me. — The gift I must give to him is that of a grandson. My three sisters all have daughters.

— Oi! I protest. — I don't think I like this spent seed bit.

— Your child is also a girl.

— That don't mean nothing.

She gives me a knowing look, which, given our history, chuffs me no end. — But it means that you are a man; that is for sure. My father is the same. He once said to me that all the stuff of man-ness has gone into him, there was nothing left over for his offspring. But I know that a grandson would warm his heart and some day I will give him one.

I'm thinking: I'd like to give you one. Maybe it's the heat, maybe it's the booze, but a nailing is *absolute* priority.

— Costas and I will live in England, close to London, she says, finally lighting up a ciggy and sticking the pack and lighter back into her bag. — He will improve his English and find acting work, while I study. Then we will have sons, many Greek sons, she smiles and raises her glass, forcing me to toast.

I'm thinking that we ain't got much time if she wants a bottling fitted in, but then she explains that she's waiting on Costas, making me feel a right cunt. I set up more drinks.

Baker ain't sticking no bun in an oven here.

Costas finally shows up. He's a skinny bloke with blond hair, looks more like a farking Swede than a Greek, and he's got a nervous way about him. First impressions ain't always right but he don't look the sort of geezer what's gonna settle down and breed a load of Finsbury Park kebab cutters.

Seph intros us and he looks shiftily at me, then her. Something's up here.

— Alright, Cost? How goes the movie business?

Seph decides she's gonna go to the shop to get some stuff. — I will leave you boys for a while to get to know each other, she smiles, happy as a fly in shit.

Sure enough, Costas ain't slow in opening up to me. — The woman is crazy. She thinks that we're getting married. Huh! Her father caught me dealing cocaine to tourists on their island. He threatened to have me locked up if I didn't go along with her crazy scheme. Said he had police contacts all over Greece and would make my life miserable. London would be nice for my career, but . . .

— A lovely gel, don't get me wrong, but she's a few bob short of the big note, if you get my drift.

Costas pulls a grim smile, and throws down the bulk of a rum and Coke. His face is tense and sweaty. He lets the tumbler hit the table in a heavy bang, which attracts the waitress, and he signals another two up. — In Greece we say that some sheep may be missing from the flock.

I nod in total sincerity. Costas ain't a happy camper. He's been made a proper Herbert. Herbertitis A, I would say. I'm warming to the geezer, though. — Her father asked me about my family. If I had brothers. For sure, I tell him, six of them, and no sisters. His face expands into the grin of a reptile. Later on he . . . he shakes his head and shudders in the heat and the waitress brings more drinks.

— Wot?

— He tries to touch me, he spits, outraged. — Like I was a bitch.

— Wot happened?

Old Cost fairly bursts into a rant. — I push him away. He says, 'That is good. You are a man.' They are crazy: the whole family. I have to get away from them all. My shooting time here has wrapped up today, but I have not told her that. Tomorrow I will go to London and stay with my uncle. Away from the crazy bitch and her fascist homosexual father. Did you know that he even gave me the ring to give to her? Picked it himself. Diamond and sapphire. For his daughter's eyes, he said. It is he himself who should be fucking her. When you hear them talk it is like that is what they both want!

I've listened more attentively than any man should to a broadside delivered at that velocity. — It don't look good at all. I drum my fingers on the table. — I'd scarper, mate, and pretty sharpish. What's it the Yanks say: get the fark outta Dodge!

Cost leans closer to me, reeking of old fags, booze and garlic. — I plan to do this. The only thing that worries me is what she will do! She is crazy, I tell you!

I think about this one. — Leave that to me, mate. It needs an Englishman's touch; stiff upper lip, keeping calm when all those around you are losing the plot. Think John Mills, Kenneth More and all that mob, I wink, giving it a little chorus of *Dam Busters*.

So when Seph returns, Costas tells her that he got a call to go back on set. She pouts a little, but he silences her with a kiss. I like it. I see a pro at work. As he goes, he slips me a little note that I'll give to her later. And hopefully, it won't be all that I give her. I slide it into my chinos pocket.

I'm pretty farked as Seph and I head for Worthy's place. She's been brighter n all, cause the drinks are fairly kicking in. — Actors are so dedicated. It is their craft, she slurs.

— Yeah. It's a tough job, I tell her, holding the door of the Cumbria open, gentleman-style, to let her in. — They'd be very hard to replace if they ever went on strike. The global economy would be well farked. What would we evah do without the likes of Tom Cruise?

She punches me jokingly on the arm as we step inside the boozer and I immediately clock Pete Worth, looking all buff and tanned, like a big farking blouse. He sees me at the same time and is coming out from behind the bar. — Alroight, sahn! Looking a bit paunchy, he goes, prodding my gut.

— Ain't got time to be in the gym twenty-four/seven like some. You steroided up or wot? I ask, grabbing his bulging bicep. — The old bollocks must be the size of dried peas by now!

— At least I'll be able to see em without the use of a mirror, you cahnt, he laughs and before I know what I'm doing, I'm sucking it in a little. It's all this hanging out with Cynth. The follow-up to passive smoking: passive calorie absorption.

Worthy don't notice though, as his eyes are elsewhere. — And who is this little beauty? Alright, darlin?

Seph looks him up and down. — My name is Persephone.

— Seph's old man's a big noise in the Greek Old Bill, ain't that so, darling?

— On the island I grew up on, my father is chief of police, she says.

— That's the whole island n all, ain't that so, gel? I tip Worthy a wink and he sets up some beers and a round of shots. He's joking with Seph about her old man's gaff and I take my opportunity to discreetly slip Cost's note into her white shoulder bag. It's like lighting a slow fuse, and fireworks are sure to follow. I'll need a few drinks for this little show.

So Worthy, a very avuncular mine host, sets us up another round. Then some more. It goes all muddy for a bit, then Worthy puts some Greek plate-smashing music on and Seph and I are giving it loads. A fat cunt in a London accent says something and for some reason I get the hump. Some time later I hear a glass smashing on the stone floor of the bar and somebody pushes me and there's raised voices. It's like I'm wearing about six balaclavas though, cause the next thing I know is that I'm falling down a flight of stairs and then there's nothing.

I wake up lying on a bed, with all my clothes still on. Somebody's next to me, I can hear loud snores. It's Seph, still in her dress. It's ridden up a bit and I can see her white cotton knickers are still on. Smoothed, bronzed thighs, all the way up to paradise. But if my memory serves, them pants should be way too scanty to contain that big, black bush, but there ain't no sign of it. She's only gone and went Brazilian on me!

Obviously, no nailing went on last night. I turn away, I'm just torturing myself; besides my farking head feels like it's gonna explode into small fragments. I recognise this gaff: it's Worthy's pad. Small front room and bedroom, kitchen, balcony. There's no sign of him, he's probably gone off on the nail somewhere.

I check the clock. It's farking morning and I've only gone and left Em all night with Cynth!

I dig the wobbly out me pocket and switch it on. Seven missed calls, and loads of messages. All from Cynth, and in tones of ever increasing panic. It's the last one that proper shits me up though: Em's gone!

I'm looking at her image on my phone's screen; a younger kid with a toothy smile, but still recognisable as her, stares back at me and I can hardly breathe. I'm trying to dial Cynth but her incoming call beats me to the punch. — Mickey . . . are you okay? Where have you been?

— I'm fine, what's this bout Em?

— She didn't come back last night. She met this boy, he was a nice lad; Jürgen, German, they were going to a disco. She's stayed out. I've tried her mobile but she doesn't get a signal over here with her service provider . . . What happened to you?

— I got tied up, ran into some old friends, I say, looking at Seph, still crashed out and snoring for Greece. I open the sliding patio doors and go out onto the balcony for a better reception. The sea looks pretty smooth and calm. The sunlight shimmering on it relaxes me a little. — My mate Worthy gave me them shots, knows I can't drink that shit, the cunt; only went and passed out, didn't I.

— Teresa was on the phone for Em a while ago . . .

Another bolt of panic hits me and my legs are pretty shaky now. I sit down on the moulded plastic chair. — You didn't say nothing about her being gone, did ya?

— Of course not. I said that she'd gone out for a walk and some breakfast with you and she'd call her back later.

If that shabby old munter back in England gets wind of this . . . — Good gel. I'm back over on the next ferry. Keep me posted.

— She'll just have gone on to a party and maybe drank too much and got her head down somewhere. You know what teenagers are like. She's a sensible girl.

I clock a big Merc going past on the coast road and I'm thinking about those farking gangster cunts. — She's only a farking kid, Cynth . . . I swallow hard, — . . . Any roads, keep me posted and I'll see ya soon.

The panic is trying to rise, but I'm fighting it down, keeping a lid on it. Think Churchill, when the Luftwaffe fancied their chances. I pull myself out of the chair and head inside. My heart jumps again as I see a note on the table. I relax a little when I clock it's in Worthy's handwriting:

Mickey,
You cunt! Trying to outdo me on the shorts, you fucking lightweight. Thought I'd best let you sleep it off. Incidentally, you caused me no end of grief last night, when you nutted my barman. I squared it but you owe me an apology, and him too of course.
Pete

Jesus cunting Christ on a mortgage in Romford. What a stupid fucker. Barman's probably some farking headcase. I'll square it with Worthy, hopefully they'll have put it down to alcoholic high spirits. Now I'm fretting about the time, as I can't recall when the next ferry is. But it's not for a bit. In the bathroom I catch a dodgy whiff from my armpits, so I peel off my gear and go into the shower. The warm water's relaxing me but suddenly I hear a blood-curdling wailing sound, followed by shouting and things smashing. I run out the shower dripping wet, wrapping a towel round me, and Seph's lying on the wooden floor, bawling her eyes out, a crunched-up note in her hand. There's a glass ashtray smashed to bits on the floor.
— He's gone . . . Costas . . .
Of course. The note I helped him slip into her handbag in my last semi-sober moment. I remember that one. I need to make sure she don't wreck this gaff, that'll be another thing Worthy'll have me for. — What's up? Take it easy, gel . . .

93

She looks urgently at me, then screams, — He is a pig, then opens her arms. — Please, Michael, hold me!

I'm on the floor with her and she's in my arms. I'm stroking her hair, consoling her. — I am so glad you are here, she wails. I'm worried shitless about Em. But then I recall, there's two hours left till the ferry and her dress has ridden up and the old fellah's desperate for the spotlight, pushing this towel aside like it's a flaming curtain . . .

5.

MARCE

Nailing her was the wrong farking move; ain't never gonna get rid of her now. Course, anybody can play Emperor within the Enlightened Realm of Retrospect, just as we can all play Cunt in the Kingdom of Trouser Wood; that ain't the bleedin issue. The pertinent topic of concern is: what do I do with a nutty Greek bird whose hair's blowing all over the place on the deck of the ferry and whose eyes are bleeding black, teary mascara all over her face? — Seph, I've got my daughter here, in Fuerty . . . and my girlfriend, well, sort of . . . I qualify. Daresay it's been a long time since Cynth was described in that way, — . . . and I can't have you around!

— Please, Michael, please, I need you . . . She pouts like a kid. — I will find a hotel over there and stay away from them if you come and see me. I cannot go home, I cannot face my father after all the things Costas said about him in his note . . . all the lies! She breaks into that farking wail again, the sort of sound you'd do anything to stop somebody from making. A nosy old couple on the deck stare at us. I give em the eye and they find something else to gawp at.

All I can do is play the honest broker. — Don't do anything rash, gel. See this as an opportunity to take stock. Attempt to divest all emotion before making decisions, I explain, trying to talk down my own mounting panic about Em. — You gotta believe that things happen for a reason. Some kind of divine, cosmic ordination. That's the word: ordination.

— But the things he said in that note . . . telling me that he had fallen in love with my father, and that was the only reason he wanted to be near me! He feared that my father only wanted him for sex, on the side!

— It's a funny old life, gel.

— But my father is chief of police, she moans, — for the whole island! He is a real man! How can he be homosexual?

That was a good move, though. My advice, that one. He listened and learned, no flies on old Costas. — Stranger things have happened at sea, gel, I tell her as the boat tears through the waves.

— It's not possible . . . it's just not possible . . .

— Maybe it's all just been a misunderstanding, I shrug, happy to see the Fuerty shoreline and Corralejo harbour coming into view.

Cynth's there at the dock and she's looking at me and then Seph in bemusement. She's got that sour, betrayed face, like she's been put in her place by younger skirt she can't compete with, which, I suppose, is the case. I put her out of her misery by introducing them and giving her the party line: — Cynth, Seph; Seph, Cynth. Cynth, Seph's an old friend who has just been, how could one put this delicately, disappointed in love. Her boyfriend's been working on this film they're shooting over here, and he's only gone and done a runner. Left her a note, the lot.

— Oh . . . okay, says Cynth, now relieved and rather sympathetic.

Seph pouts, starts grizzling and bursts into tears again, and Cynth, on cue and now delighted cause she thinks she ain't got no competition, is waiting to smother her into that ample bosom. As Seph gets the treatment and is happy to succumb, Cynth coughs out, — Still not heard from Em. This German boy she met seemed ever so nice, she pleads, her voice rising in panic. — I never thought they'd stay out, Mickey, she promised she'd be back before midnight!

— Yeah . . . I say, struggling to stay cool myself, especially as I'm thinking again of them gangster cunts. The top crowd among them maniacs these days ain't like the old school who played by a certain code. They always target the families of the geezers they want onside. Farking low-life pseudo-nonce scumbags. — Listen, Cynth, you take Seph back to base and wait there in case of Em showing up. I'm gonna go off looking for her.

So I leave them and jump in the motor in search of Em.

I'm off driving down to the Kraut side of the island, watching the vegetation get lusher and the villages get more picturesque, I hit a few bars, asking questions, showing Em's picture, which Cynth thoughtfully brought out, an update on my mobile phone edition, but there ain't nobody biting.

Then as I'm driving back into Corralejo, outside a block of shitty tourist apartments, I see em: them two geezers. Them that was in the Bull the other night.

I pull into the car park outside the gaffs and watch them. The big cunt goes into the apartments, but the little weaselly un turns on his heels and heads back out. He gets into a motor. I follow him and he parks behind the supermarket. It's empty. He gets out the motor. I do n all. My nerves are jagged with the hangover, all the booze of the other night leaving my system. Sweat's pouring off me. My limbs feel heavy. I gotta do something, but I ain't particularly great shakes at the physical side of things as it happens. I loved running with football mobs, but I was never a top lad, never a front-line troop. I'd be game enough when it came to thirty-second windmilling bouts with other mugs, but this cold-bloodied stuff was never my style. But I gotta do something. But I feel like shit. Like proper shit. Like a dirty, discarded, old brown shit sweating in some toilet that won't flush away.

The geezers might be –

No. I gotta do something –

He sees me approaching.

— Alright, John? I shout at him, pumping myself up, ramping is what I believe they call it, as the faces of every top lad I've ever known come into my head, egging me on.

— Mister Landlord, he says with a nasty smile, like he's some farking Bond villain expecting me. Well, I'm straight over and my nut's in his face, and he goes down like Cynth on a dirty weekend. The cunt obviously wasn't expecting *that*. I'm right down on top of him battering his head off the tarmac, scream-ing in his face, — I DON'T CARE ABOUT YOUR FUCKING GANGSTER BOLLOCKS, I'LL RIP YOUR FUCKING HEAD OFF AND CRUSH YOUR FARKING SKULL IN A VICE IF YOU'VE TOUCHED ONE HAIR ON MY LITTLE GEL'S HEAD, YOU CAHHNNT!

I can't hear anything except a ringing in my ears as I crack his weaselly head twice, three, four times, but then I realise that the phone's ringing *The Dam Busters* in my jacket. The geezer's lying under me, moaning and groaning, again like Cynth after a good nailing. And like her, he ain't going nowhere fast. I tear the wobbly out of my pocket and answer it. It's only Cynth. — Michael, Emily's here. Everything's fine. Jürgen brought her back. We're all having tea on the veranda. Yeah, they got a little tipsy last night and decided that it might be best not to try and drive so they sat up drinking coffee.

— Sweet. I'll be back shortly, I say, clicking off the phone. My heart sinks in my chest as I look down at the geezer.

— Please don't . . . he begs, and now his voice sounds all posh, — I'm not who you think . . . he moans.

— I . . . I . . . I try to speak and can't, so I get off him and stand up. — Look, mate, I apologise . . . I think I might have got the wrong end of the stick. I offer the geezer my hand, but he waves me away and starts to sit up of his own accord, taking deep breaths, rubbing his nut. — I thought you'd kidnapped my daughter to put the frighteners on me cause you thought I heard something I shouldn't have, which I didn't, I try to explain. — I mean . . . a geezer like you . . .

— I'm an *actor*, he moans in that posh voice.

Suddenly all I can think of now is old Costas and his stupid farking movie. — Fuck me, I gasp, and I'm helping him up. — Your mate n all?

He rubs his bonce again and keeps taking deep breaths, then bends over like he's gonna puke. After a bit he lifts up his head. — We're shooting a film . . . we were method acting . . . learning our lines.

— Fuck sake . . . I'm sorry, mate. I should have thought. I even know the farking film you're on about, I tell him, helping him back to his motor and sitting him down in the front passenger seat. — I know it might not be much consolation to ya, but you geezers are pretty good at your job, I tell him. — Had me proper wound up, you did! I laugh, but he still ain't for seeing the funny side.

Later on, when I get back to the pub, I learn that the local Old Bill found out that the businessman geezer got shot by his wife. Seems he was knocking off the au pair, and she caught em on the job and took exception. That made me think: thank fuck for gun control in England! Trees caught me in similar circumstances once and came at me with a kitchen knife. Had to scarper pronto. In another country, say like America, old Mickey here would've been brown bread. Just for a farking shag, and not, as I recall, a particularly great one at that.

No doubt the likes of Trees would say it was poetic justice.

So I had the actor blokes, Will and Tom, back at the pub for a night out on me, to show there was no hard feelings. They turned out to be decent geezers: a bit la-di-da, but alright.

Even got me some work on the film, *Old Iron*, playing the hit man's associate! A speaking part, no less, although my character was called Silent Billy. I had to say, 'Don't like the sound of this. Not one bit,' just before a bunch of us got cut down by a hail of bullets. A thespian debut. I thought: let them get their green eyes on that one back home.

Cynth was fairly enjoying playing mother hen to Em and Seph. Everything seemed sorted for a while, except that every time I looked round, and I ain't naturally what one might call the paranoid sort, they would all suddenly go quiet. What was it the old cunt said: 'When the eagles are silent, the parrots begin to jabber.' — C'mon, you lot, I demanded, — out with it. What's going on, then?

It was written all over their faces. But when they came out with it, it wasn't half a proper boot in the bollocks. — Emily's mother needs her, Cynth says. — She wants to go back.

I look at the kid. I thought that she was going to give me grief cause I had to give that Jürgen geezer a talking-to, even though I don't think nothing went on. For a Kraut he was a nice young fellah, the sincere type. Thing is, I was sort of getting used to having her around. — Em?

She shrugs and says, — I don't really want to, Dad. But Mum's really upset cause that Richie guy she was seeing has packed her in. I'm going to go back and Jürgen's coming to visit next month. Cynth's gonna take me over.

I'm instantly uplifted as I look at Cynth and try to stop a smile moulding my face into Mr Sly. — Good of ya to take her, gel. I'd go myself, but there's this place . . . I say, looking around the Herefordshire Bull, but all the time thinking about the nailing Seph's gonna be getting from now on in!

— Yeah, I thought I'd go over and see my parents, Cynth goes, — and also help Persephone find Costas.

— What . . . ?

Seph gives me a poisonous smile, which ages her about thirty years. — He thinks he can do this to me and not pay. I want to look him in the eye and tell him that he is a cowardly, lying dog!

— Sometimes it's healthier to let it go, gel, I almost plead, looking at Em and seeing the Hardwick in her and hating it. My own flesh and blood: looking like she got a career in white heather sales. In fact, the three of them seem straight from central casting for *Macbeth*.

Specially, it must be said, Seph, who's looking proper narked.

— No, I will let it go once I have looked into the eye of the coward and liar!

Cynth nods slowly in agreement. She's got a bleedin nerve acting like Snow White. A certain golfer not a million miles from here wouldn't be best pleased if he knew what she was up to when he was on the links!

Fairly bonded, those two have, but it's proper messing up my shagging plans. — Seph, you don't wanna –

— He has insulted my father, who is a chief of police. He will pay for this, and she bursts into tears again, only to be crushed back into Cynth's big floppy tits.

I let it go, cause when all's said and done, there ain't no use crying over spilt milk. As one door closes, another one opens; that's what I've always believed to be the case concerning shagging. Sure enough, a couple of days later, they're back to Gatwick on the flight, and I'm looking over at Marce. Bert was sitting in the corner of the bar getting plastered, while Rodj was cleaning glasses in the lounge. Ultimatums had evidently been issued. You could've cut the atmosphere with a knife. I nodded at Marce and dropped my voice. — Why the long face, gel?

— Bert and Rodger . . . they both say they want to be with me. I don't know, Michael, I just don't know, she told me. — It's all too much.

I winked at her, cause I knew exactly where she was coming from. — Not that I wanna complicate things, gel, but at the election back home, that Liberal Democrat geezer said, 'We are now in the age of three-party politics.' Well, I think you're in exactly the same position!

Well, she got my drift alright. — What position do you prefer? she asked, arching a brow.

And I have to say that she's certainly delivered the goods. Poor Marce: all she wanted was a good nailing and a bit of fun, not Bert and Rodj giving it the old pistols at dawn routine.

So the summer didn't turn out so bad, after all: the big disappointment being the film, *Old Iron*. It only went straight to video after me giving it the big one on the blower to the mates back home, about Hollywood beckoning and all that.

Still, you can't have everything, and as I pull a frothing pint of John Courage's finest for this tourist couple, Marce is on her knees behind the bar, her dirty, lovely mouth going to work on the old fellah, so I got to say that life could be worse. And you gotta admit that there's a lot to be said for persistence. As the old cunt said back at his posh school: 'This is the lesson: never give in, never give in, never, never, never, never, in nothing, great or small, large or petty – never give in except to convictions of honour and good sense. Never yield to force; never yield to the apparently overwhelming might of the enemy.'

Old misery-guts Rodj, cleaning up the glasses in the bar next door, daft little Bert, out on the piss somewhere, they should have heeded that advice. Reminds me though, Cynth's only due back next week; or at least I believe that to be the case. No rest for the wicked. Still, with a bit of calmness and serenity, there ain't no hurdle that can't be negotiated.

The DOGS of Lincoln Park

The city stews as the temperature soars past a hundred degrees. Their spirits muffled in the swampy insulation, some citizens veer for the lake. Many who live in apartments without air conditioning decant to the emergency cooling shelters set up by City Hall. On television, the mayor runs a hanky across the back of his sweaty, red neck for effect as he urges people to use those facilities.

Yet Kendra Cross is navigating the journey from her realty office to the small, new Asian fusion restaurant close to Clark and Fullerton with an air of insouciance. Mystic East, a manageable block away from her workplace, was where she had taken to lunching every Friday with her friends Stephanie Harbison and Stacie Barnes. Kendra seldom wearied of proclaiming that it was she who had unearthed this culinary pearl. Now she felt herself satisfyingly closing in on the weekend; all morning the lunch date had hummed urgently in her thoughts. Yes, Trent had been a washout last night, but there was the prospect of that cute rich guy from Capital Investments calling. Kendra thought that there was a mutual attraction at the meeting last week on that condo development at Printer's Row.

Also: Kendra has floated through her morning duties on a magic carpet of Xanax, the same one that takes her down the sidewalk. Taut across the face, a tight, high, blond ponytail pulling her skin tensile on her forehead swings behind her, a tail as vital as the ones on the more enthusiastic dogs which negotiate Clark. Gliding among the buffed, two-pinned, mobile mannequins, she pouts in sympathy as she regards their quad-legged companions on the leashes, the heavy tongues on some grazing the sidewalk. She thinks of her black-and-white papillon, Toto, bonding with the other small dogs her sitter looks after, just as she is set to do with her own friends.

Kendra supposed that they were typical of many young, hard-working (Stacie excepted!), wealthy urban professionals. Apart from the demands of commerce, they had been unable to come up with suitable reasons for their ennui, and had overindulged in illegal drugs and alcohol as a convenient repository for their tired, listless, alienated behavior. Then they discovered the beauty of rehab. They'd taken to showing up at lunch dates, perky, superior and focused, hand placed strategically over the wine glass, a satisfied smile at the waiter. — Rehab, they'd whisper blissfully to their dining partners, as they discreetly washed down a Xanax with the proferred mineral water.

She had left her office at the real-estate agents prompt on 12.30 and at 12.38 Kendra opens the restaurant door to let the X-ray blast of air con invigorate her. The Japanese-looking waitress, wearing a dark kimono, escorts Kendra to her seat and she looks across at the chef, his round face pockmarked at the sides, eyes harsh in this light, under his dark brows, as he takes in everything in his benignly magisterial way from his vantage point behind the sushi bar.

Within a couple of minutes, Kendra is joined by Stephanie, whom, she notes, is wearing a green business suit of a similar cut to her own, with huge Dior sunglasses pushed onto her shiny blond hair, which is cut in a dramatic wedged bob. — No Stacie? Stephanie hums, her gaze, Kendra feels, one of assessment.

— She called to say she was running late.

— Let's order anyway, Stephanie blows impatiently, — some of us have things to do.

— Affirmative, Kendra snorts, adding, — Stacie's a fucking basket case, as she tactically drops and retrieves her napkin in order to check out Stephanie's shoes, relieved that satisfying objections come quickly to mind. Fortified, she sits forward and lowers her voice. — Her stupid big mouth blew it for me with Trent last night.

Stephanie leans in, her eyes widening. Excitement and anxiety contend within her. She prays that Stacie won't appear and interrupt this story. — How so? she urges in faux concern.

— We were in the LP Tavern. With Trent, Stuart Noble and Alison Logan. Alison saw this girl and shouted, 'Isn't she from Highland Park?' I said I kinda recognized her from somewhere. Then blabbermouth Stacie cuts in and said she did psychology at DePaul, but that she was a couple of years *below us*. You could see Trent doing the freaking math there and then. He spent the rest of the evening looking at my crow's feet, Kendra explains despondently, pointedly waiting for a reassurance that Stephanie assiduously withholds. *Why thank you, fucking bitch.* — He hasn't returned my call, she moans dismally. — I'd phone again but it would come over as too needy.

And at that point Stacie, wearing a short, pink pleated skirt and matching tank top, blond hair in braids, appears in the restaurant, waving as she approaches them. She gapes suspiciously at Kendra and Stephanie. — Were you two just *talking* about me?

— Oh, wouldn't you just *love* for that to be the case. Stephanie's teasing tones are pitched somewhere between a snort and a purr as Stacie sits down. — But you *are* needy, she immediately points out to a grumpy-looking Kendra. — You need *him*. Or somebody like him.

Ignoring Stacie's widening eyes, Kendra has a thought, sparking in her mind like the wheel of an El train over a rail point.

Is Stephanie a free agent? Does she have an agenda? — Are you still seeing Todd? she suddenly inquires.

Stephanie's thin brows slant like a roof. — I guess, but he's so fucking clueless and insensitive to *my* needs, she contends. — Jeez, it's a hundred degrees outside and we don't have central air con, she purses, then quickly qualifies this, — . . . as I choose to rent a cheaper apartment because I value my work above money . . .

Kendra attempts an expression of empathy at this point, but her nod comes over as pitying and she can't stop derision and triumph molding her finely cut face, shearing it of its characteristic wariness.

— . . . which is a concept that clearly does not chime with his limited intellect, Stephanie spits in retaliation to Kendra's contemptuous expression. — So I'm stuck with those crappy fans.

— Worse than useless, Kendra hisses.

— Yes . . . Stephanie says, now more cagily, trying to calculate whether the martyr bonus points beat the cheapskate debits. She regards Stacie who is all eyes, teeth, hair – a vacancy waiting to be filled – and knows that she's made a gross miscalculation. — But the point is, she says grandiosely, — that the apartment is *sooo* gross. So I'm lying on the bed pooped, in front of the fan, after a *particularly* taxing day. I'd spent all morning talking to Sybil, that horrible, manipulative parakeet I told you about, and Benji, the aggressive tom who litters everywhere *but* the designated tray. So Todd comes through with a big smile on his face. He only wanted to *do it*!

— In this *heat*? In your *apart*ment? *Sooo* gross, Kendra scoffs, enjoying Stacie's affirmative nod.

In shared acknowledgment of her air con own goal, Stephanie winces, the ice water she sips tasting like vinegar, while Kendra grins. *That motherfucker will run,* they think the same solitary thought, but in polar opposite emotional channels.

Moving on sharply, Stephanie states, — I gave him a piece of my mind and I told him that I didn't want him in bed with me till it cooled. Of course, that simple statement of *my personal need* was more than enough to evoke the child in him, her nylonlike hair swishing and settling back as she moves her head, — That stupid pout. So moronic.

— But don't you think that all guys have that little boy in them? Kendra inquires, suddenly keen to make a common cause.

— Of course, Stephanie agrees, acknowledging Kendra's gesture. — That is *nat* the issue. The issue is 'How close to the surface is it?' In him I think it might just be a little too close for comfort. I told him, couch or cab home, buddy: you decide

Stacie's big browny-green eyes under those infeasible lashes turn first on one friend, then another, her head moving like a spectator at a tennis match.

— I admire you, Kendra purrs. — It would be great to have that sort of control over *certain other parties*.

— He's *so* much more alpha than Todd, though, Stephanie gushes suddenly.

Stacie picks up the menu card. Thinks about sashimi. Made for this weather. — Who are we talking about? she asks.

Kendra shakes her head at Stephanie, ignoring Stacie. — That's just the image he projects. To me it's a case of 'methinks the lady doth protest too much'. He's probably a fag.

— Kennie! Stap it! Stephanie squeals in jovial reprimand.
— Just because he works out?

— Who *are* we talking about? Stacie asks again.

Ignoring her once more, Kendra says, — No, of course not. He just dresses a little faggy.

— He's got style, is all, Stephanie declares, then turns to Stacie, — and we are talking about Trent.

Stacie nods. — Right. Gotcha.

Continuing, Stephanie expands: — And a membership of the yacht club. And a convertible. And a nice house on Roscoe.

— He's a sweet guy, Stacie opines.

— And rich. He's a partner in an architect's practice, Kendra says, narrowing eyes trained on Stephanie.

— A practice? Since when did architects have practices? Stacie asks, taking a drink of water which stings her teeth.

— They've always called them practices, Kendra's head shudders in irritation, — like law, or medicine.

— Oh, I'm sure that's a new thing, Stacie argues.

Kendra abruptly rises and heads for the restroom. — I think you'll find that it's always been the case, she hisses through her teeth as she departs.

When she is out of sight, Stephanie makes her hands into claws and performs an air-raking gesture. — Miaow! Looks like somebody's kitty litter needs changing!

Adopting her party-piece tones of a Southern black girl, Stacie raps out, — Stick a lumpa Carolina coal up dat bitch's white ass an she gonna shit diamond! And they high-five in triumph.

The chef coasts over to them with a tray full of small dishes. He has a habit of selecting the food for his favorite customers. To Kendra and Stacie, this constitutes special treatment. Stephanie believes it is a con and that he's just working yesterday's stuff onto them. — Very special food, for very special customers, he smiles. — Korean, the chef explains with a mirthful twist to his mouth. — Distinguishing feature of Korean food is spices. Basic seasonings; red pepper, green onion, soy sauce, bean paste, garlic, ginger, sesame, mustard, vinegar, wine.

Stacie's nodding-dog routine induces a tightness in Stephanie's chest, which is mirrored in her thin red lips.

Pointing at some small bowls of soup, Chef explains, — *Maeuntang* is spicy, hot seafood soup that include white fish, vegetable, bean curd, red-pepper powder. *Twoenjang-guk* is a fermented soybean paste soup with baby clams in its broth.

— Yummy, Stacie exclaims.

— Vegetable dish is also popular in Korea. Korean call dishes made with only vegetable *namool*. There two kind, one cold and raw, other warm and steamed.

— *Namool*, Stacie repeats.

The chef is glowing as his chest expands with pride. — Korean table settings are the 3, 5, 7, 9 or 12 *chop*, depending on the number of side dishes served. The average family takes three or four side dishes. When family hold celebrations or party, a dozen or more dishes served. Chopstick and spoons used for eating. Different from Japanese and Chinese, Korean use more thin chopstick made with metal, not wood.

— Mmm-hmm! Stacie smacks her lips.

Stephanie's eyebrows arch, her open mouth quivering slightly before settling to form an appraising but urgent smile. *Can we shut the fuck up and just eat this stuff that you've brought, that we didn't order,* she thinks, suddenly time-anxious. This afternoon will herald a potentially demanding consultation with Millie, the self-harming marmoset.

Kendra waltzes back from the restroom, equilibrium restored by another Xanax. It's not kicking in yet, and it's no placebo, but she savors the glow of anticipation, of *knowing it will* before long. Her friends note that she's changed her eyeliner from yellow to a rose color. — Looks interesting, Stephanie says approvingly, not herself knowing whether she means Kendra's makeup or the food.

— This is Korean stuff, Kennie, Stacie sings excitedly at her.

— Korean food have various side dish, Chef continues to

Stephanie's obvious chagrin. — Favorite side dish are bean-paste soup, broiled beef, fish, cabbage *kimchi*, and steamed vegetables. He accusingly fingers the various dishes like they were suspects in an ID parade. Then he taps the menu. — Full-course Korean meal called *Hanjoungshik*. Compose of grilled fish, steamed short ribs, and other meat and vegetable dishes with streamed rice, soup, and *kimchi*.

— What's *kimchi*? asks Stacie, as Stephanie swallows a long gulp of air and drums her big nails on the table.

— *Kimchi* best-known Korean food. It is vegetable dish, highly seasoned with pepper, garlic, etcetera. Served with every kind of Korean meal. Stimulate appetite like pickles. Contains amounts of good nutritions such as vitamin C and fiber. Try, he commands, looking at Kendra.

Kendra spoons some up onto her plate, then takes a small forkful. — It's very good, she nods in endorsement. Stephanie gratefully follows suit, as does Stacie.

The chef responds with a graceful bow. — Enjoy, he says, before retreating.

— I kind of like that chef, Stacie says as he departs, — that inscrutable oriental demeanor. It's kind of neat. What do you think, Kennie?

Kendra is daydreaming. She is wondering if the rich developer guy, Clint his name is, will call her. — About what?

— Never mind, Stacie wearily sings, then changes her tack: — How's Karla getting on?

— I can*nat* believe that the same sperm and egg sources that produced me provided the raw material to manufacture *her*, Kendra rants, aware that the Xanax she's popped in the restroom *is* perhaps lifting her again. — She's got one of those lame and passé tattoos above her ass that she thinks is sooo punk rock. It makes her look like a crack whore. *And* she must weigh over a hundred and thirty pounds.

— Ugh! Stephanie winces, then adds with concern, — Is she like, depressed or something?

— I don't know what shit's going down with her. Kendra shakes her head so emphatically she is moved to subsequently check that her hair is still secured back. — All I know is I had to intervene at my mom's last weekend. I pulled her over to the full-length mirror and lifted up her tank top. I pointed at her stomach and said: 'Care.'

— How did she react? Stephanie asks.

Kendra shrugs, taking in a long breath as she painfully watches a bum with a cart shuffle past the window, so gratified that he *does not stop* or turn to look in. *Thank you.* She nods tersely at Stephanie in shared relief. — The usual crappy defensive-offensive rhetoric about me being anorexic, you know how they lash out. She narrows her eyes. — You think I was wrong?

— No, not at all. I just think that the intervention could have been a little more *structured*, Stephanie offers.

Kendra considers this. Steph was pretty smart. Sometimes Kendra wishes she'd stayed on to do a masters at DePaul. Now Stephanie was almost a partner in that pet behavioralist practice on Clark, while she was stuck in real estate.

But she was *making money*.

— I ran into Monica Santiano yesterday, y'know from Highland Park. She's moved into the city, Stephanie informs them. — You know what she said to me: 'I really got to hang out with you guys.' I was like, ugh, a total DNA situation! Stephanie and Kendra high-five each other.

— I thought she was kinda fun, Stacie says. — What's DNA mean?

— Desperate and Needy Alert, they sing at her in unison. — Another one we added to our lexicon, I think it was in CJ's on Wednesday, Kendra elaborates smugly. — Where *were* you, Stace?

Stacie looks a little forlorn as the conversation drifts back to work. — How's the wonderful world of real estate? Stephanie asks Kendra.

— Still booming, and still lucrative, Kendra chirps, swinging into breezy professional mode, before something sours in her mouth. She hesitates for a second, then lets rip: — But that fat lesbo bitch Marilyn's been on my case. She's sooo disgusting, sitting there packing her face with Doritos all day and she doesn't even have a *college degree*, she rasps.

— Loo-zir! Stephanie ticks, stretching out her fingers to examine her nail extensions. They were perhaps a bit long for the metal chopsticks.

— I see her looking at me sometimes in that creepy way, and then she breaks into that revolting smile of hers. And that horrible mole on her face. Yuk! Then sometimes she'll go all girly and gross and make comments about straight girls wanting to experiment, Kendra winces. — It kinda makes me wanna puke!

— Gross, Stacie acknowledges.

— And bordering on sexual harassment. Stephanie's head twists. — Somebody oughta stick a lawsuit on that bitch's fat ass!

Kendra nods thoughtfully. Then she looks searchingly, imploringly, at Stephanie and Stacie. All suddenly raise imaginary rifles into the air, training and then firing them on invisible targets. — She's so NRA, they scoff.

The girls exchange high-fives. — Not Really Awesome, they squeal in a delighted harmony. They catch the chef observing their antics, his dark eyes glimmering, and they raise embarrassed hands to mouths to stifle their nervous giggles.

It took Kendra a while to get ready for her run that evening. The gray DePaul sweatshirt and blue shorts were pulled on quickly enough, as were the Nike Air Zoom Moire trainers, a hundred bucks a throw and selected because their color matched the shirt, but the hair had to be off the face and the ponytail tied high. Most of all, the makeup needed to be *just right*. Too little was not an option, but too much indicated a lack of serious sporting edge, perhaps even hinting at sexual laziness or passivity. This stuff she used was subtle and didn't run, not that Kendra intended to do much sweating.

Darkness is pressing down as she goes off at an even trot along Lakeshore Drive where it's cooler, the air coming off Lake Michigan smelling slightly sour, tawny and feeble, like an elderly relative doused in a favored fragrance. After several yards, boredom and fatigue gnaw at her, and she feels self-conscious and ridiculous as an elderly man passes her with ease. No matter; the best part is the slow pretend-exhausted walk back around the neighborhood. Walking with Toto got lots of attention but the problem was that the male dog walkers were invariably gay. Jogging was different. Like the Lakeshore Athletic Club, it was a way of meeting straight guys. But it was not a good method of keeping your weight down; too much like hard work. Dieting was easier, except Friday lunch, which would set her up for the weekend. It was too hot for the sweatshirt but she worried that there might be a slight distension of her stomach after that lunch. It would take till Tuesday before she could be confident about just wearing the sports bra.

Kendra pulls up to a brisk walking speed in order to enjoy the night. Looming shadows emerging from the overhead trees herald little more than the chatter of lovers or more dog walkers – this is a safe neighborhood – and she notes there is a van parked outside her block. Two men are unloading furniture. There is a third in attendance whom she immediately recognizes as the Asian chef from Mystic East. It seems like he is moving in, to her apartment complex. — Hi . . . she simpers on approach. — Are you moving in, like *here*?

The chef seems to take a while to recognize her. He squints in the darkness, holding a framed print, which he sets down on the granite curb. — Ah . . . yes. Hello. His smiling face expands.

— I'm on the second floor, Kendra explains, watching two movers engaged in a sweaty push-pull dance with one of the last of the stubbornly heavy boxes on the back of the van.

— I move into third floor, the chef tells her.

— Come and have some tea, Kendra offers, reasoning that it will do no harm to keep in with her favorite local restaurateur.

—You are very kind. Chef bows his big head slightly. Kendra holds open the doors of the apartment building as he carries the picture up the stairs. She follows him all the way up, taking in his shadowless, almost spectral form under the fluorescent stair and hall lighting. Then she hears a sniggering behind her. The moving guys. Leering at her ass. *Fucking pigs.* At the stair-bend she tugs the edge of the DePaul sweatshirt south, her only concession to their presence.

When the men are left to finish putting the last of the stuff into the chef's apartment, she takes him downstairs to her identical dwelling. Kendra feels a bit awkward as his eyes scan the clutter of her space. I should have fucking tidied up, she thinks. As she heads to the kitchen to make green tea, she notes that Toto, whom she'd left while she was running, and who was normally timid around strangers to the apartment, especially men, is enthusiastic about the Asian chef. First he licks his hand with an almost obscene look in his black, glassy eyes, and then rolls over, allowing his tummy to be rubbed.

—Very nice dog, the oriental cook smiles in delight.

— He seems to like yoooo! Don'tcha, baby? she says to Toto, — Don'tcha, sweet baby boy? Yes you do! Yes you do!

— If you ever need me to take dog for walk, the chef grins, sipping his green tea, — let me know.

— Thank you. Kendra twists her head to the side, as Chef goes out onto the stair to sign the removal docket and the men depart. They sit with their tea as Kendra tells him about the trash collection and the mailboxes, and she's unable to resist slipping in some gossip about the neighbors. Then she takes him down to the basement to show him the laundry facilities, which he seems particularly keen to view. — Very important for Chef, he explains, as they embark on the long walk down the steep and badly lit back staircase. The gate to the laundry room is heavy and stiff, and she is pleased when he comes to her aid in pulling it open. Inside Kendra clicks on a switch and there is a hum as the pitch-black cavernous room flickers into a buzzing fluorescent bluish-yellow glare revealing two washers, two dryers and an aluminum rack of bicycles. Big silver tubes carrying the air con hang overhead, snaking into the cavities of the building like space-age woodworm. — *Such* an essential for a Chicago summer, Kendra smartly informs Chef, thinking of Stephanie sweating away sourly under fans – and an enthusiastic Todd – in that antiquated condo of hers.

No, Steph would be on top.

When the tour is over and Chef departs upstairs to organize his new home, Kendra is straight on the phone to Stephanie, then Stacie, delighted as she informs them, — Chef, *our* Chef, only just moved into my apartment block!

The next morning Kendra has a crisis. Christie, her dog walker and sitter, calls to say that she had just learned that her father has been taken seriously ill in Kentucky, and she needs to go there immediately. — Thanks for everything, Kendra says spitefully down the phone. She realizes that she is going to have to take Toto into the office. It *is* an emergency. Outside is hot, but muggy and overcast. The dour, dirty sky seems to press down on her, she feels it in her ball-bearing eyes, house-brick brain and anvil jaw. Toto whines a little, dragging on his leash and panting, until she's forced to take his gasping body in her arms.

She is at her desk for about ten minutes, talking to her co-workers Greg and Cassandra, when Marilyn, hands on bovine hips, casts a shadow over her desk. — Kennie, princess, she looks at the dog, whose ears prick up although he remains sitting loyally at Kendra's feet, — Toto's a charmer, but the office isn't for dags.

— But –

Marilyn's large head cocks to the side, as she pats her stiff hair. Her voice coos, incongruously soothing, — Butts – even cute little ones – are for sitting on and getting fired, honey. Please don't ask me to get more explicit.

— My dog sitter had an emergency, I'll try to get something sorted out –

— Now, sweetheart. Her smile slides a millimetre south.

— Right, Kendra says neutrally, and picks Toto up.

Marilyn follows her out. As Kendra gets to the door, she stops her with an arm on her shoulder. As Kendra turns around, she can smell a sickly sweet corpse breath. Stroking the dog's snout, Marilyn fixes her in a flinty stare. — In case you ain't heard, hard times are ahead, baby. The condo market has gone to shit. People are like sheep. They see a few players making a killing out of condo developments and they build and build until there are too many developments and not enough people to fill them. It's a classic bubble and you can see the pin. I'm talking layoffs. Do I make myself clear?

Kendra bites her tongue. *How unprofessional is this bitch! Talking down the freakin market!* — Yes, she says blankly, exiting and heading outside. The dog is panting in her arms as she walks down the street which shimmers in the baking heat.

She hates leaving Toto in the apartment on his own, but now she has no choice. On her way back she sees Chef hanging out in the shade of the porch by the apartment entrance. He's out of his robes, wearing a blue suit, collar open at the neck, as he smokes a cigarette. The suit contrasts with the vivid red roses which climb up a wooden trellis next to him. For the first time she notes how thin his body is compared to his head. She tells him what has happened with the dog and her work. Chef explains that he is going for a walk by the lake. He has no shift until the evening and will be happy to walk the dog and look after him till she comes home from work.

Kendra is delighted, leaving Toto happily in his hands and heading back to the office. Avoiding Marilyn, she checks her messages, but there's nothing from either Trent or Clint the developer guy. When she finishes work, she returns to the apartment complex, calling upstairs first where she finds Chef cooking in his kitchen. As she crouches Toto jumps up, into her arms, delighted to see her.

— Something smells good, she says. — Has he been a good boy?

— Dog no trouble at all, Chef says and puts some food on the small table.

Kendra notes how wonderfully organized everything is. Chef must have been working so hard to get all the stuff out of boxes and set up. The front room is dominated by a huge fish tank and a collection of ornate swords which hang on the walls. — Collect swords, Chef points at himself, then at the mounted weapons.

— These look . . . Kendra can't think of a word, and then settles for, — . . . nice.

Chef takes one down from the wall. It has a curved blade

of around thirty inches, with a black leather handle a foot long. He sets it down on the table, disappears briefly into the kitchen, returning with two large watermelons. He balances one on what looks like a giant cat's scratching post that he has pulled out from a darkened corner of the room. — Stand well back, he smiles at Kendra, — blade very, very sharp. Can easy sever four inches of bamboo.

Kendra moves away. The chef takes the sword in two outstretched arms. He shuts his eyes for a few seconds and seems to go into an almost orgasmic trance. Then, in a sudden explosive movement, he twists and slices through the melon. It falls away, in two equal sides. Toto moves over and sniffs at one portion on the floor.

— Now you try. Chef places the next melon and gives her the blade by its handle. Kendra takes it and grips it tentatively. Chef moves behind her, standing close. — Take weight . . . that's good. Feel the weight. This Musashi Japanese katana. Shinto sword.

— It's kinda neat, she says.

— Imagine sword is part of arm. The edge of blade finger-nails . . . His arms circle around her, holding her lightly but firmly at the wrists. — Now on count three you raise blade and bring down on melon. Like you putting fingers through melon. One . . . two . . . three . . . Chef pulls up Kendra's wrists then pushes down, pulling his hands away at the last second as the sword falls, splitting the melon as before.

— Wow . . . Kendra smiles tensely, embarrassed now at the physical embrace and a strange charge that hangs in the air. — That was great . . .

Chef stands back, bows, and points to the food on the table. — Now eat, he urges her.

— Lordy . . . I can't . . . she thinks of her weight, — you shouldn't have done this . . . what *is* this?

— *Pulgoki*. One of the famous Korean dishes to Westerners. Means 'Korean barbecue'. Marinated with soy sauce, garlic, sugar, sesame oil, and other seasonings. Cooked over fire in front of table.

She puts down the sword and examines the fish swimming in the tank. There are two of them. — Are these . . . ?

— Pufferfish. Common red puffer. Also called avocado puffer. Not so cause taste good with avocado, but they do, he grins.

Kendra's hand goes to her mouth, which is mimicking the fishes. — Do you . . . I mean . . .

— Yes.

— Oh, Kendra says, then, anxious to ensure that he doesn't think she's offended by this, adds, — I would love to go to Japan. Eat pufferfish in a big restaurant.

— I have prepare some for now. We eat them, he says, heading to the kitchen and returning immediately with some small raw fillets of fish.

Kendra looks at the fillets, then at the tank. — Eh . . . I dunno . . . aren't they really dangerous to eat?

The chef stares at her, his eyes gleaming. — Can be fatally poisonous. In Japan they are delicacy after poison has been removed but eating can still be fatal. One hundred diners die each year from eating pufferfish.

— Is this okay? She looks nervously at the fish.

— Very good. Eat, he urges, then he lifts a fillet into his mouth.

Kendra takes the small piece of fish in her mouth. It is smooth and tastes buttery. She chews and swallows.

— With poison you feel tingling in mouth and lips. Then dizziness, fatigue, headache, cannot speak, tightness in chest, shaking, nausea and vomiting, Chef explains cheerfully.

— I . . . I . . . feel okay, I guess . . . she says shakily. Actually, she feels dizzy and sweaty, even in this air con.

Chef points at the tank. — Even though they poisonous, pufferfish popular in aquarium. Can be tame but no hand-feed because of sharp teeth.

In an instant, Kendra realizes that she's not going to die, that the nausea is largely of her mind's making. She walks over to the tank. — Can I see them puff up?

— No. Too stressful for fish to make this happen, Chef sternly shakes his head. Then he regards Kendra with those shining black eyes. — You seem like lady who loves food.

— Yes I do. I don't overeat like some, Kendra says smugly, — but I like to try new things and I'm very adventurous, she purrs, suddenly horribly aware that she's flirting with the chef.

— Me too. You can eat almost anything, Chef declares, then raises a finger, — if it is properly prepared. So you no try cook pufferfish at home!

— Don't worry, Kendra smiles chastely, aware that she's backpedaling, — I'll always come to the experts.

Toto is at her feet and she picks him up, now anxious to leave without eating any more food. — Right, sweet baby boy, we'd better get you home! You gotta be hungry too!

In her departure, she is aware that her pulse is racing as she heads down the stairs.

The LP Tavern is very dark inside, illuminated only by some indented wall and bar lights, and a bank of buzzing neon at the gantry, all glowing phosphorous blue. Until their eyes adjusted, a stranger might be forgiven for thinking that it's still the dive bar it used to be. However, the exotic and comprehensive range of spirits and beers on offer and the dress and bearing of the clientele soon dispel this notion.

Kendra is drinking with Stacie, Stephanie, and Cressida, a research assistant at Chicago University. Cressida wears her black hair short, and it glows silkily in the blue light in exactly the same way as her top. Sparkling earrings dangle like small chandeliers. The girls sit on tall stools at a round table, big enough for just the drinks and the odd elbow. Kendra admits that it is good having Chef living in her apartment complex. — He's awesome. It's unreal, she tells them. — Toto's really taken to him.

— Seems like he's not the only one, Stacie says, her tones and glance laden with coquettish inference.

— What? Kendra raises her plucked brows.

— Would you, like, well, sleep with him?

Kendra looks at her in disgust. — Don't be crazy. He's way too old. He's . . . She stops and scrutinizes her friend's face for signs of treachery. — What the fuck are you trying to say, Stacie?

— He's kinda neat though. Stacie shrugs vaguely, then offers, — I'd go with an Asian guy.

— Well, you know where he fucking well lives and works, Stacie. Go and stalk him. Kendra shakes her head but she is satisfied that Stacie is too hollow to be hostile.

— I'm not saying *him*. He *is* a little old. But as a general point.

Stephanie yawns luxuriantly, her skin stretching translucent under the blue lighting. — They're supposed to be a little, eh, light downstairs.

This comment sparks Cressida into a rage. Her pale, longish face has taken on a marine-like taint. In it her small teeth are bared, and Kendra thinks she can almost see the anger rising up inside her and spilling through them. — That's racist BS. Who makes that shit up? The black man is too big, the yellow man too small. Who, then, is just right? Who is the fucking norm? Three guesses, she sneers, and springs to her feet, heading for the bathroom.

— Oh God, Stephanie gasps, her hand going to her mouth,

— I'd forgotten all about her and that Myles guy. But I'm not a racist, how can I be? I work with members of the different species we share this planet with. If I can do that, how can I logically be opposed to different races *within* the same human species?

Stacie's brow furrows in response.

— Ignore her, Kendra tuts. For some reason she always feels uncomfortable at signs of weakness in Stephanie that some-body other than herself has managed to induce. — All that Chicago Uni bullshit. She's fucking some black professor and she can't even be pleased that she's getting some big tenured dick inside her. She still has to make herself out to be a victim. All this trust-fund guilt, identifying with minorities, it's such a bore.

Stacie realizes then that Kendra will never fuck a chef of any ethnicity unless he has his own show on television. She signals to the waitress. — I wanna chocolate Martini.

— Gross, Kendra winces. — Gimme a Stoli and tonic.

— Me too, Stephanie choruses, considering that a serious and intimidating waft comes from Cressida. You can never be totally relaxed in her company. Then she looks gravely at them and leans in. — And you'll never guess what I've heard?

They regard her, thin, plucked brows twisting in concen-tration. Kendra's hand runs over her head to make sure that her ponytail is still tight on the crown.

Stephanie bends in still closer to them, allowing them to catch a scent of her Allure. — Trent is apparently seeing, or fucking – you decide – Andrea Pallister.

— My God, Stacie says. — Didn't she flunk psychology at DePaul and have to change to, like, *art* or something?

Kendra seethes quietly, aware that their eyes are on her. — She's got *cats*, she squeaks in a petulant misery she can't quite manage to repress. — I thought Trent liked *dogs*!

Cressida returns, an air of serenity about her now, sitting down as the waitress comes over with the drinks. She orders a Stoli. Kendra stands up. — I'd better go to the restroom and moisturize. This is my second alcoholic drink.

As they watch Kendra depart Stacie tells Cressida, — We're talking Trent.

— Oh, she says, then exchanges malicious grins with the others.

As Kendra applies her tinted moisturizer she thinks about Andrea Pallister. How she would have thrown herself at Trent. How she didn't realize that, yes, some men did appreciate neediness, but generally only in short fucks. Then in her mind's eye she sees Trent's face slightly reconfigured from its iron-jawed, luxuriantly quiffed perfection; the nose more bulbous than she'd admitted, the complexion carrying a little extra flush. Perhaps a certain lassitude about the eyes and the mouth. *On the wrong drugs.* And so she readies herself to face her friends.

On her reappearance the conversation seems to strike up as if her presence has sent a signal, like an orchestera conductor waving a baton. — Never trust a guy who fucks a catwoman, Stephanie nods. — I mean, three cats! Her apartment smells so fucking gross. Who would tolerate that? Nobody but a closet slob.

— There is something just a little too gauche about him, Cressida agrees.

— That's an interesting hypothesis, Kendra says icily, her composure restored. — You know what he once said about Toto? He said, 'You could roll over and crush that little bastard and not even know it. I like dogs, but I prefer them big and robust. I wouldn't want to live with something I could kill by mistake.'

Stephanie contemplates her friends with that look of knowing evaluation they've witnessed her deploy since their first psychology seminar at DePaul. — Reading between the lines that means he's a slob. Covered in cat furs. Yuk! I'll bet his idea of a good day out is the bleachers at Wrigley Fields.

— We've all done that one, baby, Stacie yelps in a guilty delight. The afternoon shift! And she notes two young men who are sitting at the next table. *Hot, but obvious fags.*

Stephanie is nodding in the negative. — In emergencies only, and just to check out a new look on the salivating frat boys. We never went there to seriously *pick up*, not like some demented, desperate sluts. Tricia Hales, anybody?

— A total SERB, Kendra scoffs.

Stacie looks blank again, as Cressida shrugs and Stephanie nods in approval. — Self-Esteem Rock Bottom, she gleefully enlightens them.

— She's having a *baby* with that *loser*. In a *condo*, Kendra tersely observes.

Stephanie's eyes widen in horror. — They aren't even getting a *house*? God, I bet her parents are proud of *her*.

— You would *really* say that Trent's a slob? Stacie asks.

A beaming Stephanie turns to Kendra and Cressida in complicity. — Let's face it, none of us are exactly novices when it comes to analyzing human nature.

The young men at the next table are preparing to leave. As they go, one says too loudly to the other, — Oh my God, the DOGS are out tonight. The Desperate, Obsessive Girl Snobs of Lincoln Park!

The girls are stunned and then outraged as they register this. Kendra reacts first, shouting, — Don't acronym us, you faggots, *nobody* acronyms us!

— Woof! Woof! the gay men bark back at the girls, who all, except for Stephanie, manage to smile.

At closing time they walk out into the city night air, and the aroma of baking tar and concrete. Passing car headlights strobe them. Muscled and waxed young men, standing on street corners or under roadside trees, pay their thin bodies scant regard.

— I guess we asked for that one, Kendra says, — but we have got to just own that title. DOGS. DOGS of Lincoln Park, she tries it out for size.

— No we do nat, Stephanie insists. — These guys are misogynists. The sort of fags who blame their mothers for all the shit life has thrown at them.

— Honey, Cressida responds, — *everybody* blames their mothers for all the shit life has thrown at them. That's what mothers are *for*.

Bickering starts up, as Kendra is aware that tiredness has just run over her. She turns and leaves them in the street with a limp, backhand wave and heads home up Halstead.

When she gets to the stairs of her apartment block, Kendra realizes that the third Stoli was a mistake. Its charge makes her feel bare and lonely as she enters her home and the air con sucks the evening heat out of her. She presses the phone's messaging system. The developer guy, Clint, hasn't called. — Toto puppy, Kendra shouts. — Where's my baby boy? Does he love his mommy? Yes he does! Yes he does!

Strangely there is no sign of the dog. He is usually all over her. — Where are you hiding! Are you sick, baby? Kendra murmurs as she picks the handset from the coffee table and clicks on the television set. A date show flashes into her front room. The losers on parade make her happier to have come home alone. But it's too quiet. Where was that little monster! She goes into one room, then another, feeling herself being breached by a sense of imminence. The apartment is silent and she can hear her own heart thump as she checks the cupboards, under the beds, all his hiding places.

Nothing!

The dog has gone. There is no trace of him. Sensing something evaporating inside her, Kendra sits down. Gathers her breath. Then she gets up and ventures outside. Had he somehow darted out when she'd opened the door? Unlikely. She surely would have noticed. She wasn't *that* drunk. Down in the railed garden courtyard, she repeats his name over and over. — Toto. Toh-toh-oh-oh-oh.

There is no sign of him as she walks down the sidewalk around her block. Kendra is tentative, as if she expects her dog to materialize out of the vaporous night air, like a furry, floppy-eared angel. She squats in the narrow deserted street and calls his name, as if to do so will launch him into her lap from behind some shrub or tree. Soon all she can do, though, is contemplate the designer rips, frays, and distressing on the knees and thighs of her blue jeans.

Chef suddenly comes to mind. He might have seen Toto. She remembers that she had to take in a package for him from FedEx earlier; a long box. Retrieving it, she climbs up the stairs and bangs on the door. He answers, and he's still in his whites. — This came for you, she tells him, his face glowing as she hands over the box. — You haven't seen my dog around, have you?

— No, he informs her, — not seen.

— I just came back from a drink with some friends and now he's gone, she finds herself sniffing to stifle a fretful rising inside her.

They head back downstairs in the garden, where Chef, a flashlight in his hand, helps her to search again for signs of Toto. They shine the beam up to where a window is open in her apartment. It's in the back spare room, but there is no way the dog could have survived had he fallen from that height and there is nothing in the garden to suggest he had.

Back in her apartment, Kendra sits on the couch all of a

sudden aware that heavy sobs are bubbling up through her. She hears the chef's voice through her muffled confusion; insistent, instructing, and she gets up and follows him up the stairs, without being fully aware why. The pufferfish in the tank pout in scandalized outrage at her. As Chef goes into the kitchen, she says softly to them, — I'm sorry I ate your friend. Please bring Toto back.

Chef comes through with two glasses of Scotch in cut-glass tumblers. Kendra thinks briefly this isn't what she needs, then she tries to work out what it is she does need, and can't, so lets the proffered glass fill the void. Then he makes her eat something, a noodle concoction.

As she forces down the food and drink, Chef opens the box she has brought and is delighted with the sword he takes out. Unlike the other one it has a straight blade. — Ninja sword, by Paul Chen, one of best makes, Chef explains. — Ninja sword always straight, no like Shinto katana. He points at the one they used yesterday. Chef swings the sword as Kendra half-heartedly munches her way through the small supper.

— As a chef, knives very important. A good set of knives is everything. Always must respect things that cut flesh, he says.

Kendra is not so fascinated this time, in fact she feels a little sick. She can't help thinking about the danger such a weapon would be to Toto. He was so frail and small. How could anybody hurt something so defenceless? But there was evil in this world. She shakes off her melancholy thoughts. With the Scotch, the food comforts her a little and she regains some composure. — Thank you for being so kind. You like Scotch in Japan, yes?

The chef nods lightly with a dumb smile, like he doesn't quite understand her.

— Japan, it seems so mystical, Kendra continues, feeling foolish as she recalls that Chef's restaurant is called the Mystic East. — Eh, whereabouts in Japan do you come from?

— Korean, Chef points to himself. — Only came Japan study cooking. To Tokyo. But born and raise in Korea.

Korea.

And something thin and dark in the chef's smile – something that does not lend itself easily to definition – disturbs Kendra greatly. Excusing herself she heads downstairs to her apartment. Cranking up the air con, she undresses quickly and tumbles into bed. An exhausted, alcoholic sleep claims her, and she feels herself fighting in the night against its terrors. Rattling sounds fill the bedroom. She can hear Toto whining miserably, as if entombed in the walls. She rises, aware that somebody is in the apartment. Chef stands in the doorway, naked. His body is sinewy and yellow in the light. He has an outsized penis, its tip almost at his knees. The samurai sword is in his hand, hanging losely by his side. Kendra screams.

She is back in her bed. Something warm lies next to her; her heartbeat races and dips, as she sees it's just her pillow. The room is silent, save for the soft whirr of the air con.

The Saturday morning dawns muggy, the chirping of the birds in the oak tree outside particularly bellicose as Kendra wakes up, blinking in the striped sunlight pouring through the blinds. The bolt of fear surfaces in her. *Toto, oh Toto.* She rises and pulls on a Chicago Bears T-shirt, her dressing gown spilling, like so many other garments, from the wicker laundry basket to the floor. The desperate chaos of her apartment, clothes strewn everywhere, is hurtful to her, and it has been thrown into further disarray in the frantic search for Toto. Picturing the parental home at Highland Park, the stucco, the timbered gables, the electric green lawn, airy and swollen like a comforter (if only the earth really swallowed you up in that way), a sour alcoholic burping sob rises nauseously in her chest. She is supposed to work this Saturday morning but calls in, leaving a message on the answering machine. — It's Kendra. I won't be in this morning. My . . . she hesitates about telling the truth, — . . . my sister Karla . . . my *baby* sister, she says, choking with emotion as she recalls a young bathing-suited Karla with her on a lakeside beach, before an image of a galloping Toto with something in his mouth supplants it, — . . . was in a road-traffic accident . . . I just pray . . . I'm going there *right* now, and she puts the phone down.

Kendra doesn't quite trust herself to drive and calls a cab, instructing the driver to head to the city dog pound at Western Avenue, on the South Side, going towards Cicero. In her emotional state, the guilt at using Karla in such an underhand way kicks in, and she fires off a prayer of forgiveness and one of salvation for Toto. On the journey paranoia is tearing from her. It takes them an age to get onto the Kennedy Expressway, and when they get to the South Side, it's clear that the Indian driver doesn't know the city. — You do *nat* stay on 55, Kendra screeches, her nerves shredded, — No Stevenson Expressway! No, no! You come off on Damon. Then you turn on to Western!

Now her overheated mind half recalls a recent case of a Chicago Police lieutenant's dog being euthanized when it was supposed to be held for a ten-day rabies observation. The staff at the dog pound had tried to cover up the mistake and the authorities raided the facility. *What if they had done the same thing with poor Toto?*

Western Avenue is a desolate enough street on the North Side, but this far down Kendra finds the neighborhood posi-tively sinister: run-down, empty, and with an ominous air of threat. Although it's broad daylight, she is still happy to complete the short walk from the car to the building. But the dog pound merely distresses her further. Inside, all those uncared-for and abandoned animals. But a search reveals that Toto isn't one of them. — I'm sorry, a chunky Hispanic woman tells her.

She dials a cab on her cell, waits twenty wretched minutes before it comes to ferry her back over to the North Side, away from all the happy poor people, reunited with their loved pets. On the way back, the pop-up downtown area drawing closer, she can't stop thinking about Chef. Who was he really, and what did she know about him? His love of Asian cuisine and samurai swords, his keeping of pufferfish in the tanks to be consumed fresh. That sword. She suddenly shudders in her seat as she thinks of it cutting her beloved Toto in two pieces like the watermelon, his existence – and all that love – snuffed out in one sharp yelp. The cab is so hot inside and to stop her neck burning on the leather headrest, Kendra has to undo her ponytail and let her long hair fan out and act like a cover.

When she gets home, Kendra goes online, searching for 'Korean' and 'dog meat'.

Her heart pounds as she reads:

Consuming dog meat is an ancient Korean custom, its advocates maintaining that the only difference between slaughtering a dog for food and slaughtering a cow or a pig is the culture in which it is done.
   But the average Korean does not consume dog meat, as it is generally considered a medicinal dish (either to promote male virility or to combat the heat in summer).

Even more upsetting is a subsequent passage:

The dogs are often beaten to death by clubs, as a way of tenderizing the meat. Some vendors claim they put the dog through considerable pain and torment during the slaughter, as this is thought to increase levels of adrenalin and thereby improve the value of the meat as a source of added virility.

So the lesson is, if you have a dog with you in Korea, lock it up and keep it inside. It may be stolen, as dog meat is very profitable.

Kendra prints off some of the papers, then heads out into the street. Walking for a bit, she passes one blue police patrol car, then another, until they thicken, spilling out into the adjoining streets like casino chips toward their concentration in one parking lot at the side of a building that sits imposingly on the corner of a city block. It bears the sign: CITY OF CHICAGO POLICE DEPARTMENT.

The desk officer is munching takeout and drinking coffee from Dunkin Donuts. As Kendra walks in, her untied hair swinging wildly, he licks his lips. — Yes, miss? he says obsequiously, his eyes going straight to her cleavage.

— My dog has gone missing.

— That's too bad. Well, we got a little form for you to fill out with some of the details. He smiles broadly, pulling some paperwork from a box in a unit of slated pigeonholes.

— No need for that. I know where he is. I have a neighbor, she blurts out. — He's a chef. And he's always cooking!

The cop chuckles lightly to himself. — Guess that sounds about right.

— No, Kendra snaps in irritation, — he's Korean!

The desk officer looks pointedly at her. — And what has this to do with your dog?

— A chef? Korean? Hello! Her eyes go as big as eight balls on a pool table.

The policeman laughs in her face, and she can even feel some of his spittle hitting her. She rubs it with her hand. The officer looks dumbly at her in some vague lame apology, then steels himself, moving into pompous official mode. — We cannot go harassing members of the city's Korean population every time somebody's dog goes missing.

— Well, maybe you should, Kendra says, slamming the papers she'd printed from the websites onto the desk, — because it's well known that people in South Korea *eat* dogs and cats!

— We ain't in Korea, miss. They don't do that sort of thing here.

— How in hell's name do you know that?

— Well, I guess it's our different cultures. I see it as kinda about respect. Like, people in India do not believe in eating cows. They get horrified at the way cows are treated here in the USA. But they know we do things differently, so they accept it. Just like Korean folks accept that they can't eat dog here. But it's a valid point, in general terms, don'tcha think?

— No it is nat! The relationship between pets or even working animals and their owners is intrinsically different to that between humans and domesticated animals raised for food! Can't you see that?! Kendra shouts, unable to believe that the police officer is even attempting to justify this.

The officer is not for backing down. — Dunno bout that. I guess the way they see it is that some animals are raised to hunt, others to fight, others to be eaten. Besides, pet breeds ain't used for food back there in Korea.

— You don't know! Kendra wails. — I've researched this! She points at the papers. — Because dog meat is expensive, the people in rural areas of Korea will raise and kill the dogs themselves; or steal them. That chef's done something awful to Toto. I just fucking know he has!

— What kind of dog are we talking about?

— He's a papillon.

— Right. No offence, miss, but a papillon dog don't exactly constitute a banquet. Why, I doubt you'd get a decent portion of gyro outta one of them little guys, the cop smiles.

— I want him back! Will you fucking well help me find my dog!

The policeman's voice grows firmer. — Now, miss, I realise that you're a little upset here. Why don't you just go home and see if that little fellow shows up and we'll call you if anything happens this end?

— Thank you, Kendra sneers sarcastically. — Thank you so much for your help.

Outside on the steps of the station, she seethes in impotence. The only thing she can think of doing is to head home. Back at the apartment she stealthily creeps upstairs and listens outside the chef's door. There is no sound. She goes back downstairs. Her despondency is compounded further by the mess of her apartment. A huge laundry has piled up but she can't face going down into that basement right now.

Kendra decides to go and visit Stephanie at her workplace. She should be finishing up soon. Steph knows about animals and their behavior. She might be able to piece together Toto's state of mind and his likely destination, if it wasn't up the stairs and into the chef's cooking pot. She heads to the practice on Clark. — Miss Harbison has just finished a consultation, the soccer mom receptionist informs her.

She goes into Stephanie's office. Her friend is at the window, blowing cigarette smoke out into the street. — God, those people, Stephanie scoffs, looking below onto the Clark traffic, — they cannot seem to accept that they are *not* my clients. They are merely the sponsors. *Victor* is the client.

— Who is . . . Victor?

— A Netherland dwarf rabbit with an eating disorder. I felt like saying to his stupid bitch of an owner, 'Have you looked at yourself in a goddamn mirror lately? Ever stopped to consider that poor Victor might just be *modeling behavior*?' Stephanie bellows in exasperation. Then she seems to regard Kendra for

135

the first time. — But you look stressed out, honey. What's up? she asks, then wariness sharpens her features. — Like, why are you *here*?

— Toto's gone! The chef . . . upstairs, the guy from the restaurant; he's done something terrible to Toto. He's Korean. They eat dogs!

— You can*nat* be serious, Stephanie says, then she molds her face in *that* expression, the one she always thinks of as her 'clinical, diagnostic' look. It involves making her eyebrows almost collide. — Look, Kennie, Toto was — she corrects herself, — is . . . a very sweet dog, but let's face it, he has several issues.

An arrow of filial failure thuds into Kendra's chest. — You think I should have taken him to Dr Stark?

Stephanie flicks her cigarette out the window, sits down, crossing her legs. She regards her own fishnets, enjoying what she thinks of as 'the coiled-springed sexuality' of them. They were pantyhose but guys never knew for sure. You just reeled in the catch, like she'd most certainly done last night. A fortuitous chance meeting in the street on the way home, then a late drink, after the others had departed. She regards Kendra, who was just a little too quick to wind up the evening, and something approaching shame bubbles up inside her. Then she slips back into her professional mode. — Phil Stark would have identified Toto's abandonment/rejection complex straight away and drawn an appropriate behavior modification program, she briskly informs her friend. — I also think it was a no-no calling him Toto. By identifying him with the dog in *The Wizard of Oz*, you subconsciously factor in the state of his being lost and searching for home as an inbuilt element of his psyche.

— But he *has* a home, Kendra cries, — *our* home!

— Course he does, princess, Stephanie agrees, — Toto's a very loved little dog, she coos, realizing that Kendra is too distraught to be left alone. She calls Stacie, telling her to meet them back at Kendra's apartment. They leave the practice and walk down Clark without speaking to each other. As well as the intense heat, they are now assaulted by thunderous roars in the skies above them, as four jets, like birds of prey in a mechanized flock, slash through the clear blue sky.

Back at the apartment, Stacie appears and they sit together on the couch, comforting a distraught Kendra with a glass of wine. — I can't go out . . . I just feel so helpless, waiting by the phone, she says. Then there is an almighty roar from outside, the jets flying so low that the window bellies inwards. — Shit, Kendra barks in a galled enmity, — Can they not go to Iraq and do that? Is that not what it's for?

— It's just a show of strength. I find it pretty reassuring, Stephanie says. — I like the idea of us burning loads of gas in these trials.

— It must be terrible living in a war zone, Stacie shudders.

— It's kinda what they choose, Stephanie asserts. — If they don't like it, they can get off their butts and leave, like our forefathers who came here did.

Stacie seems to consider this for a while. Then she casts her eyes around Kendra's apartment. It's a mess, but it's *exactly* what she needs. — I'll bet this place is really expensive, she eventually says as she registers the empty spare room she has long harbored designs on moving into. — Can you afford it? she asks Kendra.

— Jeez, you don't *get it*, Stace. That question should be reframed: can I afford *not* to have it? Get with the Breaking News: princesses live in palaces, she shrieks, sliding a Xanax into her mouth, and washing it down with a sip of red wine.

Stephanie fidgets, looks at her watch and tries to get onto the subject of work. — Real estates's booming, right, Kendra?

Kendra would normally breezily chirp, 'More than ever,' even if the market was slow, aware that expectations drive everything and therefore need to be talked up. It was the professional way.

Now she can only distractedly moan, — Toto was an angel in the body of a dog.

— She's so upset, Stacie whispers to Stephanie, as she squeezes Kendra's knee.

Some people just shouldn't try to understand this world, Stephanie thinks wearily. Then she leans forward and touches her friend's hand. — Kennie, I'm worried about you.

— No need, sugar, I'm fine, Kendra protests in a small, reedy voice.

Oh God, compassion fatigue is kicking in, Stephanie considers, trying to convert a yawn into a smile. She just about succeeds but the strain of it makes her consider exit strategies and she's already thinking about a future engagement.

Stacie offers to stay in the spare room, but Kendra is absolutely insistent that she'd rather be alone. When they depart, she waits up, channel-hopping with the sound turned down. She can hear somebody entering the apartment complex. It's Chef; she's already gotten to know the plodding, deliberate pattern of his footsteps on the concrete stairs outside. Who else could it be at this time?

She heads out to intercept him on the stairs. — Hey, you!

— No sign of dog? he cheerfully asks.

— No . . . I've even been to the pound, she shakes her head.

— I can't sleep. I don't suppose you're in the mood for another one of those medicinal drinks you gave me yesterday?

— Very tired, long day. Chef raises his dark brows in what she takes to be a plea.

— Just a little one? Kendra purrs, thinking, for some reason, of Chef naked.

— Come, says Chef, pointing to the stairs. At his apartment, he opens the door and ushers her in.

When he moves into the toilet, Kendra waits until she can hear his urine splash, then takes her chance and goes to the kitchen. She looks through some of the cupboards. Nothing. Then she moves to the refrigerator. She looks at it, hesitating in the face of its cold, immutable form. Then the thermostat clicks suddenly, and her heart misses a beat. Steeling herself, Kendra moves over and grabs the handle of the refrigerator, yanking the door open. Squints under the light as a small carcass greets her. She almost screams.

But it's only a chicken.

She can see that. Kendra leaves the kitchen and moves across to the giant scratching post in the corner of the lounge, the one Chef uses for sword practice. Behind it is a small cupboard. She bends over and reaches for the handle.

— Do not do that, a voice comes sharply from behind her. She turns quickly, and Chef is standing in the doorway with a samurai sword in his hand. She freezes, mimicking the expression on his cold, immobile face.

The week passed without Kendra returning any calls, but Stacie was not unduly perturbed. Kennie could be a moody girl, she reasoned. A lost dog, new boyfriend, bad menstrual cramps, running out of Xanax; anything could do it, she'd joked to Stephanie. Besides, they knew where she would be come 12.30 p.m. on Friday. Stephanie, however, was a bit more concerned. How would she break the news to Kendra about her seeing Trent? It would be a tough spin. She worried that her friend had already somehow learned of this burgeoning romance, and that this was what the big sulk was all about.

Stacie and Stephanie meet on Clark. It is still hot, but the temperature has fallen a little. Smoky clouds hide the sun and the air feels heavy and muggy. When they get to the restaurant, the closed sign is up. The place seems deserted, but then the door swings inwards, and a grinning Chef emerges to greet them.

— Are you, like, open? Stacie asks.

— Always open, but only for special customers, Chef points at them. — Min go sick, in heat. Fall sleep at music concert in park. Have bad sunburn. Akiro back in Japan for funeral for one week. Only me here, but I cook very special dish for you.

Stephanie looks at Stacie, then at Chef. — Eh, have you seen Kendra?

— Oh yes, Chef smiles, — she will be here. Come!

The girls go into the restaurant and sit down, Stacie feeling more privileged than Stephanie that Chef has opened up *exclusively for them*. However, by 12.45 Kendra still hasn't appeared. — It isn't like her to be late, Stephanie muses, checking her watch, thinking that sashimi would be a good call in this heat. No rice; carbs after noon was a disgusting habit. — Probably a crisis at work. She said that bitch Marilyn had been bending her flaps, she snorts, as her thoughts turn to Trent. One more makeout session would probably close the deal and consign catwoman Pallister to the trash can of dating history.

— It's terrible when you don't get on with your co-workers, Stacie says.

How the fuck would you know? Stephanie thinks. — Well, condo developments. I ask you, she acridly observes. Trent pops into her mind again. An architect's practice; a serious upgrade on Todd. No more twentysomething loser musos, their numbers as prolific as sparrows as they hopped around the city from apartment to dive bar to gig. No more feigning interest at unsolicited disclosures of 'exciting projects'. And Stephanie and Trent had a ring to it. At family gatherings, perhaps a Thanksgiving up at the cabin in Wisconsin. *Trent and I can make it in a couple of hours if we take the convertible.* Poor Kendra. But omelette, eggs, breaking.

Chef appears with a large platter of meat. — For you to try. Very special dish.

— All protein, says Stephanie.

He watches as they prepare to take a bite.

Closing her eyes as her lips part around the morsel on the fork, Stephanie lets the buttery meat slowly dissolve in her mouth, inducing a rapturous response from her taste buds. An aura of hovering sunlight seems to melt through her. — My God, this is fantastic! So succulent. What is it?

— I love it, Stacie agrees, — it's got a really tangy, almost salty taste, but it's so subtle.

Chef contemplates her large eyes. His tongue darts over his lips to remove a layer of sodium that has frosted there. — Old recipe. They say this meat can be stringy but all is in marinade. Have to pulverize it to tenderize it first. That is secret.

— Is it pork? Stacie asks. — It sorta tastes like pork, but the texture's more like chicken . . .

— Finish meal, I show you later, he points to the kitchen door and follows his own finger through to his den.

Stacie and Stephanie sit back and enjoy their meal, as they wait for Kendra to show up.

— God, Kennie will be so jealous, Stacie purrs, — we got to try something new and she didn't!

They eat with a ravenous enthusiasm, captivated by this mystery dish; the meat tender and succulent, yet with a gamy strength to it, and it makes them temporarily forget about the absence of their friend.

Then, after a while, Chef reappears at their table. — I have something very important I must show you. Come! He beckons the girls into the kitchen. Bemused, they get up and follow him. — Secret ingredient in there. Then I have other surprise for you! Picking up a huge filleting knife from the sushi bar, Chef holds the heavy, swinging door open with his free hand and ushers them in, grinning as he lets it thump shut behind them.

Marilyn sits in the office and looks at the empty chair by Kendra's desk. She thinks: Monday, Tuesday, Wednesday, and

Thursday. A sentence escapes her mouth: — How long is that little bitch going to be ill over her freakin sister? she says, possibly to herself, although Greg and Cassandra can hear her.

About ten minutes after this Kendra Cross bursts purposefully through the door and heads toward her workstation.

— So, you've decided to grace us with your presence, Marilyn smiles caustically. — And how is your sister?

— Never mind my sister, Kendra hisses, looking over her shoulder and putting some personal effects into her bag.

— Oh, so I take it you're leaving us, Marilyn sneers. — Had a better offer?

Kendra turns around and regards her, hand on hip. — Yes I have, she lies. — You know why? she asks, and without waiting for an answer bursts into a rant: — I'll have you know that you played a big fucking part in murdering my dog, you miserable cunt, and you know why you did this? Huh? Because you've never loved anything in your fucking pathetic life. And that's because you are so inherently fucking *un*lovable.

There is a three-second total silence in the office.

— You fucking spoiled little . . . Marilyn breaks the impasse with a gasp, then whines painfully, — You don't know me, and she looks around at her subordinates in appeal, — you know nothing about me . . . Kennie, you're upset, I . . .

— I know that you're so fucking lame. She looks around at the others. — All of you are! Get with the project: the real-estate market here is dead! They cannot make the pre-sales to keep constructing those horrible fucking condos and you're all gonna be out on your lazy fat asses soon! And another thing, she focuses on Marilyn again, — you are *always* the laughing stock on our nights out, right, Greg?

Greg reddens and turns away sharply, as the front door opens and Stephanie, flanked by Stacie, steps into the open-plan office, carrying Toto in her arms. Seeing Kendra, he lets out a short volley of excited yelps. — Hey-ey-ey! Guess who showed up! Stephanie sings.

Kendra turns to face them, her mouth in a quivering spasm in response to the evidence of her eyes and ears. Her first thought is: could she be hallucinating? She'd gone up to her parents' place in Highland Park for a few days to regroup, retrench, wait by her cellphone in hope, and then, when nothing happened, to mourn Toto. In the sleep deprivation, the Xanax, and the mind-mashing heat, she no longer totally trusts her senses.

— Chef found him trapped in the vent shaft down in the laundry room, Stephanie smiles, to Kendra's bemused delight. — He must have opened that grille in your front room behind the couch and fell down there. He was okay, just a bit startled, hungry and thirsty. Chef gave him a good feed and he's fine. She pushes the dog into Kendra's arms. — Where have you been?

— Oh my God, I . . . I . . . I went to my mom's, I was so depressed . . . but he's back! My baby is back! She gasps as the tears of joy flow. — He came back . . .

—You don't make fun of me, do you? Greg? Cassie? Marilyn pleads. Then she fixes Kendra in a poisoned glare. — Get out of here! Get the fuck out! Take that fucking little rat with you!

— I gotta go, Kendra smiles at her friends, walking to the door, with Stephanie and Stacie in pursuit.

Stephanie stops, turns around, and fixes the ranting Marilyn with a look of disdain. — Advice: try cock. Or at least find a bitch with a tongue that *works*.

— Ooh-hoo! Hell, yeah, sister! Stacie choruses in black girl's voice, high-fiving Stephanie.

Marilyn screams at their backs as they go through the exit doors, — You fucking do not insult me in my place of work! I'm calling the police! It's trespass, is what it is! Trespass!

— Jeez, Stacie exclaims, as they head into the street, Marilyn's rant still ringing in their ears, — what happened back there?

— I guess I'm looking for a new job, Kendra says, filling her nostrils with the scent of Toto.

— Wow, Stacie smiles, thinking about Kendra's finances and that empty spare room.

Stephanie pats the dog's small head. — Chef was doing laundry when he heard the noise coming from the overhead air ducts. He left you a note but you'd gone. We thought you would be round at the restaurant today.

— I haven't been back to the apartment . . . I came straight here from my mom's . . .

— You missed such a feast, Kennie, Stacie sang. — Chef made us a big platter of wild boar. I got a fright when he took us back into the kitchen and made me open up the refrigerator and a big boar's head was staring at me! He's a real character!

— Thank you so much. You two are just the best friends ever! Kendra gushes, as her cellphone goes off. She digs it out of her bag with dexterity, as she's still holding Toto. — Hi-i-i . . . she coos into the mouthpiece. — Okay, okay . . . no . . . this evening at eleven round yours is fine. Okay. See you.

Stephanie feels something ominous settling inside her, ready to fall like a lump of lead. She can't speak. Stacie nonchalantly chirps, — Who was that?

— Trent. He called me this morning. Says he's being stalked by some psycho-bitch, Kendra says matter-of-factly. — Apparently he and some loser had a drunken makeout last week and she's been bombarding him with texts, emails, and phone calls ever since. You know the type, she shrugs. — I'm gonna go round and cheer him up, she smiles, oblivious to the blood draining from Stephanie's face. — But right now I think I need some quiet time with this little prince, Kendra nods at her dog, then dabs at a few tears which form over her smile, before adding, — alone. Thanks . . . you two are the greatest!

Stephanie gasps, feels giddy and weak in the heat, and can hear nothing outside of a ringing in her ears and some traffic noises. She can see Stacie mouthing something at Kendra, who is waving them goodbye as she turns and heads briskly down Clark toward her apartment clutching Toto in her arms, who sits in his exhalted position, imperious in his regard for the other dogs.

Miss Arizona

It's gotten beyond cold and I don't feel uncomfortable no more. It's nearly my time and I don't even care. Why in God's name should I? I ain't leavin without her and I sure as hell can't take her with me.

It ain't like I'm feelin anythin; my arms or legs, and I ain't even sure whether or not my eyes are open. I guess it don't much matter that all I got is thoughts. They ain't worth shit but I don't see them stoppin for a while. The joke is that it's gonna be the cold that'll take me away, when outside, beyond those thick stone walls, they got people frying in that heat. Guess we all gotta go sometime. It's just the circumstance I would never have figured in a thousand years.

I suppose I paid for my arrogance, just like he did. And yeah, I finally understand that crazy ol drunk now: just another asshole who fell on the sword of his own vanity. You get to thinkin that you're the man: the ice-cool, shit-talkin, big-dicked *artist*. Everyone else: why, they're just your itty-bitty subjects. So then you reckon this means you can just do as you damn well please. That it somehow gives you rights. But it gives you no goddamn rights at all.

When did it start?

It started and it ended with Yolanda.

Miss Arizona.

She was an ol gal, who looked like she'd been rode hard and put away wet. Yep, she said she was Miss Arizona at one time. Well, I was darned if I ever could see it. She sure was one heavy lady; I'd seen gals in Louisiana trailer parks had asses didn't wobble like the flesh on her arms did when they moved – usually to pick up a drink. Ol Yolanda had the type of red hair that might have been comely at one time, tho I reckon it had long since come outta bottle; piled high and lacquered stiff on that big piggy-eyed head of hers. Her skin was white as your momma's sweet milk; the sort that don't take too kindly to the sun, and that's one thing they got plenty of round here.

Miss Yolanda mostly kept away from it. If she were outside she'd be in the shade, sometimes sittin on the back porch overlookin that small rear garden, with its little scrap of grass as brown and dry as the ruined old ranchlands that surrounded her house. The scrubby patch sure did contrast with that beautiful, turquoise swimmin pool. Even though Yolanda often sat in a candy-stripe one-piece swimsuit (usually with a big floppy straw hat sat on her head and a robe over her shoulders, while a big fan blasted her with cool air), she never seemed to get into that pool. Probably didn't want to mess up that hair of hers. But that damn pool was kept so good I always reckoned it was a crime for it not to be used, specially in these parts. But yeah, skin like that and here she was in this place; right in the middle of the goddamn desert, a good three hours' drive from downtown Phoenix. She just sat there on that chair under the parasol, with ropes of blue vein runnin out from those pale, flabby thighs, turning coal black as they got down to her skinny calves. Yep, she was Miss Arizona. Reckon right about when that state was counted under Mexico.

I remember the first time I pulled up outside that big ranch house. I was thinkin that when somebody puts up a house that belongs in cattle country right here in the desert, you know two things right away: first is they got money, the second bein they ain't lookin for too much in the way of company.

That's ol Miss Yolanda. But it strikes me that as this looks like being my last story, it might be time to talk a little bit about myself. My name is Raymond Wilson Butler. I'm thirty-eight years old, divorced, and a native of West Texas. Before I met Yolanda I was livin in a one-thousand-bucks-a-month rented apartment near downtown Phoenix with my girlfriend, Pen. What about her? I could go on forever. But all I can think to say right now is that she sings beautiful songs, when she ain't working in a bookstore in a city mall. My life changed for the better when I met Pen. She was the best damn thing that ever happened to me.

But Yolanda was different. She changed *everybody's* life. Every single sonofabitch she came into contact with. I started seeing her through my work; every other day I'd drive out to her place. I guess I should tell you how that went.

To get to Yolanda's from our apartment, I had to drive west right out of Phoenix. It would never fail to amaze me how the city stopped so suddenly, town-to-desert within the arc of a drunkard's piss. Then you'd pass one or two subdivisions, mostly completed, some now just bein redeveloped after standin crumblin in the sun: concrete and steel carcasses, for almost twenty years. A lot of people thought land was the primary resource out here and went bust buyin it. Not when you only get around seven inches rainfall a year it ain't. The buildin only started up again when they finished the canal system, comin down from the Rockies to hook up this region with precious water.

Then, when the last of the subdivisions passed, you had a long haul through desert before you got out to Yolanda's. Driving out to see her, I always had a goddamn thirst on me. This kind of terrain didn't help the likes of me much. Cruisin down that interstate they all had a shot of trying to tempt you to stop for a cold one; Miller's, Bud, Coors, and even some of the drinkable ones. And damn, was it hot.

The particular day I'm thinkin of was my second visit to Yolanda's, the one after I had secured her agreement as to how she could be of service to me. It was midday and the sun was at its cruelest and even an old Texan boy like myself, living in LA till fairly recently, could sometimes forget how fierce it could be. Out there the bastard baked all the freshness out of the air, leaving it feelin like particles of iron in your lungs. As your throat seared your respiratory system started bangin and you sweated like a solitary truck-stop hooker gaspin goodbye as the last lusty buck in that convoy pulled on his dirty ol jeans.

My first jaunt out to Yolanda's had reminded me how much I liked to drive that Land Cruiser into the desert. I'd headed off the interstate and onto the back roads before goin right off that grimy ol track, just veerin onto what looked like virgin sand but was really more kinda broken shale; tearin through it like a wet cloth across a dusty table. You couldn't take your ass outside the car for too long, as I learned on that second visit. I had the inclination to step out for five minutes to the sound of that dirt crushin under my boot and the buzzards squawkin in the distance over some roadkill. That was just about all you could hear in this clear empty country, where the sky met the earth unbroken, every direction you turned. I looked northeast and couldn't even see an indication of the jagged, ridged mountains that were probably only a few miles away.

Takin in that emptiness and feeling the isolation, you could just about distance everythin. Through this comforting filter of solitude, I'd think about Jill and the terrible mistakes I'd made. Then I'd cheer myself at how I'd been blessed with this second chance with Pen, which I was determined not to blow.

I distrusted Phoenix, in much the same way as I did all them shabby sunbelt cities with their pop-up business districts, soulless suburban tracts, strip malls, used-car dealerships, and bad homes almost but not quite hidden by palm trees. And then you had the people; drying out like old fruit in the sun, brains too fried by heat and routine to remember why they ever did come here in the first place. And that was just the poor. The wealthy folk you only saw under glass; in their malls and motor cars, breathing in the conditioned air that tasted like weak cough medicine. I was used to heat but this place was so dry the trees were bribin the dogs.

On this day though, headin to my first proper session at Yolanda's, after my introductory approach to obtain her agreement with my business proposal, I'd got lost in my thoughts and wandered outside for a little too long. I didn't realize how that sun had got to me till I looked back at the distance I'd aimlessly strolled from the vehicle and instantly thought I'd better close it fast. The Land Cruiser looked like a mirage in that shimmerin heat; there was no way to determine how near or far it really was. I was panickin some, till my hand suddenly seemed to make contact with the scorching metal of the chassis. I slipped back into the shit-sweet coolin of the vehicle, to find my head throbbin with blood, forcin me to flop down across the passenger seat and max up that air con. It took me a good few minutes before I felt okay bout haulin myself up onto my butt. When I did, I pulled the newspaper from above the dashboard. The terror alert was green and the burn limit stood at sixteen minutes.

As I recall, that was when my cellphone went off. This registered cause it was my agent in LA, Martha Crossley, who never, ever called me on my cell. Nothin was so urgent or important it couldn't wait till I got to my landline. — Got some good news, she squealed in that high whine of hers, — you've been shortlisted to shoot the Volkswagen commercial!

— That's fine. But you know that they're going to give it to the likes of Taylor or Warburton, I told her. I ain't normally a glass-is-half-empty sort, but I knew that I was makin up the numbers on that list against the big-dicked assholes with the track records and the contacts.

— Hey! Buck up, cowboy, ya gotta be in it to win it! I'll keep you posted, she enthused, — Ciao!

I put the phone on its cradle and pulled a cold one from the icebox; not beer no more, though that terrible thirst will always be there, just waitin till things get bad. Right now there ain't no room at Ray's for that ol slut these days. I wasn't for fillin my gut with no soda nor cola either; that shit's drivin us all to a lard-assed hell, clogging arteries and sidewalks both. No, it was cool, clear water going down my hot, raspin throat, always so damn dry, and it felt good. After a while I started up the Cruiser and powered through the shale, back up onto the road.

Like I did so many times, I turned for a second to the passenger seat to imagine Pen sittin alongside me, shades on, sweet perfume fillin the cab, the painted nails on her fingers as she fiddled with that radio dial till exactly the right tune would fill up the Cruiser. It's in there somewhere and she can always find it. That's something I never could do on my own, and I guess that's cause there ain't no right tunes without that gal. That night I'd go along and hear her play her fine music and sing her pretty songs. But first I had business with ol Miss Yolanda. Glen Halliday business.

Glen Halliday, my obsession, was the all-American anti-hero. The legendary filmmaker spent his last reclusive years out here, and he spent them in the company of that woman. Yolanda was his second wife, the first being Mona Ziegler, an ol gal from his hometown of Collins, Texas. It was that town that was the inspiration of many of his films (and in my view the best of them), particularly *The Liars of Ditchwater Creek*.

Mona I'd already seen several times last year and talked to

her at some length. She'd remarried and now lived in a dull subdivision of Fort Worth. She was polite but cold about her relationship with Glen. Basically Mona reckoned that Glen just worked, and when he wasn't doin that he drank and hollered. I suppose because Glen Halliday was my hero and my inspiration, I didn't take too kindly to what I was hearing. I guess I'd put a lot of it down to Mona's bitterness and I left her to her suburban life. Unfortunately, he didn't get a better posthumous reception back in Collins. It was a small conservative town and some folks were mighty irked by the way he'd portrayed them. But I came from a similar shithole and reckoned he'd got it just about right, and nothin I heard or saw in that place convinced me of anythin to the contrary.

The desert abruptly gave way to another walled and gated subdivision, and I was thinking that those places were what Halliday railed against in his films and writings. His overridin concern was how we'd gone wrong; concrete, preachers, emperor television, and the greed of the smilin suits that made a killin from that whole crock of shit. And those raggedy dumbassed baboons that just smiled and rolled over as those jerks shafted them where the sun don't shine. I met some of those assholes back in Collins, and Glen Halliday's vision was still touchin their nerves from beyond the grave.

This subdivision was like interminable others I had passed on the way out here. They all had a huge Old Glory hangin outside in the still desert air, as limp as the dick on one of them ol fellas in the rest homes that lined the route. Then I'm through it, back into more desert land, so complete it was like a mirage recedin to nothin in the rear mirror. So I got to Yolanda's farm where they now only used the water for the swimmin pool nobody swam in, the land long turned bearassed brown.

The house itself was a low stucco dwelling. It was large

enough, but nuthin near as spectacular as the surroundin huge, perimeter stone wall, nor them big iron gates, which a wheezy, thirsty ol motor opened up when I rang the intercom. The residence was painted white, with some plants and cacti growin a few feet up its walls.

As I said, that ol Yolanda gal didn't get much in the way of company. Only other fella I saw out here was the pool-cleanin boy. That pool was always full and thoroughly maintained. Always struck me as really crazy out here, especially with her not usin it. But I guess you don't live out there alone in that kinda place without being just a little crazy.

Drivin past the pool, the boy couldn't have missed the Land Cruiser, but he didn't take no notice, just carried right on rakin up the scum from the water's surface. He had a mean face. His eyes squinted tightly, and his mouth was just as ungenerous: a tight slash under his nose. Yolanda was standin in the doorway to greet me, in that swimsuit. She kissed me on the cheek and I screwed up my nose a little; there was a strange rank odor comin from her that I hadn't noticed on my first visit. I followed her inside. Her front room was painted white, two big circular fans overhead whirling to the max. But most of the cool seemed to be coming up from the floor. She went to fix me some lemonade and I could hear her talking to herself. — Esmeralda, why are you standing around looking at me like that . . .

At first I reckoned that there was somebody else in the house, then I guessed she was talking to this cat or pooch. Then I realized it was a stuffed cat, which was mounted on an old mahogany sideboard. She was a strange ol gal, okay, but in fairness to her, Yolanda, as she insisted I called her, had been generous enough to cooperate with me in my researches on her late husband.

What I liked about being out here was that it was always

so goddamn cool, especially those slate tiles on the floor. When she came back with the drinks, lemonade for me and gin for her, I had slipped off my shoes and my soles were freshinin up real sweet. — This is so good, I told her in appreciation.

— Underground cooling. There's a refrigeration system that feeds the water we pump up from the aquifer. It supplies that pool too, once we put it through the filter, but we still get a lot of minerals and deposits. That's why I need Barry to come by a whole bunch. She pointed outside to where the pool boy was still doin his thing.

I didn't know with any great precision what an aquifer was, but the sonofabitch sure as shit must have held a whole bunch of water. I was gonna ask her but I reckoned she was the sort who could go on a little and I had my specific business. – As you know, ma'am, I'm trying to find as much as I can about Glen. He was your fourth husband, right?

— Check, she smiled, raising a glass of gin to her lips.

— Would you say you were close? I asked, then realizing how I sounded, quickly apologized. — Sorry, ma'am, I'm soundin like a local DA here. I guess I'm just tryin to understand your relationship.

She smiled at me, and settled back into the chair like a big cat, content with her drink and her audience of one. — Honey, as you said, he was number four. I've married for love, sex, and money but by the time you're on your fourth your expectations are pretty low.

— Companionship?

She flinched a little, then screwed up her face. — God, I hate that word. But it's probably as good as any, she conceded and in her voice and expression I could, for the first time, sense bitterness toward Glen Halliday.

— What did you know about his work as a filmmaker?

— Not a whole bunch, she said, takin another sip of her drink then raisin her eyebrows over the glass in classic lush style. — As you well know Glen was an independent, and I'm strictly a Burt Reynolds girl. Poor darling never had anything, he had to scrape and hustle for every dime to make his damned movies. Thought that I was money, I reckon.

I gotta say that at this point I found it hard to see Glen Halliday, Mr Integrity himself, cast as a gold digger. I'd seen him lecturing to NYU students at Hunter College, and again at Sundance, sharing a platform with Clint Eastwood. Both times he spoke with such passion and certainty. I couldn't see him as a gigolo, man-whoring his weary ol ass to get a picture made.

I guess it must've showed in my face as Yolanda felt moved to elaborate. — He got plenty pissed at me when I wouldn't sell this place.

This place was nice enough if you liked that kinda thing. But I was thinkin that if I had that ol gal's money I sure as shit wouldn't be spending the last of my days dryin out in the desert. I decided to digress and I asked her, — You pretty much settled here then, Yolanda?

Maybe it was just the liquor kickin in but I swear the wattage on her grin upped a little. — Pretty much. Oh, don't get me wrong, it ain't nothing special but it's got memories. Besides, it was Humphrey's legacy. He was my first husband and my one true love, she explained with a peachy glow. — When I pass on this'll go to our son . . . he lives over in Florida. Humphrey Marston was the one I never managed to replace, and she gave a faraway smile, — the rest never even came close.

Ol Yolanda's wrinkled lips pursed round the slice of lemon in the gin. She sorta sucked it up and kinda kissed it, before lettin it fall back into the glass. By now I was startin to get a little restless. I was sure that Humphrey was a fine man, but my business was with the other guy. — So about Glen, he was broke when you married him?

Yolanda looked a little bored, then she refreshed her glass, the act of doing so seemin to enliven her. — You know the type of films he made, she said impatiently, then softened a little. — I mean, he made them for love, not money. Anything he earned for him went on drink. A terrible lush, and such a bad drunk. My third husband Larry, Larry Briggs, he was the one before Glen, now *there* was a good drunk, she roared in celebration of the memory. — He wrote checks when he was loaded, bought gifts, pressed flesh, her voice dropped, — in bed he was just about the hottest darned thing . . . Her hand rose to her jaw. — This big mouth of mine, she cooed in a kind of simulated embarrassment.

I have to confess that I did find something mighty fetchin about her little performance, and I weren't shy about lettin her know it. — Don't worry, ma'am, as we say back in Texas, this ain't my first rodeo.

She slapped her thighs and I tried not to stare at the seismic activity that followed, as she burst into uproarious laughter. — I'll bet it ain't. You got that look in your eye! You're gonna ask me about Glen in the sack . . . right?

— Ma'am, I would never presume . . . I protested, then I conceded, — but seein as you mentioned it n all . . .

And as those words fell from my mouth, I swear that, there and then, I could feel the extent of my betrayal. What in hell's name was I doing? This was one of the great masters of American independent cinema. Up there with the likes of Cassavetes or Sayles. I wanted to write a tribute to an important, admired, and inspirational artist who'd help drag me from the sleazepits and here I was indulgin in the kinda smut I thought I'd escaped five years ago. When I was shootin those porn flicks from that San Fernando Valley lockup, just to pay the bills.

Two long years in the Valley wrecked things between me and Jill. I recall her sayin to me in one of our lush discussions, — You spend so much time shootin pussy, you don't wanna fuck it no more.

Poor gal was only half right. Cause I certainly did, but the problem was that that shit was on offer all day long. By the time I got home I guess I'd had my fill of it, but I could always use another drink. That might be oversimplifyin the matter somewhat, but I do believe that there's something about being around all that meat and sweat that sucks the soul right out of a man. I know that there are some people who can work in that industry a long stretch and just wash its stink off every night, but I certainly wasn't one of them. On the plus side I sure learned how to light a set and frame a shot.

But there I was in the Valley, a stupid, still youngish guy who should have been like a kid in a candy store, but I was miserable as a coyote with hemorrhoids and two bust back legs. Then, durin some downtime, I walked into a fleapit cinema on Hollywood Boulevard where I took in *The Liars of Ditchwater Creek*, Halliday's portrait of a West Texas town similar to the one I grew up in. That was it. I was hooked. Walking out from that ol picture house exhilarated, I wanted to do what Halliday was doing. Still do. It was both my salvation and my torment.

— Glen was fine at first, a real Texan bull as I recall, Yolanda grinned a little then let her expression dissolve into a wry smile. — But like most men it didn't last.

I didn't reckon that she was diggin me out; at that point I'd told her little about my own life, but I guess it was hard not to hear echoes of Jill's bitter asides of the latter months in her voice. I tried to remain impassive and waited for her to carry on.

— I didn't have no luck with men, she told me in a sad

lament, her mood evidently mirrorin my own. — Humphrey
Marston, he was a lot older than me, but he was about the
only one of them who left me with anything other than bills.
This is his place, sat right on this big aquifer.

That word again. I looked a little dumbfounded, and it must
have showed as she raised her eyebrows at me. — Ma'am,
excuse my ignorance, but I'm gonna have to ask you what an
aquifer is. I'm figurin some kinda underground lake?

— You got it in a nutshell, she explained, topping up her
drink. — The developers were always knocking on our door
with big checks in their hands, but Humphrey reckoned the
water was an asset worth keeping. Twenty-odd years ago, before
they brought the stuff down from the mountains, there was
enough of it here to keep a few new housing developments
and a golf course going for years. But their money didn't inter
est Humphrey. So the developers and the state fought dirty;
tried all sorts of ways to get their hands on it. Humphrey was
a very gentle fella, but he could be as stubborn as a mule; took
em all the way and whopped their asses in court every time.

— Good ol Humphrey, I smiled and raised my glass to toast
him. I was likin this ol boy more all the time.

Yolanda reached over and clinked glasses with me, killed her
gin and refueled. With her back to me, I watched the dimpled
hams spill out from under that one-piece as she poured. I looked
away as she turned around, drink in hand. — He inherited the
place from his father who wanted him to work it. But all he
was interested in was animals, she explained. — He took his
bachelor's degree in zoology . . .

She pointed at the stuffed cat, mounted on a plinth. I noticed
it was caught in that classic cat sitting pose, its hind legs tucked
under it, the forelegs extended, looking up as if expecting a
feed. — This is what he did, this was his work.

I guess I was pretty impressed by this. Most taxidermists I'd seen, and there was a lot of em in the big hunting states, they tended to go for action poses, even in domestic pets. — I like the way he got that ol boy in an ordinary cat position, rather than leapin on some invisible prey.

—Yes, Humphrey studied compulsively so that his compositions would be anatomically correct. She pointed over to a wall full of certificates and a cabinet stacked with trophies. — He was the best in the state. I used to assist him. I was so damn squeamish at first . . . Her expression went coy as her hand waved away a phantom objection or compliment.

In spite of myself, I was getting plenty curious. — What happened with you and Humphrey, if you don't mind me asking?

Yolanda looked sadly at me, then grimaced in a caustic smile. — Nothing with *me* and him, just *him*. I came home from the mall one afternoon and found him dead in his workshop. He was stuffing a raccoon when he had a massive coronary. Darned if I didn't find him right there, bent over his subject, as lifeless as that poor creature he was working on, she told me, brushin at a tear as if the loss was just yesterday. — I reckoned it was those constant battles with the developers and the state that took it all out of him. Her expression turned bitter as her incisors flashed. — Even if you beat those bastards, you always pay a price.

I couldn't disagree there. It struck me that ol Humphrey was like a hero in a Glen Halliday movie; an ordinary Joe standin up to those moneyed assholes and power trippers, just cause he could, and hell, because it was the right thing to do.

— It just made me all the more determined that I would never sell up. She shook her head emphatically. — They said that I was cutting off my nose to spite my face and that the canal waters would soon be rolling in from the mountains and that I should cash in while I could. And sure enough, it eventually did come flowin down, but not before some of those miserable rat bastards who had tried to take my Humphrey's water went bust sittin on their useless adjoining land!

And she talked on and on about ol Humphrey and I was darned if that ol gal didn't have tongue enough for ten rows of teeth. But there wasn't much I could do about it. She was upset and I had to let her go on. She told me how she'd met Humphrey at a pageant when she was Miss Arizona, and, how in contrast to the others, he was a real gent who always treated her like a lady. It sure was a strong love, no doubt about that. So I learned a lot about Humphrey and taxidermy, and while I admired this kindly ol guy who just sat on his land, stuffin animals, developers and the state, he wasn't Glen Halliday. It took me a long while to get back there and when I did I could tell it was mighty disappointin for Yolanda.

— Glen Halliday lived for his work, she said ruefully. — We got together as friends first, then got married in a whirlwind. After six months he was a lousy lay. I didn't see enough of him. He was always running off onto the set of one film after another, or hiding out in bars, she grinned at me in conspiracy. — If Glen had a *grande passion*, then, honey, I certainly wasn't it.

Emboldened by this lady's candor, I asked without thinkin, — Who do you think was?

— C'mon, darlin, you know the answer to that as well as I do, she chided, but she looked at me like she was genuinely let down. And she was right to be; it was the performance of an honors graduate asshole. In her mind I now either had balls of jello or the savvy of a virgin in a bordello. — Ms Sandra Nugent, she said slowly, her look of judging compassion makin me feel like the teenage daughter of the house who stormed out screamin 'fuck you' only to return in tears with a swollen belly six months later.

I knew full well, as did any undergrad who took an elective in American independent film, that Sandy Nugent was universally regarded as Halliday's muse. She was the actress who starred in some of his finest movies: *Ditchwater Creek*, *Mace*, *A Very Cold Heat*. Over the years they had what the likes of *Entertainment Weekly* might call 'a tempestuous on-off relationship'. She killed herself back in '86, in a roach motel in a scuzzy part of Florida. They found her with the contents of a strip mall drugstore still bubblin in her gut long after her ass had gone polar.

I'd researched Sandy extensively, prior to meeting Yolanda. The only public comment he made on her death had lost Halliday plenty of friends (sadly, I was learning that he seemed to specialize in that art). Talkin to a London magazine at the Edinburgh Film Festival back in 1990, he said, 'Nobody likes to see a good piece of ass wasted.' Of course, Glen Halliday was a chronic drunk by then. I know that ain't no excuse for that kinda talk, but I sure as shit also know that it can be a reason.

Glen Halliday was one of the most talented and underrated filmmakers I had come across. But the more I learned about him the less enamored I was by the guy. It seemed, and not only from Yolanda, that the magic was in the movies, not the man. And while I know more than most what ol John Barleycorn can do to a fella when things ain't goin his way, my hero was starting to sound like a guy who had his head up his ass.

He married Yolanda ten years after Sandy's death, then he himself apparently died of a heart attack, right here in Phoenix six years after that. Obviously the thing with Sandy, though they never tied the knot, really did seem to be Glen Halliday's big one, but she wasn't for tellin. Also, most of their mutual associates in the world of independent film had been pretty damn guarded.

But not all of them; back in New York, I had met Jenny

Ralston, one of Sandy's best friends, who'd been mighty obligin. Jenny had been mentored by Sandy and had a respectable list of indie credits and the odd Hollywood B-movie to her name. She was a dark-eyed beauty, finer than frog hair, and, maybe guided a little too much by her perspective, I'd regarded Yolanda Halliday as just a crazy afterthought, a place for drunken ol Glen to lay his tired head in this period of dark decline. But now somethin was eatin at me. I was darned if some strange loopy voice wasn't whisperin in my ear that it was this relationship with Yolanda, ol Miss Arizona herself, that was going to be the key to unlocking the Glen Halliday enigma. Perhaps this strange woman was slowly becomin more interestin to me as I was gettin a little disenchanted by her most recently deceased husband.

As we kept yakin, me tryin to keep her interest by tellin her about my life past, and the one present with Pen, which interested her more, Yolanda seemed to be strugglin. I'd no idea how many gins she'd had before I'd called round and the booze seemed to be gettin to her. I soon got to reckonin that it might be best to wrap it up for the time being. — I really enjoy chatting to you, Raymond, she slurred, — I feel like we've really connected.

— I really enjoy talkin to you, Yolanda, I told her in all honesty, despite bein a mite concerned at the way those crazy eyes kept holdin me in their gaze.

I thanked her for her time and made to leave, as I had some-where I needed to be. I fixed another appointment to see her, then headed back to the car. The pool was still ocean blue and the pool guy, skinny but muscular in his yellowin wife-beater, glanced at me for a second with hard, suspicious eyes, before turnin and rakin more gunk from the pool's surface.

I got into the car and drank my second bottle of water. I called Pen on her cellphone but it was switched off, as was her habit. I hooked another bottle into the holder on the dashboard. The road was dead as Yolanda's pets and I made good time before pullin into Earl's Roadhouse, the bar where Pen was playing. It was still pretty damn early and I could feel that ol lush pull tuggin at me, insistent as a mall brat beggin his momma for candy. Surprisingly, for a night owl, it was always in the daylight hours when the draw was strongest. But I guess there's nothin like walking sober into an evening bar full of drunks to convince you that you're makin the right lifestyle choice.

I ordered a soda water with lime from Tracey the bartender. I liked her. She had a very cold dykey thing going on with the guys who came in. It just intrigued them and made them hit on her all the more. And hit on her they did, cause that gal always dressed like a million bucks. Not in an obvious way, cause she wasn't one for puttin much flesh on show, but pretty damn classy all the same. She liked me, approved of the way I treated Pen. She told me as much one time, when she was a little drunk. Not in that hittin on you type of way, just in a mature sense of genuine appreciation. Tracey put Pen up on a pedestal. I reckoned I knew that pedestal well enough and once told Pen that I thought Tracey might be a girl's girl.

She just laughed in my face and said, — Baby, she's as straight as they come. For an older guy, you still ain't got much of a clue about women.

She wasn't too far wrong. Reckon all the women in my life had kinda said the same thing at one time or another. Jill made that point frequently, and much less charitably than Pen. My agent Martha had recently said similar stuff about Julia, the heroine in the first draft of my screenplay *Big Noise*. Or maybe she was a bit more blunt: 'She isn't a cardboard cutout, honey, she's a little paper-thin for that.'

Sure enough, a few days later we spotted Tracey throwin

gutterballs at Big Bucky Boy's Bowling with some strike-hittin real-estate-sales type of guy who was probably married, but definitely fucking her. I felt like even more of a sleazeball than this asshole looked.

It was more than just women. I guess I outta have known a whole heap more about people than I did for a fella with my ambitions. And my crazy, conceited ass thought that by doing this book and a possible documentary on Halliday, I'd grow to understand the master's mind, and somehow be able to unblock the writer in me, and become the great auteur that he was. But it was fanciful bullshit, and Yolanda Halliday was proof of that. After a couple of meetings I still didn't know what that ol gal's thing was.

The bar started to fill up, nine-to-five sorts who looked like they'd put in a hard day's work; forklift drivers, grease monkeys, retail clerks, and office types, all lookin for what everybody has looked for in places like this since folks first sat down and chewed the shit together.

Pen came in dressed in a leather jacket and tight jeans, her hair tied back in a blue ribbon lookin kick-ass rock chic. She's seventeen sweet years my junior, and her perfume smells good as she greets me with a melting smile and throws her arms around me. We kissed long, hard, and hungry, then softened it up a little and it tasted real fine and I could measure the goodness in life in the sweetest drips from those big red lips. And I knew I was lucky cause every guy, every sweaty workin stiff in that shithouse of a bar wanted to be me at that point in time and if they didn't then they goddamn well should have.

Tracey saw her come in and set her up a beer.

Sure enough, one of the ol boys caught an eyeful of that divine denim-cased rear and darn near tumped his beer. Then his mean ol eyes took their register of my own weather-beaten face, and seein that it wasn't much younger than the battered-lookin thing that greeted him in the mirror each mornin, fixed me a bitter scowl. I just gave him back a shit-eatin grin that said: Yeah, I know I'm maybe a little too old and these days definitely a load too straight for her, but it's me she's goin home with, so fuck you, buddy.

Then I ignored that sorry old fool and held up my cell-phone to Pen in a playful reprimand.

— Yeah . . . I know, she said, tilting her head to the side, — I forgot to charge the bastard up.

— But I'm the possessive type, honey, I gotta have you on call, twenty-four/seven.

She opened a couple of pop-out buttons on my shirt and put her hand inside, rubbin at the hairs on my chest. — Yeah, I know, and I love it.

— Not as much as me, baby, I told her.

She raised a sculptured brow. — But you got another woman in your life right now, the one you're spendin all this time with, she teased. — How's this Halliday woman then? Bet she was a looker, huh?

— As she keeps tellin me she was once Miss Arizona.

— Before they started keepin records, right? Pen laughed and took a big suck on her Pabst.

I felt somethin rise in me a little and forced it back down, smilin back thinly at Pen. She didn't mean nuthin by it, cause that gal ain't got a bad bone in her body. All she was doin was repeatin my own silly jokes back at me. But somehow dis-respectin Yolanda just didn't sound right no more.

Funny thing was that I guess that I was kinda gettin to like that old gal. The woman had shown me great courtesy and hospitality, but desire, no sir, no way, you have got to be jerkin my wire. Why, Miss Yolanda had at least a good thirty years and a bad eighty pounds on me. Having undergone every plastic surgery procedure known to man, her face was almost paralyzed; the last time I saw something that looked like it, it was perched on the side of Notre-Dame cathedral over in Paris.

And to my shame, I had said somethin along those lines to Pen after I first met her, set that ol gal up as a figure of fun. I dunno why. Always tryin a little too hard to be a smart-ass, I guess, then regrettin it after when the folks you shit-talk don't turn out to be so bad after all. But then the static thump of tubby fingers on a microphone head interrupted me from my thoughts.

Earl was a big and feisty ol boy, always wore those two-button brocade vests of the type JR used to sport, so damn snug you wondered how they stayed fastened, and I never saw him without his big Stetson hat. He was up onstage and he introduced Pen to a great big cheer. Then she got right up there and just blew them all away. I'm darned if that gal couldn't rock the hell out of a joint. It might have only been a sleazy little dive bar where if somebody left the door open the throatful of heat and dust that followed them in made everybody suck down another cold one quickstyle, but she was headin for bigger things, no doubt about it. But I liked it best when she put down the Gibson and picked up the twelve-string acoustic and set her sweet ass on that stool and sang those soft honey-sugar ballads of hers. They broke this old wreckage's sorry heart and made me want to set up just *one* little beer to cry into. But I knew where that would lead and as long as I had her in my arms I sure didn't need me none of that.

I loved this dirty little dive so much and the only damn reason was her. I'd first come in to Earl's six months ago, just after I'd moved to Phoenix, to try and start this damn book on Halliday. It just wasn't happenin up in that lonely apartment, so I got out for a while and drove around a little, endin up just out of town, in this place. I found it was always better to pretend to write in the corner of some bar rather than in an empty apartment. Sometimes a face or a comment overheard could lay down the bones of a character or a snatched conversation trigger an idea for a plotline. Even though I wasn't drinkin I still couldn't break that particular habit.

I hadn't been in long when she sat down next to me at the bar and asked me for a cigarette. I told her that I was sorry but I didn't smoke, and was moved to add that right now I wished more than just about anythin that I did. She laughed and said that maybe I could buy her a drink instead and I was delighted to do so. After takin note that I was passin on the liquor, she looked deep into my eyes and said, 'Well, you don't smoke, or drink, but do you . . .' and she skipped a beat, took a long drag on the cigarette that Tracey had given her, those big brown eyes full of mischief and asked, '. . . listen to rock n roll?'

When I told her I most certainly did, she got up on that stage and played me some. I guess I fell in love with her right there and then, and it's been that way ever since. I started hangin around Earl's and then another couple of bars she played, and we just began seein each other. Then, when the rent was up on her apartment she just moved her stuff into mine. One night when we was lying on our backs in bed, looking up at the ceilin after just having made love, she said, — You know, I think I'm gettin better, maybe growin up a little. I got a boyfriend who ain't an asshole.

I quickly quipped, — Just add alcohol, honey, but grinnin at her through the darkness, I was thinkin, maybe it's ol Raymond Wilson Butler here who's the one that's getting better. Cause sure as shit there ain't gonna be anymore alcohol.

I was researchin the Halliday book and bangin out my screen-play of *Big Noise*, which took up a lot of time, but I liked to go out with Pen when she played. Some of those bars were rough dives, and although she could look after herself, I guess I worried about all sorts of things, from guys hittin on her to perverts and stalkers.

But that night she was sittin alongside me in the Land Cruiser, a little tired after the gig, maybe a little drunk after the six Pabsts and four Jack and Cokes she'd had. (I couldn't help countin, I'm conditioned to do this now.) She said to me, — You know, if I came home with a guy like this before, I'd be all tough and bitter. Now I can be exactly as I like, in that I don't have to think about it.

We went to bed and slept in each other's arms. We would wait till the mornin before making love.

The next day Pen headed out to the bookstore, while I got back to *Big Noise*, and pretended I was a real writer. I wrote me a long list of what the problems with my first draft were. The main one, and I guess what most of the others kept comin back to, was Julia, my hard-assed Texan matriarch. Yeah, my agent Martha Crossley was right. She was thinner than a wet piece of newspaper. Problem was, I just didn't know who she was. At first I thought of her as based on my own momma, then a twisted version of Jill, and at one stage I even considered that she just might be Martha. Every time I clicked on my laptop though, I had the feelin that I was making this thing worse instead of better. I sat until my head throbbed, then went to the DVD and watched *Ditchwater Creek* for the hundredth time.

I realized that it was almost lunchtime and I'd achieved nothin. I tried to call Pen to meet for some lunch but her cellphone was off again, so I called in at the store. We went to a pretty gross place in the mall, where minimum-wage kids dispensed poison to the other storeworkers and housewives present. It was good to see her comin toward me, that wild mane of hair fightin to get free from the black velvet band it was tied in, and those bangles, bracelets and rings danglin from her wrists, fingers and ears. I needed to talk to somebody, and there was nobody like her.

— You're being too hard on yourself, honey; finish the Halliday book first, then go back to *Big Noise*, she implored me as we ate our club sandwiches. — Your head's all over the place. Take the advice you always give me: one thing at a time, huh?

— I guess so, I smiled, — at least if I knock out another chapter on that this afternoon, I'll feel that the day won't be wasted. Maybe I'll land that big-buck car commercial shoot, I laughed, givin up on the shit I was eatin and pushin my paper plate aside, — then at least I'd have some money and I'd have to work to the discipline of a damned schedule. Then again, hogs might just fly over the state of Texas.

Pen winked at me and made some kinda clickin noise. — You'll get it, baby. I got a feelin about this one.

— Like you had that feelin about that Majestic Reptiles video I didn't get?

— You were number two, honey, she grinned. — You're gettin closer all the time.

— As close as I'm gonna get, you mean. I'm always short-listed; the dirty ol bridesmaid who's been round the block once too often to ever get the goddamn gig.

She stood up, and brushed some crumbs from her jeans. — Well, I gotta leave my sweet little bridesmaid and get back to work, and she bent over and kissed me, then as she went, pulled out the back of my collar and tupped down the ice she'd left in her drink.

— What the f— I yelled, then laughed as it melted down my spine and the crack of my ass.

— You know I'm a bitch, she smiled, blowing me a kiss as she scampered across the mall, her heels clickin on the polished granite floor, — but I love you!

I got up and walked out to the parkin lot, my back and ass bone dry in the bakin heat by the time I got inside the Land Cruiser. I went home and did what I suspected would be the only writing I ever could: a straight hack job on my Glen Halliday book, transcribed from the tapes I'd made talking to Yolanda.

The next day I was back out to the Halliday Ranch, or the Marston Ranch as I should have probably started callin it. It seemed ol Glen was only an occasional tenant, sleepin off his hangovers: hangin his head in between shoots and hustlin for cash. I started to imagine his life with Yolanda as more like my later life with Jill; all slammed doors and long silences, punctuated by drunken, yellin rows with a sad 'where did we go wrong' lament in postscript.

Yolanda greeted me with another pitcher of her homemade lemonade, and as I stepped into the cool house it sure did feel good to get some respite from the furnace outside. I immediately noticed that she seemed unsteady on her feet. Her eyes were red and she'd discarded the swimsuit for a red tank top and white pants. Although it was nice and cool here, there were beads of sweat on her face and her breathin seemed mighty labored. — This is Sparky, she explained, pointin at a stuffed cat on her window ledge. I hadn't seen this one before. I had gotten used to old Esmeralda, but this was a mangy, mean-looking sonofabitch. — I brought him up to see you.

— Nice, I said, looking at that pouncin cat. It was as stiff as Esmeralda, but it didn't seem nearly as placid. Then I spied a small stuffed dog, some sort of terrier, standing guard outside a restroom. — That's Paul, she told me, — after Paul McCartney of the Beatles.

Paul looked a feisty lil ol sonofabitch. The glimmer in his glass eye and his full set of exposed teeth made me feel happy that his little butt was stuffed. — Humphrey do these?

— No, I did these ones by myself, she told me, moving across to her cocktail cabinet where she mixed herself a gin and tonic. — I wasn't formally trained of course, but very few practicing taxidermists are. I picked lots up through helping Humphrey. Then, when I married Dennis, I kept it up, she wheezed, as she lowered herself into a chair and bade me to do the same. I did, and placed my tape recorder on the small table by her side. — He was a big hunter, an NRA man, and he got me stuffing and mounting his prey. I did a bunch for him, but I got rid of them all after he left. She pursed her lips. — I found it disagreeable to have wild creatures killed for sport. I preferred to work on the ones I loved, as a tribute, so I'd remember them for all time.

She explained to me that the two cats and the small stuffed dog were old pets of hers. Ditto the two lovebirds in a bamboo cage she pointed out to me, hangin over the entrance to the kitchen. — I couldn't let them go, you see. I loved them so much, she said, the recall makin her a little distressed. — I was embarrassed to show you them. Do you think I'm a crazy woman, Raymond Wilson Butler?

Funny, but it didn't really bother me none. — No, not at all. I can see why you do it. Some people have their pets buried or cremated. You've got their remains there, to remind you of them.

She seemed not to hear me. — I still talk to them, Raymond, she contended, still lookin right on at me, — and I swear that there are times when I can even hear them talking to me. Does that sound strange?

— Not at all, ma'am, I told her. — I reckon that sometimes we just gotta take comfort where we can, I smiled, stretchin over and laying my hand lightly on the soft, white flesh of her arm. I could tell she was more than a little drunk, and sure enough that bottle of gin by the cocktail cabinet looked far from full.

I guess some folks might have found it a little weird, but the woman was just lonely. Way I see it was she had the money and the skill and it was a hobby that gave her pleasure; something that she had shared with Humphrey, the real love of her life, and it probably made her feel a little closer to him. Yolanda struck me as just another eccentric flutterin harmlessly in the twilight, doing what helped make her feel good. This state was full of em, ol boys and girls, brains sizzled in the heat, slowly crumblin into more desert dust.

Miss Arizona.

I thought about Dennis. If Nice Guy Humphrey was husband number one and Dirty Larry number three that must have made him number two. — What happened to Dennis?

— Oh, that was one that I did end myself. She shook her head and looked almost accusingly at me. — Right after he broke my jaw.

For some reason I sort of assumed that ol Dennis was another drunk, and one of the worst kind. — So Dennis was violent in drink?

— No, the weird thing was that he seldom, if ever, took a drink. Didn't need it to be a complete bastard. With that goofy smile and his churchgoing, sober ways, you'd've thought that butter wouldn't have melted in his asshole, she slurred, the liquor now visibly taking effect on her.

I shot a tight smile back at her.

Something flared in her eyes. — Put me off sobriety for good, she spat bitterly, movin to the glass and fillin it up. — Ironically, I met him through Humphrey, she smiled, instantly becomin more whimsical at the recall. — Dennis Andersen was one of his best clients. He seemed a perfect gentleman, and I guess to the outside world, that's exactly what he was. Then I found out he'd had two previous wives, one in Albuquerque, one right here in Phoenix, that he'd left looking like busted fruit with nothing more than a pile of hospital bills.

Unfortunately, this recollection sparked off another diatribe. The problem with this was that Yolanda was now more inebriated than I'd seen her before. She was growin mighty shrill while talking about Dennis, wailing like a tomcat in heat and highly resistant to my attempts to steer the conversation back to Glen Halliday. I started to wonder just how well they knew each other. Guess I was thinkin again about Jill and me: lovers for years, strangers at the end. And how when the love goes the stranger is the only damn thing you can ever recall.

I made my excuses and prepared to embark on that long and lonely drive back into Phoenix. It was then that Yolanda went kinda weird on me. Pulling herself up out of that old chair, she teetered toward me. — Please stay a little while longer, Raymond, she begged, — I really like talking to you . . .

She took a stumble forward and I had to catch her and steady her or I swear to God her ol blubbery beauty queen butt would have ended up on those cold tiles. — Hey, come on, Yolanda, you just had a little too much sauce and you're a little tired, I smiled, tryin to make light of things. — Maybe you should lie down. I can all come back tomorrow now, y'hear?

Her face was now rodeo-assed red and her big, watery eyes not much far from the same as she looked up at me and pleaded, — You'll bring a tape of your girlfriend singing and playing her songs?

— Sure, if that's what you want.

— I'd like that, she said, as she steadied herself. — It's so good that the both of you have a talent. A talent can never be allowed to go to waste . . .

— Well, we're both tryin, I guess. I smiled at her and made

my excuses and left.

By the time I got on to the road it had gotten plenty dark, which I didn't mind. Just drivin in that silent night, sometimes I could feel the past fadin in my synapses, and blowin through me, like a howling ghost across that desert. It made me want to stop, so I got out for a while, just to look up at that silver moon. It settled my brain, and made me focus back on the things that were important to me; Pen, my work and specific-ally the *Big Noise* screenplay and the Halliday book, in that order. The key to it was that it had to be a book about Halliday, not about an old gal with four husbands, sitting out in exile in the middle of nowhere.

When I got to the apartment, Pen was waitin up. I was tired but she wasn't and that gal wouldn't say no. Then afterwards, my head was buzzin and she was soon fast asleep. — You'd best check the messages . . . she said as she fell into a slumber, — gonna miss you, boy bridesmaid . . . or is it bride . . . ?

I looked at her, tried to shake her awake. She just turned around, eyes still shut, mouth a little open and murmured, — The voicemail . . . you gotta check it . . .

I did. To my delight and astonishment, Martha had called from LA, telling me that I'd been offered the car commercial I was being touted for! It paid big bucks, and for three weeks' work — one recce, one filming, one post-production — it would keep me on the Halliday book for around six more months. On the downside I guess it meant that the next draft of *Big Noise* would have to wait just that little longer again, but nobody, least of all my agent, was holdin their breath for that one.

I thought about ol Glen Halliday, who would have laughed in their faces and talked about the integrity of the artist to some post-grads in Austin or Chapel Hill for two hundred bucks, his gas, and a couple of nights' free minibar at the local

Holiday Inn. Or so I thought. More likely he got Yolanda to supplement things by writin him out a check. I sure wasn't going to turn into *that* version of Halliday. Pen worked long hours at that bookstore during the day and the gigs in those shitty bars at night and I was determined I wasn't going to be no kept man. And this was as near as damnit a six-figure check for three weeks' work. I wasn't even gonna debate with myself the possibility that I might say no.

I couldn't sleep, so I sat up and looked at my notes on Halliday. Just who in hell's name was this sonofabitch? A Texan who loved Texas but hated what it had become: a place where Ivy Leaguers and religious nuts could wave the flag and we'd fall in behind it and fight pointless wars for their oil. Or perhaps he was just another scumbag hypocrite who used people, women, for what he could get out of them; an insecure actress whose head he fucked more than her pussy and a crazy heart-broken ol gal sitting on a gold mine in the desert.

In the mornin I said a sad goodbye to Pen and packed up for the long drive to LA. It would take me two days. I was driving out to see Yolanda first, then I'd take the interstate. En route at a gas station I picked up the newspaper and checked the terror-alert coding (orange) and the burn limit (fourteen minutes).

Passing Earl's I saw the pool guy, Barry I think she said his name was, going in with his buddy. Something made me stop and get out and follow them inside. I checked out his pickup truck in the lot outside as I went by; an '88 Chevy with a sticker in the rear window: 'Ass, Gas, or Grass – Nobody Rides For Free.'

I squinted as I got into the almost empty bar: dark and cavernous after the blindin light outside. Barry Pool Guy and his buddy were shootin eight ball in the corner. I sat on a bar stool for a spell, readin the paper and watchin some of the play from the previous evenin's ball game. After a while, Pool Guy came up and bought a couple of beers. — Hey, you work over at Mrs Halliday's, I said.

— I work a lot of places, he snapped back, an ugly ol leer distortin his mean face even more.

I shrugged and turned back to my paper. The kid was an asshole. I finished my club soda and left the bar and climbed back into the Land Cruiser and took that long and dusty drive out to Yolanda's. It wasn't a comfortable ride. The confrontation with the kid at the bar was eating at me; it was minor pussy stuff, especially when I think of the situations I got into when I was full of liquor, but I was annoyed at puttin myself in a position where I could be rebuffed in that manner.

Anger burned me, and I guess I wasn't concentrating too much on the road. I heard a swish, then a thud, followed by an almighty clatterin sound tellin me that I had hit something. I stopped and saw the outline of a doglike figure splayed out in the road. It was a coyote, and by the looks of it a full-sized one. I approached the sonofabitch warily, but it seemed to be dead. I pushed at its head with my boot. Yep, it was gone. But the gray-and-yellow body looked unmarked by the impact of the car; it wasn't torn open, and I could see no blood from the mouth, ears, or eyes. It looked like it was asleep, as if it was an ol pooch curled up in front of the fireplace, cept its eyes was kinda half open.

Suddenly I heard the sound of a vehicle approaching over my shoulder. My heart sank as I turned and immediately realized it was a goddamn police car. One patrolman got out, and started moving slowly toward me in a loping John Wayne stride. Evidently he was worried that I still didn't take him for a grade A1 asshole, so he kept his shades on as he addressed me. — Goin a little fast, ain'tcha?

— I wasn't aware, officer, I –

179

— License and vehicle registration please.

I figured it would be pointless arguing so I complied and produced the documents. He took off his shades to study the paperwork and smiled at me. He was a country goofball; a snide, pig-eyed mutant with a small, petty heart masqueradin as a good ol boy.

He looked back at his partner in the car, a fat guy who was munchin through what looked like a taco (I knew there was a Taco Bell a couple of miles along the highway). This guy shot me a look that said, 'If I gotta get my lardy ass out of this car, there's gonna be big trouble.'

— We got ourselves a little problem, John Wayne grinned, exposin big, capped teeth. — This coyote fella, he's listed. Means a shitload of paperwork for me, all these environmental types gonna be up in arms. How far you goin, mister?

— I'm just over to Loxbridge, I –

— Fine. That's in the next county, out of my jurisdiction. Now what say you just get a hold of this roadkill and stick him in the trunk of your nice big car, and when you cross that county line, maybe a respectable few miles inside, sling him out by the side of the road? Then I can get on with doin the things folks in this county want me to do.

— Well, I –

— That would be us quits. What d'ya say?

I swallowed hard, my rancor tastin like bad whiskey in my gut. — Yessir, I appreciate it.

This prick was full of shit. Ain't no damn state in this Union gonna list the coyote as a protected species; since we killed all the wolves they were as common in these parts as squirrels in Central Park. We both knew this, of course; the mean bastard was bustin my ass just because he could.

All talk was gonna get me was a night in jail, so I moved over to the coyote and grabbed its front and back legs in each hand. I'm a pretty strong guy, around five ten and one hundred and eighty pounds, but I was strugglin in the heat with the shiftin weight of the thing. The asshole cop looked around all furtively, checkin nothin was comin up on us, then helped me bundle the ol boy into the back.

As he moved back to the patrol car, where I caught Fat Boy shaking his head in petulant disgust as he crammed more gut-filler into his mouth, John Wayne gave me a mockin salute. — Drive careful and have a nice day.

— Thank you kindly, officer, I smiled through gritted teeth.

I had a dead animal in the back of my wheels, which would start to stink it out in this heat before I got close to the county line. I was livid and I couldn't but wonder what Halliday would have done. Would he, like one of them stoical, rebel heroes in his pictures, have just taken the night in the county jail for the pleasure of comin out with some smart-ass line? Or would he have done the same thing as me? It was right about then that I got me some inspiration. I was going to see what Yolanda would make of this one.

I drove real slow, nervy after the encounter with the cop. I crossed the county line but didn't stop till I got to Yolanda's. The big gates were open and I pulled up as close to the front door as I could. Hell, it was a hot one. Yolanda opened the door, and as I went to step in, puttin my hand on the frame, a lizard jumped out from nowhere, danced over my old mitt, then ran up the side of the house. It froze for a second, pulsin slowly in the heat before slurpin into a crack in the wall like some vacuum had sucked it in.

It sure was a more sober Yolanda who greeted me this time around. — I'm so sorry about my behavior the other day, Ray . . .

— It's your home, Yolanda, you can act how you darn well please out here, it ain't nothin to do with me. I've mentioned

my past with the drinkin, so I ain't hankerin to sit in judg-
ment on nobody else, I told her. And it was true; sometimes
I couldn't believe that I'd gotten out of LA in one piece, save
for maybe a little liver damage. Now I was goin back, but this
time sober and to some proper work.

— But it was so bad-mannered, she said, rubbing my arm.
Under the cold air it made me shiver suddenly. — And you
must think me so weird, all my stuffed animals!

— No, ma'am, as a matter of fact I got me somethin that
just might interest you, and I bade her to follow me. We stepped
back outside into a heat that sucked the cool right out of me
in two seconds. Through its haze I stumbled toward the Land
Cruiser, as heavy as a drunk, and showed her what I had in
the back. It was already starting to smell, but Yolanda didn't
seem to notice none.

— Oh, he's beautiful; a beautiful boy, she said appreciatively.
— You can help me cape this one. We have to get him inside,
quick.

— What do you mean? I stood there scratchin my ass, as
Yolanda pushed a button and a motor rolled the big garage
doors open. She grabbed a trolley, which looked more like a
gurney with its alloy frame and strong wheels with rubber
tires. It was adjustable; through a handle at the back she lowered
it to the height of the rear of the Cruiser, allowing me to pull
the coyote onto it. Its body was slack in the heat, still too soon
for rigor mortis.

— Caping is when you skin out your trophy, she explained
as we wheeled the stiff animal into the house. As I cooled off,
Yolanda vanished down into the basement, returnin with a set
of white linen which she draped over the kitchen table. On
her instructions I managed to wrestle the dead beast from the
trolley onto the table. — The most deft skinning needs to be
around the delicate parts, the eyes, nose, lips, and ears, and it's

always best to leave these to a pro.

— I'm more than happy for you to run the show, ma'am, I told her as I raised my hands to my face, catching a scent of the dead animal on them.

Yolanda headed on down to the basement again, comin back with what looked like a large aluminum toolbox. — Problem is that a lot of hunts happen in warm weather and it just ain't always possible to cool the hide adequately. Most trophies are ruined in the first few hours. As soon the animal dies the bacteria begins to attack the corpse, she explained, clicking the box open. There was a power saw and a series of sharp, surgical-looking knives, as well as plastic bottles containin various fluids, some of which had the odor of strong spirit. — Heat and moisture is the ideal environment for bacteria to flourish. Caping spoils in the same way as meat does. That's why I have the big fridge downstairs. How long has he been dead?

— About an hour and a quarter. Hit him back in Cain County.

— Well, we ain't got time to waste, she mumbled, as she pulled out a knife, looking for a second like she was gonna stick it up the poor ol boy's dead ass.

— This is the dorsal method of skinning, she explained, making the long cut from the base of the tail to the neck. Knock me stone dead if that carcass wasn't pulled out in that one incision, leavin the head and feet inside the skin. There was very little blood. I heard a terrible bone-crackin sound and shuddered as she snapped the neck from the body, usin what looked like large nutcrackers. I winced as I watched her cheerfully unravel the beast, like she was peelin an orange, as she continued to enlighten me. — This is a good method on long-haired animals. Now I have to take him downstairs to freeze immediately.

She had the animal by its head, and it reminded me of a

toy teddy bear I'd had as a kid: the stuffin had come out of its body and there was just a long tadpole-like tail of cloth hanging from his neck.

— Can I help you downstairs? I asked, lookin a mite distract-edly at the pile of meat and bones left behind on the trolley.

— No, I'll do the rest later. You take that carcass to the incinerator out back. Can't miss it, it's the big rust-colored thing. We gotta burn it or the buzzards will come. Stick it in there and I'll fire it up later.

I don't mind admittin that I was a little squeamish as I got the skinned dog's body onto the trolley usin the sheet and wheeled it out to the incinerator. Out back, the house thank-fully shaded me from the sun's merciless blast, though I could feel my sweat ducts opening up. I spied an old wire broom and once I'd opened the metal door and adjusted the trolley height to its level, I used it to push the now stinkin bastard inside, as dirty big flies that had come from nowhere started buzzin round like small bats, makin my guts churn. I was happy to get back indoors to that kitchen as Yolanda shouted up from the basement, — Ray, honey, mix me a gin and tonic, will ya? Plenty of ice!

I wasn't raisin much in the way of objections to kickin back a little. I did as she requested, refilling my own lemonade from the pitcher, though I gotta say that it was tastin a little sour in my belly now. I headed back into the kitchen and poured myself a big glass of water from the dispenser on the fridge. — Shall I bring it down to you? I shouted.

— Nope, you just hang fire and I'll be up in a second.

I was so pooped after my efforts in the heat that I just lay down with my back on the cold floor, spread out like the savior on that ol cross, and God, did it feel good. I looked back at ol Sparky, then my eyes drifted across the room and there was an addition I hadn't seen before: a huge German shepherd, lying with its paws spread out in front of it.

Yolanda returned quickly and sat back to enjoy the drink.
— I'll start to mount it later, she said as I reluctantly dragged
my own carcass off that cool floor and into the chair by hers.

I pointed at the big dog.

— That's Marco, she said, — one of the best pieces of work
I've done. He was such an angel, honestly, Raymond, the sweetest puppy you ever met. Somebody poisoned him, I don't know
who, but I have my suspicions, she spat, thinking, I guess, of
one of her would-be property-developer neighbors. Things
must have got pretty ugly at one time, but I was sure as damned
that Marco's puppy years had long passed when that big sonofabitch cashed in his chips. — Anyway, she said, more breezily,
— I decided to bring some more of them up from the basement for you to have a look at.

This had all been a great education for me, but it had taken
some time and with LA and the Volkswagen shoot on the
horizon, I reckoned that commodity was getting a little scarcer.
I quickly got settled and asked her about the husband she had
before Glen Halliday.

— Larry Briggs was an alderman in town. Ran twice for
state senate. The horniest sonofabitch I met, she said fondly,
before her tone soured. — Problem was quite a few others
knew him that way too. The main difference between Larry
and Glen was that when I found Larry was after the ranch,
for the water, it came as absolutely no surprise.

— What happened to him? I raised the cool, clear glass of
liquid gold and contemplated it for a moment, then put it to
my lips.

— Who knows. I reckon he ran away with some damned
slut who fell for his smooth talk. That type never was in short
supply. He'd had it here. After two failed state senate attempts
nobody wanted him on their ticket. I wasn't going to fund his

drinking and womanizing, so he left. Last I heard he was down in Mexico. The strange thing is that in a roundabout way, I met Glen through Larry. She now sounded a little wistful. — Glen was doing a film about the water politics of Arizona and he talked to Larry and some other would-be developers. Came out here to see Larry, who by that time was gone. So we struck up a friendship. It was platonic . . . well, drink-based at first, and she reached for the bottle to recharge her glass. — I knew he was a lush from the off, but he was fun back then. I think at first he liked it here, liked being away from LA, which he always loathed, though he was always flying up for meetings.

— What about New York? How did he feel about the spiritual home of American independent cinema?

— Not a whole heap better.

That kinda made sense to me. All people who live in LA do is to say how shit it is, even if, I suspect, half of them don't mean it. In New York they all tell you how great it is and I suspect that half of them ain't properly convinced either. — I thought they'd be more understandin of what he was trying to achieve there.

— Perhaps at one time. Yolanda shook her head. — But I got the impression that he resented the new breed of independent filmmakers that were working there. I think it was because they were getting things done while all the doors were slamming in his face, she explained and she started, for the first time, to talk about Glen's work and his future ambitions.

That ol coyote had eaten into our time but it was still a good session for me, I got the best stuff yet from her. But then things changed kinda sudden when I told her about the car-ad shoot and that it would be a few weeks before I saw her again.

Yolanda looked at me like I'd just announced the death of her firstborn. I'll be darned if that blood didn't just drain from her face. — But I *will* see you again, won't I? she squealed.

I was pretty much taken aback at her reaction. — Course you will . . . that is, I mean, if you feel I ain't just wasting your time. You've told me so much already, I –

— Please come back, Raymond, she begged, hoistin herself up outta that chair as I started to rise with her, — there's some other stuff I have to tell you about Glen, some things I need to show you.

— Yes, I sure will, Yolanda . . . But can't you tell me now?

— No, no, no, she said, with a brisk shake of her head, — we don't have the time and I must let you go while I tend to our coyote friend.

All the while, though, I had noticed that after comin back from the basement the last time, she had let her hair down. At the time I had a horrible feeling it was for my benefit. This was confirmed when she gave it a fancy ol shake in my direction. Once upon a time that gesture and the accompanyin smile might have broken some buck's heart into pieces, but right now it was grotesque in its ugly ol desperation. I couldn't keep the repulsion outta my face and I guess she kinda caught it.

— I'm so lonely, Ray. So damn lonely. I was, even with Glen, she sobbed, shakin her head miserably.

— Yolanda . . .

— But you will come back to me, won't you, Raymond? she implored again, steppin forward to grab my hand in hers. Her grip was surprisingly strong. This close I could see ol-hag spines of hair sproutin from under her nose and on her chin. — I've so many more stories I want to tell you.

— You bet, Yolanda, and I pulled her close to me and we hugged for a little while. But in that embrace I felt the sorry despondency on her part and, in turn, I must confess I felt pretty damn sad for her. But when it came to say goodbye she was already distracted, staring off into space, light years away. I let myself out.

When I got outside, I twisted my Dodgers cap round to cover my neck from that sun creepin up behind the house. That asshole Barry had arrived and he was carryin a silver tank on his back, which seemed to continually explode in the dazzling sunlight. He was comin round the side of the pool and we couldn't avoid each other. Our eyes met in a now mutual sneer and I held it, forcin him to break off first, his shifty eyes contemplatin God's earth.

It was a sad-ass victory but in spite of that it flushed me with triumph for a bit, as I climbed into the Cruiser and took off, Brad Paisley's 'Waitin on a Woman' fillin up the car sweetly as I got out onto the interstate. At a station I filled up on gas and struck out for LA. Proper. I drove hard for a bit, trying to make good time on the highway so that I could goof off part of the journey along the back roads. A long red twilight, broken only by south-headin doves in flight for the river, stretched out before me as I slid off the interstate. I loved passin through them small towns, all the time hearin the thud and cranking of digging machines, and as the night fell, the barking of dogs and the mariachi music, while the low trees, covered as they were with insects, clicked, snapped, and whirred their own little tunes.

When I got to LA I was pretty beat but still runnin on adrenalin. The shoot went well. I got to be back behind a camera, and I'd forgotten how much I loved that. The concept was simple, the kind of shit that me and a million other would-be filmmakers could pull off with style and panache, without sweat touchin our ass cracks. What we basically did was to parody the car chase along the concrete dried-out LA riverbed in the movie *To Live and Die in L.A.* We emerged onto the streets outside a hospital and our faggot model jumped out with his heavily pregnant 'partner'. We finished with the byline: 'For Little Things That Just Can't Wait'. None of us was foolin ourselves it was too smart or original, but then again it was an ass-fucking car ad. The big difference was that this time I wasn't the bitter stiff in some Hollywood bar looking up from his stool at the finished product on-screen, saying how easy that shit was and how the guys who did that stuff were assholes getting paid top dollar for jack. I was the guy *doin* it. And they cut that damn check in time and whatever anyone said it felt pretty fuckin good.

Back at my Santa Monica rental at night, when I didn't have Pen on my mind, which wasn't a whole lot, I kept thinking about Yolanda and her needy hunger. Cravin so much from people but lockin herself away, just incubatin that loneliness. So that when someone did come into her life, her desperation flooded them.

My script, *Big Noise*, seemed to keep on comin to mind, particularly the character of Julia. She was the reverse of Yolanda. That was her problem, she didn't seem to need much of anythin from anyone, but was still in everybody's face. One night, looking out from my balcony toward the Pacific, which was a few blocks away but felt like about twenty miles, I got to thinkin that maybe if Julia was older, faded, less cool, less in control . . .

Suddenly inspired, I got up, went to the kitchen table and clicked on my laptop, firing up Final Draft. I sat down and I pulverized that goddamn keyboard, scarcely believing those fingers were mine. As a writer I had always been a plodder, a diligent chipper. Now I was blazin, locked into my sub-conscious, and the pages were flyin out of me. Over those next three nights I bashed out another draft, still buzzin on the adrenalin and plenty of strong, black coffee.

I ain't too stiff-assed to admit that I was tremblin with excite-ment when I took my disk down to a local Kinko's and printed off a hard copy. When I read it I couldn't believe how good it was but I tried to calm myself down. I know writers have a way of foolin themselves that what they've just done is *the one*. Sure, I figured that I should maybe stick it in a bottom drawer for a few weeks, see how different it read once I got a little distance from it. But for some reason I didn't, I just read it again and went with that feelin, emailin a copy straight over to Martha.

The next mornin she calls me, her voice uptempo. I'm more excited than ever but I soon hit the earth with a bump. — Sorry, darling, I'm delighted that you've finished another draft of *Big Noise* and I'm happy to receive it, but I haven't checked my email yet. It's just that I have some very good news.

Then she tells that I've been offered this video shoot I'd been previously told I'd just missed out on, from this guy representing this hot new British band, the Majestic Reptiles, who were going to be touring out here next spring. The dude they had lined up had been in a motorcycle accident and had to pull out. And the money was good. Maybe not as good as the car ad but it sure wasn't bad and it would be good to have somethin else on my showreel, which you couldn't file under 'fucksploitation'. I'd probably only got the gig as I was available in LA at the time, but fuck it, sometimes you need a goddamn break. Things were certainly lookin up, but my mind was elsewhere. — But you will look at the new draft of *Big Noise*, Martha?

— I promise you I'll read it right now, if you promise that you'll lighten up a little and celebrate your good fortune. Deal?

— Deal.

I was as good as my word. To celebrate I took two ol LA-based friends, Brett and Evan, out for a drink at the Chateau Marmont. For a bit it was just like old times except that I was the only one who wasn't on the sauce. I kept thinkin bout what a motley crew we were; the porn rigger with ambitions to be an art-house writer/director, the standard LA wannabe-actor/bartender, and the songwriter who gigged in sleazepits like Pen's, but who wanted to write film scores that would make Mancini wet his pants. As was our sad routine, we'd sit there fantasizing about our imaginary movies, casting then rejecting everybody who came in: Keanu, Kirsten, Val, Bob, Colin. Then, through their increasing inebriation, Brett and Evan made me painfully aware that I was the cold ass sipping the mineral water. As they blasted off to that other planet, I could feel their resentment bubblin thinly under the surface of the evenin. They grew belligerent and bitter as they decried the success of others, while I sat bored and tight-lipped for the rest of the night. I felt a blessed relief when it was time to piss in the fire and call a halt to proceedins. I ran them home to Westwood and Venice Beach respectively, the broken, desperate dreams of drunks crashin around in my ears. I couldn't see no role for me in their lives but as permanent designated driver. Which is another way of sayin I could see no goddamned role at all.

Then the next day Martha called again. I swear to God I'd talked to her more in that last week than I had in five years of being on her agency's books. But when she started to speak I didn't know which one of us was the most awestruck. — I can't believe what you've done with *Big Noise*, honey . . . it's a work of art . . . no, forget that, a work of genius!

It was me who couldn't believe what I was hearing. This was Martha, and that gal had never exactly been prone to hyperbole. But then again, I guess I hadn't given her nothin much to get carried away about. — I'm glad you like it –

— Like it? It's so completely realized . . . and Julia . . . she's totally unrecognizable from the first draft. Look, I'm sending this straight off to Don Fennel in New York with a 'read immediately' tag stuck on it. God, what a streak you're on right now, honey!

I called Pen with my good news and she decided to take a

few days off to fly to LA, which cheered me up no end. Every spare moment I got we just hung out in Santa Monica; makin love, watchin television, eating pizza and Chinese, catchin rays and lookin out to the ocean. One day we were just hangin out on the beach at Venice, watchin some surfer dudes doing their thing and somehow the 'M' word came up. I dunno who started that kind of fool talk, but it all ended with me asking, 'Will you?' and her saying, 'For sure.' As we trawled round Santa Monica until we found a suitable ring, we were both joyous, and even the fact that she had to head back down to Phoenix couldn't take the goofy smiles off our faces.

We floated around on cloud nine, makin plans, or rather scenarios of happiness; moving up to LA and finding our own beach apartment, taking Pen to meet my folks who were gettin on and who'd appreciate new, younger blood in the family. Life couldn't get much better than this, surely. Then Martha called sayin that she wanted to meet me for dinner. She wouldn't tell me what it was about but she sure sounded excited. We arranged to meet in a restaurant on Wiltshire and for the first time she was earlier than me. More importantly, she was lookin like the cat that got a whole big bowl of cream.

— I don't quite know how to say this. Don Fennel loves your script so much he wants to produce *Big Noise*. He's confident he can raise the cash. You did say four point five million dollars, right?

I was so convinced that she was dickin me around, I wasn't even slack-jawed about this 'news'. Don Fennel, after all, was one of, if not the, hottest indie producer in America. — Don't do this, Martha –

— I told him that you had to direct and he was cool with that, she said. It was round about then I saw she wasn't jokin and I had to stop myself shoutin at the maître d' for a vodka Martini. Martha pointed to the glass of Dom Pérignon she'd already had. — I know you don't, but I *must*. Darling, Fennel absolutely loved the showreel. If you can shoot it for four point five million –

— Of course I can!

— Then it's definitely going to happen!

— *How* can he love the goddamned showreel? It ain't nothing but a handful of ads, pop vids and a couple of shorts that did zilch at the half-assed festivals they got screened at! I gasped. I couldn't believe it. This just all seemed too good to be true.

— I tell you, I've never seen Don Fennel so excited about a script. I said to him, 'It reminds me of Halliday.' He just scoffed and said, 'When was Halliday ever as good as that?'

I almost fell off my chair at that one! The world had gone crazy! I'll swear by my momma's sweet life on a warehouse full of Bibles that it was the best week of my life! As I got back down to Santa Monica, Pen was packing her bags for Phoenix, and her eyes widened as I punched the air. I grabbed a hold of her, coughing out my news and we bounced on the bed laughin and foolin, until our eyes met in some primal gaze and we were helpin each other out of our clothes.

Afterwards, she sat up in bed and lit a cigarette. She rolled her eyes and said, — Now, honey, I *really* have to go.

The band's shoot was scheduled for two days but took the best part of four. This was all down to the lead singer, who, like many of that breed, was a sullen, irritating, uptight asshole. At first he said that he didn't want to be in the video. I told him that it was a long way to come from London just to catch some rays and get decent sushi, which he didn't much appreciate. Then he wanted to wear a stupid leather jacket and a deerstalker hat and cavort with a bunch of models done up as cheerleaders. I was probably emboldened by my stock risin so dramatically lately, so I cornered their manager, a nice guy called Asad, and told him, — Tell that Limey bag of shit we do this my way or I fuckin walk.

To his credit Asad did, and after a band meeting, they decided that I *was* the man in the chair. The singer asshole, Tommy Sparrow they called him, well, he was hostile for a bit, before he did this complete about-face, spendin the rest of the shoot following me round like a fuckin puppy dog, telling me I was cool and wanting to get loaded with me. With his attention-seekin, he was still a tiresome pain in the ass, and I think I even preferred him sulky. Nevertheless, we finished the shoot if not on time then on budget.

All this and the other shit had shown me that I wasn't really interested in Yolanda no more. I had all the material I needed on Glen Halliday. And that was who the book was going to be about, a great artist that was at the height of his powers, not some ol lush in decline with a drunken nutcase recluse of an ex-beauty queen turned crazy old crone.

All I needed from Yolanda was some specific information about the circumstances of Glen's death. But while I was here in LA I had another opportunity to find out who the hell Glen Halliday was. There was a woman he spent 'a lot of time with' when he was out here, according to Sandy Nugent's buddy, Jenny Ralston. And Halliday was out here a lot. Although he did most of his shooting on location in Texas, or occasionally Florida, he had a contact in an LA studio lab, and they let him do for cheap all his editing and post-production up here. He was also in town a lot on that relentless hustlin for cash merry-go-round that dominates the indie film scene.

His friend's name was Andrea Lyons and she lived up on the hills in Pasadena. Andrea's home was a smart colonial-style dwellin in an affluent neighborhood favored by Hollywood types. A big convertible sat in a three-car garage. Andrea herself was well groomed in a trashy kind of way, quietly smug with her lot, looking pleasantly surprised by the hand life had dealt her. She gave off the smell of a cocktail waitress who had snared and married the suit at the bar with the big bucks. There was somethin kind of upliftin about this gal, somethin that raised the spirits. I didn't ask about her husband but I guessed that he was working away on some business trip, as she was very candid about her relationship with Glen Halliday. She told me that she and Glen were an item when he was in town. — I knew that he was hooked up with some mean bitch down in Phoenix, she said, taking a big drag on a Marlboro. — She had this useless old water farm but wouldn't sell it.

So there it was, straight from the horse's mouth. Glen Halliday *was* a gold digger and he was cheatin on Yolanda. I had this information confirmed and I now didn't know whether I would bury it or use it.

One thing I figured for sure was that it was time to get the hell out of Arizona. It had served its purpose. Pen and I decided it made sense to move up here and Evan knew enough people in town to get her gigs. I reckoned I'd now be making enough to help her in her music career, just as she'd helped me in my screenwritin one; get her some studio time, good backing musicians, and a quality demo tape knocked out. Hell, I was even thinkin of her and Evan in terms of scoring *Big Noise*.

I loaded up the Land Cruiser, paid my dues on the apartment, booking it for another six months for Pen and me, so we could find somewhere good at our leisure. Then I headed out of LA. This time on the drive down there were no self-indulgent detours, it was interstate all the way. When I crossed the state line into Arizona, I called Pen but her cellphone was switched off; again, no surprises there. I dunno why she bothers with them at all. You could see where she got the habit: bookstores, the stage, recording studios. When I got tired on the road I checked into a motel and watched trashy TV. I felt high, like I wanted to celebrate, so drove to a truck stop and instead of liquor bought a tub of Ben & Jerry's and headed back to my motel. I watched some reruns of *Sex in the City* feelin like a goddamn pussy without really caring too much about it.

The next day I was up later than I intended. Hadn't slept so long or so well in an age. Sun was near as damnit overhead by the time I got back on the road. After drivin most of the day, when I got to the apartment there was no sign of Pen, and her mobile was still switched off. It was a Saturday, and she never worked the bookstore those days. I figured I'd take a run out to Earl's Roadhouse. It was dark by the time I got there, and I entered with anticipation, though I guess I was also a little tentative in case that asshole Barry was in. But I hadn't seen his truck outside, nor, for that matter, Pen's car. Ol Earl spots me right away and comes across. He told me that she ain't on tonight and that she ain't stopped by.

I looked behind the bar. No Tracey. Of course, it was her night off every other Saturday and she and Pen often went out for a drink together. It was their night to grab a bite and sink a few beers and I couldn't begrudge them that; not being a sauce hound anymore I always worried that I was maybe just a little borin in company. I reckoned I'd leave them to it and elected to drive out to Yolanda's, calling her first to check that it was okay. She seemed flustered – probably drunk – but was pleased to hear from me. She told me that she had some company she needed to get rid of and would appreciate it if I could hold off for a while. That suited me fine. I went back to the apartment for a while, lookin over the latest draft of *Big Noise*. This, I said to myself in satisfaction, was why I met Yolanda. I got so carried away I guess I lost track of time. An hour had passed. I called Pen again, without expectin much, knowing that when she and Tracey got together it was party time. Then I headed outside and back into the Land Cruiser and out of Phoenix. The dark sky seemed infinite as I cruised down the highway, thinking about Yolanda. This would be my last interview with her. I was kinda concerned that she'd go all psycho-bitch on me after the last time, but I'd never seen her so calm and serene. There was a wild glint in her eye and a crooked smile on her lips as she stood in front of me wearing a white smock and black slacks. — I seem to apologize to you a lot lately, Raymond. I'm sorry if I was rather undignified at our last meeting, she said. — But I assure you there will be no more apologies.

— No problem, Yolanda. I raised my hand, brushin off her concerns. — But I gotta tell you that this is probably gonna be our last meetin. Got some good news workwise; I'm movin back up to LA, then I'm shootin a movie down in Texas.

— I had kind of anticipated that, she said, with a kinda grim, distracted cheer. — You're an ambitious man, Raymond Wilson Butler. You're definitely going places.

I guess I was finding it hard to keep the crap-eater outta my smile. It was true. I *was* goin places. Yolanda got some drinks: a gin for her, and my usual lemonade. I ain't sure whether it was cause I wasn't gonna see her again, or perhaps I was just being an arrogant jerk, too flushed with my recent success, but I decided to ask her about her plastic surgery routines. — You . . . eh, I touched my own face, — had a little work done?

— Stating the obvious, huh? She laughed, not at all offended.

I went to protest but she silenced me with a grandiloquent wave of her hand.

— Don't worry none. It was a long time ago and he wasn't exactly the best guy in Beverly Hills, she grinned. — In fact he wasn't in Beverly Hills at all, just some rat-bastard suburb in Houston. She laughed loudly at her own wit. Her face looked more gargoyle-like than ever at that point, nerves frozen with bad cutting and the stretching of old dead skin.

— What made you decide to go under the knife?

— It was Larry Briggs got me into that. Thought if I looked a little bit like how I used to, back when I was queen of this damned state, then I might be good for some votes when I was on his arm. I admit, though, I didn't take too much pushing. She smiled sadly. — One strives to keep beauty with one.

I looked over at ol Sparky; way the light hit his glass-eyed stare it seemed alive, feral. Then there was Marco, forever loyal, waitin patiently by the door.

She caught my eye on them. Gave me a nod that was slow, knowin, and that creeped me out a little. — The coyote is done. I'll show you him in a little while; he's down in the basement. We have to think of a name for him though, Raymond. I think that you should pick one.

I was thinkin about how that mean coyote followed me everywhere, like I couldn't get rid of him, and then I recalled Tommy Sparrow, the lead singer in the Majestic Reptiles. — Thank you, ma'am. How does Tommy sound to you?

— Tommy it is, she said with a grin as wide as the Mississippi.

— To Tommy the coyote. She laughed and raised her glass and I found myself guffawin along with her.

When we stopped, it was with a nervous silence on my part and a cold detachment on Yolanda's. I came clean and told her that I was shiftin the emphasis of the book squarely back toward Glen's work, and away from her story and his personal life. She looked at me quite harshly for a split second, and I don't mind sayin now that her glance set something crawlin down my spine. Then she seemed to grow more thoughtful, noddin slowly as if to encourage me to go on.

I sure didn't want to sit around here much longer. There was just one thing more I wanted to know about. — I need to ask you, ma'am . . . when Glen went . . .

— What makes you think he's gone?

A sudden big chill came over me, and this house no longer seemed cool, but as cold as death. I forced a laugh. — Yolanda, I've seen the headstone in the cemetery. His place of burial, back in the family plot in Collins.

— C'mon, honey, she said brusquely, standing up and moving over to the door leading down to the basement. I followed her down the metal steps. We came into a small room; it was nowhere near large enough to run the full length of the house. It had a concrete floor and stone walls, which had been white-washed. There was a reinforced steel door and a porthole window next to it, all steamed up with condensation. She unbolted the door and ushered me forward. — You can go in, but be very, very quiet, she whispered. I hesitated, but only for a second, intrigued as to what in hell's name was going on in there.

Because I suddenly saw it all in my head: Halliday was still alive! I had this fantastic vision of him bent over the desk of an editin suite in a secret basement studio, splicin together his masterpiece. I was so convinced, I was even startin to rehearse my greetin in my head.

Mr Halliday, sir . . . this sure is a surprise.

As I stepped over a metal ridge at the bottom of a door frame and into the room, a mist nipped at my eyes. This place was so cold, like a great refrigerat— I turned quickly, alarmed, but the door slammed shut behind me. I pushed hard but I could hear the bolts slidin over. I banged on the door with desperate ferocity as the cold stung my bare arms. — Yolanda! You fuckin crazy . . . but I could feel the fear rising up in me with the cold, takin the fight from me. — C'mon, cut it out . . . I was pleadin. — Look, we're gonna stay in touch . . .

And then I saw her face in the porthole; monstrous, bloated

and white as her voice crackled from a speaker above me. — They all want to go, but they never can. We all stay together. Always.

—Yolanda, this is crazy . . . and I turned to take in the room as my eyes adjusted to the mist. Then I could see them all standin, the four of them, lookin at me, their timeless eyes of dead glass starin ahead.

Glen Halliday, those coal-black beads sunk into his hangdog face. That red and dark blue gingham shirt and those stonewashed blue jeans that were a kind of trademark. The still thick gray hair, slicked back. He even has a bottle of beer, a Coors Lite, in his hand. And then there are the others; Humphrey Marston, with that look of intense concentration on his face that he must have brought to his job, sittin at his desk workin on a small animal. Standin behind him, Dennis Andersen, a rifle slung over his shoulder. He's replete with that toothy, wholesome smile which probably never left him, even as his finger squeezed on the trigger to blow away some animal, or the back of his hand snapped out to bust a woman's chops. And then there's Larry Briggs, standin at a lectern, immaculately suited: rakish and shifty, even in death.

The four horsemen of her own personal apocalypse: that twisted ol witch. I pulled my cellphone out of my pocket. — Goddamn you, you sick old fuck –

—You won't get a signal in here, my darling. This 'sick old fuck' has had the walls lined. It's signalproof and soundproof. So please do spare yourself the terrible indignity of shouting and screaming for 'help'. Poor Glen was such a terrible baby. A man so cynical about life in his latter days, but how he begged to hold onto it when his time came. Strange that, don't you think?

I ignored the crazy old hag. There had to be another way

out of this place . . .

Her voice was rantin on, cracklin through the speakers. —
Who the hell do you think you are, Raymond Wilson Butler,
with your artist's conceit, thinking you can come into my life
and take, take, take, just like the rest of them, get me to spill
my guts and then walk away when you've had your fill? Cause
it don't work that way, honey! Not here!

Then I saw the door to an anteroom and made toward it.
The coyote was standing there, hunched, ready to pounce
through the mist. — You can't go in there, I got Tommy to
guard it, you see, Yolanda's voice mocked.

I moved forward warily but as I got closer I saw that the
coyote was as dead as a dodo. Sure enough it was the old boy
I hit; twisted into an action pose by Yolanda's craftmanship. I
kicked it over and my hand gripped the cold brass handle on
the door.

— I really wouldn't go in there if I were you, angel, she
cooed.

— Fuck you, you fat crazy ol bitch!

I pulled it open and as soon as I registered what was inside
I fell to my knees. All I could do was scream no no no over
and over again, as I looked up at her chemical-gray skin that
devoured the meager light in the room. She had a guitar in
her hand, and her mouth was open, blastin out a silent power
chord, frozen that way for all time.

— Such a lovely girl. I went to see her play and then I
invited her to come around. I think you'd made her a little
curious about me. It took me a while to do her, we had to
work very hard through the night to finish her, Barry and
myself. He's my son, you know: and such a big fan of hers.
But we wanted her ready for you. This will be your little place
together.

As the cold slowly starts to seep into my bones, because

she's turned it up now, all I can do is sit here in a defeated heap as my head starts to spin and I hear her voice, ol Miss Arizona, sayin, — You'll always be together now, Raymond, we'll all be together!

Kingdom of Fife

I.

JASON AND SEXUAL JEALOUSY

Ya hoor, sor; the conversation in this place wid make a pornographer blush. — You ken Big Monty, it's no as if eh isnae well hung or nowt like that. Eh'd goat a hud ay that crystal meth fae some boy in Edinbury n it wis up like two fuckin cans ay Tennent's, yin oan toap ay the other; his words, no mine, the Duke ay Musselbury says aw sagely, liftin the pint ay Guinness tae ehs lips n takin a swallay. Thir's a ridge ay foam, or cream as the Porter Brewery chaps in Dublin wid like ye tae think ay it, hingin fae the dirty ginger mowser oan ehs toap lip. Early Scturday n we're the only cunts in the Goth, wur local boozer. Great place, the Goth, an awfay warm howf, wi aw thon mahogany-coloured wood everywhaire. Thir's a big screen opposite the bar for the fitba, usually just Scottish (borin, only two teams kin win), or English (worse, only one team kin win), bit they sometimes show Le Liga or the Bundeslegia. Thir's a big partitioned pool room at the side, surrounded by gless, makin aw the bams in thaire look like goldfish.

No thit thir's any in the day. The hale high street's as deid as a Tel Aviv disco flair. Means thit the Duke's goat a captive audience ay two fir ehs tale. — Bit eh's cowpin ewey at this piece n she's no jist takin the fuckin loat, it's rattlin oan the sides, man! This is yin dirty hoor, wider thin the fuckin Nile, ya cunt. Aye, dinnae talk Mississippi tae me. So eh pills oot n turns ur ower n whaps it tae ur up the fuckin chorus n it's as tight as a drum n eh's gittin a decent ride oot ay it at last. The Duke lits oot a wee belch n settles ehs beer oan the bar.

— Phoa, ya cunt, thit ye are, says Neebour Watson, takin oaf ehs silver-framed specs for a wee polish.

The Duke ay Musselbury's fair shakin yon big, baldy napper ay his; ehs ginger ponytail's whippin acroass ehs back. — Naw bit, wait till ye hear this: it's a fuckin total miscall, man, cause this bird's been oot oan the fuckin peeve fir a few days ehrsel n as soon as ehs fuckin knob's in her choc-boax aw this diarrhoea's right under ehs foreskin, like fuckin chip shoap sauce, nippin away at the cherry n that, eh.

Ah sees the Neebour Watson's eyes starin tae water under they specs, fair cascadin away n aw: like the contents ay a hoor's gash at the end ay a line-up.

— She's tweakin oan the crystal n aw, the Duke explains, — gaun fuckin mental, n she sais tae um, 'Ah'll fuckin bend it, ah'll fuckin brek it oaf ye,' n she's backin intae the cunt n it's like yon irresistible force n yon immovable object, eh.

— What happened? the Neebour Watson asks, pickin a bit ay crust ootay a nostril. Eh examines it, rolls it, n flicks it oantae the flair ay the Goth.

The Duke's foreheid wrinkles in distaste. — Well, this is in the hotel, yon yin in Dunfermline thit thuv booked intae. Whit's it called . . . glorified knockin shoap . . . the Prince Malcolm, that's the yin. So Monty's that aroused eh batters the gless on the fire alarm panel by mistake wi that fistfil ay sovies oan ehs mitt n it aw goes crazy . . .

Ya cunt! Ah'm thinkin: The Prince Malcolm Hotel. That's muh ma's power base. Works at the reception n everything, wi yon smarmy cunt she's shaggin, Wee Shitey Drawers Arnie.

— . . . fuckin polis, fire brigade . . . the loat. An embarrassin situ fir every cunt. The Duke picks up ehs pint n takes another gulp.

Then the Neebour turns tae ays n goes: — Your ma no work thaire, Jase?

— Aye . . . ah goes. Wind-up bar steward kens full well what the situ is thaire.

But the Duke ay Musselbury inadvertently spares muh blushes as ehs no wantin the tale tae run away fae him. — So eh's giein ur the message, the dirty wee hoor. N ken whae it wis? That hoarsey lassie n aw; the doctor's daughter, her thit steys oot oan the road oot tae Lochgelly. That Lara Grant, eh sais, ehs chin juttin oot. Then ehs tongue lashes oot like a lizard's, lickin the foam oaf ehs tash like the snaw oafay a car windscreen. My spine goes a bit stiff at this news, but the Duke jist looks slyly at ehs n sais, — Aye, you used tae sniff aroond eftir thon, eh, Kingy?

— Still stalks it, Neebour laughs.

— Jist tae keep muh haund in, ya hoor, ah explains, but it's like aw yon fuckin oxygen in the Goth Tavern jist burns up cause thirs nane gittin intae ma fuckin lungs any roads. The object ay ma desire n that big ugly cunt Monty . . . and in muh ma n Wee Shitey Drawers's fuckin hotel n aw!

This big-moothed baldy ponytailed ginger Duke ay Musselbury cunt wi the yellay teeth n the tash . . . disnae like bein the bearer ay bad news or nowt like that. — Aye, ah thoat that wis your wee floozy, eh goes tae me.

Well, ah kin feel muh haund tightenin oan yon gless n this cunt is gaunny git it fir spreadin lies, bit ah think, stoap, Jason, stoap n think . . . it isnae the wey, ye dinnae shoot the messenger.

But no Lara, fir fuck sakes, muh first girlfriend. Well, ah suppose Canadian Alison wis the *real* first, if wir talking ridin.

— Aye, wir you no knockin her oaf years ago whin ye wir daein the jockeyin? the Neebour enquires, sweetie-wife that eh is. Kin see thon cunt wi a heidsquare oan, up the street at the Premier Bingo, ya hoor sor.

Ah jist nods, — Aye, she's right intae the showjumpin, so thir wis a mutual interest in the clop-clops, ken?

— Ye cowp it back then? the Duke asks.

— Wi went oot for a bit but she wis jist a wee lassie at the time, ah sais, outraged. Some company's ye find yirsel in, yir better asking whae *shouldnae* be oan the register.

— No a wee lassie now but, eh. Pits it aboot big time by aw accoonts.

— Aye, pub accoonts, ah goes.

— Ah dinnae hud wi this virgin-hoor way eh classifyin lassies, Neebour goes, — fundamentally flawed, if ye ask me.

The Duke shakes ehs heid. — At least wi cannae git accused ay that in Fife. Thir aw fuckin hoors, n thir husbands, faithers, boyfriends, brothers n sons n aw!

N wi raise wur glesses in toast. The Kingdom: non-sexist as fuck.

Then the Duke says, — That Lara, but; hings aroond wi Tam Cahill's lassie.

— Aye, ya cunt, ah goes, — Wee Jenni.

— Ye might no huv rode them but yuv been sniffin aroond enough, the Neebour says. — Hud yir forty wanks oot ay thaime, eh, Jase?

— Mair thin jist forty, ya hoor sor, ah'm in five figures. Hud mair pleasure oot ay they lassies thin any big lyin cunt like Monty, ah goes, drinkin up.

That leads the Neebour oantay some speculation. Eh takes ehs glesses oaf n polishes them n rubs at whaire thuv been indentin intae the side ay ehs neb. — Gits me wonderin whit lassies wid think if they kent thit we spent that much time wankin aboot thum? Aw that effort ay thought and willpower gaun intae creating they carefully constructed scenarios? Aw they fuckin Hollywood porn blockbusters that play in yir heid every other night, wi some dozy wee hoor that works in Greg's cast as lead lady!

Ah looks at um as ah finishes muh pint. — Ye pit it that wey, ya hoor, thir bound tae be flattered! Fuck sake, ah wid be if ah found oot thit somebody ah barely kent existed wis spending aw that time n effort oan ays! Ah'd shag the cunts oot ay pity!

Neebour shakes ehs heid n pits the specs back oan. — Disnae work that wey, bit. They'd jist think thit ye wir a filthy fuckin perve whae led a sad life. Female sexuality, ya hoor: it's different goods. It's aw aboot ethereal forces n that; thaire fuckin frigs. Hoarses n Knights n castle towers n aw that shite. That's how they posh burds are aw hoarsey types, eh goes, warmin tae ehs theme. Hus tae be said that the Neebour is the fanny expert here, being as eh wis once mairried. — Back at yon skill ah said tae that Irene Carmody lassie, mind ay her?

— A fit yin, as ah recall, ah nod, tryin tae conjure up an image.

Neebour's face goes sad and doleful. — Tried tae be candid at the pleasure images in ma heid ay her in the buff n in threesomes wi me n yon Andrea McKenzie gied ays. Did ah git complimented oan ma taste n ingenuity? Like fuck. She only telt her faither n the cunt grabbed a hud ay ays outside the chippy n telt ays tae stop making lewd propositions tae his lassie! Some people, Neebour shakes ehs heid again, — think they'd nivir pilled the wire in thir puff.

As entertainin as the sexual politics ay the Central Fife male might be, ah'm fir the oaf.

— Where ye headed, Jase? the Duke asks.

— Might take a wee walk up the street, call intae muh turf accountant.

So ah heads outside intae the fresh air, and sets off doon the main drag.

The toon might huv seen better days but the high street still supports plenty a waterin holes. JJ's and Wee Jimmie's are the yins thit ah use, apart fae the Goth, which gits a rep as an auld boys' pub n it is, ah suppose. N thir's Partners Bar ower the road; might be a place tae take a burd at night, but no durin the day, no, sor.

Ladbrokes versus Corals, whae's gaunny git ma cash? Corals is a Hun shop, but the toon's long hud that sort ay Gers vibe in general, ever since Jim Baxter, accordin tae the auld man. Ah opts for Ladbrokes but thir's nowt grabbin ays oan the caird. Ah realise thit ah'm starving but, so ah heads outside tae git a scran.

Ah'm huvin ma lunch in the Central Perk café, the one that they named the place in the telly series *Friends* eftir. Oor yin's named eftir its proximity tae Central Perk, hame ay the Blue Brazil. Much, much aulder thin thon daft wee New York perk ay the same name.

Ah decides against the chips and peas n opts fir a fried egg and black-pudding roll n a mug ay tea. It's empty, bar two young lassies wi a bairn in a pram. Funny March day: rainin but also surprisingly hoat. One lassie's wearin a white anorak, n she takes it oaf n announces tae everybody, — Ah'm roastin wi sweat! The other yin's jist goat a white cotton top oan n she protests, — What aboot me, but? Ah'm soakin wi rain!

Ah think it might be Soakin Wi Rain's bairn, cause the waitress lassie goes tae talk tae Roastin Wi Sweat.

Ya cunt, ye couldnae sexualise they lassies wi Timmy Leary's fuckin stash in ye. Ah only gits the horn oan whin this rid-heided wifie wi front protrudin teeth comes in. It's like some cunt's tried tae pannel thum fae the *inside*. Thir's that many dirty cunts aroond, ah'm thinking mibbe yin ay thum goat carried away wi the fistin, ya hoor sor, n somehow that made ays think aboot Big Monty n Lara.

Goat ays aw aroused n ah hud tae nip intae the bogs at the back ay the shop wi the obligatory 'For Customers Only' notice, soas thit ah could huv a wee chug tae masel. Hardly room tae swing a cat bit ah still manage tae bang oaf some paste intae the sink. Ya hoor, strikin a blow fir the oweraroused n undersexed everywhaire!

The heid's birlin whin ah goes back oot, n the choppers woman's standin thair lookin at ays, but thirs nae ming comin oot ay the bogs so ah'm awright. Fortunately maist people think thit yir jist daein drugs oan the premises.

Ah gits a T/5 bill and settles up.

Struttin doon yon high street oan a Saturday; creditors tae be avoided, debtors tae be pursued, n how thir nivir the same. Aye, ye find oot yir standin in the food chain in a place like this. The laddie King: constantly flirtin wi relegation, but somewhat above the likes ay Richey the Assaultee, whae ah see headin up the slope tae the station, nae doot huvin jist come oot the New Goth.

Cannae beat this toon though, chips n mushy peas for £1.90, keep ye gaun aw day. Mixed wi a couple ay black golds n even yon Gillian McKeith burd wid be cautious aboot cuttin intae yin ay they logs! Wid she no, but!

But ma egg and black-puddin rolls wi the mug ay tea set ays back £3.05, seriously eatin intae black gold funds. So ah heads ower tae the jobcentre tae check what's up oan the computer, but thir aw minimum-wage jobs n thir aw nation-wide. Thir's only one thit's local (if ye count Dunfermline as such which ah dinnae):

LABOURERS IN DUNFERMLINE, £5 PER HOUR, 40-HOUR WEEK.

It's 8–5 Monday–Friday wi nae weekend work, temporary fir six weeks. That's two hundred quid a week before deductions ay tax, national insurance, which leaves 170, which is nae wage at aw. If ah dinnae gie the auld man rent n cut doon oan the black gold n avoid ma creditors (and new debtors) that means ah could save five hundred in six weeks. Ma hairy hole. They say experience no essential as trainin will be given but thill nivir huv a runt like me workin oan a site.

Ah comes out intae a surprisin sun glintin in ma eyes, n the first person ah sees sittin oan the waw is oor disgraced ex-minister, Jack 'Jakey' Anstruther, whae's indulgin in a fortified wine ay some dubious vintage.

— Jason King! eh shouts at ays. — Any luck in the employment market?

— Naw, Jack, it's jist no happenin, buddy. Nae vacancies for commie ex-jockeys.

Jakey laughs n the wey that probably causes another few blood vessels in ehs swollen rid coupon tae rupture. That hair's still stickin up, like yon Don King boxin promoter hoor. Along wi the doolally eyes, it gies um a permanent air ay shock, like a bairn whaes fingers uv located they three wee holes in the waw. The auld coat's seen better days; mair ripe thin the fruit oan sale at Central Perk merkit. — Funny, son, it's the same fir commie ex-Church ay Scotland Ministers, eh laughs, hudin the boatil oot tae me.

— Eh, naw, yir awright, Jack, no ma tipple, ah tell um. Dinnae like tae refuse a drink, but ye are what ye peeve n despite ma financial worries ma position as a champion ay the black gold pits ays a guid few notches above the El-D and Buckie boys.

Ah leave the auld man ay the cloth tae ehs fun. Ah clocks wee Jenni leavin the leisure centre, the pride and joy ay the Beath, but like Lara, skilled in snobby St Andrews. Thaire's a wee yin whae isnae half shaping up, ya hoor! Possibly been daein that Pilates class. That's at the very same venue whaire ma grudge Scottish Cup tie wi the hoor Mossman will take place. Ya cunt, ah git a check ay thon rounded erse ay hers as it slides intae the front seat ay thon motor. Makes ays gled ay jist emptied the tank or ah'd be tempted tae fire yin oaf in broad daylight!

Instead, ah head back up the street. Ah wince every time ah pass thon Spider's Web Tattoo Parlour. Saved up like fuck tae git the big hert wi ALISON oan it, jist afore the hoor kicked ays intae touch. The Canada boy, a Lochgelly cunt, hud sponsorship tae the colonial lands, n better prospects wi yon pipe fitter's papers under ehs belt. Wisnae aw the cunt hud under ehs belt accordin tae her, a contention made in aggression whin oor parting goat a bit heated.

The Clansman's ower the road, wi thir Crazy Vimto cocktail, or £2.50 fir a WKD Blue wi a shot ay port, n ahm fair tempted, bit that Big Monty jist might be in thaire. Instead ah head intae the bookies n look at the form, hopin tae crack the code tae untold riches.

2.

JENNI AND DEATH

I rise and move over to my computer and spark it up, checking my emails. One from last night, from Lara, who in any case, is coming round later.

To: mscahill@hotmail.com
From: msgrant@gmail.com

Jen

God, I hate this town. This county. This country. I want
out. If it wasn't for Scarlet Jester, the stables, the
competitions, and of course, your good self, I hesitate
to think how unbearable it would be. Just coming back
from the (highly successful – if you've got it, flaunt it!!)
tournament in Ireland, walking down the high street
the other day, en route to the leisure centre, I was
reminded of Ginny Woolf's great words: 'On the
towpath we met and had to pass a long line of
imbeciles . . . everyone in that line was a miserable
shuffling idiotic creature, with no forehead, or no chin,
and an imbecilic grin, or a wild, suspicious stare. It
was perfectly horrible. They should certainly be killed.'

That's how I feel about them all in this town.
Particularly that weirdo, Jason King, who literally
drools at the mouth every time he sees me. To think I
once hung about with him!

Hope Midnight is shaping up. Fiona La Rue and all
the stables very pleased with me right now.

Anyway, see u tomorrow.

Love
Lara xxx

Cocky fucking bitch, but it perfectly encapsulates how I feel,
not just about Cowdenbeath, but about this house. I update
my blog in MySpace, checking out what some of the usual
suspects have been up to. Then I pull on a sweatshirt, leggings
and trainers, which are in a sports bag at the foot of the bed,
and tiptoe downstairs.

I'd intended to sneak into the little gym and use his cardio
equipment. But he was there with his new dog. It was harnessed
onto the treadmill and running along. He spends all his time with
it. He looks at me, and the dog mirrors his action, glancing sadly
from the side. — Just building Ambrose's legs up, he says, with
some guilt. — He's quite weak for the sort of dog he is.

— Why not just take him outside? I ask him. He looks
repulsive and brutish in that vest and those uncool, old man's
tattoos. They're so thuggish, and devoid of style: a dragon, a
skull and crossbones, a saltire and my mother's name in a scroll.

— He keeps me company when I work out, he says, moving
across to the bench press by his multigym. — You're welcome
to join us, he says, noting my tracksuit.

— No . . . I'm going to the leisure centre.

He shrugs and starts to bench-press his weights. His round
face goes an unfeasible crimson shade and his eyes bulge. The
dog's tongue is lashing out as it pants heavily. I find myself wondering which of them will die first. Then I get to thinking: Would
I cry at his funeral? Probably. What a depressing thought.

I leave them and get into my Escort and drive down to the
centre. I do some stretches, then twenty minutes on the treadmill

and another ten on the Stairmaster. I check my weight: ten stone two pounds. A three-pound loss since last week! After a shower I have a coffee, read a section of my novel, Danielle Sloman's *Reluctant Survivor*. It's about a girl, Josephine, who is in a coma following a road-traffic accident. She's willing them to pull the plug, but the doctors and the family refuse to do so. Now one of the doctors, Steven, has fallen in love with her. Meanwhile, Josephine is recounting her life from her vegetative state, little knowing that her fiancé, Curtis, who was HIV-positive, has perished in the crash. After a while, I drive home.

I have some gym aches so I run myself a bath, remembering that Lara's coming over later and we'll probably take the horses for a canter, the state of Midnight's leg permitting.

I stretch out my own legs in the bath; they are so ugly and stumpy I want to die. No shape to them at all. I turn the jets on so I don't have to see them through the frothy bubbles. I find myself contemplating the possibilities of suicide by wilfully drowning oneself. Yes, obviously, by jumping from a boat into a stormy sea. But could you drown yourself in a bath? Would this be possible with solemn intent?

It would take a Herculean exercise of will. We would really need to *want* to die, but for longer than the second that it takes to jump over a cliff.

I fall back, sliding down into the tub made slimy by the bath salts and let myself go under the two feet of water.

I want to die.

R.I.P.

JENNIFER LOUISE CAHILL
1987–2006

Beloved daughter of Thomas Cahill and Margaret Mary Cahill née Alexander,
Much loved sister of Indigo Sunita Cahill

I can't do it. I can't open my mouth and swallow, can't even stop expelling air out from the holes in my nose. I just can't. Then I force myself to try to take it in, but as soon as a trickle of water hits my lungs my body shoots bolt upright as I cough and splutter it out. The bathroom floor is soaked. My eyes sting with the bath salts that have dissolved into the tepid water. I'm gasping, my body a machine, a biomechanism with a sickening power over my will, filling itself full of air, fighting back, overcoming my conscious desire. Surviving.

I gather my breath as the pounding in my head subsides. I write in the condensation steam on the blue tiles:

I WANT TO DIE

Then I obliterate it with a sweep of my hand. Cancel that thought: who would look after poor Midnight?

Downstairs I can hear my mother at the door. She shouts up the stairs: — Jenni! Lara's here!

Best-friend Lara. Back from Ireland, basking in her triumph, coming round here to gloat. And then I hear his voice, a low grunt. He'll be sniffing around her, his cock stiff in his trousers, his tongue hanging out. Just like his poor miserable killer dog that accompanies him everywhere.

I haul myself out of the bath and, wrapping a towel round me, I dry off, throwing on the clothes I looked out. Those green tight combat trousers Lara thinks are cool will do for me. I know this by the way she looks at them. If she didn't like them the bitch would say, 'Oh, they look so good on you.' I hear my mum's voice again; insistent and desperate, possibly aware that she's two-thirds destroyed. (The best two-thirds.)

— Come on up, Lar, I shout.

— We're going to the stable to check on Midnight, my

father shouts in his gravelly tones, straitjacketed into an ill-fitting corset of nonchalance.

— Fun, I snort. *Like he cares.*

— Come down and join us, he shouts again, in a patently insincere tone. Of course, he doesn't want me there. He wants to ogle Lara, maybe even feel her up. He's scum. But so is she. She's a slag. Once when we were drinking she even confessed that she 'quite fancied' him. I think she said it just to shock, but all the same, what a sicko way to talk about your friend's dad.

All the more reason to spoil their party.

I leave it for a bit, waiting until they go outside. I can see in my mind's eye the dog following them, always a few paces behind. Both the pooch and my dad from the back: squat, square, thuggish versions of their particular species.

I hear him shout, — Stay, to the dog. From behind the frosted bathroom mirror window, I see them joking and laughing in a nauseatingly flirtatious way, her anoraked and wellingtoned back following him into the stable. Then I creep downstairs and run out, suddenly joining them. — Hey, I say breezily, studying first his expression then hers, looking to see how my unwanted presence has impacted on them. They stand a little apart from each other, and it might be my imagination, but their faces seem eaten up with guilt and disappointment.

Lara has cut her brown hair short and slightly spiky on top. With her upturned nose and freckled face it gives her a mischievous, pixie-like look. Her eyes are her best feature, almond-shaped, glowing, a warm brown, that and her mouth, those full lips which hide small, white teeth, till she smiles. She's seven stone and never had a spot in her life. She's rich, an only child, and she gets everything she wants. She's my best friend and I fucking hate her.

Midnight is in the stables, standing beside Clifford, Indigo's pony, who is his companion animal. Originally bought for that purpose was Curran, the psychotic pig, who makes both animals lives a misery with his butting and nipping. Even the dog keeps away from Curran.

Lara explains to me that she's driven over to give Scarlet Jester a break after his Ireland exertions. — He looked peaky and was a wee bit snottery. Fiona's looking after him at the stables.

She keeps him at Fiona La Rue's stables, which is only a mile down the road, out of town. They take better care of him there than we evidently do with poor Midnight. He's strained a tendon in his front lower leg and has been on anti-inflamatory drugs. Dobson the vet came over yesterday to check it, massaging the tendons and ligaments and manipulating the foot to assess freedom of movement. Midnight hurt it when I was riding him over the boards at home a few weeks back.

As the vet urged, I try to replicate his actions. Then I put on Midnight's harness and walk him around the field, leaving my dad and Lara in the stables. I can hear her laugh, shrill, insistent: desperate to affirm some comment he's made in his phoney James Bond voice. I stroke Midnight's long, velvet-smooth face and watch his nostrils flare. — It's a good thing I've got you, Midders, I tell him in a whisper.

3.

THE FIFE STYLE OF PLAY

Back in the New Goth for the evening, enjoyin a decent pint ay the black gold. Now ah ken thit oor Celtic cousins acroas the Irish Sea will tell ye thit the black gold ower here tastes like it's been strained through the bloomers ay a seasoned Lochgelly hoor, but this ey fair hits the spot fir me.

— The cunt's mad. Stab-yir-faither n shag-yir-ma mad, Neebour says, talking aboot Monty. Aye, thon hoor's a wrang yin awright.

Bit ah'm no wantin tae talk aboot bams, no the now, so when wee Reggie Comorton, Mister Reflected Glory himself, starts oan aboot this Mossman boy ah'm playin the morn in the Scottish, ah gits right intae the discussion. — Ya hoor ye, the cunt's no goat a flick in um. Boy's a fuckin slider, ahm tellin ye.

So Comorton, looking like auld Peter Falk's *Columbo* in this dirty wee overcoat, turns tae me n says, — It's the Fife style ay play. Yir still trapped in the Fife style ay play, Jason. The game's moved oan.

— What ye tryin tae say Comorton?

— Eftir yon twa thoosand n twa World Cup they selt nearly one million Subbuteo pitches in South Korea. Think wir gaunny huv it wur ain wey in Fife forever?

Ah looks tae the Neebour tae see if yon bourgeois revisionist sentiments are bein endorsed, but ehs goat that staney coupon oan. No thit it bothers me. As ah'm short ay black gold tokens, n ah've goat the big game oan the morn, ah takes ma leave n gits hame tae ma residence, jist roond the corner next tae the railway station. Central Fife: as central as it gits.

Ah gits up tae ma room n pits oan ma Cat Stevens album, skins up n starts tae huv a wank thinkin aboot yon Lara n her chunkier wee pal Jenni, jodhpur-clad erses bouncin oan yon saddles, sweaty wee minges batterin oaf yon hoarses' backs as they brek intae a trot, n ah manage a fair auld spurt *withoot* video assistance! Whoa, ya cunt ye! Tea for the Tillerman. Aye, sor.

Some ay they equestrian-orientated lassies'll take some satis-fyin n aw, ah kin tell ye. Thir's been a few thit huv hud that hymen burst acroass the back ay a hoarse, ahm stressing through sportin endeavour, nowt untoward, ya hoor sor! Been a guid few marital ceremonies throughout the ages declared null n void oan the absence ay thon elastic twang on the end ay the cherry oan the first night in yon marital bed, but it kin happen in pure innocence wi a sportin maid. Funny tae think ay that perr Princess Di as a wee thing huvin tae go through the indignity ay the 'intact fud test' before her marriage tae Prince Charles. Nae danger ay thon Camilla needin tae subject that aulder clam tae the same scrutiny! Progress, ya hoor, whin fem-inism finds its wey intae the royal gynecological services! Bit hoarses n lassies; aye, once yuv hud that sort ay power between yir legs yir standards might jist go up a wee bit!

That Lara; eywis tidy, but awfay snooty, even back in the day. Went oot wi her whin she wis fourteen n ah wis twenty-one. Ah hae ma doots thit her faither, Doaktir Grant fae yon practice oan the Lochgelly Road, wid huv blessed a fully-fledged sexual relationship back then. Academic point cause she gied ays ma marchin orders jist eftir the fuckin stable ah wis attached tae did, purely by coincidence ah'm sure! Ah reckon she still huds a candle fir me, but. But aw aye, sor, ya hoor ye, it wid take some satisfyin these days, by maist accoonts.

Mind you, thir aw boozer accoonts, and by thaime every cunt takes some satisfyin. Telt muh auld man aboot this n he sais it wis much different in his day. A lassie wis gled ay a length back then, n accordin tae the auld yins they aw went oaf like nuclear bombs. 'A sexual fuckin utopia, right here in Fife,' tae paraphrase the auld boy, ya hoor.

Ya hoor sor, ah'm better gittin back wi that Alison Broon, she wis the lassie fir me. Ah wanted tae git back the gither wi her, bit as Scottish Subbuteo Cup Champion. Fower n a hauf inches didnae bother that wee yin. Or so she sais at the time. Mind you, she's in Canada n she's married. Three bairns n aw, they tell ays.

Too far away tae contemplate a visit oan the mere speculation ay a ride, so ah gits oot the Subbuteo n practises for the game the morn. Ah've jist goat Cowdenbeath and Dunfermline set up whin the phone goes. Ah cannae hear the auld boy in the hoose, eh must be doon at the library reading socialist tracts, so ah runs doon n picks it up.

— Kingy! What kept ye? You been huvin a wank?

It's ma auld mucker Kravy fae Spain. — It's pointless lyin tae ye, buddy; aye, a substantial chug wi the usual suspects oan the jukebox.

— They hoarsey lassies? Dae you never change the record?

— If it isnae broke thir's nae need tae fix it, sor.

— Sorry if ah put ye off yir stroke.

— Thir's nae danger ay that, ah goes, n ah ken it's just phone lines n thir aw the same, but ah git a wee hunch eh's a wee bit closer thin Spain. — Whair ur ye?

— Jist this minute walked intae the New Goth, Cowdenbeath, Fife, Scotland. Where else?

— What aboot Spain, ya hoor?

— Hud tae come back tae look eftir the auld mare. She hud a faw while pished n smashed her hip comin doon they big steps outside the Miners' Welfare.

— The Fountain Bar n Pool Hall as we call it now.

A wee silence, then eh goes: — Aye, ah heard they hud changed it. Now thuv changed the auld mare's hip n aw.

— Sair yin.

— Aye, but they reckoned it wis riddled wi arthritis anywey, so they stuck in a plastic joab, the hoor explains. — Ye comin fir a pint?

Ah'm thinkin aboot the contest versus Moosey-Face Mossman the morn. — Ah'm a bit short ay the sheckles, bro, the giro ay last week bein jist a nostalgic memory.

— Ah'm in the chair. Goat enough narks tae pit Boots oot ay business n aw.

Well, thir wis nae mair tae be said!

Jist then ah heard the door open n the auld boy came in wi a cairry-oot. — What up, bro? eh sais, then regards Cat Stevens oan the stereo n looks at ays, shakin ehs heid as eh lays the bevvy oan the table. — Nae cunt listened tae Cat Stevens, even back in the day. It wis wankers' music, even back then. Thon 50 Cent boy's the man.

The auld man listens tae the likes ay yon 50 Cent aw day. — How kin ye say that, Faither, eftir raisin me oan Eldridge Cleaver, Bobby Seale n Malcolm X? The black man's loast it; jist wants the bling, the hoors n then tae off ehs brothers. Like the Fifer, ah suppose.

— The black cunt's still goat the anger but, son, that's what we Scots huv loast.

— Ah widnae be sae sure, Faither, the Young Team here are a bit fuckin radge.

— Bit it's aw chivs, son, nae shooters like the black man in the USA, eh slurs. — Yi'll never overthrow the white man in Westminster wi chivs.

Ah kin tell thit the auld boy's been oan the sauce awright, n ehs goat mair, as eh reaches intae the bag n cracks open yin ay the hauf-dozen Tennent's n thir's a wee boatil ay the Johnnie Walker n aw.

Eh nods at me, as if ah'd want tae share it, n normally ah wid, but the day ah've goat a better offer n ah cannae be bothered listenin tae his shite.

So ah wis right roond tae the Goth, tae meet Ally Kravitz, ma handsome big biker buddy whae absconded tae Spain aw they years ago. N eh looks good n aw. Still goat that thick black mop ay hair n the skin nice n tanned; that Romany look thit the less charitable might – and do – describe as 'gypo'. It's great tae see um. Mind you, thir wis eywis a wee element ay betrayal in the friendship. Whin Kravy first goat the bike, the pair ay us wir gaunny head south tae Spain, n jist leave it aw behind. Then along came Shona Cameron n it wis nae contest. She goat the Spain berth oan the back ay the boy's bike n ah started tae git served up the Miners' Welfare follayed by the Goth.

Twelve years doon the line but, ehs back. — What happened tae the jockeying? eh asks ays.

— Nivir took oaf. What aboot Spain then?

— A spiritual land, man, says Kravy takin a big gulp ay cider, — a deeply spiritual land. Shona never got it. Every land has its own voices, they just blow in the wind. Shona never heard the voices, ya know?

— Aye.

— The wind in her hair, she looked like a dream, but she didn't hear the voices that carried on the wind, y'know?

— Fuckin right, ya hoor.

— Knew you'd get it, Jase, kent you'd get it instantly.

Kravy had only been back once, fir eh's step-auld boy Coco Forsyth's funeral, ehs de facto faither, the sperm and surname donator's ID bein shrouded in mystique apart fae the name and nationality. Apparently, eh wis a Russian that docked in Rosyth fir a day n Kravy's ma fir a night before settin sail fir the auld USSR, n leavin a free berth fir Coco Forsyth tae push intae. It wis a hert attack thit oaffed perr Coco. No sae much ay a drink or tabs man, but would stick a block ay Lurpak oan every slice ay toast eh goat doon ehs coupon. This bein Fife, thir wis nae shortage ay thon. Ya hoor, even yin vice kin be fatal if it's taken tae thon extreme! If yir lucky ye might git away wi a yellay caird fae the referee wi the scythe afore the end ay the official three score n ten. If yir really spawny ye might even git a wee bit stoppage time oan toap, though no much ay thon gits played in the Kingdom, but, it has tae be said.

Eh takes me ootside and shows me the latest beast ehs been riding throughoot Europa, a Thruxton 900, a premium job fae the Triumph stable. — Great feel tae it, Jase, a responsive 865cc parallel twin engine, Kravy waxes. — Comfortable fir trans-porting fanny long-distance as well; preload adjustable front and rear suspension. Add tae that aluminium rims, grippy tyres and floating front discs and you've got the goods tae make any discerning buxom young peasant wench who is fed up wi her one-hoarse toon want tae jump on the back first and think about payment-in-kind eftir!

Ah'm impressed but even mair so whin we git back inside n eh sets up a couple ay voddy n Rid Bulls tae accompany muh black gold n the cider he's oan.

— The mother awright, Kravy? Ah nivir even heard aboot her accident.

— Aye, she took a tumble oan the icy steps whin she wis pished ootside the Welfare. It wis the indignity ay it aw; ehr skirt rode up wi it aw displayed fir the whole ay Fife tae see! Ehs voice drops menacingly: — A couple ay the young team took some revealin shots ay her wi the cameras oan thir mobile phones. Posted thum oan YouTube n a Blue Brazil website n aw!

— That's gantin, so it is, ya hoor, ah says, making a mental note tae check oot they sites oan the Net facilities up the library. They banned ays a few months back fir lookin at porn but they cannae git ontay ays fir a Blue Brazil yin. Ye might only git a few hundred along tae Central Perk tae see the boys play, but it sometimes seems thit jist aboot every single peyin customer hus ehs ain website. Once ah git money ah'll be gittin ma ain computer then thi'll be nae stoappin ays! Ah look ower tae Neebour and the Duke, in the goldfish bowl next door, oan the pool table, then droap my voice: — She wis wearin knickers, but, right?

Kravy pouts and shakes ehs heid. — Fuck sakes, Jason, it was a Saturday night up the Welfare n she's a single woman! That Blue Brazil site is gitting fuckin well checked!

— That fuckin Young Team need tae be taught no tae cross the bastard line, Kravy sais, then eh thinks aboot it n hus a wee laugh. — Fuckin Fife but, what ye gaunnae dae, man? Listen, gie's five minutes tae drop the bike oaf back roond at the auld mare's, then we paint this toon, nay, this coonty, a deep shade ay rid!

— Menstruatin gash rid, wi the commensurate touch ay darkness, ah venture.

The boy laughs. — You're a bam, Jason, but you're the only cunt in this place oan my wavelength, he smiles, slapping ma shoodir.

— Ah'm in thaire, bro, ah grin, watchin um depart. Soon ye kin hear the big metal beast striking up a roar outside n turbo-fartin its wey across toon.

Wi a jaunty spring in ma step, ah steal ower tae the pub noticeboard where ah find a new page fae the *Central Fife Times and Advertiser* stuck up oan it:

The competitors lined out once again in Necarne Castle's picturesque walled garden for the final class of the Fermanagh Council Championship on the Sunday afternoon. There was an international flavour to this year's festival with visiting pony teams from England and Scotland. The Scots also sent junior, young rider and senior teams to compete against their Irish hosts. Lara Grant, a member of the Fife Bavarian Warmblood team, won the prestigious Mourne Rosettes Medium Championship with Scarlet Jester.

Aye did she no, ya hoor ye! 68.25% oan advanced test 106. Nae clementary, novice or intermediate crap for that lassie! Oan the back ay thon Scarlet Jester n aw!

The Neebour Watson comes ower. — Neevor mind the fuckin chuggin away tae posh lassies in jodhpurs that widnae gie ye the shite offay thir bits. Ah'm no wantin that Subbuteo hand weakened fir the morn.

— Ya hoor sor, ah goes back tae the cunt, — it's no like that at aw. It gie's the hand fuckin strength.

Neebour looks at ehs gless in ehs haund. — Ah'll tell ye what'll gie yir haund strength sor, is diggin intae yir pockits n setting up another pint fir yir neebs here.

Ya hoor ye, n thaire ah wis wanting tae keep the last fiver fir a fish supper n a boatil ay Irn-Bru doon at Marco's. Best-laid schemes, ya hoor sor. But Kravy sais thit eh wis wedged up. Aw the better fir yon Jocky Mossman laddie when eh goes tae the table. Fill yir nostrils wi that guff, ya hoor thit ye are!

Kravy comes back in, nods tae the Duke and Neebour,

whae's gone back tae join um at the table. Then eh drums ehs fingers oan the bar. — No that struck oan it here, Jase, eh sais in a low voice, — Fancy comin back tae mine? Fridgeful ay beer and a gram ay coke, n eh's still lookin ower tae the pool room, — . . . which ey splits better two weys thin fower, man.

Ah kin hear the Fife slippin back intae Kravy's accent, sneaky as a hoor oaf a shift intae a morning oafice cleanin job. — Bring it oan, big baws, ah goes, suppin up ma black gold. N wi head oot wi some wee waves tae the soor-faced cunts ower at the pool table. Good tae see yis, dinnae want tae be yis!

4.

HIS GIRLFRIEND

The sunlight suddenly pours in through my window from behind a cloud, cutting across Lara in a dramatic sweep as she lies sprawled across the bottom of my bed. I sidle away from it in vampire panic, squinting as I move back against my headboard. I feel very spotty and it'll show up everything. Touching my face, I wince as an angry boil throbs under my skin. I'm bloated and cramped and my period is due. I can tell that when it starts I'll be bleeding for days like a stuck pig. One good thing is that it means I'll drop another couple of pounds of repulsive girl-fat, hopefully ducking under the ten-stone mark, when it comes on.

Lara, or Ms Grant as I often call her, we use the liberated prefix with a compulsive irony that depresses us, takes one more puff on the joint and puts it in the ashtray, passing it over to me. — Do you think Will's girlfriend is good-looking, Ms Cahill? she asks me yet again.

I take a long toke and settle back against my stacked pillows. — The point is he obviously does, I curtly inform her. I'm loath to go through all this tiresome 'you're much better-looking than her, if only he could meet you he'd realise there and then you'd be our next anorexic Queen' shit with her. Aka the usual crap she evidently needs to hear so much. — Besides, Ms Grant, don't you think he's a bit young to be going bald?

— No, he's so dishy, she says dreamily.

Lara floats in and out of people's lives, well, my life, as it suits her. When she comes back into my orbit after living on Mars or wherever, I'm expected to kick everyone else out of it, in order to make room for her. She undermines my other friends, and does it very well, pointing out negative qualities I'd previously been blind to, but in a very benign way, making it hard to take offence. Then, once she has you all to herself, she vanishes. She stops calling and texting and is reticent about returning messages, making you feel very needy. If I challenge her about her disappearances, she'll tell me that she has 'boy issues'. She always has loads of boyfriends but is the kind of girl who somehow escapes the slag reputation. At least with other girls. Some of the boys she sees, I wonder what they say about her. — What about that big guy you've been seeing in Dunfermline, are you going to see him again?

— Yeah, for sure, she says, but in a very unsure manner, then ventures, — He's kind of fun, I suppose, in a thicko sort of way. He's uncomplicated, she thoughtfully states. — Confident. In bed, if you know what I mean, and her eyes charge with light and she looks searchingly at me.

I nod, too quickly. I don't want to talk about sex or to hear her talk about sex and she knows that so that's what's going to happen. The sun's gone behind a cloud. The room has turned a murky blue.

— But why are we talking about *my* sex life, Ms Cahill? she asks with glee. — You're the one who so badly needs to get laid!

— I need to leave home, I tell her, passing the joint back.

Lara flicks the ash off the end of the joint. — Yeah, but not if you want to keep jumping. It's hard to do equestrian sports in Fife from a flat in Edinburgh, she says, then considerately adds, — but not impossible. You could always put Midnight in stables.

— I couldn't, not now. He's not used to it. It would break his heart . . . and mine, I miserably concede.

— Well, that means that you're basically tied to being here as long as you want to jump with him, she contends, and not without some smugness.

— I know, I know! I moan, pulling my knees up under my chin. — That's the fucking choice! Riding horses and competing with no social life and living at home with my fucking parents in this shithole, or having a proper life somewhere, but giving up the horse.

— Put him in Fiona's stables, Jen. It's practically next door! Your dad wouldn't mind shelling out.

I look evenly at her. — That's the point. He thinks I can't look after him. It would be a great victory for him, and confirm that I'm as useless as he thinks.

— Can you look after him?

— Yes! I snap, guilty at the thought of his damaged leg. — It's all I do! I'm in the stable mucking out, feeding, every day. That's why I packed in uni! That's why I stay here in this shithole!

— I suppose Fife isn't that bad. You just need to get out more, Ms Cahill, she says, looking over at the pile of CDs on my table. — Everything's gloomy if you're sitting in your room listening to Nick Cave and Marilyn Manson all day. Come out with me and Monty and his friend. We're going somewhere special on Tuesday night.

— Where?

Lara glares intently at me, her eyes staring me down. A smile plays across her ruby-painted lips. — It's secret, you have to promise that you'll never tell.

I'm now interested in spite of myself, although I'm trying to affect bored. — Why the big mystery?

— Cause it's not, well, it's not strictly legal.

— Is it some kind of party or rave?

— No, don't be daft, she says, looking at me in that patronising 'I'm so worldly' way that always nauseates.

— What then?

— Promise first.

— Okay, I say, — I swear on the life of both my parents. She shakes her head firmly in the negative. — Swear on Midnight's life.

No way. — Oh for fuck's sake, either tell me or don't, I snap.

Lara contemplates this ultimatum for a while, regarding me as if I'm an insolent wretch. And I can't help feeling my growing discomfort at her impending disapproval. Just when it gets unbearable and I'm moved to apologise, her face softens. — Okay, she purrs, and then grins, — actually, we're going dog fighting.

5.

DISCIPLINE

The last couple ay days shot by like a crack hoor oan crystal. Partyin at Kravy's aw day n night, shootin aroond oan the back ay ehs bike. Crashin oot n wakin up tae aw they take-away cartons n empty cans litterin the flair. One or two auld Chinky tinfoil efforts, but mainly boaxes fi Sandy's Pizza Hoose oan the High Street. Ah pit it doon tae Domino's sponsorin *The Simpsons* oan Sky n Pizza Hut sponsorin it oan Channel 4. So wi went fir a few outlandish creations wi loads ay pine-apple n that, aw inspired by the tarry.

But sometimes ye hae tac wrap it up, and just go hame tae sleep. So ah take that long walk past the auld Soviet-style building ay the now renamed Miners' Welfare Institute. Aye, the Iron Curtain came doon in Central Fife as much as it did in East Europe and the frozen winds ay the marketplace huv been blastin us since. In capitalist development wir much mair along the Bulgarian-Romanian lines, thin the likes ay the Czech Republic or any ay they new trendy Baltic States. Mair cappuccino outlets in Tallinn or Riga thin Central Fife: that ah'll wager!

Then ah come oantae the roundabout at the Bruce Hotel. It's been a niggly hoor ay a winter but this is aboot the first real spring day. So ah'm oantae the high street and past the Goth, duckin doon the lane at the station intae the hoose. Hand tremblin in the lock as the key goes in. Thir's nae sign ay the auld boy thank fuck, probably doon the library again, readin the Marxist propaganda thit still slips through the cooncil's net. Thank fuck fir dissidents! Thir's a letter fir ays ehs left oan the mantelpiece. Ah open it up:

Dear Mr King,

We have received several complaints about your behaviour during yesterday's Scottish Cup tie at the Cowdenbeath Leisure Centre. Your opponent, Mr John Mossman, has made a formal complaint to us. The association's supervising officer and referee, Mr Alasdair Sinclair, has filed his own report. I have to inform you that your behaviour is totally unacceptable to the East of Scotland Table Footballing Association and in breach of our Rules of Conduct, with specific reference to rules number 14 (c) and 27 (b and c).

It has therefore been decided that you will be banned for two years from all association competitions. Your return to competitive table football will be dependent on a six-month probationary period, during which your behaviour will be closely monitored. You will also, of course, forfeit the cup tie with Mr Mossman. Under the rules of the association I am obligated to inform you that you have five working days within which to lodge an appeal.

I should add that we have also received complaints about damage to Fife Council property at the venue. A noticeboard was torn from its mountings in a senseless act of vandalism. We cannot say for certain who the guilty party was, but the caretaker, Mr William Carter, and Mr Sinclair have intimated their suspicions to both the council and the association.

Yours sincerely
Oliver Mason
Head of Disciplinary Committee
East of Scotland Table Football Association

Fuck sakes! Ah cannae even mind ay playin thon tie! Ya hoor ye sor, fuck yir kip now, fuelled by outrage ah'm right doon the Goth n ahm showin thum aw the letter. The Neebour Watson screws ehs face up at ays n goes, — Ye no mind, ya daft drunken hoor, ye showed up wi Kravy, oot yir face. Ye broke two ay the boy's players wi yir clumsiness. N eh kent ye wir coked up and oan thon base speed, it wis obvious!

— How the fuck wis it? ah plead.

— Chowin through yir ain bottom lip n drappin blood aw ower the pitch. Ye'd huv tested positive in a drugs test, ya cunt thit ye are!

Fuck aye, n if it wisnae aw comin back tae ays now. The leisure centre; ah hud that big half-time line fae Kravy. Ah won n aw! — That wis jist a wee tickle, tryin tae straighten masel oot, ya hoor ye. Beat the boy fair n square, two-nil.

— It wis three-two, Jason! For fuck's sake, man, Neebour Watson goes. — Ye even ripped doon the big DAFC notice-board in the corridor, sayin they shouldnae huv this in Cowdenbeath, thit it wis the unacceptable face ay globalisation.

Ya hoor: ah'm swallayin here like a Kelty lass. — That's aw aboot security, a separate issue. The fact is thit ah won the game!

— Well, neebs, that's no what the top brass say. The Neebour Watson shakes ehs heid like a dug comin oot ay the sea n Comorton's noddin away like a toy yin in the back ay a motor.

— We'll see aboot that, ya hoor ye. Ah stick the letter in ehs face. — It says ah kin still appeal.

— Naw, naw, naw, neebs, yuv goat it aw wrong; they jist pit that in tae cover thir erses. Tae thaim a successful appeal wid be like an admission ay defeat, the Neebour Watson contends n Reggie Comorton's noddin like the wise auld sage. That'll be right! That cunt, wi ehs degree in Wisdom-Eftir-The-Event,

Skill ay Retrospection, University ay If-ah-hud-that-Prince-William's-connections-up-in-St-Andrews-ah-widnae-be-sae-marginalised.

So ah state ma case, ay which ah'm certain. — What's the point ay huvin agreed procedures, ya hoor, if yuv made up yir minds awready? Twa sides tae ony story, neebs. Ah'll go roond tae the boy's hoose, ya hoor sor, plead ma case. Fling masel upon the mercy ay the coort!

— Naw, naw, naw, Jase, the Neebour goes, — you're talkin aboot how things *should* be, but the high heid yins, once they've made up yir mind, that's you snookered wi a capital 'S'. N the thing is, eh says, shakin ehs heid, — we cannae even gie ye a game wursels, even jist muckin aboot like, cause that's in breach ay the association's rules.

Ah cannae believe whit ah'm hearin here! The table-top version ay the beautiful game n ah've been frozen oot. — Ya hoor sor, ah tells thum, — ah'm still the best Subbuteo player Fife's ivir produced!

Neebour pills me taewards um, droapin ehs voice soas Comorton cannae hear um. — Everybody kens you've goat talent, neebs. Naebodies disputin that. But yir yer ain worst enemy. N ah'm no jist talkin aboot metters ay discipline.

N now eh stands away fae ays n looks at Comorton. Ah shot the hoor a look ay betrayal. Yir men Strachan and McLeish might say thit auld Jock Stein wid huv taken yir Auld Firm intae the English Premiership if eh'd goat the chance, but everybody kens thit the Big Man wis a true Scot n cut fae different cloth thin the modern-day money-mad charlatans wi thir ego n ambition. Ah'm bein punished cause ahm a purist, an idealist oot ay time! Ah look at Comorton, the moneyman, whae clawed ehs wey tae Kirkcaldy call centre supervisory level n now spouts the doctrine ay wur ain Adam Smith as corrupted by yon Nazi Hayek cunt n that English Thatcher hoor; a man whae wid destroy the table-top version ay the beautiful game . . .

— We're also talkin aboot yir resolutely dogmatic adherence tae the Fife style ay play, the quisling hoor says. — Everybody in the modern game gits a wee bit ay purchase, a wee bit ay slide oan the baw. Aw aye, ye kin beat aw ay us easy enough, but at the highest level the boy thit kin dae a disguised slide hus a competitive advantage. End of.

So ah drank up, sure ah did, sor. Suddenly, ah didnae like the company nae mair. In the big picture bit, it wis a guid thing ah vacated the premises cause ah heads doon the street n ahm thinkin thit ah might chap oan Kravy's door, see if ehs ma's oot ay the hoaspital yit. Then ah catches sight ay the two ay thum, up oan thir hoarses, trottin doon yon lane: Lara Grant n Jenni Cahill. So ah croutches doon behind the bus shelter tae lit them go past soas ah kin mibbe git masel a wee deek at they tight jodhpur-covered erses but it's a walk, no even a trot, far less a gallop, n thir's nae sign ah yon mawkit jakits ridin up tae expose the peaches below. Ah huv a sneaky wee rummage in the doonstairs department, n couldnae even git the heid ay it up! Ya hoor ye; perr source material!

So ah follays them, keepin in at the big stane waw wi the overhinging foliage, blendin in like that big *Predator* cunt, thon crab-couponed Rastafarian hoor fae space. Ah'm thinkin aboot how drugs've ruined ma sportin career, ah'm no gaunny git any serious copy in the *Central Fife Times and Advertiser* now; naw, thill only be the wee blurb Jason King dsql v J. Mossman, ya hoor sor. Aye, right next tae they equestrian notices tellin us aw aboot yon Lara n Jenni's 'mare' substantial achievements.

A bit ay jiggery-pokery wid dae but, aw aye sor. Nivir mind the edge ay sexuality thit sportin success brings, ah'll cut tae the chase n git the wee felly sucked dry right noo in antici-pation ay greatness tae come, if it's aw the same tae youse!

Ya hoor sor.

Ah could fair dae wi a wash n a chenge ay clathes eftir fuck knows how many days oan the black gold, ching, base and takeaways, but ah elect tae keep up muh pursuit ay ma intendit. Mind you, it's poor stalkin terrain; soon we're oot ay toon n ah'm exposed, walkin behind thum doon the country road. Ah thinks, thill huv left that dykey La Rue's ridin skill n be headin for yon big house, the auld ferm thit the Cahills boat years ago. New money thon; the haulage business. Scab lorries fae the strike back in 1984 some say, well, ma auld boy tae be specific. Aye, ya hoor ye. Mind you, any cunt wi money's bad money tae the auld boy.

Funny, but wee Jenni's the snootiest yin oot ay the twa, bit they eywis say that aboot new dosh. Bit it's an awfay state tae git intae. Ah'm waitin fir thaime tae go intae yon Clark Gables wi the horses n mibbe git a peek at thum, yon Lara n Jenni huvin that dirty fun thit ye ken aw lassies secretly want tae huv. Mibbe wi the hoarses gittin involved n aw! Aye, yon Scarlet Jester n yon Midnight.

Gittin between thir legs but, ya hoor sor!

So ah'm walkin doon the side ay the barn on ma tiptoes, making sure thir's nae light in the kitchen ay the Cahill hoose, a bad bastard yon auld Tam, whin the big door swings open n thaire they are staundin thair, watchin ays! Rumbled, ya cunt! That Lara gies ays a wee smile n looks at ays while Jenni goes that snooty wey, — What do you want?

Ah'm well flustered here but ah tough it oot. — Eh, saw yis gaun doon the road n ah came by tae offer muh congratulations, aboot yir win ower in Ireland, ah sais tae Lara. Might be nowt ay her, bit what thir is hus gone tae the right places. Aye, she's filled oot yon jodhpurs n that blouse since her n me hung aboot the gither, ah'll tell ye!

— Thanks, Lara goes. N ah'm sure that wee yin must be a

bit guilty oan hudin oot oan ehs in the minge stakes aw they years ago. As an apprentice jockey ah wis the local hero; could've split every fuckin gash in the Kingdom back then, ya hoor sor. Bit no me; goat aw worried aboot the size ay the wee felly here, n it took a dirty big auld hoor fae Ballingry tae pop ma cherry! Said tae ays it wis best sex she ivir hud in her puff n aw! Even allowin fir hoor's licence, it wis fair balm tae the auld ego, ah kin tell ye that! So if ah'm gaunny talk masel intae a threesome now, ah'd better git the auld gab gaun. — Aye, ah read aboot it in the paper. 68.25% oan advanced test 106! Oan Scarlet Jester thaire, ah nods ower at the hoarse.

The Lara lassie looks at her Jenni mate wi a wee smile, then back at me.

N ah'm jist staundin thair, ya hoor ye, cannae think ay nowt else tae say. — Did you go ower tae Ireland as well then, Jenni? ah asks in mountin desperation.

She looks at ays n sweeps her dyed black hair back fae her face. Liked that wee yin better whin shi wis a blonde. The burden ay bein a gentleman, ah suppose. Mind you, she's fair shaping up n thon fat's no hauf been trimmed back. — I wasn't competing, she says like shi's upset aboot that. — My horse was lame.

Felt like tellin her ah've hud ma share ay lame rides n aw, but thir's Goth talk n thir's posh fanny, and yuv goat tae keep that wee bit sophistication gaun. Ah feel a bit sorry fir Jenni bein Lara's mate: that yin isnae hauf 'filly' hersel.

Ah notices thir's one ay they wee studs in Jenni's nose. Aw aye, ah bet that wee yin could yaze thon ridin crock, ya hoor ye. — Ah hud a guid wee win at the table-top beautiful game, ah tell thum, — Aye.

— That's good, that Lara goes.

— Aye. Thing is, they might be takin it oaffay ehs. Thir wis a bit ay difficulty wi the discipline, ah telt thum, n ah cannae take muh eyes oaffay that ridin crock yon wee Jenni's hudin.

Ah'm wastin ma time thaire, ah'll never be popular wi thon family. Thir wis a time when her faither came intae the Goth wi a couple ay fellys, one ay them fae the cooncil. One ay the boys wis sayin something aboot Kelty n of course ah couldnae keep ma big mooth shut. Ah goes, 'Ya hoor ye, only hoors n miners come fae Kelty.' So big Tom Cahill, this Jenni lassie's faither, he looks at me aw hard n goes, 'Ma wife comes fae Kelty.'

Weel, sor, ah jist says tae um, what pit does she work in?

Thoat the big cunt wis gaunny banjo ays right thaire n then in the Goth but everybody starts laughin so eh hud tae climb doon n join in. But Lara's faither, the doaktir, he never hud a high opinion ay ays either. Whin ah wis workin at the warehoose, the hoor wid peer at ays ower the specs n go, 'Surely not *more* back problems, Mr King.'

Now that Jenni's lookin at ays aw that impatient wey, the yin the successful ay the toon tend tae display in thir dealins wi the undercless. — So is there anything else, eh . . .

— Jason.

— Anything else we can help you with? she says again, n now that Lara's starin right at ays, waitin oan a response, ya hoor sor.

— Eh, naw . . . ah'll be oan ma wey up the street. Jist wanted tae say well done.

— Thank you, Jason, Lara sais, then turns tae Jenni quickly and goes, — I hope you manage to sort out that little discipline problem, and they baith huv a wee snigger tae each other.

Well, ah turns oan ma heel n ah'm doon that road aw hoat n bothered. If ah wis a sortay James Bond type ah'd uv went: 'Well, there is a little something you could help me with, but I think we should all retire to the barn to discuss it, ya hoor sor.'

Oan the road back intae toon, it's stertin tae pish doon. Thir's some craws pickin ower a deid rabbit thit's been blootered oaf by a passin car, so ah sooks doon a snottery gob n lits it fly n it slaps one craw oan the back ay the heid. They reckon (or at least the Neebour Watson does) thit it makes the other yins tear the cunt tae bits, bit the hoors've goat too much meat tae be bothered wi that the now so that particular hypothesis remains not proven. Disnae matter but, it wis a result, speed and accuracy, ya hoor, n ah sing in celebration: — Thir wis a wee cooper wha lived in Fife . . . nickity knackety noo the noo, eh goat ehsel a durty big hoor ay wife . . .

But then ah sees this van comin towards me n it's slowin doon. It's thon Tam Cahill, n the big cunt pills up n gits oot. — Aye, aye, eh goes.

Ah wanted tae say tae the boy that ah wisnae stalkin ehs lassie, it wis hur mate, ya hoor, strictly speakin it wis ma auld paramour Lara, but ah dinnae think eh's the type whae worries about hair-splittin.

— You're Jason, eh?

— Aye.

Eh nods n looks ays up n doon. — You trained as a jockey, eh.

— Long time ago now, neebs, ah tell um.

— What ye up tae work-wise these days?

— No much.

Eh does that slow nod again, but eh's lookin at ays right in the eye. — How dae ye fancy daein some casual work for me? Nothin too taxin: jist some stable work, muckin oot, feedin n general stuff. Gie ye a bell when ah need ye, cash in hand, eh winks.

There wis me thinking ah wis gittin pilled n aw. Naw, but, it's a fuckin stalkers' paradise! Oan the firm, ya hoor! — Aye, sound.

— Geez yir mobile number, eh sais.

This occasions a wee bit ay embarrassment oan ma behalf.
— Eh, muh mobby is oot ay commission right now. But ah've
goat a landline.

The boy's lookin at ays as if eh's made a big mistake, seein
the dirty drink n drugs grime oan ays, nae doot catchin the
whiff fir the first time. — Geez it then, eh gasps aw exasperated. Kin awready tell eh'll be a cunt tae work fir. But if eh's
daein ehs haulage shite n ah'm in the stables, it should be a
sweet case ay neer the twain. — How dae ye git oan wi dugs?
eh asks ays.

— Love thum, aw kinds, ah tell um. No thit ah hud yin
since Jacob, the German shepherd-collie cross thit died wi a
lump in ehs throat whin ah wis seven. Cut ays tae the quick,
yon did. The auld girl said somethin aboot cross-breeds eywis
dyin n wi should've went pedigree, n the auld boy called her
a fuckin Nazi hoor. Aye, they wir nivir that close.

The auld boy said that she only wanted tae mairry him
cause he'd goat her up the duff. She'd been dumped by this
Greek waiter whae'd headed back hame eftir the family restaurant in Kirkcaldy went bust, brekin the auld mare's hert. Eywis
a speculative venture fir the seventies: back then the Chinky
wis probably exotic. She suffered fae a bout ay depression but
comfort ate her wey through it, pittin oan loads ay weight in
the process. Then the auld boy fired intae her up the Miners'
Welfare and bairned the hoor n ah wis the result. So ah cannae
really complain but what the fuck, ye eywis think thit what
yir folks dae before ye came along is nowt tae dae wi you.
Supposed tae be grateful tae them fir the gift ay life; fuckin
nonsense. Wi aw intuitively ken that thir's aw they souls in
heaven thit ur gaunnae git allocated tae some cunts anyway, if
they dinnae shoot one oaf.

So ah shakes Tam Cahill's hand and ahm a semi-workin man

again. Stable haundin wis nivir ma thing, but. Ah wanted tae be a jockey but ah wis never that keen oan fuckin nags; best appreciated fae Ladbrokes, they cunts. But it fair held ays back, that attitude did. N tae be honest ah eywis shat it when they bastards goat gaun fill pelt. Like Kravy oan thon fuckin Triumph Boneville bike; ah dinnae really like it oan the back ay that hoor.

Darkness faws like a workin hoor's keks: sudden but yet predictable. Ah gits hame, n tae celebrate my new employ makes masel a fried egg sanny n hus a read ay the paper, which irritates the fuck oot ay me. The *Central Fife Times and Advertiser* says that Dunfermline Pathetic huv selt 3,500 season tickets so far. I'll no be fuckin well addin tae that list any roads! Shouldnae be huvin information aboot they cunts in the Cooden media! Hoors've goat thir ain fuckin press!

The Auld Boy's in; either here or the library ur the only places yill find um. The Goth n aw: but only around last orders. Nivir leaves the hoose much as eh's badly disfigured oan yin side ay the coupon due tae a burnin accident. Back in 1989 ch set himself oan fire. He blamed the cheap, flammable shell suit eh wis wearin, while the auld doll blamed the fags. Dinnae think that the auld mare wis that sold oan ehs coupon any roads, so wee Shitey Breeks moved in n whisked her oaf doon the road tae a life ay Dunfermline decadence.

The auld boy looks at ays, then sits doon wi the *Record* and starts shakin ehs heid at the news. Eh's soon back oan ehs favourite subject, the seventies and the betrayal ay the workin cless. — The tax rebate, ye nivir git thaim now. Eywis came at the right fuckin time n aw. Aye, the seventies. Great times, then along came that English hoor n fucked it aw up. It's aw fir the rich now, the whole fuckin country. That's nivir a Labour man, no wi a mooth like thon. That's a hoor's mooth thon. Must huv been worth a fortune at that posh Fettes school wi a mooth like that; aye, well sought eftir, ah kin fuckin well bet ye! That Eton Tory wanker that's gaunnae replace um: a fuckin clone!

— Thir's a loat tae be said fir progress but, Faither. Some ay they great auld seventies institutions wir bad bastards; like the chip-pan fire disaster. The microwave, deep-fat fryer n the late-night takeaway's done fir aw that.

— Aye, ah suppose thir's been *some* kind ay progress, eh sais as eh rips intae ehs Pot Noodles. — But ah blame Scargill, should've goat a fuckin mob doon they Hooses ay Parliament, torn it apart brick by brick and stoned every yin ay they public-skill cunts tae death wi the rubble.

— Elites'll eywis try tae impose themselves ower time but, Faither. The day's revolutionary vanguard are the morn's rulin cless.

— Aye, bit that's how ye need permanent revolution but, son; build a set ay non-hierarchical structures . . .

Ah'm lookin oot the windae n ah see thit the wheelie bins huv been left oot in the street n need pit back in the front gairdin. — Aw structures by thir nature ur hierarchical but, Faither. N people dinnae want permanent revolution, they want tae jist chill oot sometimes.

The auld boy slams the Pot Noodle carton doon on the table. Eh twists the fork tae gain control ay the stringy noodles thit dangle fae it. — So what's the answer then? Drink, drugs, the chippy n mair Tory rule? The cornerstanes ay your life?

— Ah'm no sayin that.

— Defeatist talk, son, eh sais waving ehs noodle-filled fork around. — That's the problem wi your generation, nae collective consciousness! Ye should be doon that library fillin yir heid wi political n social education soas yi'll be well placed tae take advantage whin the upturn comes! The likes ay Willie Gallagher and Auld Bob Selkirk wid be turning in thir graves!

— Ah doubt they'd be much impressed wi your gangsta rap stuff either, Faither.

Eh turns they blazin een oan ays: — Thir's mair real politics in yin line ay 50 Cent thin in a hundred albums ay that hippy poof that you listen tae!

Fuck sakes, thir wis me hopin tae enjoy my fried egg oan Sunblest n Lurpak, garnished wi HP Sauce and pepper, but that's aw fucked now.

6.

ANNIVERSARY

One of the saddest things imaginable is seeing my mother in her workout gear, putting on an exercise DVD, getting about five half-arsed incompetent minutes into the forty-five-minute programme, then switching it off and going into the kitchen. You see the tear stains on her fat cheeks and her flustered air as you approach her. Then you check the chocolate biscuits in the big, plastic Tupperware box and they're about 50 per cent down.

— It's our anniversary today, Mum almost absent-mindedly announces as she starts to tend the plants with her clippers and watering can. I can see from the display on the DVD that the recording is still in the machine, playing away to nobody. Out of boredom I'm sitting on the couch with Indy watching cartoons on another channel.

— So how many years have you been married? Indigo asks.

Just then my dad comes in. Mum's about to say something when he replies, — Who cares aboot that? Love's aw chemicals, he snorts. — It's aw just a big con, like that Valentine's Day.

My God, he's so crass. — You don't know what you're talking about, I tell him. — Besides, you're a hypocrite. You've got Mum's name tattooed on your wrist.

He looks at his wrist, and then gapes stupidly at the cartoons, Scooby Doo and Shaggy running from a very unscary monster, then turns to me with a tight smile on his face. — You're ideal-istic, you're young. You'll see sense and grow oot ay it.

I glance up at him. — Like you did when you were young? Indy looks at him too.

— I was never idealistic, always a realist, me. He shakes his head, collapsing into the big chair. — I was too busy making money so that you and your sister could ride horses and grow to hate me, he laughs, reaching across and flicking Indy's long tresses.

— I'll never hate you, Daddy! she screams and leaps from the couch and jumps on his lap.

My dad makes a big fist and plants it softly on her face. — Naw, no you, hen, cause you're a wee smasher!

She reciprocates the gesture and they box and play-fight for a bit. I can't stand this, because part of me wants to join in. I stand up and move off. — Give it five years, some hormones and a bit of perspective, I say, heading for the door.

— Who rattled your cage, Lady Muck? he bites.

Mum looks around slowly in stunned incomprehension as she skooshes the cascading spider plant. I point at my own forearm. — You read what it says on your own wrist if you think that you were never an idealist. You're a coward, that's all.

— Mind what you call me, hen, he snaps. — You're cross-ing the line.

One of his favourite sayings. I get out and bound up the stairs, two at a time. I've become an outcast in this family. The little brat is the mainstay of their lives now; she's like a drug, reducing them both to baleful, fawning idiocy as soon as she walks into the room. I'm the embarrassment, the troublemaker, and the one who reminds them of how they've failed. The money shelled out for Stirling University, which I flunked, now more for Midnight, who is probably fucking lame because of me forcing him to jump a fence that was too high for him just to keep up with that bitch Lara and Scarlet Jester, and I'm nowhere near as good as her.

I lie on my bed listening to Marilyn Manson's, '(s)AINT' from my favourite LP of all time, *The Golden Age of Grotesque*, and reading my Danielle Sloman. I saw that guy on his motorbike, the good-looking one, who lives in Spain. He had the creepy wee Jason stalker on the back with him. I wish it was me that was on the back, and my fingers rub against my crotch when there's a knock on the door and he barges in, obviously still upset. I move my free hand to my book. — You should be oot in that stable kicking that horse's erse instead of lying around here listening tae that crap.

I look up from *Reluctant Survivor*. — The vet said that Midnight was to rest. He's not finished his course of anti-inflammatory drugs yet.

— Did eh say that you wir tae rest n aw? Eh should be in they stables ay La Rue's, where eh kin git taken proper care ay.

God, change the fucking record! — I've done everything Dobson told me –

— Aye, that Dobson's a waste ay space, he looks at me, — kens absolutely nowt. N how are ye gaunny beat that bools-in-the-mooth Lara wi a milkman's hoarse like thon? Aw that parasite does is eat eat eat. Ye stick a nosebag in front ay him n eh'd keep eatin till eh burst. Ah hope you're no overfeedin him.

— Oh please, do stop wittering on. I turn away. The coarser he gets the more proper I become. It's practically the only game we play where I always win, as he ends up sounding like a village idiot.

But this time, he's a thin smile playing across his face. — Tell ye what though, the weight's fair flyin oaf ye, hen. That's the wey tae beat that yin, ah kin tell ye! Keep up the guid work, he winks.

The horrible thing is that this is his way of trying to bond. He leaves me and I feel defiled and unclean. I want to go out to the Burger King. He really knows how to get under my skin. What did my mother see in him? There's nothing between them. I can't even think what there once could have been. I think of the photos of them young, her pretty, him still the same. I try to imagine a man emotional and tender enough, even for a few fleeting minutes, to get a woman's name carved into his skin. How I'd love to resurrect that man of then, if just for a day.

The alienation between him and my mother is such that he can't even bear to spend any time alone with her on their anniversary. He's therefore insisted that we all go out 'to celebrate as a family'. He might have taken her, us, out to Edinburgh or Glasgow, or even Dunfermline or Kirkcaldy. Even the simple kindness of making that small effort is beyond him. He's marched us down to La Ducal; the nearest you'll get to fine dining in Cowdenbeath.

— Push the boat out, my tongue drips sarcasm at the news.

— La Ducal is lovely, Mum bleats in piteous gratitude.

— I cannae drive due to our friends in the Fife constabulary, he reminds me.

Funny, but it never seems to stop him when it's work. I almost feel like volunteering my motoring services but no way: I'll need a drink to get through this. — What about public transport? I ask.

— Ugh! Ming-ing! Indigo screws her face up.

— I cannae be bothered waiting on trains and the taxis are a rip-off, he explains. — It's settled then. Cowdenbeath's finest it is.

To be fair La Ducal is pretty good, a lot better than somewhere in a town like Cowdenbeath has the right to be. At least you have decent tapas and cappuccino. If you don't look outside it's possible to kid yourself on that you're somewhere else. As the *Sunday Post* put it: 'Good food, friendly service, nice surroundings.' It's a pity about the dining company, but you can't have everything.

— This is nice, Mum says. If they stuck her in Auschwitz in the forties she'd say the same thing.

— So how many years *have* you two been married? Indy asks, crunching on a breadstick.

— Eighteen and counting, Dad smiles, knocking back his wine and refilling his glass. I hold mine out for the same treatment. He looks warily at me, but tops it up all the same.

When the main course arrives, Dad's mobile goes off. — Oh Tom, Mum thinly protests.

— Have to take this yin, he winks at her. — Excuse me a tick, girls. How goes? his voice spits into the phone. — Just a minute, he tersely says as he departs out into the street. I see him through the window, holding the phone like it was a robot device sucking the life out of him, moving like he's burning or badly needing to pee.

I don't know what he's up to but I know it's no good. The only reason I care is not because he's ruined this already fucked-up night, but that he's dragged me out to make small talk with these two while he hatches his pathetic schemes. — Wonder what he's playing at? I muse.

— Need you ask? my mum says, then adds, — Work. He never stops, she rolls her eyes wistfully.

I want to shout into her stupid face, 'What he's up to is fucking somebody else, and that's if you're very, very lucky.' But I don't. And the only reason I don't, I consider with a reflective shudder, is because I don't even care enough about their sordid business and their dull lives. I want to go. To get out of Cowdenbeath, Fife, Scotland, and out of that house for good.

7.

APPEAL

They fair set upon ays awright, yon time, they fuckin Dunfermline boys. Big Monty jist stood thair grinnin, n eh's since goat mobbed up wi thum. A fuckin traitor as well as a liar. Accused ays ay instigatin trouble. Fair tanned ays in n it hurts ma pride as a Cowdenbeath man, tae come oaf second best tae thcy hoors. Aye, even if thir wis a tidy wee mob ay thum, it cannae be disputed thit me n Boaby Shek fac the Chinky took a hoor's erse ay a panellin.

The kung fu films, ya hoor; when ah befriended um ah thoat thit the laddie Shek would be able tae hud ehs ain, mibbe ken some ay they moves. But aw eh does is read comic books n listen tae the likes ay Coldplay n Marillion n tell every cunt aboot the time eh studied engineerin at Heriot-Watt before eh flunked oot. Even hud ehs gaun doon tae Haddington wi um, n stalkin the lead singer Fish aka Derek Dick, at the boy's hoose. Ah've ey been mair a fanny stalker thin a celeb stalker, but Sheky insisted. Worse thing wis thit ah wis the one thit hud tae go in n git ehs autograph, Boaby jist turned intae a twelve-year-auld lassie. Eh managed one partin shot, took um ages tae git it oot: — Any new . . . any new . . . new projects . . . any new projects in the offing? And then the cunt ran away wi embarrassment before the bemused Fish could reply. Left me oan the doorstep explainin tae the frontman thit it wis a minor form ay Tourette's thit Boaby suffered fae, n the boy jist nodded sagely before eh goat shouted back intae the hoose by some supermodel bird.

But Haddington's much preferable tae Dunfermline. Fife ma hairy hole; it's an Edinburgh suburb. So even though 'thon place' hus bad memories, ah wants tae see what kind ay a gaff this hoor fae the East ay Scotland Table Fitba Association's goat. So eftir a guid shower and change ay clathes, ah gits a quick one in the Goth. Thir's a choice ay the 15, 30 or 19 buses tae Dunfermline up the road, but ah cannae be ersed walkin up thaire, so ah faw oot ay the boozer intae the station.

Ah keep tellin folks thit ah stey in Central Cowdenbeath. Ye kin gob n hit ma hoose fae the railway station platforms, ya hoor. Ye see the block ay cooncil dwellings wi the wheelie bins ootside, rubbish n recyclin; black for the black diamonds, blue fir the Blue Brazil.

Oan the choo-choo, wee Richey the Assaultee comes tae punch ma ticket. The boy's a local legend; eywis in the Central Fife media fur gittin battered by youths, totally unprovoked, ah should say. Mind you though, some wid say thit the ginger heid wis provocation enough, no thit ah wid number masel wi they bad bastards.

When the boy goat a start at ScotRail the high heid yins couldnae believe thir luck. An abused ginger stepchild wi a pair ay een that made yon Bambi look like the shark oot ay *Finding Nemo*, and eh wis comin tae work fir thum in front-line employment! Of course, they wanted Richey as poster boy fir thir anti-violence against staff campaign. Telt the hoor ehs look possessed jist the right amount ay pathos. Said thit eh could be a celebrity, like thon black hoor wi the bottom-ay-coke-boatil glesses fae the Halifax.

Richey weighed up the proposal, balancing the pros and cons, but opted tae stey relatively anonymous. Said that eh didnae want tae be even mair visible tae 'disaffected youth in the local community whae already see me as a bit ay an author-ity figure thanks tae the uniform'. His words, ya hoor, no mine.

Heard the story ay ehs stepfaither tons ay times, the boy wi the fast, hard hands. Even tried tae cooncil the cunt in the Goth oan mare thin yin occasion. In ma ain wey, ah wis yon Alexander Shuglin wi the black gold standin in fir the E. Anywey, Richey apologises fir stampin my ticket. — It's no me that's chargin ye, Jason, it's ScotRail, the perr cunt pleads, big eyes waterin, like ah wis gaunnae machete um oan the spot. — See if it wis up tae me . . .

— Nae worries, man, ah tells um.

Eh looks at ays n goes, — You're a true friend, Jason. Ah count you as a friend. Ah hope you feel the same?

— Aye, Richey, course ah dae, ah tell um. Thank fuck it's time tae disembark. Thon cunt wid talk umsel intae a doin; ah wis feelin ma bile rise n ma fists involuntarily clenchin n unclenchin jist bein around the cunt.

Dunfermline. Oot the fuckin train n yir stuck at the bottom ay a fuckin hill ootside the toon. How kin *this* be Fife's top toon whin it's no even oan the main rail line? Ah'd rather huv one ay they Kirkcaldy cunts thin yin ay they hoors any fuckin day, ah kin tell ye.

It's a big hoose, like one ay they granite-type yins they goat up in Ebirdeen. It's jist gittin dark whin ah'm chappin oan the door n a fat wifie in a big print dress comes tae answer. She's goat short, black hair n beady eyes n the sort ay voice thit says 'see how superior ah am tae a wee dwarf ratbag like you'. — Yes?

— Eh, ah've come tae see her man. Mr Mason. Eh, Oliver, ah elaborate, thinking thit the hoor shouldnae pit ehs first name oan the paper if eh doesnae want ays tae yaze it.

She pits a lemon-sucker ay a coupon oan n goes inside and shouts, — Oliver! Someone for you!

A minute later this boy wi thinin grey hair comes tae the door. Eh squints at ays ower a pair ay glesses. Looks a wee bit like an aulder version ay the Neebour Watson. — Who are ye and what d'ye want? eh snaps at ays.

Ah shows um the letter. Eh takes ehs specs oaf n pits thum in ehs cardigan pocket. Eh reads it, then looks at ays wi disgust oan ehs coupon. — You come to *my* home, upsetting *my* wife, disturbing me with this *trivial* matter!

— Sorry, neebs, but yir letter says thit ah jist hud a few days tae appeal. Dinnae trust yon post so ah thoat ah'd come in person, ken.

— Channels, Mr King, channels! In writing and to –

Cause the boy minds ays ay the Neebour, ah git a bit emboldened and cut the hoor oaf. — Bit ah thoat, mibbe be mair civilised, meet the chap, take um fir a pint up the East Port or something, state ma case, man tae man . . .

Eh thinks aboot this fir a bit as eh looks ehs up and doon, then stares at ma feet for a second or two. Then eh looks ays in the eye. — Hmm . . . alright, I'll be round the East Port in five minutes. The lounge. They do a nice pint of Guinness there. You a stout man, Mr King?

— I'm mair thin partial tae a wee drop ay the black gold, Mr Mason.

— We're getting off on the right foot here, Mr King. See you in five, the wee boy winks.

So ah'm sittin in the East Port n ah sets up the Guinness and sure enough auld Olly Mason comes in. Ah points tae his settled pint and he smiles. — Sorry, Mr King, misjudged ye a wee bit there. Thought you were one of these maverick types. I've no time for those who would try tae ride roughshod over procedure, Mr King: a right way and a wrong way to do everything. Nonetheless, your presence here shows that you have passion for the game and we always need that in Scottish Table Football.

— It's ma life, ah tell um, takin the opportunity tae move

strategically closer tae um, tae make room fir a bunch ay workies that come in.

— Well, as irregular as this is, I'm prepared tae give ye a hearing.

— Yir a gentleman, sor.

Eh pits the gless ay black gold tae ehs lips n takes a sip. Ehs ratty wee eyes focus oan me. — One thing I will insist, though, is that due to the somewhat irregular nature of this appeal, everything that passes between us is treated by both parties in the strictest confidentiality.

— Goes withoot sayin, neebs. Ah'm sure thit yir gaun oot oan a limb here n ah appreciate it.

Eh nods impassively. — State your case please, Mr King.

So ah talks aboot the specifics ay the case, n aw the while chs lookin at ays, like ehs measurin ays up. — If you don't mind me asking, Mr King, what height are you?

— Five two, well, five one and a half if ye want tae split baw hairs.

Eh sits back in the chair n eh's nearly purrin like a pussy. — Marvellous . . . and you're so very slight and slender, I'm guessing around seven and a half stones?

— Nearer seven, ah telt the hoor. — Cannae pit oan weight, no fir the lack ay tryin. Used tae be a jockey, ye see.

— Ah . . . cut short by injury, was it, your career?

— Mair a wee growth spurt. At fower seeven ah could've been officially registered as a dwarf. Total short-ersed heaven, ah contends, enjoyin the black gold. Ah'm nae fan ay Dunfermline as a toon, but this East Port's a fair auld oasis. — Aye, ah explains, — then ah hud this daft wee growth spurt n that wis me five two before ah kent it. Story ay ma life, the extra inches eywis gaun tae the wrang department!

Olly boy looks like eh's sizing ays up again. — Yes . . . that's about the same height and weight as my daughter was, he sniffs, lookin a wee bit sad. — The amazing thing is, you've even got the same colouring and similar features to her. Those eyes . . . gazelle-like, I always used to say . . .

— What happened tae her?

— A tragedy, King, a tragedy. Olly shakes ehs heid n sips at his pint. — A young girl cut down in her prime in a horrific road-traffic accident. She'd been at one of those bloody raves and the idiot driving the car was probably out of his head on drugs . . . well, he lost control and my Kathleen was taken from us, he sais aw wistful n pathetic, ehs voice brekin up.

What could ye say tae thon? Eh tells me thit she wis jist nineteen n aw, same age as Lara. She wis ehs pride n joy, the boy explains.

Then eh pills ehsel thegither. — Sorry to go on, he says then looks at ehs watch. — Listen, why don't you come back to mine for a malt? We've still got lots to discuss.

Well, a huv tae say that ah'd kind ay thought that wis it, but obviously no. — I can ensure that the reinstatement takes place, he turns and looks at ays like a polisman as we walk past the Carnegie Halls lit up for a performance, — but I cannot condone vandalism. You had nothing to do with the damage to the noticeboard?

— Oan muh ma's life, a plead in sincere tones addin, — Word oan the street is it wis a disgruntled element within the Cooden support, wi it bein a Pars noticeboard n aw.

Olly thinks aboot this for a wee bit. — Yes, sadly we in Dunfermline have our share of bad eggs too, Mr King. But I can see that you're cut from different cloth.

So wi gits back roond tae auld Olly Mason's n thirs nae sign ay the wife. Eh seems tae read ma mind. — June's at the Rotary club, she's always there. Eh leads ays intae this big front lounge. Then eh picks up a photae oan top ay the piannay. It's a young lassie. — Kathleen, eh sais, hudin it in front ay ays.

Ya hoor sor, a lovely wee bird n aw. Life kin be gey cruel. — Aww . . . ah goes, soundin like muh ma hearin aboot a dug that's been run ower.

— Follow me, Mr King, he says n then the hoor bounds oot and up a big auld staircase n ah'm strugglin tae keep up wi um. N thir's nae sign ay that fuckin bevvy yit.

— Jason, ah goes.

Eh stoaps n looks doon at ays fae ower ehs shoodir. — Let's keep it on a semi-formal basis until we've done business, that is if you are the type of person I can count on to do business with?

— For sure, ah sais.

Eh nods in conspiracy n wi go intae a bedroom. It contains nae Margaret Thatcher but thir's loads ay lassies' clathes hingin oan the racks. — Kathleen's place . . . just as she left it . . . I never . . . eh starts sobbin softly, takin oaf ehs glesses n rubbin ehs eyes. Then eh picks up one ay the hangers wi a Next top oan it n holds it against ays. Lookin at ays for a second, eh pills it away. — You wouldn't . . . no, I'm being silly . . . forgive me, King, put it down to the lunacy of the bereaved . . . when you've lost everything you go to a point beyond desperation, you'll attempt anything to alleviate the pain . . . foolish, I know . . .

— Eh, what? ah hear masel say. — Ah'll help ye oot if ah kin.

Auld Olly's lookin at ays wi they big moist eyes n ah'm thinkin aboot yon *Bambi* film. Me n the auld girl watchin it thegither, that sad bit whaire the ma dies. Muh ma sayin, 'That could be me n naebody wid care,' n me gaun 'Ah'd care, Ma, ah'd care, ah'm yir wee Bambi,' n her replenishin her sherry gless n gittin aw tearful. Poignant times indeed, sor, afore she shunted ower tae yon Dunfermline four-poster n Shitey-Ersed Arnie, n the recollection ay thum fair gits me gaun. Perr auld Olly. — Anythin ah kin dae . . .

— Well, you could do me one hell of a favour Mr K— . . .
Jason. You see, I never got a chance to say goodbye to Kathleen
and you remind me of her so much . . . I know I'm being
stupid and it's such a self-indulgent favour to ask . . . but it
would be very greatly appreciated.

I'm thinking, perr boy, if ah kin help him n help me at the
same time, ya hoor sor, ah'm in thair. Ulster, Palestine, Fife; lit
the healin process begin! — Anythin ye like, Olly.

— Well, I was thinking that if I could ask you to slip these
clothes on . . . it's crazy, I know, but if I could pretend that you
were Kathleen, it would only take a few minutes, I would be
so grateful . . . so that I could say goodbye and achieve, I don't
know, I think that 'closure' is the fashionable term these days.

— Well, aye . . .

— Like a glove, Jason, lad. These clothes would fit you like
a glove.

Ah look thum up n doon. Some nice stuff here, awright.

— That ah'll wager, sor; that ah'll wager.

So ah wis game, if it meant helpin the perr boy n at the
same time silencin some ay the critics in the New Goth, who
would jist love tae see the King ay Fife cast aside oan the
Subbuteo scrapheap. So ah'm intae the gear; blouse, short skirt,
stockins, sussys the lot, and of course the high heels, the boy
bein particularly delighted that the shoes fitted.

Then eh comes through wi a wig n a make-up box, which
ah'm a wee bit perturbed wi. — I can't believe it, you look
just like her as she dressed in her final days as an insurance
broker at Scottish Equitable . . . He hands ays the wig n the
make-up, ya hoor. — To crave your further indulgence, Mr
King, the uncanny resemblance you share with Kathleen would
be completed with these accessories.

— Eh . . . okay . . . ah say tae the boy. In fir a fiver, in fir
a score.

— Go easy on that make-up though, Mr King, let under-statement be the watchword. My Kathleen was never a tarty sort of girl.

— Ay that ah've nae doots, Olly, ay that uv nae doots, ah tell um, n ah settle doon in front ay the mirror. — Tell ye whit, ye did mention a wee malt whisky, well, ah widnae mind yin now fir a bit ay Dutch courage!

— Of course, Olly says, exitin the room, — do forgive me . . . Jason. My manners are failing me.

Ah hear his clump doon the stairs n ah'm done n nae time n ah've goat tae say, looking no too bad in thon fill-length mirror. Ah head doon the stairs n Olly's thaire wi two big Scotches.

— It's amazing . . . I can't believe it! You look more like Kathleen than . . . please, sit down.

So ah sits in the big easy chair n eh gits doon at ma feet n then eh starts kissin thum, in the shoes, n eh's gaun, — I'm sorry, darling, so, so sorry, eh bleats, suddenly, loudly, then ehs heid's buried oan ma lap!

Ah'm jist lookin at the tap ay the hoor's heid, the shiny dome wi the strands ay grey across it, no kennin whair tae pit ma coupon.

Eh's still gaun oan aboot how sorry eh is, so ah jist says softly, — It's awright, Dad.

— Say it again . . . eh goes, aw urgent.

— It's awright, Dad . . . Daddy . . . really, ah goes.

The Olly boy's sobbin but ah feel ehs elbay digging intae ma leg. Eh seems tae go aw stiff fir a while, breathing heavily, then trembles and says, — Thank you . . . thank you, oh my God . . . in a long gasp.

For a few seconds eh's lyin relaxed at ma feet, nae tension in ehs boady now, then thir's the sound ay the key turnin in the lock n eh shoots bolt upright. — Jesus Christ! It's her, back from that stupid Rotary club. He looks at me like eh's aboot tae shite ehsel. — Look, you'll have to go, an eh's oan ehs feet n eh starts pushin ays oot through the kitchen and oot ay the back door!

— Bit ma fuckin clathes, ya hoor ye, ah canny go oot like this!

— Please, Mr King . . . Jason, my wife will . . . the trauma of seeing someone who looks so like our daughter, it would kill her, she wouldn't understand. Do this for me and I'll ensure that your appeal is successful, I promise!

N ah'm left standin ootside in the back gairdin, in fuckin drag, ya hoor sor, wi no even a light tae git back tae the Beath! Railway ticket in the fuckin pocket ay the jeans upstairs n aw, ya hoor! No thit ah kin git oan the train lookin like this; the pity displayed by Richey the Assaultee wid be bad enough, but huvin tae come doon the hill in fill view ay the Goth at closing time? Git tae fuck!

The only thing tae dae is try tae walk wi as much dignity as ah kin. Ah gits roond the side ay the hoose n intae the street and an auld wifie wi a dug looks at ays. Ah'm tryin tae think ay the body language ay lassies thit ah've stalked, n ah endeavour tae keep the erse wiggle tae a minimum n lit they fuckin heels dae the rest. So ah heads oot eastbound, past East End Park, towards the big roundabout where thir's nowt tae dae but git the auld thumb oot cause it's pishin doon ah'll never make six miles in heels!

8.

TRANSIT

The boys meet us in the café in Dunfermline Glen late afternoon. We're all on the Kenco coffee, when one of the boys, the big one Lara's been fucking, Monty, she calls him, pulls a small bottle of whisky from his pocket. He is wearing a T-shirt with *Guns n Roses Appetite For Destruction* emblazoned across it. With his huge hands, as big as my father's, he pours some in Lara's, and then does the same for this other guy, whom he's introduced as Klepto. He gestures towards mine but I put my hand over it. — I don't drink and drive, I tell him.

The big lad has grey skin with incongruous orange freckles peppered across it. He looks like a pitta bread with measles. His blond hair is cut short, greying at the temples. He's a monster and I can't help thinking about the sort of sex he and Lara have.

Monty shrugs and this Klepto character says, — Very sensible, with a wry nod. He's a skinny, wiry boy with big buck teeth and very cold, dark eyes, which seem to permanently stare.

Monty leans back in the seat and stretches out, showing off his muscular build. He's not overweight, but he doesn't have the bodybuilder's sculpted muscles like the guys I see in the gym, though his biceps are huge. I've seen it before in some of my dad's acquaintances: it's all building-site work. — So yis ur lookin fir a wee bit excitement the night then, girls? he asks like a threat.

It unnerves me, and I think even Lara as well, as she laughs a little, spitting out a defiant, teasing, — Come to the right place, have we?

— Defin–ite–ly, Monty smiles.

A little later, as we head out to the cars, I whisper to Lara, — He's certainly no Prince William.

Lara's features are set in neutrality. She's freezing me out. My heart skips a beat as she gets into Monty's car. I can't disguise my apprehension, and Monty notes it. — Klepto'll go wi you, make sure ye dinnae git lost, he says darkly.

The van sets off and after standing in the rain for a second or two, I reluctantly climb into the car, opening the passenger-seat door to let Klepto in, and we head off in pursuit. The rain is falling heavily now, thick dollops on the greasy windscreen, and I switch on the wipers.

Klepto sits back in the passenger chair. The seat belt runs in parallel with the diagonal line on his jumper. I can feel his eyes on me, sizing me up. — So what's your story, then, Jenni? Ye goat a felly on the go?

I start to feel very cold, and I turn up the heater. — Yes, I'm seeing somebody.

My instinctive response tells me that I want to put some boundaries up between this guy and me. I obviously didn't say it with much conviction, as he smiles and tells me, — Ah dinnae believe ye, then he adds, — Cause that's no what yir buddy says.

That fucking bitch: trying to set me up with this loser. — I don't really care what you believe, I tell him.

His voice rises slightly and I can see the menace in his eyes. — Hi, dinnae git snooty, hen, he snaps, and it now seems too hot here in the car. Thankfully, his tone goes back to playful. — Okay, if you've got a felly, what's ehs name well?

— Jason, I say suddenly.

— Jason, Klepto says softly. — So where's this Jason the night then?

— He had to go and see some friends, I tell him.

I'm hoping that this will stop his cross-examination. It's a forlorn anticipation though. — Funny how yir mate disnae ken anything aboot this Jason felly, he grins. I can barely see the van ahead.

I decide to keep focused on the road and ask, without looking round at him, — Does your friend know everything you do?

— Monty? He laughs. — Aye. Pretty much.

This seems to spark off a thoughtful period and thankfully he's silent for a bit. I turn the heating down and look out to the sodden brown hills that shiver in the rain. Just when I'm starting to relax, his eerie voice fills the car again.

— Bet you've got a few boyfriends though. Tidy lassie like you, they'll be queuin up.

I try to ignore him, but I can't help feeling sickeningly flattered. There are so many boys whom I'd like to hear say that to me, but him . . .

— Tell ye what though, Jenni, kin ah ask ye a question?

How can you respond to something like that? I can't even shrug it off. I look straight ahead at the road through the wipers.

— Is that a yes or a no?

— Ask if you must, I huff in defeated tones. Then annoyed with myself for conceding ground, I snap, — I'm trying to concentrate on the road!

It doesn't phase him as he advances his predictable but scary proposition. — Do you think if somebody is gaun oot wi somebody, they should be allowed tae snog other people. Jist snog, likes.

Even through my anxiety and distaste, I can't help thinking

how I'd actually enjoy this sort of flirting, if the guy asking the question wasn't a gormless, chipmunk-toothed psycho rapist. — Depends, I spit out.

— On what? he says, his mouth hanging open.

I'm recast in the patronising moron's role again. — On what both parties have agreed, on the type of relationship they have.

— Aye, he nods stupidly.

And there's something about that stupidity, that level of predatory cretinism in *my* car, that makes me react in a way I shouldn't. — Aye, I echo, — and whatever my circumstances, I can't believe that there would ever be a time when I'd want to snog you. So I'd appreciate it if you talked about something else, or better still, just shut the fuck up.

I don't look in his direction, but I hear his breathing change. It becomes laboured, as if forcing against the air conditioning of the car. Then his voice, strangled, throaty, rasping like a buzz saw rings in my car. — You think thit yir fuckin shite disnae stink, eh, ya posh wee hoor?

My confidence starts to evaporate. I shouldn't have said that. I was winning. — Look, I'm trying to drive.

— Good, you jist keep drivin, he says and he leans across and puts his hand down the front of my jumper!

I fucking don't believe it! — Fuck off! What the fuck are you doing! I slam on the brakes and thankfully there's nobody behind us. I push his hand away. — Get out! Get out the fucking car!

— Make ays, he challenges, his eyes like that of a half-starved bear in a nature documentary.

I get my mobile phone from my bag. He snatches it out of my hand! — Give me that back!

— Uh-uh. Gie's a wee flash ay the tit n ye git it back, he grins, putting it behind his back. I'm not going to wrestle this pervert for my phone. That's what he wants!

Instead, I try to reason with him. — Look, Lara's going to call me if we're late.

— Naw, ah reckon thit her n big Monty'll be gittin busy somewhaire, he grins. — C'moan, a wee flash ay the tit n ah'm happy. Ah'm a man ay muh word. Otherwise, he raises his voice, — it'll just have tae be a smack across the fuckin chops.

For fuck's sake, how can this be happening? I look at the door.

— Dinnae start wi that, he snaps. — Dinnae be silly, now. Aw ah want's a wee flash ay yir tits. Ah'll keep muh hands tae masel. Scout's honour.

— If it means that fucking much to you, I curse in impotent rage. That fucking bitch Lara slumming it with psychopaths and dragging me into her shit! I open my blouse and pull up my bra. — There. You've seen my tits. Happy now?

— Ecstatic, he laughs, as I rearrange my clothes. — As ah sais, ah'm a man ay muh word. Just got muh rep as a ladies' man tae think ay. Now, when ah'm sittin in the pub n if the talk gits smutty, ah'll be able tae describe your paps. And that wee mole on the right tit.

— God, you're so pathetic.

His smile vanishes again. — Shut the fuck up and drive.

I do exactly that, through my anger and humiliation. I hate myself for getting stuck with a psycho bully in my car, but most of all I fucking hate Lara. At least the moron shuts his filthy mouth, except to bark the occasional direction.

We cross into Clackmannanshire, pulling off at this farm near Alloa. It's a slip road with an unmarked entrance that you'd pass without thought if you didn't know it was there. Soon the asphalt vanishes and turns into a gravelly mud. The farmhouse looks run-down and has a big barn, with lots of cars parked outside it, many of them big 4x4s. I can't wait to get out and I do it too quickly, my boots sinking into thick mud. I want to say something to Lara, but she's got that nutter Monty with her. — Got a little bit lost, she smiles.

— See youse did n aw, Monty sniggers at Klepto. He has his hulky pitbull terrier with him, which is thankfully muzzled. It comes over to me and sniffs at my leg.

— A wee bit, but it's the detour thit makes it worthwhile, that fucking inadequate sex offender, Klepto sneers. — Ah did see a couple ay nice wee hills on the wey oot, he bends down and slaps the dog's muscled sides.

I swallow hard and move away from them, looking over to the barn. There's a guy on the door, and Monty nods at him and we go inside. It's packed. Old doors, turned on their sides, are bolted together to form a ring, which seems about twelve foot square. The ring is covered in old carpet, presumably to stop the dogs from slipping when they attack each other. I have to admit that the whole grotesque pantomime is oddly fascinating.

After a bit, the owners come into the ring with their dogs, a Rottweiler and an Alsatian. They hold them in different corners behind scratched lines, where they look at each other like boxers. Apart from a skinny man with slicked-back hair, who is presumably the referee, they are the only other bodies in the ring. The atmosphere is becoming murderous. The faces on the men in the barn are uniformly demonic, and I feel like I'm in the middle of a strange nightmare. Lara looks fascinated, yet as horrified as I feel. The referee suddenly barks: — Release your dogs!! And the animals charge towards each other, converging savagely in the centre of the pit, in a snarling, tumbling flurry.

A cheer goes up and the crowd scream rabid encouragement at the demented beasts. But there seems little action; it's a strange impasse where it's as if the dogs' faces are superglued together. Then a chant – 'fanged, fanged, fanged' – starts up, gaining in volume and velocity. Monty puts his big face in between Lara's and mine and explains, — When one dug bites through the other yin's lip, they become fanged. Stops aw the action.

It didn't stay stopped for long, as the handler came into the ring with a stick and puts it into the dog's mouth, prising its jaws open. — The handler's goat tae work the brekin stick intae the dug's mooth tae brek the grip, Monty gleefully explains.

His muzzled dog is very disciplined and shows no reaction to the carnage in the ring as it stands by his side on a choke-chain leash. — Kenneth here's a face dug, no a throat dug. A bonus, he explains with obvious relish. —Very few throat dugs are quick enough tae go for the kill and rip a throat oot. Some that git lucky might be able tae make the other dug pass oot if they kin git a guid grip ay its throat and cut oaf the oxygen supply, he explains, looking contemptuously at the dogs in the ring. — These urnae proper fightin dugs, he explains, — A pitbull worth its salt wid dae baith ay thaime at once.

Separated, the dogs charge again, converging into one snarling beast and whacking the door in front of our legs with force. They separate again and charge, the Alsatian seeming the more aggressive. After this exchange, the Rottweiler's face is ripped and it whines horribly. I want to cry 'Stop'. — See, Monty says triumphantly, — thon Rotty's goat a grip three times stronger thin the Alsatian, but the cunt's nae fuckin hert. Maist throat dugs git one shot n aw they git is a moothfae ay fur. Once the face dug starts rippin up thir coupon thir bottle jist goes n that's thaime beat. It's like a boxer wi just one punch, tryin tae land that big right aw night, but gittin picked oaf wi the jab n the combos. Pit bulls are the real fighters; the rest is just exhibition stuff. A freak show, he laughs, — we're the main event. This is steeped in tradition; the rules have been set for years. It's sport, jist like bullfightin in Spain, he says grandly.

Lara shudders. — I think it's horrible, she says, and then looks at him and smiles. — But kind of fun, too.

The Alsatian has the whining and fretful Rottweiler in a grip in the back of the neck. The poor creature is paralysed with fear and just shivers and whimpers and cowers low as the Alsatian stands over it growling through its nose. One old guy, demented, scary, raising a half-empty half-bottle of whisky, roars: — Kill the cunt! A big guy with a shaven head and heavy black Stone Island jacket greets Monty and passes a ridged mirror to him. It has lines of cocaine chopped onto it. He takes one and passes it to Lara, who passes it to me. I decline, I want to get high, but not with these fucking people. I notice that Klepto takes a line.

— I think that's the way it's gaunny go the next round, Monty sneers.

Eventually, the owners pull the dogs apart. The Alsatian is muzzled and the Rottweiler's owner looks at the dog in disgust. What I take to be some kind of disgraced vet, but I realise is actually the drunk with the whisky, is tending its wounds with some dark stuff from a bottle which I assume is an iodine solution. He applies it while the owner holds the dog's face.

— Cunt cost me five hundred quid. Bastard, Stone Island moans. — Ronnie's patter's shan. That fuckin dug couldnae fight sleep.

— Eywis bet wi the puss dug, Mike. See how you fight whin yir face is gittin ripped oaf ye! Monty says.

I'm enthralled, even as the cold seeps into my bones and the shivers pulse with strobe light-like regularity through me. Lara, emboldened by the cocaine, now seems to be enjoying the carnage. — That was great, she says. Then she looks at me, and says, — What? That's what they're born to do. Like horses are meant to run and jump and be ridden, those dogs are born to fight. I don't really see the problem.

— The problem, I start, dropping my voice and whispering urgently in her ear, — is not the dogs. It's the people here, and as I study the faces of the men around me, one across the ring snaps into recognition. It's my *father*, talking to a small, bald man! Thank God he hasn't seen me! I step back in panic and pull Lara aside.

— I have to go. Now.

— Why? Wimping out, Ms Cahill? she asks smugly, — Monty's dog's fighting next!

— It's not that. My dad's here! I don't want to see him!

Lara grinds her jaw and raises her eyebrows. — Well, I'm staying. This is fun.

— Don't tell him I was here, I say, stepping back a bit more.

Klepto looks at me. — *That's your faither?* Tam Cahill?

— Yes! I hiss. — Please, don't tell him I was here.

The colour has drained from his face. — There's nae danger ay that!

I push through the crowd. Somebody gropes my arse. I turn around to see Stone Island's bullet head skewing with a saucy wink. I push on and an old guy laughs and says, — Aye, it isnae Crufts, hen! I get outside and into the car. As I drive off, I can see my father's 4x4 is parked alongside some other vehicles, on a tarmacked forecourt on the other side of the barn. I head away from that terrible place, getting on the road back through Dunfermline towards Cowdenbeath. The drizzle has turned into a downpour.

I'm so glad to be on my own. I'm thinking about my dad and the dog. Oh my God. Surely not . . . Ahead, there's a solitary figure standing half in the gutter, lurching into the road. Astonishingly, outside of Dunfermline, somebody is thumbing a lift. It's a girl. I pull up and stop as she comes running towards me.

But it's not a girl. It's a guy dressed up in woman's clothing and I know him!

I wind down the windscreen. — Why are you dressed like that? What are you doing out here?

He wraps his arms around himself. He doesn't have a coat! — It's a long story, could we mibbe no discuss it in the motor?

I open the front passenger seat. As he gets in, all I can think of is how womanly his legs look, in their soaked tights. I feel a wave of jealousy, my own are so shapeless and chunky under those jeans.

— Where ye been? he asks.

— Seeing friends, I say quickly. — More to the point, where have *you* been?

Jason looks at me with these almost permanently startled eyes of his. I consider, with a chilling realisation, that it was his name I used to try and get myself off the hook with that pervert. It was the first one that came to mind when he asked about my boyfriend! And now he's dressed as a girl. — Ah goat involved in amateur dramatics. Ah wis playin a lassie in this drama. Up at rehearsals in the Carnegie Hall, likes. Aye, n ah went fir a wee swallay, n one became several, n ah goat masel locked oot! Thing is, aw ma clathes n cash were locked in the dressin room! Could only happen tae me, he smiles woefully.

As we drive into Cowdenbeath, I tell him about Hawick and my diminishing hopes of making the tournament. As we get down the high street he seems agitated.

— Eh . . . obviously, ah widnae mind if ye could droap me oaf right at ma door. People might, eh, misconstrue things . . .

I find myself laughing uncontrollably as he sinks down into the seat, directing me to the small housing scheme behind the railway station. — Fuck, and he ducks further down as he sees some people coming out of that dirty old pub on the corner. — It's the Neebour Watson!

Once the guy he doesn't want to see passes by, we pull up outside Jason's house. — Jenni, could ah ask ye one mair wee favour? Wid ye mind tappin oan the door n askin ma auld boy tae git ma parka, trainers n tracksuit boatums?

I'm a bit reluctant to do this, but he seems so desperate. — Well, okay . . .

I get out the car and go down the path. Loud rap music blares from inside as I bang on the door. Eventually a man with a crumpled, yellow face opens up, it's like it's been burned down one side. On the other side he looks like somebody semi-familiar, but it's not an older Jason. The noise is almost deafening, and he goes inside and turns it down. As he reappears, I tell him the story Jason told me. He shakes his head doubt-fully but tells me to come into a hallway. Everything looks old and smells of deep-fried food. — Sorry aboot yon racket. 50 Cent, he nods, then complying with Jason's request, runs up the stairs, returning with the items. I take the clothes out to the car. I stay outside as Jason struggles into the bottoms and trainers, and then wraps himself in the parka.

He gets out of the car, then stops to look at me. — Thanks for that, Jenni. Ah owe ye a favour. He smiles broadly and it transforms his face; all teeth, eyes and enthusiasm. — You're a top lassie: too cool fir school, likes.

He goes into the house and I head home, thinking that Jason's a lot sweeter and a damn sight more interesting than I gave him credit for.

When I get home my mind is turbulent with the events of the day, so I sit up to watch the repeat of a brilliant docu-mentary on the death of Kurt Cobain. I like this time; when everybody else is in bed and I have the place to myself and the television is actually watchable. Cobain was a genius. To be able to choose death over adulation: isn't that the ultimate moral courage, of the type we all want to possess? My eyes mist up. I fantasise about Kurt coming into Cowdenbeath on a big motorbike, taking me on the back, driving out of town and eventually travelling down dusty, southern European peasant roads, then stopping to make love on a Tuscan hilltop in the sun. I'm about to have a frig when I hear the front door opening.

It's very late, who the fuck –

Then Dad comes in, with Ambrose, whose face is covered in bandages! Dad's uncharacteristically coy when he sees that I'm still up. — Eh . . . awright?

I approach the dog, only one sad eye visible through the gauze. — What the fuck's happened to him? I gasp, as if I didn't know.

My dad looks down at the poor creature. — Some Rottweilers, two of them, they set on him in the Glen this afternoon. Poor bastard nearly lost an eye. Had to get his face stitched up at the vet's.

— And you let that happen to him?

— What else could I dae? he bleats, then adds, as I spring off the couch, — Since when did you start tae care aboot the dug?

— Since you've been fucking exploiting him like you try to do with everything that comes across your path! I scream at him. I hear him protesting about waking Mum and Indy and I slam the door to drown him out.

Sure enough, Mum's on the top of the stairs in her night-gown, pleading, — What's wrong, Jenni? What is it?

— Ask the fucking monster you were daft enough to marry! I bark as I go into my room.

— You'll respect your father and this house, young lady! she squeals and I hear him placating her on the stairs. I don't know which of them is worse: him with the morals of a sewer rat or her, who possesses the brains of a gerbil.

9.

IN THE GOTH

The Neebour Watson is makin a guid point in the Goth, one that's teased the mind ay the speculative-natured man fir a long time. — Ah dinnae see how lassies git aw funny aboot they VPLs; like thir no sexy, n a pair ay drawers wi a Calvin Klein label stickin oot ower the tap ay yir jeans is meant tae be.

— Ken full well whit ye mean thair, ya hoor ye; saw that Lara gaun ower yon hurdle oan Scarlet Jester, the black undies showin through yon white jodhpurs. Aye, ah played that yin back a thoosand times oan the DV.

— Whae shot it?

— Me, ya daft hoor! Fae yon Perth tournament last year, ah turns taewards um, — oan the video camera Sheky borrowed fae the local FE college. The main campus in Halbeath Road in Dunfermline, that is, no the poxy wee outpost the hoors have oan the industrial estate doon the road, ah explains tae the Goth guid n great.

The Duke ay Musselbury comes in, clocks ma near empty gless but makes nae move on ma behalf as eh sets ehsel up. Noted, ya hoor sor.

— Ah heard thit hur n yon Jenni Cahill ur gaun doon tae the Borders, Hawick like, fir the big tourney doon thaire, ah tells thum. Aye, she fair saved ma life wi her motor, that wee yin last night. Took ma explanation charitably n aw. Quality behaviour in a lassie, that.

The Duke looks at me like ah'm a bam. — Ye gaun doon?
— Well, aye. Ah mean, yuv goat tae support two guid Fife
lassies against aw yon Perthshire rich-bitches. Patrotic duty as
an ambassador for the Kingdom, ya hoor.

It's guid tae git some peace, here in the Goth. The auld boy
kept playin yon 50 Cent track 'Many Men (Wish Death Upon
Me)' ower n ower again, louder every time. N him jist sittin
in yon battered chair, aw teary-eyed, sippin a can ay Stella.

10.

TANNING

I lie in late till the Bastard goes to his work and Indy goes to school and the Non-Event is at the shops, so that I don't have to face any of them. I'm in a house of monsters, and they fill me with a sick loathing. When the coast is clear, I have a long and delicious frig, imagining myself on the back of the bike of Ally Kravitz, Lara said the dishy guy who hangs around with Jason was called. I can feel the Mediterranean sun on my face but it's just my own blood rising to the surface of my skin as I come in jarring, violent convulsions. I've had sex with just two guys before; neither has felt as good as when I do it with myself.

I pull the duvet off myself to cool down. After lying in a dizzy stupor for a while, I get up and get ready. Then I'm off in the car and to my step class at the sports centre. The strange old drunkard who sits outside there says something to me or about me. Surprisingly, it didn't sound that uncomplimentary. — Whatever, I shrug back, heading inside.

I put in a good session. Afterwards there's a text message from Lara on my mobile and I meet her in the Alpha Leisure Tanning Studio in the high street.

We go into adjoining booths. There's only a flimsy partitioning wall dividing us as we climb onto the beds and they start up with an almighty whirr and an intensive explosion of light that still bursts formidably from under my protective glasses. It's okay at first, as I think of tropical beaches, and it's hard to believe I'm on Cowdenbeath High Street. But after a while it gets really hot and I start to get a different image in my head. I see myself as a barbecued chicken on a spit. I swear I can even smell myself cooking. — I'm not sure about this, Lar, I shout through to her from under the banks of light, my bare arse hard against the cold glass. — I think I can feel myself burning. This can't be good for you.

— Nonsense, Ms Cahill, comes her disembodied voice from the adjacent machine, — it'll do you the world of good. Once you get rid of that white, pasty skin, you might be tempted to buy some more colourful clothes instead of black all the time. It'll be great for Hawick.

— How will it? It won't make Midnight's leg any better or make us jump any higher.

— You want to look your best for the photographers there. I've heard that there might even be some TV cameras, for that STV show, *Country Pursuits*.

Afterwards we go to the leisure centre coffee bar. I'm think-ing about that horrible Klepto, and Jason, the weird but sweet stalker, and my fucking father and poor Ambrose the dog. How it seems to be my lot to be surrounded by the creeps that Lara draws into her orbit.

When I get home and check on Midnight in the stable, Dad appears with Indy and he's on one of his recurrent themes. He says I'm 'overhorsed' on Midnight. — He's an experienced old stager but ye need a fitter, hungrier animal if you're tae compete properly. There's a well-schooled six-year-old for sale. See if you like him. He's a gelding but he's goat stallionesque spirit. The owners even said it was a mistake getting him done, as they should have bred from him. An Oldenburg warmblood. You cannae beat German horses. A thoroughbred as well. Horses like him dinnae come along every day.

Indy goes into the stable to check on Clifford the pony. My

dad walks towards the fence and shakes it. Poor Ambrose trails pitifully behind him, face still taped together. — How is his face? I ask, following them.

— Twenty-two stitches. Looks nasty, but it's superficial. He's three-quarters pitbull. He ought to have fought back! He looks at the dog in an angry contempt.

I think of Monty, and Kenneth, his killer dog. — Funny how the dogs went straight for his face. There are no marks on his body.

— Aye . . . that's dugs for ye. They dae that.

— Especially if they're trained, eh?

He looks searchingly at me for a bit, then shrugs. — Best check up on that stable. Fuckin minging, he goes.

— I try, but it needs so much work, I protest. — And there's Indy's pony and the companion animals, and I'm lumbered with the lot!

— Thir's a solution tae that, he says.

He's going to go on about boarding Midnight with Scarlet Jester in La Rue's stables again. How many times do I have to say it to get it through his thick skull that it isn't going to happen! — I know what you're going to say, I snort.

— I hear ye aboot the stables. He raises his palms. — I think we need somebody tae help us thaire. Ye cannae git staff they days, eh, he smiles, and I force a response. — I might just ken somebody, he winks at me.

— Okay, I say quietly back. I realise that I've just entered into a pact with him to say no more about Ambrose's wounds, in order that I get him to pay somebody to skivvy in the stable. It dawns on me that I'm probably as shallow as he is, possibly even more.

II.

EAST PORT

The next eftirnoon ah'm back in Dunfermline, sittin in the East Port wi Olly Mason, whae's goat ma clathes in a placky bag n is aw fill ay apologies. — I'm so sorry, Jason, but my wife wouldn't understand this need I have to seek a symbolic communion with my daughter. June's a wonderful woman, but a terrible reactionary: not open-minded like you or me.

Fair kens how tae ego massage, thon hoor, ah'll gie um ehs due. Thir's geishas spent years learnin thir trade thit couldnae git that close. *Things They Dinnae Teach Ye At Kelty Business Skill*, right enough. Eh's fair found ma clitoris, any roads. — Well, ah pride masel oan bein a free thinker in the best Fife traditions, ya hoor sor.

Olly nods in the gesture ay mutual understandin employed by learned men the world ower. — What you did yesterday helped me so much, eh says, liftin the black gold in a toast motion that ah'm moved tae reciprocate. — Consider the ban rescinded. I've been onto the committee and they've agreed with my recommendation that we acted too hastily and that the Mossman result should stand, and that Jason King will play Derek Clark from Perth in the next round of the cup! Cheers!

— Cheers! Delighted tae be ay service, Olly, but it wis an awfay loat ay bother gaun through the toon in drag.

The hoor's brows knot, as weel they might. — Yes . . . I'm so sorry about that.

This is a rerr pint ay Guinness, though. Ah lick the inevitable

278

foam mowser fae ma toap lip. — Aw's well that ends well. Goat picked up in the motor by a nice wee lassie ah ken. A nae-questions-asked type. Wee goth bird, likes, but no in the sense ay the boozer, ah hastily add.

— Excellent . . . excellent. Listen, Jason, how would you feel about helping me out again? Olly pleads. — That last session, it was so . . . cathartic, a couple more at the same level of . . . intensity . . . would surely see me able to move on . . .

— Well, ah dinnae –

— Of course, I'd make it worth your while, the boy cuts in. — How does fifty pounds suit?

Ah thinks aboot this for a minute. Hermless stuff, by any just accoont, sor. — Ah'm game, but if thir's any chuggin involved ah'm wantin a ton, ah tell um. — Nae offence, but bein in the presence ay another man's climax disnae dae nowt fir ays; specially whin ah'm the only skirt in the room, ya hoor!

Olly looks sadly at ays as if tae acknowledge that it's aw jist business. Aye, cash nexus, relationships, as auld Karl sais. Then eh gies a slow nod. — That would be fine, provided I can record the proceedings? They will, of course, be exclusively for my own personal . . . therapy only. This I guarantee.

Ah think aboot this for a while, n shrug. — Awright, cause auld Olly doesnae seem the sort ay felly whae'd want anybody else tae ken aboot this.

— It's June's shopping day in Edinburgh, eh explains in a low whisper as we kill wur pints n head back tae the hoose. What one does fir one's love ay the beautiful tabletoap game. But if we huv tae prostitute wursels tae thon pimp commerce, then lit's git the fill goin rate ay bawbees. Basic trade union principles, ya hoor.

Olly's set up ehs camera n tripod n wir soon at work. Ah think ah pit the make-up oan a wee bit better this time roond, daein the lippy like the auld girl used tae. Olly's stagin things much mair now n ahm fair huvin tae work fir ma sheckles. The hoor likes ays tae huv a faraway gaze, while hudin different books he's gied ays like *Little Women* or *Jane Eyre*, like ah wis jist contemplatin a sentence in the work, likes.

Next thing ah ken is ah'm sittin oan eh's knee, n eh's goat ays reading passages oot loud tae um. Simulatin yon coachin gied tae the Kathleen lassie as a young thing, nae doot. Ah fair goat a beamer whin eh telt ays thit ah hud that 'quality ay innocence' aboot ays. Really made ays determined tae go oot n git ma hole, that yin did.

Olly's breathin went as shallow as a hoor that says 'ah love ye' n ah wis certain thit perr Kathleen's dress wid need a guid cleanin.

Whin ah gits back intae civvies n meets the hoor doonstairs, eh goes, — I think I'm almost there, Jason, negotiating those troubled waters of grief with that harbour of serenity almost in sight. Eh, any chance of just one more visit?

— Mibbe will cry it quits fir now, Olly. Ah mean, nae offence, everybody's goat thir ain wey ay dealin wi bereavement, but ah'll leave you tae sail this particular ship alaine, if ye dinnae mind, ah'm moved tae tell the hoor.

He nods in slow understandin, n coonts oot the notes, handin thum ower tae ays. — Fair enough, but if you ever change your mind, you know where to find me, eh sais, showin ays oot. Ah shimmy doon thon gairden path, giein um a wee wave, spankin that wedge in ma back poakit, n ah feels fabby, ya hoor sor.

Eftirwards ah stey in Dunfermline huvin arranged tae meet Kravy. We plan oan gaun up tae the Queen Margaret hospital tae see ehs ma. Ah takes a look around the centre for a bit but ah sees that Monty comin oot ay the newsagent wi two or three ay they boys that gied Sheky n me that skelpin thon time. Ah turn the other wey and thankfully the hoors are too loast in thir ain drama ay fag-crashin tae register muh presence. Close shave! Ah consider gaun tae see the auld doll at her hotel, but ah dinnae want tae risk bein frozen oot by the Sperminator, thon wee cunt Arnie. It's gittin near time tae meet Kravy any roads. Darkness descends like a hoor's proverbials as I get oot the centre and oantae the main drag. The city chambers looks like a fairy-tale castle wi its turrets as it juts oot intae the street. Ah turn doon the hill and git intae Tappie Toories, a hostelry kent way beyond the borders ay Fife as it wis once owned by the late, great Stuart Adamson, formerly fae Big Country and the Skids.

Ah've jist set up some black gold whin ah hears the roar ay a bike engine ootside n then Kravy walks in. Ah set um up a lager. — What's in the bag, Jase? eh asks.

— Eh . . . set ay clathes. Left thum at this bird's the other night whin ah hud tae dae a runner.

— Anybody ah ken?

— Ask nae questions yi'll git telt nae lies.

So wi hus a quick Artooro, then ah climbs reluctantly oantae the back ay his bike up tae the hozzy.

Whin wi finds the ward ehs ma's sittin up in her kip. Thir's a congealed penne picante on a wheelie table by the side ay hur bed. Her beak's streamin, like she's been daein tons ay coke. — How goes, Mrs Forsyth?

— Ah seriously doot thit ah'm long fir this world, Jason, son, already spoke tae Faither Maguire. She looks tearfully at Kravy. — Ah jist wish thit muh boy wid come back hame n meet a nice Scottish lassie n settle doon.

— Ah prefer Spanish burds but, Ma, Kravy sais, — especially the chunkier yins. Eh traces oot a fill rather thin oorgless figure. — Barry rides; it's the Latin spirit. Thir's this chick ah've been slippin the doadie tae up in Setubal, intae threesomes, the lot.

Kravy's ma sits up n pushes the trolley table away fae the bed. — Huh, we did aw that sort ay thing n aw, son. Hear him, she turns tae me, — thinks eh kin shock ehs auld mother.

It fair leads yin intae contemplation, but. — Funny, Mrs F, aw the auld yins up the Goth say the same thing. Tell ays thit pre-Aids, thir wis some vintage ridin gaun oan in Fife. The young team ur aw intae it as well; that Ballroom up the road, um telling ye, ya hoor, ye'd end up oan the register jist walkin in thaire oan a Saturday night! Aye, it jist skipped a generation, or at least ma pert ay the generation! Lorenzo's n aw, ah tell thum, now in effervescent form, — the Miners' Welfare back in Cowden cannae compete!

— Aye, bit this yin here, she looks at her laddie, — still thinks thit eh's invented sex. Besides, whin ye git tae ma age ye realise thit thir's mair tae life.

Kravy looks contemptuously at his striken ma, gypsy-broon lamps risin up ehs foreheid. — Aye, n you're tryin tae tell ays thit they injuries ay yours wurnae sustained in the hunt fir a lum sweep? eh sneers. Fuck me, ah widnae be able tae talk tae muh ma like that. The chops wid be mair fuckin tanned thin that wee Lara's chorus eftir a session oan yon sunbed!

— I was having a social glass of wine on a night out with some of the lassies from the bingo, his ma protests in formal tones.

N that's whit maist ay the evening consists ay: listenin tae thaime windin each other up. When we git oot, it's brass monkey weather n ah dinnae feel like gittin oan the back ay yon bike. Ah'm almost tempted tae elaborate oan my porky pie aboot seein this bird in Dunfermline, tellin um ah'm gaunny meet her, then sneakin oan the 19 or 30 fae Halbeath Road, or even doon tae the station. But ah swallay hard and climb oan the back.

Kravy accelerates away that quick my bowels and hert are

still in Dunfermline whin the outskirts ay the Beath ur comin intae view!

God, it's great tae git oaf that fucker. Whin ah arrives hame, muh auld boy goes, — That gangster hoor, thon Tam Cahill, he wis oan the phone fir ye. Ye want tae keep away fae thon scum, thon's a wrang yin.

— Thoat you wir intae gangsters?

— Gangsta's son, thir's a big difference.

— Aye, right, ah go, too tired tae argue, whit did eh want?

The auld boy forces oot some air as ehs lips purse. — Ah dinnae ken. Telt um tae fuck off.

— Ye didnae . . .

— Naw, bit ah felt like it, the auld man scowls at ays. — Dinnae be bringin trouble tae this hoose.

— It's only aboot some stablework, ah tell um, raising they palms in appeal.

— Thir's nae employment that's stable right now, the hoor says, totally missin muh drift. — No fir the workin cless at any rate.

Well, ah didnae fancy another lecture oan politics oafay him, so ah flung oan the glad rags and opted tae go oot tae Starkers niteclub, owned by redoubtable Fife businessman, Eric Stark. When ah git thaire, the sign has been vandalised, the activity ay the Young Team ah'm wagerin, as the first 'R' hus an 'L' painted ower it. It's an awfay young crowd. Thir's two lassies sittin at a table aw made up n wi aw the slap oan it takes ays a while tae recognise thum as Roastin Wi Sweat n Soakin Wi Rain. One ay them waves at ays. — Ah ken you fae somewhaire, she threatens.

Ah fell like sayin, 'Cowdenbeath, perchance?' but ah sits doon cause tae muh surprise Roastin Wi Sweat looks the pert wi the warpaint oan. It wid take ah few mair nips inside ays before ah'd plunge thon pork bayonet intae that Soakin Wi Rain, but. Hobbies include: pregnancy, cigarettes and daytime television.

— Did you no used tae stey next door tae Alison Broon? ah asks Roastin Wi Sweat.

— Aye. Her wee sister Evelyn used tae be muh best pal.

Wee Evelyn, wi the braces oan the teeth. Doaktir Lecter, ah used tae call her; only in jest but, ya hoor.

— Thoat ah wis yir best pal, Soakin Wi Rain cuts in, really pit oot.

— Aye, but she used tae be, but. Yonks ago likes, Roastin Wi Sweat hastily pacifies her.

Ah'm thinking aboot they braces again. Wonderin if the grown-up Evelyn could be induced tae wear thum in a one-off, purely fir the purposes ay giein oral pleasure, ya hoor. It moves ays tae enquire, — Whatever happened tae wee Evelyn Broon?

Roastin Wi Sweat takes a fag oafay Soakin Wi Rain n lights up. — She went ower tae Canada wi Alison n her man. They sponsored her. Think she's goat a felly now, ah ken she's goat a bairn.

— What aboot Alison?

— Last ah heard she hud three bairns, Roastin Wi Sweat goes n Soaking Wi Rain nods approvingly.

— Aye, jist goes tae show, eh. So what aboot you ladies? Any of youse enjoying that fine institution of motherhood?

— What? Soakin Wi Rain goes.

— Youse goat bairns?

— She's goat two, Roastin Wi Sweat points at Soakin Wi Rain whae glows in a bovine pride.

She's giein me the look like ah'm now supposed tae say 'ye dinnae look auld enough'. — Whaire ur they the night?

— Muh ma's goat thum, she says. Then she screws her face up and goes to her mate, — Watch muh coat, um gaun fir a pish.

As she departs Roastin Wi Sweat turns tae ays n discloses,

— She's up the duff again. It's his, she grasses, pointin ower at this wee guy fae the Young Team, whae isnae that wee. In fact, eh's a monster; shaggy black hair, a white shirt and a bottom drawer ay a chin hingin open tae catch any stray flies. — Big Craig thaire. He screwed her when they wir baith steamin in the perk. That's three bairns wi three different fellays, Roastin shakes her heid in somethin like disgust. — Ah mean, ah want bairns, but wi jist one nice felly, whae wants tae be wi me. She takes a drag oan her fag, and looks around hopefully. — That's no too much tae ask, is it?

Ah'm thinking thit in this place, ye might as well wish fir the fill set ay lottery numbers.

Anyway, the stink ay desperation is social bromide, so ah move oaf patrolling the dance flair in search ay better prospects. Maist huv been sectioned oaf as Young Team property, bit. Every time ah try tae make eye contact wi something decent, a steely glint ay the type usually found sandwiched between two swathes ay Burburry check comes intae view.

Whin ah say thit the fanny isnae bitin, ah mean thit ah could be standin 'starkers' in an Edinburgh sauna wi a wad tied roond the wee fellay and ah'd still be oan a KB.

Ah git a bit humpty and order a lonely pint ay lager at the bar. Then ah hears this voice in muh lug. — Every cunt's entitled tae a wee bit social exclusion, Jason, but there's nae need tae monopolise it. Come and join us.

Ah turns roond tae see yon big Tam Cahill. Eh points ower tae the roped-oaf VIP section whaire some big hitters oan the Central Fife social scene are sittin gathered. Thir's that boy Sammy F Hunter, him that wrote the science-fiction novel aboot the asteroid hittin Fife n nae cunt giein a fuck. That wis years ago, but jist whin ehs star wis oan the wane, along comes yon Hurricane Katrina in New Orleans n they call the cunt a visionary, sayin thit eh predicted exactly the American government's response tae yon crisis! Thir's a big Fife literary presence right enough; if ah'm no mistaken next tae Sammy we've goat the poet Ackey Shaw, reckoned tae be yin ay Jim Leishman's greatest influences. Eh penned the pamphlet 'A Hermless Cunt' which the literary magazine *Chapman* gave positive reviews tae, aye sor.

Ya hoor, once ye go under yon rope ye step intae another world; a veritable galaxy ay champagne ice buckets, sunbed hoors n big deals talked, a wee bit ay Stringfellay's relocated tae Fife Central.

— Jason King. Wur great white hope at the sport ay kings at one time, Cahill addresses the company. — Was formerly signed up to Cliff Redmond's stable in Berkshire, right, Jason?

Ah hate this bit cause ah ey end up huvin tae explain why ah nivir ran, lit alaine won a pro race. What kin ye say whin yir life began at fowerteen n wis ower at eighteen?

— Aye, ah goes.

Fortunately, the onus is taken away fae ays as Tam Cahill turns roond tae Sammy F, n goes, — This man here wis an apprentice jockey n aw.

— Aye? Ah'm surprised, n the sci-fi scribe looks like he is n aw.

Tam pats the boy's ample gut and goes, — An apprentice Jocky Wilson, that is.

Everybody hus a wee laugh, n ah'm thinking that old Tam Cahill isnae such a bad felly eftir aw.

12.

TRADITIONS

I had terrible dreams last night. I curse myself and my stupidity and weakness with that Klepto idiot. I curse Lara, for getting me involved with scum like that. Most of all, I curse him. I won't forget it either; one day, some way, I'll watch the bastard squirm as I kick in his buck teeth.

I go downstairs to get some breakfast. I'm planning to head to the leisure centre for the kick-boxing introduction class. The steps are too boring, and I want to be able to punch and kick hard. It seems to be a required skill in these parts. I'm sitting at the breakfast bar and I start suddenly as I look beyond the partition into the lounge and see a figure rising in the semi-darkness from the settee. I'm about to scream, when I realise it's that creepy wee Jason!

— Eh, hiya . . . he says, rubbing the sleep from his eyes. — Ah met Tam last night . . . we eh . . .

My dad appears in the doorway, trussed loosely in his dressing gown. He rubs at his eyes. — Morning, he says in clipped tones.

— Ah, Tam . . . wis jist telling Jenni here how I was a bit the worse for wear the other night and you played the Good Samaritan and took me back here tae crash on yir couch.

— Aye, my dad says, suddenly becoming animated, — but ma charity isnae boundless, Jason. So once you've hud yir slice ay toast or whatever that garbage is, he looks at my high-fibre cereal, — you can git tae work muckin oot in thon stable. Sweat some ay that bad beer oot ay ye!

— Ah'm oan the case, Tam, he says, rising, — ready for a fill day's shift!

Jason helps himself to some coffee I made, and a couple of slices of toast.

— So, you're going to work in the stable, eh? I ask.

— Aye . . . Tam . . . yir dad, reckons that I've a good wey wi animals. Ah'm cleaning them oot, feeding the hoarses and takin that dug fir walks. Yir faither reckons he needs mair exercise.

This is a double-edged sword. I'm far from happy that I have another weird acquaintance of Lara's hanging about, without me even being consulted as to who looks after Midnight, but I have to say that I'm delighted at all the time this is going to free up for me!

My dad comes back in, with Ambrose on the chain leash.

— Aye, yir a proper Dr Dolittle, Jason. Ah need your skills with animals, son, and he hands poor Ambrose over to him.

— He's a beauty, Jason says, warily taking the leash. He looks shocked at the wounds in the dog's face. — What happened tae ehs coupon?

I'm about to say something, but I stop myself, remembering the tacit pact, of which, I suppose, this Jason is now a part. As my mum and Indigo come through, my father repeats the lie.

— A sair yin, Tam, fir the boy, likes, Jason nods.

Mum picks up her coat and takes Indy out to the car to run her up to school in St Andrew's. I start to head out after them, but I decide to hang around outside the kitchen door.

I hear my father's voice, low, conspiratorial. — Three-quarters pitbull, one-quarter retriever; a killer with intelligence. You huv tae look eftir him while I'm no aboot. Ah dinnae trust the missus, fuckin shite-for-brains, tae dae tae it right, n ah widnae trust him aroond the wee yin.

— What aboot Jenni?

— She's no interested, he scoffs dismissively. — Aw she cares about is that scabby auld hoarse ay hers.

— Eh . . . awright, Tam. Ye mentioned something else last night? this Jason tentatively asks.

— Aye . . . see how ye go wi this yin first, his voice rises, and I can sense he's coming back out, so I head into the hallway and slip out the front door. I see Lara coming by on Scarlet Jester. I'd forgotten that we'd arranged to have a session with Fiona La Rue at the stables. — Hi, Lar! I shout, moving over to her. Jason and my father have appeared on the doorstep behind me and are both waving at us or should I say her, then they look at each other, each of them suddenly seeming uncomfortable.

— Hi, Jen! Hello, boys, she smiles, getting down from Scarlet Jester and putting him in the stable beside Midnight and Clifford the pony. Curran the pig scuttles to the back of the pen and they all seem pleased to see each other. Except for poor old Ambrose, whom my father ties miserably to the post outside. Then he goes inside and Jason starts cleaning out the stable. Lara and I talk about the forthcoming Hawick show and after a bit we harness up the horses for a light canter across the field, but Midnight is struggling and can barely break out of a walk. I can tell he's distressed as he pulls forward, tearing the reins from my grip, which he never usually does. We decide to stay here and Lara calls Fiona La Rue to reschedule. Midnight and I have to watch Lara and Scarlet Jester flying over the small jumps.

I take him outside the stable, keeping on his halter and bridle, and clip him to the posts with the horse ties. Removing the bridle, saddle and saddle pad, I start to groom him. With the hoof pick that hangs on the post by the ties, I do his soles, one by one, taking special care with that sore front left leg. A heavy snort tells me he's in discomfort, so I leave it. I get the curry-comb and start rubbing in circular motions. He loves this and settles down into a steady rhythmn of breathing, dozing contentedly.

I see Jason come out of the stable, big welly boots covered in horseshit. He looks at me and Midnight and his eyes are bulging out of his head. Then he gives me a strange wave as Lara comes over with Scarlet. — Hello, Jason, she smiles coolly as she dismounts in an easy athletic sweep. — Helping out here?

— Eh, aye. Hiya. Aye, a wee bit ay assistance, he says.

Thankfully, Lara wants to go into town, and we restable the horses and jump into the car. As we depart I look back to see Jason gaping at us open-mouthed and slack-jawed. My dad appears and shouts something at him and he springs to attention.

In the car, I turn to Lara: — It was Monty's dog that did that to Ambrose, wasn't it?

— Yes, but he didn't know it was your dad's dog at the time.

— What difference would that have made?

— Quite a lot, from what I gather. I think he's a bit wary of your dad, Lara says, her eyes wide with excitement, — like he's some kind of gangster.

I roll my eyes in disdain.

Lara seems impressed though. And I recall the satisfying fear that Klepto scumbag displayed when he found out who my father was. — Well, she contends, — it's better than having a doctor as a dad!

But I think some people in this town have overactive imaginations. — He's a boring old haulage contractor, I say dismissively, — and he's too sad and depressing to be scary.

We do a workout at the centre, and then have a coffee. Lara's self-obsession starts to niggle, and I soon find myself wishing

I was alone so I could read the final third of *Reluctant Survivor*. I've got to the bit where the handsome Dr Shaw has kissed Josephine tenderly on the mouth. He becomes aroused by the action, and starts to shower her still body with kisses, eventually performing cunnilingus on her. She wakes up, stunned, shocked and ultimately relieved as an embarrassed Shaw has to tell her everything. It's just getting really good. Instead I have to listen to Lara going on about this Monty, my stomach churning whenever that Klepto creature's name is mentioned. I want to tell her, to tell *somebody*, about that bastard.

When we get back, Lara gets Scarlet and heads off home. Jason's gone and Dad comes out as I'm putting Midnight back in the stable. — Ah want tae see you compete wi that wee yin wi the bools in the mooth. N that hoarse is fit fir the knacker's yerd. Eh huds ye back.

I look at him in an angry panic, thinking about what he did to poor Ambrose. — If you ever hurt Midnight . . .

He extends his palms in a gesture of mock innocence. Ah ah'm sayin is that we need a proper team, nae lame ducks . . . or hoarses. Ah mean, look at ma business. At ma place we're a team. If somebody isnae pillin thir weight, then off they go: right doon the road . . .

— Midnight stays. He'll get stronger, I know it.

— Mibbe, my dad says doubtfully, — but think ay what ah said aboot thon gelding.

13.

EXILE ON HIGH STREET

A fightin dug, ya hoor, that's the furry Fife fashion acces-
sory ah'm draggin aroond wi ays doon Main Street n up
tae the High Street. Ambrose, they call him. N eh's no that
bad once ye git used tae um; thon nippy wee cunts ootside
the chippy gied ays a wide berth whin ah strutted doon the
street wi him on the chain, suren they fuckin did!

Cahill obviously thinks the jockeyin backgroond and the
coort appearance that the Neebour Watson and me hud on
thon hare-coursing rap a couple ay years ago (slipped through
the hoor's fingers as under Scots law ye kin only be prosecuted
for poachin) makes ays a bona fide black-economy man ay
sport. N whae am ah tae disabuse the hoor ay that notion?
Specially whin it's cash in hand fir me oan top ay the giro, jist
fir cleanin oot yon stables n gittin a wee deek at ehs daughter's tight erse as she pits yon big hoarse through ehs paces.
Ah'm waitin fir her tae go ower they wee jumps, but she tells
ehs thit ehs leg still isnae up tae it. Eh's fuckin middle leg surely
is, but. Ah couldnae believe masel the other day. Ah wis muckin
oot in the stable watchin her groomin the cunt whin eh wis
tied up under the canopy. Snooty wee Lara wis gaun ower they
fences fir aw they wir worth n ah wis in stalker heaven.

Then ah sees Jenni rubbin the hoarse's back wi the comb.
This yon black cock starts tae telescope oot ay its sheath;
like yon Darth Vader's light sword, ya hoor. There wis me
standin thair wi a daft wee smile oan ma face tryin tae git

292

some attention, but thir's nae wey a dwarf laddie like me could compete wi thon!

As guid as the stalkin at the Cahill ranch is, ah quite like taking Ambrose oot. The problem is thit walkin the dug stoaps ye fae indulgin in the key pleasures ay the socially marginalised; namely the lunchtime pint ay black gold doon the Goth. But then ah think, one swallay does not a summer fuck up; a quick yin, then wi kin mibbe head doon the coast.

The lads ur aw in, n thir pretty wary ay the dug. N ah'd like tae see Big Monty Fuck come ahead whin ah'm hudin this boy's leash. — S'awright, ah says tae the Neebour Watson, — this boy widnae hurt a fly, eh no, Ambrose? Eh'd take your hee-haws right oaf but, wid eh no though, ya hoor sor!

The Neebour stands back n the Duke's no gittin that loud in the mooth, tell ye that fir nowt.

— See that boy got done the other night there, that Mason felly, Neebour Watson tells ays.

— Whae? the Duke asks, keepin ehs eyes oan Ambrose.

— The table-fitba supremo, Neebour explains, then turns tae me n says, — Jist as well eh overturned yir ban first, Jase.

— Aye, right enough, ah goes, tryin no tae sound too concerned, bit ah feel ma haun tightenin oan the leash ay Ambrose, whae's lyin doon, assumin the pub-dug position.

Neebour's switchin intae sweetie-wife mode as eh cannily regards Ambrose. — Surprised thit Tam Cahill never mentioned it tae ye, neebs, wi you spendin that much time up thair thit yir vernear pert ay the faimlay!

— Specific tasks though, ya hoor, ah swings Ambrose's leash, bit no enough tae disturb the boy oan ehs choke, — animal husbandry. Thir's a wee oinker n a pony n a durty big hoarse wi the sort ay tackle ye neevir see made ower at Central Perk, if yis git ma drift. Gelding though, nae use tae um, but it doesnae look like that fae whaire ah'm standin!

293

Ya dirty big fower-legged long-faced hoarsey bastard that ye are!

— Aye, thir hung awright, they beasts, the Neebour says.

Ah'm tryin tae change the subject here, bit the Iron Duke's oan yin, n eh goes, — Aye, that dirty Mason cunt wis grassed up by a couple ay wee laddies fae the skill. Eh used tae pey thum tae dress up as lassies n then eh'd go and huv a wank ower thum. Apparently some mair came forward eftir the other yins blew the whistle.

— Mingin hoor. The Neebour shakes ehs heid.

— Aye, says the Duke as ah keep ma cooncil, jist like auld Ambrose whae's lyin thair quiet, nostrils gently expanding, making soft wee wheezy noises, almost like a cat purrin, — spun thum this story thit eh hud loast ehs daughter in a car crash n thit they wir the right height n weight n size n could they dae him a favour n dress up like her. Well, the gullible wee bams felt aw sorry for um, n went along wi it. Eh peyed some ay thum n aw, so eh wis at it fir ages! Took photaes n made films tae! Aye, Andy the polis, yon big Hun fae the craft: he telt ays they found tons ay material.

Fuckin hell. Uncle Davie's a grandmaister up thon lodge. He'll surely keep a lid oan it. Faimlay. Surely.

— They types are ey weird though, ah goes, — ah eywis thought thir wis a touch ay the Tam Hamiltons aboot yon yin, ah elaborates, feelin disloyal tae perr Olly, bit wantin tae lit the trail go cauld.

— Dirty bastard, exploitin naieve wee laddies like thon. Ah ken whit ah'd dae wi the hoor, the Duke goes.

— Eh nivir touched thum bit, jist hud a wank ower thum, Neebour sais, turnin tae me wi a big grin splittin ehs coupon.

— Mind you, Jase, what did you huv tae dae fir um tae git that ban overturned fir ye? Your size ah'm bettin ye could've fitted easily intae they lassie's clathes! Did eh huv a wank ower you n aw, ya hoor ye? Eh laughs, but eh's starin at me and the Duke's lookin wi serious intent n aw n ah'm thinkin: muh whole credibility and future in the Kingdom is determined by muh next response. It's like huvin the baw in the shooting area oan the Subbuteo table, the game's tied n thir's jist time fir this yin shot. Stey cool, Jase. — Nowt like that, ah goes. — Ah jist sucked ehs cock, that's aw.

The Duke lits oot a volley ay laughter n Neebour does n aw, then pats ays oan the back n sais, — Ah widnae fuckin well pit it past ye; anything tae git that ban rescinded, eh!

— Ya hoor, ah wish ah'd hud the option ay suckin ehs cock or gittin dragged up, insteed ay haein tae listen tae the hoor gaun oan aboot proceedures and protocol and standards ay behaviour. Wid've been a loat less fuckin demeanin, ah kin tell yis.

Thir cacklin away n ah gits the round in. Bit that wis a narray escape, n ah wis tempted tae make another joke bit it's best no tae owerplay the auld haund. It's time tae look forward wi focus, and the main thing is thit ah've goat that Perthshire cunt Derek Clark in the next round. A hame tie n aw fir the laddie Clark, the venue bein the Salutation Hotel in the Fair City. St Johnstone v the Blue Brazil; mair thin a clash ay two individuals, toons or coonties. Nothin mair thin a desperate battle fir supremacy between two diametrically opposed philosophies ay life!

Bring it oan, ya cunts!

Neebour sterted gaun ower auld times, talking aboot the Horse ay the Year Show at Wembley Arena, when wi baith worked doon thair oan the caterin. — Caroline Johnson oan Accumulator; now there was a filly worth ridin.

Of course, ah'm moved tae reciprocate the inane grin oan the hoor's coupon.

— Accumulator of course, wi bark in unison.

It fair gits me in recall mode. — Ya hoor ye, thaire's me tryin tae dae muh best wi the grub n aw they posh cunts ur giein ays it tight. Ah mean ah ken the Hoarse ay the Year Show's thir big bash n that but thir's nae need tae git as wide as thon. The old colonel boy wi the tash started bellowin at me like eh wis muh auld man n it wis last orders at the Goth, ya hoor ye!

— Aye, some gey nippy fuckers thair, Neebour agrees.

Ah nivir said nowt, ya hoor ye, but ah kin fuckin well tell yis ah wis straight tae that packet ay rat poison thit they'd pit doon in the stockroom, n ah goat chefin fir the Kingdom, did ah no, but.

Couldnae believe the read in the paper the day eftir:

Commander Lionel Considine-Duff, OBE CBE RN (ret) was discovered dead at his home in Belgravia in the early hours of this morning. His maid, who alerted police and ambulance services, found his body when she went to wake him for his morning breakfast. Considine-Duff had been complaining of chest and stomach pains following an enjoyable evening at the Royal Horse of the Year Show at Wembley Arena. Formerly a keen equestrian himself, he retired from political life after having suffered two mild strokes.

Political correspondent Arthur McMillan writes: 'Buffy' Considine-Duff was a knowledgeable, compassionate back-bencher whose distinguished military and sporting careers meant that he was disinclined to climb to the top of politics' greasy pole. Having previously been satiated with the demands of high office and the spotlight, Buffy was happier to stay in the background and serve. A tireless lobbyist for the oil industry, he also strived ceaselessly on behalf of his Wessex constituents. His personal life was colourful. Thrice-divorced Buffy was prone to admitting that the type of filly that gave him most pleasure invariably had four legs. When having quaffed a little too much of his favourite tipple he was prone to loudly exhorting 'two legs bad, four legs good' at anybody from the two-legged variety who incurred his displeasure . . .

N it went oan like that, so it did, ya hoor ye.

Ah sup the last ay the black gold and gie Ambrose a very gentle tug, and low and behold the boy's oan ehs feet n wir oot the door. Goat the hoor eatin oot ay muh hand here!

14.

VET DOBSON

Dobson has just finished another examination of Midnight's leg. The trot was too much for him, now he's hobbling again. I phoned Fiona La Rue who came round straight away, then on her advice, I called Dobson. Now it's not looking good. The vet's face briefly crinkles in distaste as the horse excretes. Clifford the pony brays as Curran the pig (named by my father after the policeman who busted him for drink-driving) headbutts the back of his legs. — Will he be okay for the Hawick competition? I ask, knowing what the answer will be.

He looks sombrely at me, then at my father. — I'm afraid not. Look, Jenni, I'm sorry to say this, the words spill grimly from those rubbery lips in that hangdog face, — but I think we may have to face up to the fact that Midnight's leg makes him unsuitable for showjumping. It's a very high-impact sport, and it's only going to make this weakness worse.

Clifford the pony makes a playful whinny, as if in celebration of the news.

My father has been standing over us; one hand stuffed into a pocket, the other pulling on a cigarette. Rolls of fat hang from his chin. It's as if seeing him from this angle is showing me how much he's aged and I now feel a strange tenderness towards him. Which evaporates instantly when he opens his mouth. — Telt ye, he says, shaking his head knowingly, a sneer cutting his face, igniting his features, pulling them north. — That hoarse is gaun naewhaire but intae Spiller's pet foods.

I swallow hard and look in appeal to Dobson, who shakes his head in disgust. — He's a perfectly healthy horse, Tom, there's absolutely no question of him having to be put down. It's only tendonitis, but he needs much more rest and another course of anti-inflammatories will do wonders. I would say, though, that competition jumping is very unlikely.

— So eh's washed up, that's what yir sayin? My dad looks aggressively at the vet.

— I wouldn't put it like that, Tom, Dobson whines. — He might still be suitable for lighter use; pleasure or trail riding, hunter-jumper, dressage and such. It's just that showjumping is very hard on horses and his leg has a weakness.

My dad flicks the cigarette out of the stable. — Dead wood, that's what I call him. He shakes his head. Midnight looks so depleted, his eyes so sad, I almost want to scream at my father to shut up. — We bought him as a jumper, a *competitor*. Now he's going tae be another parasite whae does nowt but drain resources, he says, pushing his hands into the pockets of his jacket and looking around in contempt.

Who the hell does he think he is? What does he know about horses?

— Midnight's a Cleveland Bay, I protest, — they're really carriage horses, I explain to the old fool as I stroke Midnight's face and whisper calmingly in his ear. My dad and that pig, the one that's supposed to be a companion, they spook him. It's funny, but he's okay around Ambrose the dog.

— Aye? Well, ah'll mibbe buy ye a carriage fir um, he says facetiously, — then ye can dae they horse-drawn tours ay the Beath. That's aboot his dead strength n you might even make some money instead ay spending aw ay mine on lost causes!

I'm outraged at his crassness and selfishness and all I can think to say is, — I didn't ask to be born!

— It's aboot the only thing ye huvnae asked fir, he scoffs.

Dobson the vet looks nervously at us and says, — I think I should be off. And I'm thinking to myself what a fucking good idea that is.

15.

PERTH PACK

Mindful ay the lessons ay previous abuse, ah took it easy in preparation fir the next roond ay the Scoattish. Ah goat a nice bit ay haddock fae Boak's at the Central Perk market: protein, ya hoor. The laddie even dressed it up in breedcrumbs, so ah fried it up at hame, mine in a sanny on Sunblest, Lurpak, pepper n HP, in front ay *Scotland Today*, the auld man, a traditionalist, at the table wi ehs Pot Noodles oan the side, hummin yon 50 Cent's 'What Up Gangsta' under ehs breath.

A double feast n aw, cause later that night Kravy treated ays tae a big curry at the Shimla Palace. The only time ah've been in whin it wisnae thir eat-aw-ye-kin Sunday buffet. Felt like a fuckin sultan whin ah got back hame. Fir synergy purposes, ah hud a guid auld ham shank tae some Asian porn, blawin muh load as the vindaloo still bubbled in ma belly wi the lager. Nae black gold or grinnin Scandinavian sirens wi a curry: a chap needs a sense ay propriety.

The next morning ah'm oan the back ay Kravy's bike n wir tearin through the Beath high street like a thirsty Kelty hoor oaf the backshift wid a six-pack. Wir gauny hit the trail fir Perth n ah feel like tellin the Kravitz laddie tae cool they proverbial jets, but it wid be an exercise in futility. Thankfully, eh does slow doon though, whin eh sees the twa lassies gaun past oan the hoarses.

— Better no spook they gee-gees, eh shouts, or something like thon as eh slows tae a halt beside the lassies.

— Hi, Lara (whae's clad tae chug tae, by the way) shouts at us, — where are you off to?

— Perth, ah goes. — Goat a result. Common sense prevailed at administrative level n ah'm back in the cup. Gaunny progress fir the Kingdom, show thum whaes philosophy ay table fitba will win through in the end. When's yir Borders tourney?

— Thursday, Lara goes.

— Might even take a wee jaunt doon thair oorselves, eh, Kravy, support the lassies, likes, ah ventures. Kravy jist shrugs non-committally. Eywis been a cool yin. Bit ye kin tell thit they dark, broodin looks huv goat the birds' gashes fair waterin. N ah'm thinkin it widnae be a bad result if ah jist left the field clear fir him wi Lara, n concentrated ma efforts oan that wee Jenni Cahill lassie; peach ay an erse oan it! So ah says, — Ye headin doon then, Jenni?

— I'd entered but I've had to scratch. Midnight just isn't ready, she says sadly. — The vet has even said he might not be able to jump in competition again.

— I'm sure he will, Lara smiles.

— Right, Kravy goes, — hud on tight, Jase, you've got a tourney to win, n eh kicks oot n wir tearin up the road n by the time ah'm relaxed enough tae look back the lassies n even the hoarses ur jist dots.

Ya hoor, ah dinnae like aw this swervin in n oot ay traffic oan the motorway! Thir's nowt ye kin say but, ah jist try n think ay the next life, wonderin if thir might be some sortay arrangement whereby Fife becomes the new Sussex, a county ay affluence within the realm and Scots withoot sectarian lean-ings can sing 'God Save the Queen' wi an absence ay irony! N ma dreamin works tae an extent, bit whin wi stoap oaf at the Little Chef for a coffee b/w one ay Mr Kipling's fir the sugar hit, ah'm shakin like a Hill ay Beath hoor thit's been gittin pleasured wi a pneumatic drill insteed ay a vibrator.

— Ye okay, Jase? Kravy asks.

— Nerves, ah tell um, — no through bein oan the bike, ah lie, — ah'm an ex jockey eftir aw, well, trainee, bit it's this forthcomin game wi Clarky. The boy's good, n ah'm feelin the weight ay the coonty's expectations oan they shelpit, roond shoodirs ay mine. Bit the better the stage fright, the better the performance, ya hoor.

Kravy looks deeply intae ma eyes. — You've goat the spirit, the soul n the passion. Eh'll no live wi you, Jase.

— Steady on, ya hoor, ah sais, a bit embarrassed by the emotion oan display in the Little Chef. That's the problem wi we bonnie laddies: cannae trust oorselves around sports. Ah think it wis the great bard Rabbie Burns that once said: 'Cocaine n fitba mak homosexuals ay us aw.' Or mibbe it wis this coonty's ain Ackey Shaw.

Whin we rolls intae the ancient toon ay Perth, the sickenin wealth oan display makes ehs want tae git a squad roond fae Cowden wi a few vans, tae start instigatin oor ain form ay socialist redistribution ay loot. Fuck thon pie-in-the-sky promises the frocked n collared defenders ay the status quo advance (auld Jakey Anstruther excepted): lit's hae it here and noo. But ah huv tae admit thit ah wis partial tae yon Salutation Hotel; mahogany wid everywhaire, as auld skill as a Kelty hoor that utters thon reassuring words 'whin ye talk size in oor game, it's eywis wad rather thin willy'. N ye'd hae tae huv a harder hert thin mine no tae appreciate thon portraits oan the waw ay several recent VIP visitors; Sir Bob Geldof, MPs Boris Johnson and Tommy Sheridan, Clarissa Dickson or whatever ye call thon fat yin that cooks, the yin that didnae die, n Frank Bruno. Nae Jason King yit, bit that yin's impendin, ya hoor; aye, impendin.

N whin wi gits tae the Moncrieffe Suite, where aw the tables ur set up fir this round ay the contest, thir's a buzz ay expectancy in the air. Pure sporting theatre! Ah'm stridin around, sizin up ma fellow gladiators whin ma hert twangs as ah sees the disgruntled collaborator Mossman, well in the Clark camp, rootin fir yon Perth cunt, ya hoor. Fuckin Dunfermline: the capital ay Vichy Fife. As ah head tae the toilet ah'm even treated tae Mossy's wee stage-whisper tae Clarky, intended fir ma ain delicate lugs: — Ah hope ye annihilate that dirty wee jockey.

Ah turn tae Kravy in the bogs as wir sprayin the porcilin wi urine. — Did ye hear that Mossman cunt callin ays a 'dirty wee jockey'? At least some ay us tried tae make wur mark in the world ay sport!

Kravy shakes it oot n zips up. — Ah thoat eh said 'dirty wee jakey', Jase.

— That's awright then, ah goes, thinking again ay wee Jack 'Jakey' Anstruther, n hopin, in spite ay muh Marxist-Leninist leanins, that if thir is a god, then the hoor's a Fifer rather thin a Perth cunt.

Bit fuck divine assistance: that Mossman's ungracious behaviour wis aw the motivation ah needed. Ye could breeng in wi the likes ay him but Clark wis a different matter: the laddie hud some talent. Ma tactics wir tae play the passin game, retain possession, jist keep the Clark fellay away fae the table soas eh couldnae establish any momentum, thus frustratin the hoor. Ah kent the boy hud cavalier tendencies and thit eh goat a bit nippy if eh went too long without gittin a flick.

So ah did jist that; keepin the baw, no in situations ay threat at first, but slowly weavin muh men intae place, n waitin till ah wis in a good position afore any goal attempt. Muh first yin came whin ah deflected a shot oaf his defender (meant, by the way) tae take the lead. The second wis a long-range strike fae the midfield whaire the baw wis jist oan the shootin line n the player trundled intae the net eftir it. Ya beauty! The

Clark felly showed ehs displeasure in thon second concede, knockin ehs goalposts n net aboot, forcin the ref tae huv a wee word.

Ah kept hud ay the baw n ran the clock doon, and it steyed at two-nil.

The cunt nivir even accepted my gracious offer ay a pint ay black gold at the bar eftir. The drink eftir the contest is the symbolic cup ay friendship; even Sir Alex and thon wee fuckin dago cunt'll share a bottle ay rid wine eftir a game, win, lose or draw. Nae time fir thon unsportin behaviour.

16.

GYPSY BOYS

I'm playing Marilyn Manson in my room, thinking about how I can get out of 'supporting' Lara in this Hawick competition. I'm zoning out to 'Better of Two Evils' and I hear a strange whistling then a clearing of a throat, noting that my father has materialised before me. He didn't knock; he just opened the door and came inside. Now he's standing at the bottom of my bed. — Can ah have a wee word?

Try stopping him. — Whatever, I shrug.

He turns down the sound on the stereo and lowers his bulk into my big wicker-basket chair. It creaks under him. In the last week or so, he's talked to me more than he's done in years. Evidently, he now considers me worth saving. Of course, it's what he considers me worth saving *for* that's the big worry. However, I cross my legs and make a passable stab at being all ears.

— Ah'm hard on you, he concedes, then adds with a surprising degree of conviction, — but it's only cause ah dinnae want tae see ye waste yir life.

— It's my life, is all I can think to say in retort.

— Dinnae gie me that, he says gravely, as if he expects more understanding. — I'm hard on you, only because ah ken you've got what it takes.

In spite of myself I feel the nauseating elation of his flattery rising up through my frustration. At least in his own inept way he's trying. — I'm not a showjumper, Dad, I tell him, the words almost choking in my throat. — You can get me the best horse in the world and I'll never be as good as the likes of Lara.

— Aye ye will, my father retorts with a calm, empathic certainty that annoys me. — Ah've been watchin you lately, the way you've slimmed doon. The weight's been fawing off ye!

— I don't want to talk about it –

— Your mother goes on about anorexia and all that pish. That's jealousy talking, that's aw that is. She couldnae pass the confectionary coonter in that newsagent, and ah've seen her, at thon supermarket checkoot, he says in a derisory manner, — crammin they chocolates intae her puss, never able tae git enough, like some demented junkie. It's sickening. That's somebody that's no right in the heid, that!

It's his *wife* he's talking about. But he's right. He is so fucking *right*. — Dad –

— Ah ken that you're different, Jenni. Ah know that ye go tae that leisure centre regularly and work oot.

A spark of pique ignites in me. — Is nothing fucking private in this fucking place?

— Hey! Mind the language! He pouts, then says in placating tones, — I'm no criticisin ye. It isnae meant tae be a *criticism*. Ah think it's great. N it shows you've got discipline and pride. Cause you've got *me* in ye, his weather-beaten, leathery face crinkles. — You're a Cahill, he boasts proudly. — Yir always welcome tae use my gym, you ken that though, eh?

My stomach is churning. Observing my dad trying to be nice is much more disturbing than watching him being obnoxious. He just isn't cut out for it.

— You've got to think of your future, Jen. If you don't think you're gaunnae do it in showjumping, then you could do worse than learn the ropes ay the haulage business.

What a truly fucking sickening thought. — I doubt that it would be my thing, I quickly respond.

He laughs derisively and lights a cigarette, ignoring the No Smoking signs I've put around the room. The big pub ashtray is under the bed, where it'll stay. I'll not have him smoking filthy minging tobacco in my room. — Too common for ye, is it? Aw they nasty trucks n sweaty drivers? Dinnae forget that it was that business that put food on your plate and fed that useless four-legged parasite in that stable doonstairs. Aw they trips abroad, aw they tourneys, aw that equipment, aw this land. Ah dinnae see ye turning yir beak up at that! Ah blame masel fir spoilin —

He stops mid rant, seeming to see what he's doing. — Thanks, I say.

— For what?

— For reverting to type. You actually were starting to sound like a decent human being for a second or two there.

— You . . . look, he says, fighting down his exasperation, as he stands and looks around for an ashtray. He gestures towards one of my plants and I shoot him a look that says 'don't even think about it'. He moves to the window, takes two quick puffs and flicks the cigarette outside. — Dinnae be like that. C'mon. Gie it a try. At least come in wi me and see how the business works.

— I'll consider it, I tell him, basically just to get him to go.

— That's ma girl, he says encouragingly. I lean over to the stereo and turn up my music and he takes the hint and leaves, screwing up his face and putting his fingers to his ears.

17.

BIKE CRASH

So wir comin tae the outskirts ay the toon, and ah'm think-ing again, thank fuck we've made it, that Kravy cunt is fuckin fearless, weavin in n oot ay traffic, aw they fuckin lanes, like we were icons oan a PS 2 game, but now Cooden is in sight! Wur tearin roond the bend at high speed . . . but then wir gaun naewhaire . . .

. . . ah'm oaf the bike n ah'm sortay flutterin through the air like a butterfly, n ah seem tae be gaun that slow that whin ah come tae rest it'll be like oan this bed ah pillays but then ah feel this impact, it's like an explosion but yin comin fae *inside* ay ma boady! Then, for a bit, thir's a strange peace. It's like huvin aw the rest ah've ever been promised, before ah n git woke by a rustlin sound aw ower n aroond ays. Eftir a bit ah realise thit ah'm lyin stuck in the branches ay a tree.

Ah look doon n thair's Kravy sitting up, but slumped forward at the bottom ay this big oak tree next tae mine, like ehs huvin a wee nap. Thir's like this big streak ah dark rid paint runnin up the tree above him. It looks fresh. Ah cannae see whaire it's come fae. Ah hear a craw screechin. Then ah see where the stuff oan the tree's come fae, Kravy's neck. Cause thir's jist a rid stump wi a bit ay bone in it comin oot ay the boy's shoodirs. Cause the hoor's heid's missin.

Fuckin

Eftir checkin baws, eyes, airms, legs n that order, n aye, thir aw thair, ah starts tae climb doon. Muh hands are tearin and bleedin oan the branch n the foliage but it disnae bother ays as ah feel fuckin weird: sortay numbed and wired at the same time. Ah gits tae the bottom ay the tree tae git a right look at Kravy. Ah moves closer.

Aw ya hoor, aye, ah wisnae seein things.

Eh's nae fuckin heid.

Thir's jist a stump ay neck, ah kin see the spine, it's been severed cleanly like by a fuckin guillotine, blood still bubblin fae it, pumpin up oot ay the body which is twitchin away like eh's comin up oan a pill. It's still like eh's muckin aboot, playin some sort ay daft trick, n ah'm looking around fir the heid, expectin tae see it wi a big grin. Thir's nowt but, Kravy's gone.

Ah feel rain droplets hittin my heid n shoodirs, n ah look up. Yin lands rid oan muh white T-shirt. It's Kravy's blood, sprayed up intae the leaves n branches ay the tree, now droapin back doon oan ays.

Turnin roond n lookin up the bankin, pittin ma hand ower muh eyes tae keep the sun n blood oot ay thum, ah see the bike lyin oan the road where it skyted ower. A car's stoaped and cause ah'm covered wi Kravy's blood this auld boy in a checked jaykit's goat oot n eh's shoutin at ays, sayin, — Ur ye hurt?

— Naw, ah'm awright, ah shouts back.

— But you're covered wi blood!

Ah start tae laugh at that. — Aye, ah say, for some reason thinking ay the lassies Soakin Wi Rain n Roastin Wi Sweat. Ah could be the felly fir the threesome wi thaime, right enough. — Ah'm Covered Wi Blood, ah admit, lookin at the claret oan my ripped airms n no really kennin or carin whether it's mine or muh boy's. — But muh mate . . . eh's loast ehs heid.

— It's easily done, the speed those things can get up to, the auld boy goes. — It's so dangerous driving a motorbike. Was he on drugs?

— Jist a wee bit ay tarry n a pint at the Sally up in Perth, ah say as the boy moves ower tae the verge. Eh sees Kravy's body and goes, — Oh my God . . . it's a real person, his head's missing . . . oh my God . . . n eh starts tae boak n lurches back tae the motor. Then eh's straight on the mobby.

Aw ah kin think ay is ehs ma in the hoaspital, n for some reason her gash that Kravy came ootay aw they years ago, so cruelly exposed by the Young Team oan thon Blue Brazil website.

N ah kin see whit's happened, ya hoor; the sharp edge ay that road sign thit says 'REDUCE SPEED NOW' hus been bent ower, by some Young Team vandal, nae doots, n Kravy's come oaf the bike at speed wi me n ehs heid's been in line wi it .

Aw naw.

The sign has an edge ay rid blood oan yin side, specklin oot across it. Like a fuckin guillotine; Central Fife, totally fuckin medieval, ya hoor.

But whaire's ma boy's heid?

Ah dives right intae the thick bushes and rows ay nettles, lookin for the heid, it's still gaunny be in the crash helmet, it'll no huv gone far, surely. Then ah hears the cloppin ay hoof oan the road n voices n the auld boy's sayin, — Don't look, girls, come away . . .

N ah hears Jenni, — But it's our friend . . . then she shouts, — Jason! Are you okay!

— Please, stay back, there's been a terrible accident! the old felly says.

Ah'm waist-high in jaggy nettles but turns n looks up n ah sees Lara's hudin back, looking aw shocked but Jenni's comin forward. — JASON!

Ah goes, — Aye, ya hoor, ah'm awright, bit ah cannae find ma mate's fuckin heid, eh no.

So ah'm still rummagin aroond in the big forest ay jaggy nettles lookin fir Kravy's heid in the rid helmet, but ah feel muh legs gaun n ah try tae squat doon for a bit, jist like, tae rest fir a bit, but ah feel ma stomach risin up n me cowpin forward, n when ah wake up ah'm in the fuckin hoaspital, ya hoor!

18.

HEAD

His friend was so good-looking; the beautiful boy who left this town on his motorcycle and made a new life in Spain. I had visions, dreams, of him taking me there with him, on the back of it, or anywhere away from here.

But to my great surprise I'm relieved that Jason's alright; that it's his friend who's gone and not him. — I'm going to go and visit Jason up at the hospital, I say absent-mindedly, as I load some crockery into the dishwasher, first pushing Indy out the way to get the door open, as she's slumped over the worktop, reading a comic.

— That ham shanker. It would have been better off if he'd went the same wey as his daft mate, my dad moans, as he spreads himself some peanut butter on his oatcakes.

I don't rise to his bait, but then my mother, who is sitting at the kitchen table doing her nails, chips in. — He has a family and friends of his own, Jenni. You have to wise up to people like that. They do tend to take advantage. They just can't help themselves.

— Like Dad did with you, I respond.

— No! You don't know what you're talking about – she trills as I head out towards the door, then screeches in panic, — Come back here when I'm talking to you!

I laugh loudly, continuing my exit. — Under no circumstances. You're so inherently trivial and inconsequential!

— What does inconsequential mean? Indigo asks, looking

up from the comic. She's now sprawled right across the worktop, like a cat.

— It doesn't mean anything, my mother shrieks. — It means that Jennifer thinks that she knows best, as usual! And you: get down from there and sit on the chair!

I hear Indy saying something under her breath as I depart, then voices getting raised. I enjoy a buzz of gleeful satisfaction, happy that I've wound them all up. Outside, it's a miserable day, dirty rain falling in sheets and you can feel the bronchitis incubating in your chest. So I drive up to the hospital in Dunfermline, where I went with Jason when he was admitted yesterday. When I get onto the ward there are screens around his bed. I feel panic rising inside of me, envisaging him fighting for his life, but they're suddenly whipped open as a red-headed nurse appears. As she removes Jason's bedpan I catch his bulging eyes ogling her.

He registers me and breaks into a big, if slightly guilty smile.

— Jenni!

— Hello, Jason, I grin back. He doesn't look too bad, apart from one side of his face, which has come up in big, blotchy white spots where he collapsed and fell into the stinging nettles.

— Sit yirsel doon, he urges. — Heather wis jist seein tae muh, eh, pressin needs, if ye ken whit ah mean.

— How are you? I ask, looking at the steady beam that ignites Nurse Heather's face as she goes about her duties.

— Ah'm brand new, but thuv telt ays tae keep still till they git the rest ay they X-rays back. Aye, Heather, fae Tayport, he says as the nurse smiles thinly at me and departs with the bedpan, Jason's offerings covered by a paper towel.

I sit down in one of two hard red plastic visitors' chairs. Jason's locker is stocked with Irn-Bru and grapes. He seems better than when they brought him in yesterday, a lot more settled. He thought he'd fractured his arm, but the X-rays revealed that it was just bad bruising. He had some lacerations on his back that needed stitches, but it was a really remarkable escape. — I can't imagine what it must be like, I'm asking him, — to survive when your friend dies . . . tell me again *exactly* what happened.

— Ah appreciate ye comin, Jenni, he says, — but ah'm no gaun through aw thon again, ah telt ye it aw last night.

— Of course, of course, I nod sternly. — You have to rest, it must have been a terrible shock, I appreciate, looking at his big, confused eyes. — Still no word about his head?

Jason suddenly slaps his own forehead with his good arm, and seems in real distress about this. — Nup, thuv hud Fife's finest oot aw night n aw mornin combin the area n thuv still found zilch. Ah cannac believe it; it's in a rid crash helmet, for fuck's sake!

There's something that's so wonderful, magnificent and *symbolic* . . . about such a death. It excites me. — I *love* the idea of his beautiful head, like that of a disembodied angel, floating around looking down on us all. That perfect, wonderful face that won't age or be corrupted by life; he'll stay as beautiful as Kurt, Princess Di and Jimmy Dean, forever young!

But this thought doesn't seem to console poor Jason, who is so upset. — Aye, but ehs ma's a green grape n shi's wantin a fuckin open-casket joab! So ah've got tae find that heid. If the fuckin bizzies cannae dae it, n ah hae ma doots aboot Fife Constabulary's commitment tae this case, then ah'll need tae get oot thair masel!

— You can't, Jason, you have to rest, I urge.

— Aye, ye talk aboot ehs beautiful heid, but it'll no be that beautiful once the craws n rats n worms git a haud ay it, he says in horror. And it *is* such a terrible thought. — Yuv goat tae help ays, Jenni, ye huv tae dae me a big favour, he begs.

I'm looking into those crazed eyes, which remind me of the

fighting dogs back in the barn, and I feel that I can't really refuse. — What?

— Go tae ma hoose n tell muh auld boy that ah need some clathes. Then bring thum back here fir ays.

I know where his house is, from when I dropped him off when he was wearing the sort of clothes I don't think he'd appreciate me getting him now. He tells me the exact address again. — Okay, but on one condition, I tell him, — I come with you and help you find the head.

It takes him all of two seconds to agree to this. — And see if ye kin git hud ay a pair ay gairdin shears.

— That shouldn't be a problem. But why?

— They jaggy nettles ur fuckin gittin it, he says angrily, fingering his lumpy face.

I prepare to depart, and feel moved to give him a chaste kiss on his sweaty brow. Just then, a painfully thin woman with made-up eyes and long, brown hair, comes hobbling in on a walking frame. — Mrs Forsyth . . . Frances . . . Jason says sorrowfully.

She moves over to the bottom of his bed. She looks at me, then at him, and then bites her lower lip for a bit. Then she speaks in a slow, sad voice. — This coonty took muh son, Jason. It took muh laddie. Ah ask masel, why did eh come back, whin thir wis nowt fir um here . . . ?

— Eh jist wanted tae be wi ye whin yir wirnae well, Jason says sadly.

— Aye, that's what ah thoat. So it wis ma fault. Ah kilt um! Muh ain flesh n blood, and she looks from Jason to me.

— Naw . . . ye cannae say that, Jason gasps. — You ken Kravy, ehs a free spirit. Naebody ever telt him tae dae anything eh didnae want tae dae. If anything it wis ma fault, fir littin um run ays up tae Perth fir that daft table-fitba game. Ah should've goat the train or bus!

The woman, Mrs Forsyth, looks so spectral, as if she's just emerged from a three-thousand-year entombment. — They said eh hit a road sign that wis buckled, she sadly muses, — bent back by human hand, she almost howls, the lips in her ash-grey face trembling.

I feel moved to say something, so I cut in. — The kids do that. Vandalism. They twist the road signs.

— This horrible coonty swallowed up ma bairn, she cries in pain, then turns her walking frame and starts moving away. She twists her head round, — Get oot ay here, Jason, you n aw, hen: git oot while ye still kin.

— Mrs F, Jason pleads, — lit me dae one thing fir Kravy . . . n fir you n aw.

She stops and turns at an angle, so she can bend round to see him.

— Ally's funeral. Eh wisnae intae aw that Christian shi— nae offence. Aw ah ask, is let me organise a send-off the boy wid be proud ay.

— Dae it, son. Any kind ay service ye want. Aw ah want is tae see um onc mair time, in an open coffin.

— But Mrs F . . . Jason begs.

But she's manoeuvred her frame round, and she's off.

As she departs, Jason says to me, — Ah've been thinkin aboot that fir ages. Gittin oot ay here, ah mean. In fact, that's jist aboot aw ah think aboot.

— It's all anybody thinks about, I tell him. — That was his mother? Ally Kravitz's mum?

— Aye.

— What a terrible way to lose your own flesh and blood. Something you've grown inside you . . .

— Aye, perr hoor's hud nae luck at aw, Jason observes, and he now seems tired as he stares off into the distance. — First her man Coco Forsyth cashes in ehs chips, then she's caught

compromised oan the steps ay the Welfare, and now this . . .
He suddenly stares intently at me. — I need one mair favour.

— What?

— Ye ken yon auld boy that sits oan the bench ootside the
sports centre?

— The tramp? That disgusting old man?

Jason seems a bit upset at my description of this down-and-
out. — That's the boy, he says glumly.

The nurse enters to check his charts and Jason lowers his
voice, forcing me to move in closer. He smells of a sweet, fresh
perspiration, almost like girls' toiletries. And he tells me what
he wants me to do.

— You can't be serious, I gasp.

— Nivir mair, he says earnestly.

When I get home I check on Midnight in the stable. A sinking
feeling hits me as I can sense that something isn't right. The
stable door is open. A wave of panic moves through me. I go
in and for less than a second I'm relieved, as he's in the stable,
but he's lying down, on his side. Something horrible rises in
me. I fall onto my knees and burst into tears. His breathing is
shallow and he's making a horrible dry wheeze.

The feed hatch has been left open.

I run into the house and scream at my mother to call the
vet. Indigo comes running back out with me to the stable.
Dobson soon comes by, but by the time he does Midnight's
gone. I hold Indigo in my arms, we're both in tears. Clifford
the pony sniffs at Midnight's body, then lets out a distressed
bray. After examining him, Dobson puts his hand on my shoulder. — It looks like extreme colic; he's eaten himself to death.

A car pulls up and my father gets out and comes across to
the stable. He puts on an expression of contrived shock and I
can't look at him. — I'm sorry, hen, he says.

— Keep the fuck away from me, I snap, pushing him in the chest. — You did this! You wanted Midnight dead! I'll never ride another fucking horse as long as I live!

— But, princess . . .

He's giving me Indy's title now, he hasn't called me that in years, probably since I had a period. — Do fuck off! I storm away and head to my car.

— Go then, my dad shouts, — go away and greet like a daft wee lassie tae that dippit boyfriend! If you'd let me pit him in La Rue's stables where he could have been looked after this would never have happened!

As I head to the car I can hear Indigo bursting into tears and my father comforting her. — It's okay, hen, it was an accident. There, there. He's at peace now.

I drive off and I'm crying and laughing at the same time. I think about Jason; how if he'd been there he would have noticed that my dad or somebody had left the feed hatch open. After a while I just seem to find myself in the B&Q garden centre, looking at shears, thinking about the damage you could inflict on somebody with them.

I have a coffee at the new Starbucks as darkness falls. I get into the car and I drive into Cowdenbeath. I'm thinking of my dad, a man who loves himself, but who's a parochial failure, never leaving this place, never really testing what he's got inside; just content to lord it over the people he works and drinks with. Or the uptight Dr Grant with his practice on the hill, like his father, the one who sent all the silicosis-ridden miners back down the pit to dig up more coal as they coughed up their lungs. Then there's snotty Fiona La Rue: all those so-called successful people in this town; as beaten and insignificant as the supposed plebs they despise.

I feel a burning rage against everything and everyone in this world, and somebody's going to pay. I realise that I'm carrying the shears with me. And there he is, right by the leisure centre, still barely compos mentis. That disgusting, foul old tramp.

I'm breathing heavily with the horror of what I just had to do, when I get to Jason's house, right behind the railway station. I ring the bell and his father comes to the door. That terrible mark on the side of his face: I can't help but stare for a second.
— Aye?
— I'm Jenni, I gasp. — I'm a friend of Jason's. I was here before.
— Aye, ah mind.
— He said I was to come and take some clothes into the hospital for him. They said he can wear his own clothes.
He looks doubtfully at me for a second, — You his official fashion consultant? Cause yir no daein much ay a job.
— No, I start, — I'm only trying to help.
Mr King graces me a sympathetic nod. — Okay, hen, ye'd better come in. Ah've no long done a washin.
I follow him inside and through to the kitchen, where he starts laying out some clothes: jeans, T-shirt, jumper, socks, underpants. — Right, thanks, I say, as he puts them into a plastic Co-op bag.
— Ah think ehs shoes are still in the hospital, but thir's trainers here onywey, he says. — Tell him I'll be in the morn tae see him.
— Righto, thank you, Mr King.
Jason's father is very chatty, but he's quite eccentric and has some strange ideas. He tells me that he has 'irrefutable evidence' that the council had got a team of trained cats to rip open bin liners so that they could introduce wheelie bins to the area. Apparently a contractor who manufactures them is a business partner with a prominent local councillor. — It's

aw profit n personal gain. Ah'm gonnae write tae Gordon Broon, ya hoor. If wi still hud the likes ay Willie Gallagher in Parliament n Auld Bob Selkirk up the toon hall . . .

Midnight's gone.

Midnight was all that was keeping me here. I can see that with him around I would never leave. My father . . . he did me a fucking favour! He set me free!

. . . so if ah wis any young person, n ah keep sayin that tae oor Jason, ah'd git right oot ay here. It's no a place fir the young. No now. As 50 Cent said: Git rich or die tryin. What huv they goat tae keep thum occupied here but mischief?

— Yes. I think you're right, Mr King, I struggle to break him off, making my apologies.

I get into the car and drive back out to Dunfermline and the hospital. Back on the ward, the visiting period is just about over as I hand the bag to Jason.

— What took ye? he snaps.

I look tearfully at him. — It's Midnight, he's dead. Somebody left the feed hatch open. It should never have happened. We all knew he was prone to gluttony with feed . . .

— Aw naw . . . ah'm sorry . . . he says.

— If one of us had been there we could have saved him. It takes a long time for a horse to die of colic. I should have checked on him! I as good as killed him!

— Naw, Jenni, it wis probably jist an accident . . .

— My father said that he should have been in La Rue's stables where they would have regularly monitored him! He was right. I fight against a sob. — I'm just a selfish, spoiled brat; insisting I had my own horse at home! I fucked up. I failed to look after him like I've failed at everything else!

— Naw, Jenni . . .

— It was my father that did it; I know it was! He killed Midders to replace him with a stronger horse so that I could compete with Lara. I now let the tears come. — I used to have a silly dream, Jason . . . I hear myself ranting, — I dreamt about riding Midnight out of Cowdenbeath for good . . . right away from this place . . .

— Aye . . . riding fantasies . . . Jason says, his mouth hanging open. — I'm sorry, he goes, and he looks so distraught. — Ah blame masel, ah mean, if ah hudnae been in here he'd huv been looked eftir.

— No, it was him, that bastard. Indigo's pony was fine!

Jason gets out of bed and moves over to me in his striped pyjamas. He puts an arm round my shoulder, then steps closer and he hugs me for a bit. It feels good. He smells nice. I could stay like this forever. Then he pulls apart and looks around and whispers urgently, — We'd better nash, visitin time's up.

He tells me to keep a lookout, as he gets dressed. I comply, but I have a strange and strong urge, which I resist, to turn round and watch him changing.

Oh, Midnight. This fucking place! I'm getting out of here! For good.

— C'mon, he whispers, and we creep along the hospital corridors. As we go outside an orderly approaches and at first I think he's going to stop us, but he merely asks for a light. Jason hastily obliges and we head out and across the car park into the motor.

We drive back into Cowdenbeath and through the town and back out to the bend in the Perth Road. I pull the car into a gravelly lay-by beside the turn and climb out. I get the torch I keep in the breakdown kit in the car boot. We vault the crash barrier, Jason with a wince as he put the weight on his bad arm, and I shine the light into the nettle bush. There's nothing visible for yards and yards besides these big plants, some of them shoulder-high to us both. As we start to push through them, I realise too late that their foliage has concealed the fact that they're on a slope and I feel myself being propelled forward and I grab out at Jason. Then I scream as I think that we're both going to fall, but he steadies us. — Fuck! he snaps. — Muh fuckin airm!

— I'm so sorry, I forgot, I gasp, my breath steadying.

— Slow . . . he pleads, as he swings the shears and starts chopping through the nettles. He's panting and sweating as he hacks deeper into the growth. The moon casts a silvery light over the fallen plants who lie like stricken soldiers on a battle-field. — There! he shouts, as my beam illuminates something red.

Then his face suddenly creases up in anger. His boot swings at the object, launching a traffic cone into the air, which flies a few yards, landing deeper into the back rows of the nettles.

We plough on for what seems like ages, but uncover nothing. I've been stung in the hands and ankles through my gloves and socks and I detest nettle stings from my childhood. In the numbing cold a despair almost overwhelming at the futility of it all sets in, and I'm about to suggest packing up and trying again in the morning, when something reflects off the torch beam.

There it is: the back of the red helmet.

And we know what's on the other side. — Look, Jason, I urge, but I don't really need to bother. He's seen it and I swear that his eyes could light up this wasteland.

Jason looks at it in a powerful reverence, then bends down and slowly picks it up. — It's heavy, it's . . .

He turns it round. I shine the torch into it. The face is white and blue around the lips and eyes. He rubs some leaves and dirt from it. It hasn't been eaten though; it's still recognisable as Ally Kravitz. — Sorry, mate, Jason says, and cradles it to his chest.

I see what look like drops of rice falling from the bottom

of the helmet, onto the ground. I shine my torch and see them wriggling under its beam. — Jason!

He turns the helmet over and the red-bloodied stump is crawling with maggots. —Ya fuckin . . . ya fuckin hoors! Jason wipes them off with his bare hands, then hugs the helmeted head again. — Ah'll no let these cunts get ye, mate, ah'll fuckin no, he sobs, tears splashing from his big eyes onto the top of the red crash helmet. After a passage of time he looks at me miserably, and nods, then he puts the head into a bin liner.

— Let me see him again, I beg.

— Naw, Jason says, tears streaming down his face, — naebody's seein um. Ah dinnae care what they dae wi the rest ay um, but this heid's gaun back tae Spain, wi me!

I put my arm around his shoulder as he sobs heavily, keeping his grip on the bin liner. I realise that I'm crying too, thinking of my beautiful horse.

19.

FUNERAL

Sunday ah felt it aw comin oot; the aches, pains, nettle stings
n the dirty black depression. That wis the worst of aw: like
yir giein some invisible fat cunt a collie-buckie. The auld boy
goat a prawn vindaloo takeoot fae the Shimla as a treat, but
muh hert wisnae in it. Ah brightened up a bit when yon wee
Jenni Cahill came roond, even if she kept askin ays whit ah'd
done wi Kravy's heid. Ah kept ma cooncil, ya hoor, but it wis
hard as she's a persistent yin. Whin she left ah wis even too
doon and exhausted tae entertain masturbatory thoughts, n her
wi that scarlet-rid lipstick oan n aw. The only thing thit cheered
ays up wis the browse through Central Perk merkit, n the big
styrofoam boax fir keeping beer n sandwiches thit ah picked
up at the stall.

— Be good fir the summer, fir picnics, Mrs McPake fae oor
wey said tae ays as ah went doon the road wi the hoor.

— Aw aye, ah nodded.

Monday ah felt better. Ah hud tae: thir wis Kravy's funeral
tae organise. Jenni let ays yaze her computer tae send emails
tae Kravy's mates in Spain. Ah found some addresses in this
book eh'd left at ehs ma's hoose. Ah didnae think they'd make
it at such short notice, but they hud the right tae ken. It took
ays a while tae git the two grams ay coke n the big lump ay
base that ah needed for wur boy's gig. Hud tae go ower tae
the city, the fuckin loat. Ah dinnae like gaun ower the brig at
aw. The city's fine but as soon as ye leave the centre in search

ay collies it's a different place aw thegither; fill ay psychos whae kin smell the fuckin coonty offay ye fae fifty yerds.

A joab well done, but. So Tuesday morning saw the funeral take place at Kirkcaldy Crematorium. Ehs ma wanted the Dunfermline Crematorium, same 310 quid tae the council hoors, and easier tae git back tae the reception at the Welfare, but ah talked her intae Kirkcaldy. Ah couldnae huv lived wi masel if the laddie hud been sent off oan Vichy soil.

It wis a weel-attended do, right enough, ya hoor sor. Kravy might huv turned ays back oan the Beath but the Beath nivir turned its back oan him. Besides, naebody likes tae see a young cunt die. Nae Spaniards made it ower, but thir wis stacks ay wreaths sent through Interflora n loads ay touchin messages oan Jenni's email, which she goat printed oaf n stuck in a folder wi a big Spanish n Scottish flag oan the front, which she then presented tae ehs ma. Ah huv tae hand it tae wee Jenni, she played a blinder. She wisnae pleased at aw at huvin tae approach Jakey Anstruther, especially wi upset aboot her perr hoarse huvin jist kicked it, but she helped ays git the auld minister oanside.

The boy's sermon wis the undoubted highlight ay proceedins. Ah hud tae git um a wee bit tanked up first, but no sae much that eh widnae be able tae perform. Whin eh staggered up tae the lectern at the chapel ay rest, ah feared the worst. — Hullo . . . eh slurred. — Gid tae see yis aw . . . one or two auld friends . . . n some strangers . . .

Thir wis a deathly silence. Kravy's ma looked at ays fir a second or two. She wis still nipped that the heid hudnae been recovered, so thir could be nae open-casket viewin. Hud tae keep it fae her; couldnae lit the woman see the maggots eatin intae um. Jakey, though, soon started tae find ehs stride.

— The aulder yin gits the less yin is taken by aw this churchy shite. It's aw driven by fear; thon fear that wuv no been guid enough tae git selected fir the trophy-winnin team n need tae stey in a satanic version ay this doss. But Ally Kravitz wis nivir plagued by they fears. They cried him a free spirit, but what in the name ay sufferin fuck is that? Ah cry him a Fife spirit, eh bellows, now it's like the auld felly's never been away fae the pulpit. Ah saw a tear run doon Mrs F's cheek at that yin.

The nods ay approval ur enough tae send Jakey intae oratory hyperdrive. — Think aboot this coonty, a place what gied the world capitalism, and yit wis one ay the first places tae realise thit capitalism wis shite and steadfastly opposed it. For mair thin any ay they Weedgie chancers wi thir Paddy-teuchter pish, or they snobby English connivin Embra hoors, this coonty is a microcosm ay the true spirit ay Scotland. N Allister Kravitz, a bold, internationalist laddie ay passion n soul, wis, ah'll declare, a microcosm ay this damned coonty, a place thit yit might huv the key tae baith global and national salvation within its borders!

Kravy's ma is smiling through her tears and the place is now a furnace ay emotion. — Ah want yis now tae pray fir the soul ay Ally Kravitz, *especially* if ye urnae given tae prayer. Cause *ma* God might jist listen tae ye! *Ma* God will be seek tae fuck ay hearin the same voices; askin um fir a new car or hoose or speedboat, or tae endorse another fuckin barbaric war fir eyl!

Thir's a huge cheer echoes round the chapel ay rest. Even the Iron Duke's goat a tear n ehs eye, ah swear tae fuck. Ah cannae see Call-Centre Comorton, but it's ma belief thit the revisionist wee Tory cunt is hudin ehs dippit heid lower thin a snake's erse right now. Jakey's still daein ehs nut n aw. — Ma God wants a bit ay a fuckin change, n eh wants tae hear fae somebody whae wants nowt in return except they wee things wi cry liberty, justice n equality! eh roars, then wheezes a bit, takin a swig ay Buckie tae calm um doon. — Jesus fuck almighty, eh smiles, — ah'd forgotten how guid it wis tae be up oan this pulpit wi a fuzzy heid fae the night afore n bolstered by a few drams ay the Deevil's elixir. It's in this state – jist a baw hair fae demonic possession – that ah feel closest tae Oor Saviour, n ah'm talking aboot God, no that wanker Jesus fuckin-erse Christ. N as a last broadside against they snooty cunts doon in George Street, ah'd like tae thank Jason here, fir giein ays the opportunity tae stand n dae this at a Fife pulpit in honour ay yin ay its finest sons, Allister Graham Kravitz. Ay-fuckin-men, ya hoor, sor.

N eh steps doon tae a massive applause and a standin ovation that goes oan till eh left the chapel, as the coffin went doon.

Ootside, it's me n Kravy's ma sayin thanks tae the mourn-ers. — It wis Jason, ah hear her say tae muh auld man, — he wis the one that made the whole thing special.

It's back tae the Miners' Welfare fir the do eftir; sausage rolls, egg n cress, fancy cakes, tea, whisky, the fuckin loat, wi pit oan a guid spread. The wee collections in the toon's boozers peyed fir it aw. Jakey is in ehs element; people ur plyin um wi drink, telling um tae stert ehs ain church; a real Church ay Scotland. N it hus tae be said, eh's scrubbed up well fir the do. Thir's nae whiff oaf ay um but wino n eftirshave. Ah wrap an airm roond ehs auld shoodir. — Ye took the words oot ay muh mouth, ah telt him. How dae ye follay thon?

Jakey winks at ehs. — The laddie might huv been a fickle, drug-dealin hoormaister, but, n here's whaire it gits crucial . . .

Ah join in chorus: — Eh wis *oor* fickle, drug-dealin hoor-maister!

Jakey laughs n ah pat um oan the back again. — Whit ye gaunny dae, Jack? Ye canny sit oan that bench the rest ay yir days.

Eh gies a wee shrug. — No that bad a place tae be, Jason. Still goat the C of S pension. Huv tae confess thit since ay loast yon tenure ay the Manse things huv been a bit slack.

— That wis ower ten years ago, ya hoor.

— Eleven n three months, son, and it's flown like a hoor's bloomers off a washin line in March. But what can ye dae against the Calvinist repression ay the Kirk?

— It wid huv helped if ye believed in Jesus Christ, though, Jack. They wir bound tae git upset wi that.

— Nonsense! Very few ministers, when ye get them on thir ain, will admit tae believing aw that Christ-wis-the-son-ay-God garbage, eh snaps in scorn. — Wi aw huv tae go along wi this Hans Christian Andersen-Lewis Carroll shite world view tae appease the brainless elements, but maist ay us are educated enough tae ken that's jist wee bairns' nonsense. Besides, it wis the hoorin thit finished wi me n the Church, no a disbelief in some moanin-faced auld hippy!

Ya hoor, ah wis nearly compelled tae rise tae Cat Stevens' defence thair, till ah realised eh wis talking aboot that other cunt. Ah wis intrigued tae ken a bit mair, but eh wis gittin loud n thir wis duties tae attend tae, so ah made ma excuses n mingled.

Mrs F, as wis her due, goat a wee bit drunk n emotional, n the auld boy wis gallant or opportunistic enough tae take her hame (delete tae taste, ya hoor), nae doot keeping a guid tight hud ay her gaun doon they steps ay the Welfare.

So later ah hud thum back upstairs at mine; me, wee Jenni, the Duke n Neebour Watson, wi the remains ay Kravy in the urn, well, maist ay um. Aye, the open casket wis nivir gaunny play. Snooty wee Lara nivir showed up fir some reason, Jenni reckons she wis oot wi thon Big Monty cunt.

— This is sick, Neebour Watson goes, as ah mix up some ay the boy's ashes wi the coke n speed n rack up the lines oan ma copy ay *Tea for the Tillerman*.

— Sick yir minging furry hole, ah retaliates, savourin the delicious feedback ay a sexy wee giggle fae Jenni. — Kravy wis a free spirit; he wid huv goat aw the New Age significance ay wir ceremony, ya hoor, ah explain tae thum.

— I think it's so beautiful, Jenni says, squeezin ma thigh, n thir's a wee bit ay blood rushin tae the auld hee-haws here.

— I wish I could have done something similar for poor Midnight.

—Ye cannae compare a hoarse wi a human being, the Duke goes.

Wee Jenni shakes her heid emphatically. — We all love beautiful souls, primal souls, whichever vessel they're housed in, she says. Sweet wee chick, but mibbe a wee bit oan the doolally side. Kent ay should huv gone the fill hog n pit thon new Marilyn Manson CD ah boat oan display.

— The boy will live oan in us aw, ah sais, gaun doon oan the first line.

Well, it wis no a bad hit but ah huv tae say thit it might huv been a bit better without Kravy bein in the mix. Awfay rough oan the beak n the lungs. No thit ah wis grudgin the boy, likes.

Ah gies Jenni the second snort, n she fair hoovers it aw up. Eftir, she throws back her heid, wrinkles her beak fir a bit n her eyes water up, but she fights it back.

— Awright? ah asks.

—Yeah . . . it's quite nice, she grins, taking a big breath. — I just find the idea of him being inside us all really exciting! She sneezes, then squeezes ma leg again.

The Neebour n the Duke take thir shoat. Eftir a decent passage ay time, ah say tae thum, — Right, folks, ah'm gaunny huv tae chase yis oot. Aw except you, Jenni, we've goat a wee bit ay private business tae discuss, ah explain, as the lads file despondently oot, nae doot Goth-bound fir last orders.

Once thir oot the road, ah git tae the wardrobe. Ah take oot the styrofoam beer-carrying box. Openin it up, wi look at wir boy again, liberated fae the middle ay some shoodir-high jaggy nettles. Ghostly white, but blue aboot the eyes n lips, like a plasticine model ay ehsel, n startin tae seriously ming now.

— What are we going to do wi him? she gasps.

— Ah've goat an idea. N it's goat tae be done soon. Eh's in bad shape n ah'm sure thir's still some ay they maggot hoors in the neck. Bit first wi hae another line, in tribute.

As she goes doon oan it and gits the buzz, she says, — I haven't done coke for ages; not since Lara and I went up to St Andrews and tried to gatecrash Prince William's graduation ceremony. She had a friend who graduated at the same time. We didn't get near the Prince, though.

— A sensitive laddie, ay that ah've nae doots, ah tell her, but muh eyes nivir leave perr Kravy's deid lamps in that rid-helmeted heid.

20.

FLOORED

Iwake up on Jason's floor. I think it's the next morning. He's lying next to me and we're both fully clothed. So nothing went on. My sinus stings with the speed, cocaine and ash mix, and my throat feels like sandpaper.

I stand up and crouch down over him, kissing his forehead, but he's dead to the world. I go downstairs and head out into the street, just as his dad is coming round the corner, and he looks as sheepish as I feel as we give each other a thin grin of acknowledgement.

I'm suffering badly with this hangover and I know that it's going to get much worse once the cocaine and alcohol still in my system start to wear off. I recall Jason playing some interesting music, the likes of which I've never heard before. I climb into the car, which has been parked outside all night.

As my backside makes contact with the seat I feel wetness on my arse. I've probably been sitting in something. My armpits whiff a little. I should go home, shower and sleep, but I'm restless and excited and I go up to see Lara. When I get to the house, Dr Grant answers, his face lined, lean and tubercular. It's as if the respiratory diseases he diagnoses in the district's former mineworkers have somehow, by a strange osmosis, filtered into his own lungs. You can see why Lara loves to go out and fuck cavemen. How else would she get a reaction from this repressed, stoical figure? Despite the fact that she's 'grown out', as she puts it, of Marilyn Manson, there's still an anger in her that runs deep. Her habits are still the same and they're worse than mine. She's just good at the civilised veneers. Fuck that, I've seen what that shit does. My mother being a case in point.

— Is Lara in? I ask him.

Dr Grant looks through me. This man loathes himself and the world in equal measures. He just nods at the stairs and I go up. I wonder if he can see the sticky wet patch on my bum.

I knock and go right in to her bedroom. Lara's sitting up on the bed reading her magazine and a purple-and-black eye looks out from over the top as she lowers it. — I can't go into Dunfermline today, she says.

— What happened?

— What do you think? she challenges, and then adds cheerfully, — My bastard went psycho on me. I told him it was over. We argued. He wanted, you know, one last time.

I think about that scumbag Klepto, and how far evil trash like that would actually go. — Oh my God! Did he, you know –

— It wasn't rape, far from it, she says, now smirking. — I was quite turned on at the idea. More than him when it came down to it. She shakes her head contemptuously. — He couldn't perform. I was a little too scathing, and well, he didn't take it so good. She now stifles a sniffle, seeming flooded by a rush of angry despair.

— Oh love, I cry and I open my arms and take her in them.

— You're sweet, she says as she breaks off our hug and looks miserably at me. — It's my own fault. I should have known better. He's bad news. So is his friend. You just think, I don't know . . .

I'm almost going to tell her about that horrible Klepto, and I can't help but finish the sentence: — That you can change them?

Lara laughs loudly at me. — Fuck, no. I'm not that stupid, Ms Cahill, she snorts, as I realise that I'll never confide anything of importance to her, ever again. — You just think that they might be a little grateful to spend time with somebody who has an IQ and who doesn't want to be pregnant. I was wrong. Now this fucking bruise won't go down for Hawick. I'll look like some schemie crack whore from Glenrothes!

— It isn't so bad, I tell her, getting out my make-up bag. — Let's see what we can do.

21.

JASON'S MUM

The auld girl's gittin gey meaty: especially roond the airms. She's still goat that stiff blonde hair piled up and lacquered in place n thon foundation thickly caked in layers oan her coupon. She's an awfay short-erse though; ah take thon vertically challenged gene offay her n it's a persistent but disturbin thought that ah wis ripped oot ay her gash ower a quarter ay a century ago. — What the hell huv ye done tae yir airm?

— It's jist bruising, ah explain, n tell her the story about perr Kravy.

She listens in open-moothed silence, eyes bulging oot like she's done a strong line ay coke. — Are ye happy, son? she keeps askin ays. — N ah'm no meanin just aboot perr Allister; ah mean apart fae that. Are ye happy *in general*?

— Aye, too right, Ma, ah tell hur. Then she gies ays that look and goes, — But ur ye *really* happy?

When ah say nowt, she does as she eywis does n blames ma faither. — That man spreads misery like ah spread butter on toast when ah dae the breakfasts here. Wanted a Marxist state which wis bad enough, but eh wanted everybody else tae bring it intae being. He wouldnae git oaf his erse though, no Alan King. It was aw ah could dae tae get him up in time for the bus for the picket line.

— How's this new yin treatin ye then? ah ask hur, even though eh's no that new now; its been fifteen year, longer thin she wis wi the auld boy. But ah still cannae even bear tae say

335

the wee cunt's name. Ah like the fact that even though eh's bigger than me, every hoor prefixes his name wi the term 'wee'. Ah mean, ah git called 'wee man' sometimes, but naebody gies ays that 'Wee Jason' treatment. Ah call it r-e-s-p-e-c-t, ya hoor.

Muh ma looks balefully at ays. Ah suppose yon Bambi moment wis the high-water mark ay wur relationship n yin that wir eywis baith subconsciously strivin but failin tae recreate oan oor very occasional meetings. — Look, Jason, ah'm no sayin that Wee Arnie's perfect; ah mean, whae is, n what relationship is? But he's been here fir me when ah needed um, n she sortay looks doon at her missin tit, no thit ah kin mind ay which yin they loped oaf, n they baith look the same wi that big rid jumper ower thum. Suckled oan they hoors ah wis; in a bizarre wey it makes ays gled thit ah goat ma share before they surgeons did thir deed.

— Listen, Ma, ah need a wee favour.

— Thoat that's how ye might be here, she says tartly, gaun tae her handbag.

The alarm bells tell ays it's time fir Alan Wells meets Davie Hulme in Fife Centrale, as a wee sprint tae yon moral high groond is called fir. — Naw, it's no that, ah goes. — Ah need tae borrow yin ay they big pots fae yir kitchen.

She looks a bit relieved, then guilty, then perplexed. — Yir no plannin oan cookin soup, ur ye? Mind the last disaster whin ye tried tae cook soup? Still, ye wir jist a wee thing then, she goes wistfully. Then she looks up at ays wi interest. — No nestin ur ye? Nae sign ay a girlfriend?

Thinkin ay thon wee Jenni, whae left early this morning eftir 'steyin the night', ah goes, — Well, thir is a wee romance, fledglin ah stress, but, fledglin.

— When dae ah git tae meet her?

— Soon, if ye lend ays a pot, ah tell her. Aye, wee Jenni

went right oot fir the coont last night. Apart fae thon wank wi the cum splatterin across the tight buttocks ay thon stretch black troosers, ah wis the perfect gentleman. Went back oot like a light masel eftir that yin. Heaven through a haze that smoky rid thit it might huv been the other place, ya hoor sor.

So wir doon in yon big kitchen n ah gits a hud ay this big cracker ay a pot thit's hinging up oan the waw, ideal fir ma needs. Ah pits it ower ma heid n it fair rattles.

— Git yir heid oot ay thair, laddie, it's fir food!

— Sorry, jist messin aboot, ah tells her in echo, then pills it oaf.

— What ye wantin wi a big stockpot like that? You openin a soup kitchen fir aw the deadbeats back in Cooden?

How soon they forget. A wee bit ay the sophisticated life in Dunfermline, n thir soon throwin thir loat in wi the bourgeoisie. This toon got airs n graces whin they opened that Costa Coffee. Ah kin jist hear her and the Wee Shite now – thon Wee Spermin Rhino – wi thir M&S cairryer bags under thir airms, makin a pit stoap before loadin up yon hatchback. Aye, thon stage whisper, 'Make mine a large mocca!' Ah'm no risin tae nae fuckin bait here, but. — Ask nae questions n ah'll tell ye nae porkies.

She rolls her eyes and lights up a fag and takes a big drag oan it. — What ur you up tae, laddie?

— Nowt dodgy, n you shouldnae be smokin thaim, no eftir yir cancer.

She shivers at ma use ay the word. — It wis tit Big C, no lung Big C.

— But it's no gaunny help.

She shakes her heid. — Ah reckon ah've hud aw the Big C ah'm gaunny git. The breast thing wis ma ain fault, gaun oan aboot gittin they implants aw the time.

— But ye nivir actually goat nae implants, did ye?

— Naw, but ah *thoat* aboot it, she looks skywards, — n it wis *His* wey ah mindin ays thit ah'd been thinkin aboot frivolous empty things. For that ah gie thanks.

The Wee Shite got her intae God-botherin years ago. — Mair likely it's his wey ay mindin ye that ye bide in Fife, ah tells her, grabbin the pot.

She gies ays a sour pout at that yin, n nods tae the pot. — Well, jist you mind n bring it back!

— Course ah will, Ma.

— N in the same nick that ye took it away in. N if ye want a hat ah'll buy ye a baseball cap, right?

— Aye.

— Mind then. Wee Arnie's a stocktaking demon and Chef's a stickler for cleanliness.

— Nae bother.

She sticks a bin liner roond it fir ays. — How ye fixed for money, son?

— Brassick, ah instinctively goes, although ah'm flush right now wi Cahill's pey-oaf fir special services rendered and the auld 'Egyptian fae Cairo' hittin the mat yisterday. Even sorted masel oot wi a second-hand computer for a hundred quid fae Ideal Computers, next tae the toon hall. An investment awright: new(ish) technology, ya hoor.

She fishes oot her purse, lookin sharply at ays, thon flinty gaze fair mindin me ay the times back in the hoose whin its contents wid miraculously vanish. At the same time ah'd be aw emotional as ah stockpiled loads ay model-aircraft perts nivir tae be assembled. — Take this, son, and she hands ays two twenties.

— Ma, ah goes in gratitude, — ah dinnae ken what tae say, so ah'll keep it short n sweet: awright.

N wi that ah snaffle the auld hoor's guilty pey-oaf n pick up the pot n head back tae the Beath.

22.

NEW HORSE

L ara has taken my advice and come out with me to the leisure
centre. At first she was reluctant, and she refused to remove
her dark glasses till we got there. I half expected her to emerge
from the changing room into the gym with them still on, but
they've been replaced by blobs of foundation. We do a full
session; weights, step class, Stairmaster and the exasperatingly
boring treadmill. It takes ages as she vanishes to apply fresh make-
up before every new activity. Thankfully, she's knackered and has
to stop long before *I* run out of steam, something we're both
silently aware of! Afterwards, we go to the tanning studio. I've
been telling her about my dad going on about this new fucking
horse, and Indigo's moaning about it all the time as well.

We're both a reddish brown, and when we get back to the
leisure centre sit at the coffee bar with still mineral water. Lara
plays with a choc-chip cookie she'll never eat, and she's another
one who won't let the new horse thing go, venturing, —
Indigo has a point. You'll need to get something anyway, as a
companion to her pony. Therefore, it might as well be a horse
you can ride and you like. If you leave it, that spoiled little
bitch will probably end up getting another pony!

I bristle at that comment. Indy *is* a spoiled little bitch, but
she's *our* spoiled little bitch. The terms 'pot' and 'kettle' spring
to mind.

— It's too soon, I say harshly, – and I don't think I want
another horse –

Lara raises her eyebrows in exasperation. — At least come and see what this gelding's like, she argues.

I shake my head and watch a girl I used to go to primary school with struggle with a pushchair, toddler and a tray with two plates of chips and two cans of Coke on it. — You're not listening to me. I want to get out of this place. I've had it.

— It's the same everywhere, Lara says. — You're just feeling a bit down.

— No, I need to get out, I state emphatically. I can't believe her great love affair with this town, county, country all of a sudden. All she usually does is criticise the place and everyone in it. In fact, I learned this all from her. It's how we became friends! Whatever became of Virginia Woolf?

— But you're an excellent jumper. With this new horse —

— No way. You know as well as I do that I'm a shite showjumper. I was just doing it to please my father, and to please you in some way, cause you're my friend. I scrutinise her for a reaction to that statement but her caked and tanned face is Botox immobile. I smile grimly and tell her the truth that I, and everybody around me, needs to hear. — I love horses and I loved Midnight, but I am not, and never have been and never will be, a jumper. And you know why?

I look searchingly at her. She's all ears and I really do believe she expects me to say something like 'because I'm too fat'.

And she's obviously irked when I tell her, — Because I simply don't want to. I love horses, being out with them, riding them, but I'm just not interested in showjumping. I'm not bothered about pushing them or myself to go faster, turn quicker, jump higher. Actually, I don't give a flying fuck, I pompously contend. — In future I'm only doing shit that *I* want to do.

She looks at me in open-mouthed incredulity for a few seconds. I've never seen her look so dumb. When she finds her voice, she moans, — But everybody wants you to do well!

— Fuck everybody. I'm only going to turn into my mother if I don't get of here.

— But you can't leave me here! Lara wails. — *I* can't go. I've got Hawick, then Bedfordshire, then —

— You'll find other horsey friends, Lara. Don't worry about that, I tell her. — It's not like I'll be vanishing off the face of the earth. We'll still be mates, I say and I feel giddy with exhilaration as I realise that I will, soon, actually leave here; that it's gone from being a fantasy to an inevitability and I'm not in the least bit scared about it.

— How do you fancy going out clubbing tonight? Lara says, more needy than I can ever recall her. — Just you and me? In Edinburgh? We can stay over at Sophie's and —

— Nah, I can't, I tell her with great satisfaction, — I'm meeting somebody later.

There is a pout of hurt sadness on her face. How many times, I consider, must I have looked so equally pitiful to her?

23.

TREVLIN

So ah've goat wee Jenni Cahill sittin in the Goth wi me, n it's like wir an item, gaun oot n that. So ah should be chuffed, but ah cannae stoap thinkin ay perr Kravy, the laddie thit came back tae Fife tae look eftir ehs ma n ended up decapitated. Nine years in Spain, tearin like a hoor through Europe, then back in Fife fir yin week, takin a nice and easy bend (wi me oan the back) n the bike jist leaves the fuckin road n that's it; baw oan the slates, game a bogey.

The road must huv been fucked; surely groonds fir a claim ay compo against ma injuries, afore ye even accoont fir the emotional damage incurred through the loss ay ma best buddy. Perr Kravy. Ah'm sittin here wi it aw; the posh bird by ma side, place in the table fitba semis, the money in the poakit, the pint ay black gold in front ay ays, n they two jealous auld celibates the Neebour Watson n the Duke ay Musselbury standin miserably up at yon bar, forced tae contemplate ma success. But in ma ooir ay triumph, thir's nae satisfaction.

Aw ah kin dae is talk aboot the perr laddie. — The Kravy fellay's words wir prophetic, ah tells Jenni. — Once eh says tae ays, 'If ye want tae live a long life keep away fae the blaw n dae plenty trevlin. Otherwise it's far too short.'

— I'd say ironic rather than prophetic, wee Jenni speculates, — with his own life being so short and . . .

— Naw bit, hear ays oot, ah insist. — Aw they years thit eh trevild roond Europe oan thon bike wir marked by the concept ay difference. By new experience, the assimilation ay different sights, smells, sounds. Aw that ingestion ay new lingo, new culture. Burn the different neural canals. That disnae happen if ye git stuck own the blaw in an auld cunt's toon like the Beath. Ye cash in the 'Egyptian' n live fir the weekend, n very soon aw the weekends ur just the same. Eh's awready hud a longer life thin me if ah lived tae be two hundred! Smokin dope n steyin in the same place compresses time. Trevil, n meetin new people, eywis expands it. Ah widnae say it's physics but it's true aw the same. Dae you want tae stey here aw yir puff?

Jenni rolls her eyes. — Certainly not. I've no intention whatsoever of doing that. Do you?

— Naw, bit ah probably will.

She looks a wee bit pit oot by that. — Why?

So ah try tae explain, without seemin too sorry fir masel, thit ah'm jist no like her, or even Kravy. — Cause ah've no been able tae accrue the type ay skills thit might help ays function somewhere different. Ah'm jist a short-ersed wee bampot fae Fife thit cleans oot stables.

— Well, I think you're cute, she says, like she's a wee bit drunk. No used tae black gold or tarry, ah'll wager. Well, no in the quantities we've been daein it ower the last few days. Ma quantities.

— Aye, but in a short-ersed wee bampot fae Fife thit cleans oot stables sort ay wey, ah laugh, then git serious. — But ah'm gaun tae Spain, ah'll tell ye that much. That's fuckin defo n –

— Shh, you talk too much, she says, n ah'm aboot tae take umbridge when she goes, — Kiss me, and her lips brush against mine n then wir snoggin. Ya cunt, it's like ah'm gaunny shoot ma muck thair n then, in ma troosers in the corner ay the Goth!

Whin we back off, ah glimpses across tae see certain parties

343

at the bar tryin tae look everywhaire but wir wee corner. Then Jenni picks up the vibe cause she says tae ays, — I don't suppose we could go back to yours?

N ah croaks oot, — Aye, n ah'm worried aboot bein able tae staund wi this thing in ma troosers – fower n a half inches muh erse – but ah gits tae muh feet. Ah dinnae look acroas tae the bar as we leave the Goth (ah even leave half a pint ay black gold!) but ah'm hopin thit the boys huv clocked every-thing. Jason King, Depertment S, ya hoor: the 'S' bein fir Shaggin!

Wi git intae the hoose n ah pops muh heid intae the front room where the auld boy's watchin the eftirnoon nags on Channel 4, racin pages oan ehs lap. — Dae you never git any tips fae thon stable ye wir attached tae? eh asks, turnin roond tae regard ehs sole offspring (or so ah've been telt).

— Naw . . . no fir a while . . . eh, look, Faither, jist gaun upstairs wi Jenni tae listen tae some sounds.

— Christ, Jason, yir twenty-six years auld, eh scoffs. — Ye dinnae need tae use bairns' euphemisms fir sweepin lum!

Ah'm hopin thit Jenni didnae hear or pick that yin up, but wir up the stair n intae the King boudoir n things ur movin fast. Wir pillin oaf oor clothes n she's goat wee spots on her chist but no the actual tits, if ye ken whit ah mean, n a big mole oan one ay the paps. She's goat that wee rid thong oaf n aw; game as a partridge, this yin, n thir's a hoor ay a sight mair bush thin ah'd speculated aboot; bit ay a surprise, thon. Still mibbe it wis Kravy's ma's shaved blat that pit they thoughts intae muh mind.

Ya hoor, it's a wee bit ay a sensory overload . . .

24.

SNOGGING

I just want to fuck him, I like him and I want him: his skinny light body, his crazy eyes and his barely repressed air of madness. Also, the history with the bitch Lara makes him even more appealing. She confessed that when she was younger she actually wanted to shag him.

But Jason seems a bit weird, like he doesn't want to get undressed, and I'm sitting here in the nude and he's not even made an attempt to take his clothes off. I'm wondering if he finds me too fat, too repulsive, because he's so thin. — Don't you like me? I ask.

— Naw . . . you're gorgeous . . . he pants, open-mouthed.

— Get undressed then, I urge.

— Thir's somethin thit ah want tae show ye first, somethin thit ah did for ye, he says, and he opens this large cupboard which houses a water tank but he reaches down to a boxed-in shelf underneath. He pulls out what looks like a human skull!

Of course . . .

— Alas, poor Kravy, he says, then he lights a candle on a plate and carefully places the skull on top of it. The flame burns through the eyes, sending a yellow glowing light across the room. It looks beautiful; the amazing light is back on in Ally Kravitz's eyes. — It's . . . so . . . lovely, I tell him. And it is.

— Ah hud tae dae it, Jenni. Jason's dark eyes glint in the

candlelight. Yon blue flesh wisnae daein um justice. Eh wis mingin. The maggots . . . it wisnae him. Ah biled they hoors tae death. The skull, but. It hus a kind ay . . . purity.

— It does, Jason. It's what he'd have wanted. I know it. But what did you do with the flesh, brain, eyes . . . all that stuff?

— Took it in a Co-op bag n buried the hoor under the turf behind yin ay the goals at Central Perk, Jason smiles sadly, then falls back on the bed. He kicks off his shoes and pulls down his jeans and shuts his eyes.

I move over to him and pull off his T-shirt in one motion. His body is the colour of milk. He's shivering, trembling, but still just lying there. As the light glows and flickers around us, I suck at his nipples, biting into one until he gives out a sharp yelp of pain and the dark red blood trickles down his chest.

Then I pull off his pants and take his penis in my mouth. It firms up under my touch, and I can feel it expand in my head. It tastes briefly salty but that goes as I work it, tongue on its tip, mouth and hand moving down the shaft. After a bit I think he's going to come so I stop and whisper to him, — I'm the jockey, and I can't make out his gurgled response.

I climb on him and edge him into me. I start to ride him slowly, taking him further in, moving up and down on him in the candlelight from Ally Kravitz's burning dead eyes.

Jason is the most passive boy I've ever been with, although, I suppose, he's only the third I've had full sex with. He lies back muttering deliriously and I ride him until I start to come in small bursts, ending in a demented crescendo. I want to just keel over but Jason holds me up under my armpits (he's deceptively strong and the sinew and muscle strains in his lean body) and then he comes in juddering, eye-popping convulsions, so violently that for a second I worry that he's having some kind of fit. — Ya hoor . . . he gasps.

As I feel his spent prick deflating inside of me and falling out, like a ripe piece of fruit from a tree, I roll off and curl him into me, wrapping his thin frame in my arms. — That was . . . so . . . good, I tell him, as we cuddle together on the single bed.

— Ballingry lass . . . she once said the same thing, he mumbles, drifting off into sleep.

25.

TWELVE INCHES TALL

Ah walk intae thon Goth Tavern, a guid twelve inches tawer in height n jist aboot the same again in the trooser department, ya hoor ye! Ah'm at the bar but no really listenin much tae the Celibate Club ay Neebour Watson, the Duke ay Musselbury n Reggie Comorton cause ah've made a connection wi Auld Erchie the bigamist, whae normally drinks in Jimmie's.

Erchie wis a long-distance lorry driver. Eh hud twa faimlies fir years, yin here in Fife, the other one doon in Hull. Hud tae come clean, whin Kenny, ehs son up here, met this bird oan holiday in Tenerife. They goat it oan, wir drawn tae each other beyond the usual hoaliday romance, so she came up tae see um. Erchie's jaw fair droaped awright whin Kenny brought her hame; turned out it wis ehs daughter fae Hull! Aye, Nadia, her name wis. Sparks fuckin flew awright, but baith wives reasoned thit as eh wis the breedwinner thir wis nae point in grassin the cunt up. So they basically shared um; kept the same arrangement gaun, half the week each. They agreed thit Erchie wis awright fir half the time but any mair wid've been too much.

Erchie's tellin ays about history, it's ehs favourite subject, or 'Scottish History S' as eh calls it. The boy's a fuckin PhD in post-war ridin in Caledonia. — When they hud that Cuban missile crisis the number ay illegitimate births nine months later went through the roof. Bastard bairns everywhaire!

— How come?

Eh coughs n swallays doon what wis comin up, the hoor stickin in ehs gullet like a cat's furbaw. Once ehs eyes stoap waterin eh goes, — Well, they reckoned it wis aw comin tae an end. Wi aw they Yank bases in Scotland, wi wir in pole position fir a tannin fae they Soviet ICBMs. So every fucker went mental. Strangers jist went hame n shagged each other daft. Lassies banged any cunt they could git thir hands oan.

Aye, it came back tae me that fuckin instant; as soon as they fuckin Twin Tooirs went doon ower New York, ah wis right roond tae Lara's wi ma new Slipknot album, six tins ay Rid Stripe n a chicken jalfrezi fae the Shimla. N Cat Stevens n aw, jist as backup. She wis oan fuckin hoalidays in the south ay France, nae doot in the airms ay some garlic-smelling Froggy cunt fill ay insincere fears ay impendin apocalypse!

— Apparently that Lara wis even gaun up tae St Andrews tae stalk thon Prince William, ah'm telling the boys, drawin in Neebour Watson n the Duke tae the fold. Eftir whit Jen's telt ays, it's open season oan yon hoor. — Aye, ah goes oan — she's goat a big fancy fir um. That wid be some foursome right enough, though wir talkin aboot outside the duvet here; nowt against the Windsor boy; a sensitive laddie, ay that uv nae doots, jist dinnae like the idea ay other cock sharin ma kip!

Erchie hus a laugh at that yin, n the Neebour gies a peely-wally smile while the Duke signals up a round ay black gold. Fuckin wonders'll nivir cease!

— Imagine if yon Lara ended up banged up but, Wills takin the responsibility n the ensuin male child becomin heir tae the throne, the Neebour says, — but then an even bigger shock if eh's a wee cunt thit wants tae ride hoarses, aye, but hus innate skills at table fitbaw as well as as penchant fir the tarry!

The Duke guffaws at that yin, n ah hae tae admit, ah'm no above haein a wee chuckle masel.

— Aye, ya hoor, ah sais, — the Kingdom is right; pump in some Fife DNA tae perk up that stagnant auld aristocratic gene pool. Been done in the past. Perr midwife wid fuckin feint when she saw the bastard hud a chin like Dan Dare! Aye, mibbe ay wis too hasty in rulin oot two-a-sides under the duvet!

They aw huv a giggle at that yin n wi bang the glesses ay black gold thegither like in days gone by. But no quite, cause eftir this scoop ah'm gittin picked up by Jenni n wir gaun through tae Kirkcaldy tae thon poetry slam thit she's goat ma name doon fir. Showed hur some ay the stuff ah'd been writin whin ah wis tarried up; cathartic originally, helped ays tae git ower the shock aboot Kravy. She takes a wee sketch at it n says ah've goat talent. Ah'll take that, ya hoor.

Even the auld man's comin roond. Showed um the poems n aw, n eh wis well impressed by some ay the political content in a few ay thum. — Fuck me, eh goes, ehs eyes bulging, — ye do listen tae ays eftir aw!

— Nae fuckin option, huv uh, ah sneers, but it fair made the auld cunt's day. Mine n aw, hus tae be said.

26.

FIFE POETRY SLAM

The half-filled hall is still implausibly smoky. My feet stick to the worn carpet as I pass several trophy-filled cabinets and settle in my seat at the bar. Jason's very nervous. — You'll be fine, I tell him.

His eyes have never left a skinny anaemic-looking guy with black hair, who sits over in the corner. — Aye, but Ackey Shaw's readin the night n aw. Ma debut, n ah'm oan the same bill as ma mentor, ya hoor.

As the MC announces him, Jason stands up and makes his way past the tables to some cheers as he skips confidently onstage up to the mike and adjusts it down to his height. With his mittened hand, he pulls a pair of reading specs from a case in the inside pocket of his overcoat and puts them on. Then he goes back into a small leather case he's been carrying and produces a sheath of pages. — This yin's fir the soccerati, he announces. — It's called: 'John Motson on the Death of Sylvia Plath'.

There is respectful silence. Jason starts to read from the first poem, reciting in an exaggerated English accent:

> — *Sylvia Plath*
> *took an early bath.*
> *Quite remarkable!*

I don't get it myself as I haven't a clue as to who John Motson is. But quite a few people in the crowd laugh. I watch the guy he calls Ackey Shaw, who is nodding in quiet endorsement. A studenty couple at the bar I talk to seem to think that Sylvia Plath would see it as a tribute, so that's good enough for me. Jason's obviously a talented wordsmith and it's evident that he loves the applause. Seeming to grow in stature, he looks over to me and smiles. — Thanks tae Jenni ower thaire for encouraging me baith tae write, but also tae perform.

And he gives me a wee wink, which makes me blush.

I now realise that I was so wrong about him. To think I thought that he was just a sleazy wee pervert. He's not; he's excellent. Even more forceful on his next poem, Jason clears his throat, letting the chatter of the audience subside into a hush, then states with strident pride: — This yin's called 'Eulogy Fir Robin Cook', whae last year, or wis it the year afore that, anywey, whae tragically passed away.

> — *Edinbury's mobbed the day*
> *but awfay circumspect*
> *fir a Scottish statesman droaped doon deid*
> *n it's time tae pey respects*
>
> *Eh did ehs bit fir freedom,*
> *Fir justice n fir truth*
> *No like thon toss in Downing Street,*
> *The yin wi the hoor's mooth*
>
> *Erse-lickin yon Yankee cunt*
> *Oan the issue ay Iraq*
> *And sendin oor lads tae the front*
> *N some widnae come back*
>
> *But Cooky had his principle*
> *His courage, gall and pluck*
> *'Where ur they WMDs then?'*
> *'Thir no thaire — git tae fuck.'*

Auld comrades oan the benches
They were craven, timid swine
Thir erseholes in tight clenches
As they towed the perty line

The track his only respite
Fae the Middle East debate
The Tory press cried him a traitor
Wi thir Arab racial hate

Eh died up in the hills eh loved
Nae doaktirs oan alert
Bit it wis the liars doon in London toon
Thit broke that brave, brave hert.

The crowd really seems to lap that one up, especially Jason's dad, who is at a front-stage table with some of his friends drinking. He claps in a demented manner, whooping and cheering his son. — You is ma niggah! he shouts, pointing at Jason.

Ackey Shaw gets up and graciously says, — Excellent stuff from Cowdenbeath's very own Jason King there, before launching into his own set.

After the event, Jason greets me at the bar, ordering drinks for us both. He opts for whiskies, not his usual tipple. He tells Ackey Shaw, who looks a little bit bemused, — One ay your best lines: whisky n freedom gang thegither, then announces, — *Slainte!*

People are coming over to congratulate him on his performance. His father seems to be holding back, then steps forward. — Ye made me proud up there, son, he says, all watery-eyed.

Jason seems bowled over by this. — Well, ah've no eywis been a source ay that fir ye, Faither.

His dad's eyes widen, and for the first time the father and son look very similar. — What d'ye mean?

— The jockeyin wis a failure. The hingin aboot here oan the dole. The lack ay interest in the political struggle.

His dad shakes his head sorrowfully. — Aw, son, ah'm sorry. Dinnae listen tae the likes ay me. These are different times. You always make ays proud, and he looks over at his friends, — me wi aw ma homies here n aw. Now you git oan through tae Bathgate the morn and git in the final ay that cup.

Jason's face scrunches up in pain, like he's eaten something nasty. — Faither, ah'm thinking ay blowin that yin oot.

— Whit dae ye mean, son?

— Wi reference tae one ay yir ain great literary heroes, Faither, Alan Sillitoe: *The Loneliness ay the Long Distance Runner*, ya hoor.

— A great book, son, his dad acknowledges as he hands me a pint of lager I didn't even see him getting up. — Excellent film n aw; Tom Courtney, ah think ah'm right in sayin.

Jason nods at a settling Guinness, blackening up on the bar. — Aye, bit mind the central thesis ay thon work but, Faither: sometimes ye kin only win by no takin part.

I take a sip at the lager. It's very gassy, but I can't stomach that gut-rot Guinness Jason loves so much.

His father smiles at me, then nods back to Jason in enthusiasm. — Whin the odds are stacked against ye, optin oot ay the system is the only wey. Like the boy in the book that won yon race but refused tae cross the line. The ultimate rebellion, son, n yin muh man 50 Cent understands only too well, he says, and then asks in concern, — What you goat planned?

— Dad, Jenni n me ur thinking ay gaun tae Spain. Fir good, likes. Kravy's got mates ower thair, Jason explains, — n ah've been in touch wi thum . . . on the Net, likes.

— Go for it, son! That's excellent. His father takes a swig of his pint, gulping it back. — Ah wid n aw if ah hud ma

youth, n if ah hud a wee belter like this yin, he smiles at me,
— aye, ah'd be right oaf tae Spain in a flash!

I feel my face igniting in a smile. — Your dad is so sweet,
Jason, I say, and Mr King goes a little coy.

— Ye'll be awright oan yir ain? Jason asks in some concern.

A mischievous glint comes into his father's eye. — Whae
says ah'll be oan muh ain?

— Aye?

His father winks and lets a smile mould his face. I notice
that there's something different about him. It's the burn mark,
it looks faded, but I can see he's just put some cosmetic foundation on it. — Maybe this old niggah got moves too. Watch
this space, but ah'm sayin nae mair except: oot ay adversity wi
can find triumph.

— A sentiment ah hertily endorse, Faither, a sentiment ah
hertily endorse, he says and puts his arm around me and we
have a little snog.

— Enough ay thon! Mr King snaps. — Mind, this is Fife!
Dampen yon ardour n buy yir auld felly a beer. Ah saw that
boy slip ye a double score fir this gig!

— It's my shout, I say, pushing up to the bar and shouting
them up. Before I leave this town I want them all to know
that I'm Jenni Cahill, not Tom Cahill the haulage guy's
daughter!

27.

DEMISE OF AMBROSE

That wis a great yin in Kirkcaldy last night, then ontae that perty in Glenrothes. Wee Jenni liked it n aw; hud plenty joints and even a couple ay lines. Glenrothes isnae Fife, but. They filled the place up wi Weedgies back in the sixties. Three tae fower generations doon the line thir still no assimilated intae the local population. Instead it's real Fifers thit gie it aw yon 'by the way' shite n swan aroond in Auld Firm replica tops. Some social experiments ur doomed tae fail here, like the preservation ay the native rid squirrel fae yon incomin American grey hoors.

Ah also git the wee notion thit Tam's beginnin tae suspect that somethin's cookin wi me n ehs firstborn, cause eh gies ays a call first thing in the morning. So ah huv tae head up early doors. Ah mind ay Jenni no being happy aboot cutting oot early, but she said she hud tae drive her ma tae the city.

Ah lits masel in the hoose wi the spare key Tam gied ays, hopin a might catch Jenni fir a wee grope and snog. But thir's nae cunt hame; she's already gone intae Edinbury shoapin wi her ma n yon wee spoiled Indigo. Thir's a note n a pair ay car keys.

J
Decided to get train. Take car if you want.
J x

So ah borrow her motor, thinkin thit ah'll take the dug doon tae the seaside at Abby-Dabby, cause it's a hoat yin awright, sor. Mair like a summer's day!

The water wisnae even like thon oily pish thit ye normally git in the Forth Estuary, it wis St Andrews-style; cobalt blue and as calm as a well-shagged, wedged-up hoor wi hur purse in her drawers. Tae ma mind then, thir wis nae bother aboot flingin yon bit ay stick in; jist a wee bit driftwid fir the boy tae fetch. Cool doon the pantin beast, likes. Didnae want um gittin aw nippy in yon heat n takin a chunk oot ay some cunt's weddin tackle. Like mine. Aye, ye kin git awa wi murder wi fower n a hawf inches by flingin hawf a dozen Bicardis intae the mix, but three n a hawf n ah'd nivir work again. No in this fuckin coonty any roads!

Aye, Ambrose is gaspin in yon heat. Felt fair sorry fir um, so ah did.

So ah picks up a long, slimy bit ay driftwid n birls n launches the fucker oot as far as ah could. Afore ye could say 'Jim Leishman' the dug's flyin off intae the sea eftir it, bobbin up n doon, that retriever gene still active even eftir three generations, ya hoor ye!

Thing is thit perr auld Ambrose nivir looked back once, even wi me shoutin the bastard's name at the top ay muh voice. Jist that wee heid bobbin away, gaun up n doon like a . . . well, then thir wis nowt.

Ah'm standin oan the beach oan muh Jack Jones n big Tam Cahill the haulage gangster's pride n joy, ehs fightin dug, is oan ehs wey tae bein washed up in an Amsterdam canal!

Ridin ehs daughter, now ah've fuckin drooned the cunt's dug!

Ma heid's birlin. The only thing ah kin think ay is thit nae cunt saw ays come or go; ah hud the run ay the hoose. They'd aw left early tae go tae the city n Tam wis at ehs work, leavin Ambrose tied up in the back gairdin. Ah drives right back tae Cowden n perks Jen's motor. Ah steels masel up fir a performance, then bells Tam at the yard. — Awright, Tam? Whaire's

yon dug ay yours? Naebodie's aboot n ah'm twiddlin ma
thumbs here. Will ah pick um up at the yard, aye?

Thir's a wee silence, then eh goes, — What . . . eh's no here,
eh's tied up at the back. Left um thair this mornin!

— Eh's no thair now. Would the lassies no huv taken um
wi thum tae Edinbury?

— Would they fuck! Fucken do not believe . . . is Jenni
thaire?!

— Naw, they wir aw away by the time ah goat roond; hud
a wee bit ay a late yin last night. Ah couldnae see them takin
the dug so ah assumed you hud um.

Another silence, then, — That wee hoor's done somethin
tae ma Ambrose! She accused me ay fuckin oaf that useless
kerthoarse ah hers n she's done somethin oot ay revenge!

— Ah widnae be jumpin tae they conclusions, neebs, ah say.
Then ah ask, aw uneasy, — Ye dinnae really think she suspects
onything aboot yon hoarse, dae ye?

— Ah dinnae ken that ungrateful wee bitch's state ay mind
. . . n eh stoaps fir a bit, — you fuckin tell *me*, Jason! N it's a
voice ay accusation right enough, ya hoor.

— Hud yir hoarses! What ye oan aboot, Tam?

— Well, yir ridin her, aren't ye?

— Whoa, Tam, hud oan thair, man –

— Dinnae deny it, lover boy. Ah ken; ah've seen her fuckin
diaries, eh sais, then adds, — . . . which wis an accident, as ah
wis lookin for information about what she kent aboot that
hoarse, right?

— Eh, aye, fair enough, Tam, ah goes, but that cunt's oot ay
order. Nae wonder Jenni wants oot ay thon hoose.

— So you say nowt tae her aboot it or the twa sides ay yir
jaw'll nivir meet again!

— Ah widnae say nowt, Tam –

— Mr Big Shagger. Eh makes a fartin noise doon the

phone, then ehs tone changes. — Ye fair surprised me. Ah thoat ah kent everything thit went oan in this toon, he says in disappointment. Then ehs voice goes aw stroppy again. — Ah gie ye a key tae ma hoose n ye repey me by knobbin ma wee fuckin lassie!

— It wisnae like that, Tam, it jist happened, wi jist started seein each other.

— You kin ride whae ye like but ye dinnae fuck wi Tommy Cahill!

— Ah ken that, Tam, fir fuck's sake, ah'd nivir dae that! You've been good tae me n ah appreciate it.

— Gled some cunt does, eh sais, awfay piteously in ma book. Eh might be a bastard but ye git the impression thit eh's quite lonely and a bit sad underneath it aw. No thit somebody like him wid ever admit it, but. — One question. Did you and her touch ma dug?!

— Naw! Ah've grown awfay fond ay Ambrose! Ah'd nivir dae nowt tae um, ah squeal in ootrage. One thing the auld boy taught ays: if yir gaunny lie make it as close tae the truth as possible.

— Right. Hopefully ye ken better.

— Too right ah do, Tam. Ah work for you.

— Aye, and dinnae forget it, the hoor threatens. — Now ah want ye tae find that fuckin dug. Some cunt's taken um n you'd better find oot whae!

— Dinnae worry, Tam, ah'm right oan the case, ah say, then ah git a wee thought. — Jist thinkin, Tam, whae wid it benefit if Ambrose wis oot the wey?

— Jenni!

— Ah hae ma doots, Tam, ah'm sure she'd huv said something tae me, or ah wid huv kent if somethin wis up wi her, ah endeavour tae explain. — Whae else? Mind, Ambrose is a fightin dug . . .

Thir's a long silence.

— That big fuckin scrotum-faced Montgomery cunt . . . he fuckin dies! Eh started knockin oaf that posh wee Lara whin ah wis aboot tae move in . . .

Ah think ay thon Calculon, the robot actor oot ay *Futurama* and his barry catchphrase: 'That's what I wanted you to think.' — Dinnae jump tae conclusions, Tam, lit me investigate, ah tells um, leavin the haulage man seethin oan the end ay the line.

Still, the wee seed's been planted. No even sae much ay a seed as a hoor ay a field.

But ah go back intae toon wi a heavy hert. Ah nivir did tell Jenni whit happened tae Midnight. The hoarse might no huv been much ay a performer but the hoor wis certainly fuckin well hung. So ah suppose thit ah agreed wi Tam Cahill's course ay action, cause ah wis jealous. His big back between her legs, n her gaun, 'Midnight fuckin this, Midnight that,' aw the fuckin time. So ah thoat that wi yon hoarse away the lassie might huv peyed a wee bit mair attention tae me. Worked a fuckin treat n aw! Soon forgoat about perr Midnight whin she hud a new pet!

She's been tryin tae git ays intae aw thon pseudo goth stuff; read Sylvia Plath poems, Anne Sexton, and that kind ay gear. Does nowt fir me, bit ah go along wi it soas tae git her intae ma twin interests ay ridin n Cat Stevens (pre-Islamic incantation, ah stress), ya hoor. One thing she did gie ays thit ah loved: that novel *Reluctant Survivor* whaire the boy brings the bird back tae life by lickin her oot. Ah think she might be tryin tae tell ays somethin here. Thir's yin chapter thit's practically a guide tae cunnilingus, n it's goat a fuckin dog-ear, ya hoor!

Steven hadn't told Josephine, that although he did find her body irresistible, he prided himself on his ability to give good head. Eating pussy was an obsession for him, and he boasted to Tom in the locker room after the workouts or squash games that there was no woman he couldn't get a response from. So, to some extent, she was a vanity project for him. Nobody was more surprised and delighted than he was when his skills proved to be effective.

Ah read oan, thinking aboot aw the stages. Spread the flaps tae isolate the pubic hair n git it oot the road. Save up a loat ay gob n splash it oan, letting it roll fae yir tongue oantae the pussy. Keep the first licks nice n slow, n dinnae be feared tae git a bit vocal tae show thit you're intae it. Test the clit softly fir sensitivity reactions, seein if the burd goes nuts the first time ye hit the spot, then it's game on, or if it might be a longer haul. Dinnae be worried aboot gittin the fingers gaun; thir's a loat doon thair tae play wi!

Ya hoor; ah nivir kent thir wis that much in it!

So ah'm sittin at hame, watchin eftirnoon telly, wi a hard-on. It's yon *Richard n Judy*; husband-n-wife team; aye, ya hoor. Could even see a wee future fir me n Jenni in a similar kind ay role, though mibbe jist Scotland rather thin UK-wide.

Whin ah hears a knock oan the door ah ken it's her. She gies ays a kiss n the wee felly doonstairs is right up oan parade. Ah dinnae ken if it's pressure on the thigh or the light in ma eye, but her ain een fair sparkle wi shaggers glint n wir helpin each other oot ay wur clathes as we head up the stairs tae ma fusty single kip.

Aye, ya hoor, nae wonder she gied ays that fuckin novel!

Eftir the event wir makin post-coital plans fir a sportin double-heider. Wir gaun doon tae Hawick tae see Lara in the event the morn, then back up tae Bathgate that evening fir the semi against the hoat tournament favourite n current holder, Corstorphine's ain Murray Maxwell. They say thit whae wins this yin wins the cup. But Jenni's a wee bit contempla-tive. She's gaun oan aboot Tam n the dug, Ambrose; him n yon other dug fightin. She tells ays how she wis thaire wi Monty n thon chipmunk-toothed hoor fae Dunfermline.

— I hate these bullies. I wish somebody would put them in their place. All of them, n she's lookin at me wi intent.

— Eh aye, nivir liked that Monty or ehs mate, ah goes weakly. But the thoat ay fightin Big Monty. Back at the skill ah'd uv raised they white pair ay hoor's knickers up the figurative flagpole in the gesture ay surrender, afore ye could say Mixu Paatelainen. Big Monty, Wee Jason. The fitba player, the ugly, craggy centre half, versus the wee jockey. It wid be 'attach yir teeth tae ehs baws n hud oan fir dear life', like that nippy wee dug in the news thit saved its owner fae gittin mauled by a bear ower in America. Yir one chance in they circumstances, aye, ya hoor, sor.

Aye, they halcyon days back at Beath High. No that snobby wee Lara n Jenni went thaire but; bussed up tae St Lenny's for Posh, Rich Bairns up in St Andrews. Mind ay thum climbin intae that Mrs Grant's motor in they school uniforms. Ya hoor, ah used tae mind ay it every night!

28.

HAWICK AND BATHGATE

We're heading down to Hawick in the car, following the horsebox driven by Dr and Mrs Grant, and containing Scarlet Jester. Jason was sweet to volunteer to sit in the back and let Lara and myself be up front together, not that I particularly wanted to be beside her.

When we get down to the showgrounds, we head to the tented marquee café to relax for a bit. Well, Jason and I relax. Lara goes up to get some coffee; she's nervy and antsy. Jason's been strolling around, checking things out, letting on to everybody. I saw him introducing himself to an old couple: — Hello, I'm Jason King, he says, flashing a toothy smile and extending a hand that they feel moved to take. I can't stop sniggering at his antics, but perversely, he seems sincere enough. — Goat tae make an effort tae be social, likes, especially wi the auld folks. Thi'll no be oan this planet much longer; aw that accrued wisdom gaun tae waste, he says sadly. Then he looks up at the blackening Borders sky. — Thir's some big cumulus clouds ready tae pish doon oan thir parade. Hope Lara's ready tae gie thon hoarse the ride ay its life, he winks at me.

I nudge him in the ribs and we both get the giggles, then go for a little stroll. I stop and say hello to Angela Fotheringham and Becky Wilson. Becky isn't competing either. — To be honest, she tells me in hushed conspiracy, — it was all getting a bit too much like hard work.

— Tell me about it, I grimace, looking over at oddly nervous Lara, who's networking like her life depended on it.

Becky and I swap numbers on our mobiles: hers is a new one. Jason is watching them depart. — Stop checking out their arses, I chide, — you've got a girlfriend now. At the very least I expect you to be subtle in your leering.

Jason looks sorrowfully at me. — Sorry, doll, force ay habit.

— Well, cut it out. You don't catch me staring at boys' packets, I tell him, 'you don't catch me' being the operative part of the comment.

Poor Jason just says, — Right enough.

He's such an innocent, deep down.

We come across a big, beautiful-looking bull at one of the shows. Its intelligent stare seems to unnerve Jason. — What's up?

He shakes his head. — Yon bull's giein ays some fuckin look awright; sly, evaluatin, wise. Last time ah saw yon expression wis the face oan muh ma's fancy man in yon snobby wee hotel, ya hoor, he nods at the bull. — Ah ken you awright, Wee Arnie, ya cunt, he says. Then he turns to me and adds in conspiracy: — Yon look thit sais 'it might be a good idea tae discourage Jason fae comin roond sae much'. Aye, aye, ah ken.

— Don't be so paranoid, Jay, I laugh, grabbing his bony arse. — When you win at Bathgate tonight, I'll fuck you senseless.

His eyes bulge out so severely it's like a movie computer-generated special effect. — But what if ah git beat?

— Then you can fuck me senseless.

His jaw drops to compound the effect of the eyes.

The buzz goes around that there's free champagne in the sponsors' tent, so Jason and I are right across. We're enjoying the bounty with restraint as I have to run Jay to Bathgate for the tournament, but Lara's appeared and she's still a suffering bag of nerves. I hear her going on to some toff about Princess

Di. — The latest theory is that she was murdered because of her views on Palestine.

Jason's picked this up and looks aghast. —What fuckin views oan Palestine? Git tae fuck! he snaps in irritation like a little terrier. Suddenly it's all very testy between the two of them. The toff takes his leave, and not very discreetly either, swanning off in disdain.

— Thank you, Jason! Lara spits. — Do you have any idea who that was?

— Some hoor, says Jason, mimicking the toff's arrogance and heading off himself, circulating like he's to the manor born.

That's my boy!

It becomes more than apparent that Ms Grant is not pleased with my choice of partner. — I'm trying to get in with the sponsors and you bring *him* along! She squeals as Jason shamelessly steals over to her uncomfortable-looking father and mother, engaging them in conversation. Dr Grant is looking away, while Mrs Grant is struggling with a pained face. What's even more delicious is that I know Jason knows just how much he's winding them up, and is thoroughly enjoying it! So am I.

— But he's fun! I protest, enjoying her discomfort. The bruise has faded a bit, but you can still see it. Of course, I'd previously told her that it was completely invisible.

—You haven't been, you know . . . ? she asks.

I shrug nonchalantly. — I'm saying nothing, Ms Grant.

—You have! With a stable boy! With a failed jockey! A stalker midget, a drug addict . . . how horrible . . . Then she sees I'm not amused. — But Jen, you could do better. You're so pretty.

— Don't worry about me, I tell her. — I'm fine. I'm getting shagged. That was my big problem, remember? Well, problem solved.

— But *Jason* . . . he's stalked us both all over the fucking country! Lara gasps.

I stare into her bruised eye. — Yes, I know that I don't have your immaculate taste in the opposite sex.

— Gosh! Her hand instinctively goes to her eye. — It really doesn't show, does it?

Then a voice booms through the tannoy, telling Lara to go to the paddock and ready Scarlet Jester.

— Maybe a little, I concede, — but it's really nothing to worry about.

She looks wanly at me, touching her face, and heads off in trepidation.

— Good luck, Ms Grant, I shout.

I have to hand it to Lara; she is a good horsewoman, and a gutsy competitor. In spite of everything, she pushes Gillian Scott all the way for the cup. But Gillian is gangly, spotty and an awkward mess out of the saddle. Her teeth are more prominent than those on any horse in the tournament. The television people go through the motions with her, but what they really want to do is talk to the sexy, feisty loser, Lara Grant. No, you can't worry about our Ms Grant. She's a Nazi monolith and some day she'll rule the world. But I have to admit to being concerned when she comes storming up to us, in a real state of agitation. — It's a disaster! she shrieks, tears in her eyes.

— Second to Gillian Scott isn't a disaster, Lara. She's won –

— No! The interviewer made a joke about my black eye! On camera!

— Thi'll edit that oot, surely, Jason says, strutting over, champagne glass in hand. Lara's bottom lip trembles and she breathes heavily through her nostrils like a snorting dragon. I doubt she's ever hated anybody in her life as much as she detests Jay right now, although the TV presenter must come a close second.

366

— Never mind though, second isnae bad, Jason says at that moment, and I have to stifle a chuckle. — Better tae huv fought n loast, that's ma stance. He turns to me with a thoughtful nod, his bottom lip curling out. — Onywey, we'd better be shootin oaf, if yi'll pardon the expression!

—You going to come along to Bathgate with us? I ask Lara.

She bubbles back at me: — I can't go to Bathgate . . . to some table-football game! Don't you see! Everything's ruined! And she runs across to Dr and Mrs Grant, collapsing sobbing into her father's thin chest. Her mother strokes her hair, looking accusingly over at us.

— My God, she's such an emotional retard! How old is she! I find myself squealing with sheer, unbridled delight, and utter shock. — What an outburst! I never, ever knew that she was such a daddy's girl!

We go to take our leave and Jason waves and shouts over at them, — See yis, well! As we head to the car he says to me, — Never liked thon Doaktir Grant. Eh wis ey a right tight hoor wi they lines whin ah worked in the warehoose.

Climbing into the car, we set off for Bathgate. The second glass of champagne was a mistake and I drive slowly and with great deliberation. I keep thinking about something that's been concerning me and I decide to raise it with Jay. — She was only fourteen when you went out with her. Wasn't that a bit dodgy?

Jason does that crazy thing with his eyes, then hunches his shoulders back. — Whin ye pit it like that, mibbe it wis, but ah nivir saw it that wey at the time. Ah mean, thir wis nae hanky-panky, it wis jist a friendship brought aboot fae a mutual love ay the hoarse. Besides, she wis probably mair experienced thin me at the time!

That's the amazing thing about Jason, he actually *boasts* about his celibacy. This marks him out from any other boy I've ever met. — I wouldn't doubt that. I don't mean it as a slur on you, Jay, but Lar's always been a busy slut.

— Aye, but thir wis nowt like that wi us. The odd wee snog, but maistly, as ah sais, it wis the mutual love ay the hoarse thit brought us thegither. The rest wis aw platonic.

I look steadily at him. — She'd have fucked you back then if she thought you were up for it. I turn back to the road, then accelerate past a camper van. — She told me that.

I watch his eyes bulge out a little further as he sits in silence.

We get into Bathgate and on the Whitburn Road stands the rather imposing Victorian building, the Dreadnought Hotel, with its five spires and five bay windows. We go inside and a receptionist ushers us through to the nightclub, which is the venue for the semi-finals.

This guy Maxwell is the tournament favourite, and he's brought a few supporters from Corstorphine with him. They wear maroon Hearts football tops with 'Maxwell No 1' in white letters on the back. However, some of the Fife boys from the Goth pub are over, and Jason's dad is down with some friends. One of them is the old down-and-out minister, who seems to have got himself together a bit. I catch his dad looking at the confident, swaggering Maxwell, and saying to Jason, — Niggah don' fool nobody. I can see the pussy in his eyes.

Jason doesn't respond, just clenches his jaw.

The crowd is fired up. They've obviously been drinking, especially the Fife contingent. I change my mind about the disgraced minister as he slurs something I can't understand at me. At least he doesn't smell too bad, though. Jason is obviously nervous. — Okay? I ask.

— Ya hoor, ah dinnae want tae lit every cunt doon, he says to me, holding out trembling hands.

— It's okay, Jay. Just do your best, I urge.

He nods tersely and heads to the table.

It's a very tight game but Maxwell seems to be at the table more and Jason is finding it hard to keep possession. His jaw is tight in concentration, but he gives out the odd exasperated 'shite' or 'fuck'. It's just a hiss, really, and it's at himself rather than his opponent, but the referee gives him some disapproving glances. Then Maxwell opens the scoring and there's gloom and doom in the air from the Fife camp, as several overweight, bespectacled guys in maroon tops jump around.

Then suddenly, Jason is awarded a penalty, which Maxwell hotly disputes. Jason converts it and we all go crazy, setting up a chant of 'Blue Brazil, Blue Brazil, Blue Brazil . . .', which we're told to cease by the officials. For the first time, I realise, I really feel like I'm part of my town, like I belong. And that's not something to be celebrated; in fact, it's the saddest thing I can think of: enjoying myself with a bunch of strange permanently pre-adolescent misfits at a table-football tournament. And worse: I feel anything *but* sad at the moment.

— Eh's takin a pummellin, but, his friend Colin Watson, or 'Neebour' as they call him, whispers in my ear. But Jason's goalkeeping is inspired and he makes several brilliant saves as Maxwell's shots rain in on his goal. They go into extra time and still can't be separated. It comes down to the penalty shoot-out.

At first I thought I was imagining things, but now I'm sure that Maxwell's been staring at my tits before and during the game. It has to be the case; I'm the only female here. Inspired, I take off my jumper. Underneath it I have the sleeveless T-shirt and the Wonderbra, showing the rack off at its best.

I'm standing behind Jason, who's positioning his keeper for Maxwell's penalty. I can see Maxwell looking from me to the goal and back to me. I look straight at him and slowly lick my lips. He shoots, and Jason saves! I make sure I stay behind

Jason as he converts to Fife cheers at the other end. Already, the poor Corstorphine lad is almost in tears at what he perceives as the injustice of it all. — This is nae wey tae decide a place in the final ay a major tourney, he bleats. — It's a joke!

He scores his next one, but he's still disconsolate, as Jason converts to go two-one up. Maxwell seems to sink into a seething depression and the referee urges him to take his third kick. He thrashes it and it rebounds straight off Jason's keeper and bounces right down the table. After a cheer, there's a ghostly silence, then a roar as Jason coolly converts, punching the air, and it's three-one. Chants of 'so fucking easy' come up from the Beath mob, only to be silenced by officials making disqualification threats. We all shut up.

The referee gets the broken Maxwell to take his fourth. He needs to score his last two and hope that Jason misses his last pair, just in order to force more penalties. Maxwell scores, and it seems to energise him as he forces his face into a twist of defiance. It's now in Jason's hands. This for the game. Our hearts sink as he blasts high and wide.

Maxwell goes up to the table. I'm right over the defending Jason's shoulder, looking at Maxwell. He won't look at me. I wait till he goes to take the flick and I quickly pop out my breast, hoping that the umpire doesn't see. As my cleavage is hastily secured the ball flies wide and the Fife crowd cele- brates, with chants of 'Blue Brazil' filling the air, and Jason is in the final of the Scottish Cup!

He gets up and shakes the hand of the referee, then the disconsolate Maxwell, who reluctantly proffers his mitt, but can't look at him. — A wee announcement, Jason says suddenly, raising his voice, as shushing is urged by the Beath boys, and the crowd falls silent. — Ah'm no gaunny take part in the final ay the Scottish Cup. He shakes his head to incredulous gasps. — It's up tae youse what ye dae, he says, turning to the officials.

— Ah hereby forfeit this game in favour ay ma very gifted opponent, Murray Maxwell. And ah take the opportunity tae wish Murray all the best fir the final.

Maxwell is walking away, shaking his head. A fat guy tries to lift his arm, but he brushes it off.

An official comes up to Jason, obviously panicky. — But this is most irregular, Mr King! We at the East of Scotland Table Football Association —

Jason cuts him off. — Youse at the East ay Scotland Table Fitba Association need tae git laid. It's a bairn's game fir retards. Grow up, ya fuckin tubes!

— Mr King — the official briefly blusters, before walking away, shaking his head in disgust.

Jason's dad grins and looks at his son in admiration. — Ain't cutting no deal with that muthafuckin DA, he shouts. Neebour and the Duke are looking at each other, nodding in agreement. Everybody in the Fife squad laugh, as the Corstorphine lads hang their heads and start to sneak out.

I see Maxwell turning away, shaking off the overtures of another official. — I'm no taking part in this disorganised crap, he spits. — You let people into this tournament who bring it into disrepute! I lost under the association rules! It's over, do you hear?! Over!

In the pub across the road, Jason's dad approaches with some drinks he's got up. — Well done, son.

— Aye, ah held ma bottle in the shoot-oot, Faither.

— Naw, son, thon speech, he says, all misty-eyed, and the disgraced minister nods in approval. — Pure James Connolly or John McLean. A sort ay 'I stand here as the accuser, not as the accused' speech fae the dock, pittin authoritarian structures oan trial in thir ain fuckin coort, he turns to me, raising an eyebrow, — if yis'll pardon my French. Aye, he says to Jason, — ah saw the spirit ay Auld Bob Selkirk and Willie Gallagher

371

thaire, son. The very spirit we need tae turn yon so-cried Kingdom intae the fully-fledged Soviet Socialist People's Republic it wis destined tae become!

Jason looks at the dirty reverend. — It wis Jack here that wis the inspiration, he says, and the drunk ex-man of the cloth beams.

We slam our pint glasses together and toast the forthcoming communist revolution. If my father could see me now!

29.

OLD FOUR-LEGS IS BACK

So ah'm back in the morn and it's a nippy heid wi aw last night's champers n lager: the tipples ay the workin man n wummin. But even though ah'm ridin ehs lassie, thir's nae escaping merkit forces: Tam Cahill still wants a fill shift in the stables. Ah'm graftin like a hoor servicing a trainload ay tweakers, only the odd glad eye fae Jen brightenin up the day.

But we couldnae believe it whin the RSPCA boys showed up at the Cahill hoose n opened the back ay the van. There wis auld Ambrose in a cage, but still wi thon bit ay driftwid in ehs mooth! Eh widnae lit it go!

Evidently the daft mutt jist kept swimmin, driftwid wedged intae they jaws like a hoor's haund intae yir pocket, n the current fae the tidal Firth took um as far as Leith whaire eh washed up. The polis n the authorities wur alerted by a lone angler whae saw um paddlin, cream-crackered, intae Newhaven harbour.

So Tam Cahill's gaun, — That's him! That's muh boy! N they opens the cage n the dug ignores um, jumps oot n bounds ower tae me droapin the bit ay driftwid at ma feet.

Ah bends ower n pats the laddie's heid. — There's a boy, there's a boy, ah goes n looks up at the rest ay thum.

— He never let thon bit ay wid oot ehs sight, even when he was eating, one RSPCA man, a boy wi a military tash, goes. — Woe betide ye if ye tried tae take it oaf him!

— Aye, ah looks roond nervously, — ah used tae chuck um things tae fetch.

Tam disnae notice but, eh jist goes doon n leads up the dug.

The other RSPCA boy, a clean-shaven hoor, goes tae Tam, — Those scars on his face and body, sir, how did he come by these?

— Mauled by Rottweilers, Tam tells them sadly, and this cunt is yin plausible hoor, ah'll gies um that. — Two ay thum set upon him in Dunfermline Glen; the mess they made ay him. Eh turns tae the dug as if lookin fir backup, — Thought wi wir gaunny lose ye . . . again, ya wee rascal! Aye, they fair made a mess ay um, eh, boy? eh sais sadly, then turns tae the uniformed men. — They pit thum doon, of course. It wisnae the dugs' fault; ah blame the owners.

The clean-shaven RSPCA boy disnae look impressed, mind you.

Tam seems tae recognise this and changes tack, gaun intae ehs wallet. — Right, chaps, how much is it ah owe yis?

Clean-Shaven shakes ehs heid. — It's all part of the service.

— Then it's an excellent service, neebs, Tam says, — but what aboot a wee drink oan me? Ah really cannae thank yis enough for finding him and bringing him back tae ays.

Clean-Shaven looks at ehs mate Tashy for a second. The hoor looks like some cunt's rammed a white-hoat poker up ehs erse. — Thank you, sir, but there's no need. However, if you want to make a donation to the RSPCA, that would be most welcome.

— Coont ays in, Tam beams in contentment.

— Unfortunately, we can't take cash here, Clean-Shaven says, — but we do have forms for you to complete.

— Right . . . Tam says deflatedly, cause the cunt kens that ehs been huckled!

Tashy goes back intae the car and comes oot wi a set ay

forms which Tam fills in, ehs jaw droapin a wee bit, then the boys take thum n jump back intae the motor n speed oaf.

Once thir oot ay sight Tam boots the dug in the side n perr Ambrose lits oot a sad yelp, n cowers away. — See what you're costing me, ya cunt! Fuckin twelve quid per month on direct debit! He wellies the perr boy again n muh hert rises tae muh mooth.

Jenni jumps across in front ay um. — Fucking leave him! *You* did that to his face, at the dogfight! I know because I was there!

She picks up Ambrose's leash. Tam's just standin thaire, glaring daggers at me.

— What? ah goes, in appeal. — Ah didnae take her. Ah've no been tae any dugfight in ma puff!

— Let's get away from this psychopath, Jenni shrieks and pills Ambrose doon the path n ah look back at Tam, shrug n follay.

— Whair ur you gaun, lover boy? You've goat work tae dae!

— Sorry, Tam, ah'm wi Jenni, ah say, and ah feel a bit bad cause it's goat tae be said that Tam's treated me awright.

— Fuck off then! Pair ay yis! See how long ye last without me peyin for everything! Fuckin parasites, the lot ay yis! N eh turns n heads back intae the hoose.

Jenni's takin Ambrose tae the car n ah'm followin. It hus tae be said thit ah'm happy tae get in as ah dinnae fancy stickin roond here wi him in that mood. Naw, sor, ya hoor. Jenni starts up the motor, n pulls oot ay the drive. Whin wi hits the road she says, — He's an animal. I have to get out of this place now. We have to take Ambrose with us or he'll go the same way as Midnight!

— Aye . . . lit's git back tae mine. Ah'll say goodbye tae ma faither. Tell um wir away. Tae Spain!

— I can't fucking wait, Jenni hisses, then breks intae a big smile. — Oh Jase, it'll be so fucking excellent!

We drive intae the toon for a bit, stoapin at the offie fir a wee boatil ay champers tae celebrate. Headin back oot ontae the street, wee Jack Anstruther's there, lookin a bit pished, but definitely smarter in ehs appearance. Showin ehs face in the Goth a lot, by aw accounts. — Awright, Jack? Mind ay Jenni?

— I certainly do, eh smiles, n lifts her mitt fir a kiss oan the back ay it. Fair play tae her, she manages tae maintain a smile. A lassie pushin a pram passes ays, n Jenni lits oantae her n thir soon bletherin. Just then, the Neebour Watson comes intae view, carryin what looks like a box ay tools.

— Awright, Neebour? Moonlightin?

— Jack, Jase, eh goes. Then eh moves in closer. — Ask nae questions n ah'll tell yis nae lies, ya hoors.

Ah asks Jack in a low voice, — Ah nivir goat the real story as tae how the Kirk gied ye yir marching orders. It wis hoorin, right enough?

Jack shakes ehs heid in disgust. — Despite ma detailed citations ay scripture that made ridin hoors acceptable, it fell oan deef ears in George Street.

The Neebour looks outraged at this. — But no in the church, durin the Sabbath, in front ay the congregation!

Ah laughs loudly, noddin ower tae Jenni and the bird, who ur startled. Jakey resolutely shakes ehs heid at the Neebour. — Ah'd peyed fir twenty-fower ooirs n tweenty-fower ooirs ay wis gaunny git. Ah couldnae help it if yon snooty Elders came in early wi thir fuckin wives tae arrange flooirs n caught ays wi the bird in midcowp across the altar. Tell ye whit, but, Neebour, Jason, eh sais tae ays, ehs wee face gaun aw lecherous leprecaun. — It wis worth it. The best ride ah hud, n the lassie, she even said the same hursel. Nice young lassie; Ballingry, if ma memory serves ays right.

Ah jist aboot felt thon boatil ay champagne ah wis haudin slip through ma fingers. Ah made ma apologies n goat Jen, n wi piled back intae the motor.

Whin we git back thir's nae sign ay muh faither, but thir's a note oan the kitchen table, written oan a Ladbrokes' bettin slip.

Miners' Welfare at eight the night, a surprise party. Got some news.

— What the fuck's gaun oan here?
— I don't know, but we have to go to the party, Jenni says. — We'll take the champagne. Then we get out of here, just driving through the night . . . on the motorbike.

Ah dinnae really like the sound ay that. Temptin fate big time, especially eftir Kravy. Dinnae want tae be seen as an unromantic shitein cunt, but. — Eh . . . what aboot Ambrose?

— I know somebody who'll look after him. We can send for him later. I want to get out of this place on Kravy's bike. Her wee lamps light up like a Kelty hoor thit's goat a Christmas bonus. — It would be so symbolic, don't you think? It's what he'd want, I'm sure of that!

How the fuck does she ken what eh'd want? She nivir even spoke tae the boy. Still, ah'm no arguing; she's the one wi the tits n fanny, n it'll be a long time afore ah'm satiated enough tae turn ma nose up at thon currency! Ah'd defo rather go by the fuckin motor masel, but it isnae the time tae discuss the issue. Ah'd been hopin, as should uv happened, thit the bike wid uv been written oaf, but the fucker hud an even mair miraculous escape thin me. Wi pit the champers in the fridge n leaves Ambrose doonstairs n head up tae ma scratcher fir a bit ay recreation. It takes a bit ay pleadin, but eventually Jenni lits ays go oan toap, eftir the fourth go.

Ah've worked oot thit if ah achieve five orgasms a day till ah'm thirty ah'll huv hud a roughly average sex life. Cannae make number five though, that wid require chemical assistance, cause ah fair shoot ma load ay gravity-assisted spunk intae her. That's whit gaun oan top does fir ye!

Sleep hits ays like a sledgehammer. Ma last thought as ah drift under: Ballingry? Whaire the fuck's that!

Whin ah come to, thir's still nae sign ay ma faither n it's dark outside. My eyes are blurred wi too much sex-sleep, that comatose state when yir plunged right doon intae deep sleep n come up quickly, like a diver thit gits the bends. Ah kin make oot the digital crystal display oan the cloak:

8:57

— Wake up, Jen, ah shout in panic, — we've goat tae be up the Welfare!

She rolls ower. — For fuck's sake, Jason, give me five minutes to revive!

But ah gits right up and whips oan the keks, strides n then the rest ay the clathes. Fair play tae her, she follays suit. Ah'm watchin her gittin dressed n it turns ays oan that much ah feel the wee fellay risin again, but ah decide tae hit the bog n gie they choppers a brush tae git rid ay the scum ay sleep.

Ah cannae believe ma eyes whin wi git up the Welfare, Ambrose oan the leash. The place is mobbed n thir's a big banner up, a sheet wi words in black paint which spell:

CONGRATULATIONS FRANCES AND ALAN

Aw ah kin think is thit one's the auld man's name n the other's the name ay Kravy's ma! Muh freaky speculations git confirmed whin she waltzes ower drunk, n flashes a ring oan her engagement finger. The auld cunt's been oan that bus tae Dunfy visitin HM Samuel, the hoor!

— Spur ay the moment, homes, the auld boy says a wee bit coyly, his airm roond Kravy's ma. — Thir hud ey been a spark, but we wir eywis baith involved. Then ah stoaped leavin the crib . . . the auld boy involuntarily touches his foundation-poodired puss.

— Thoat this stallion had broken ootay the stable n taken the high road, Kravy's ma, Frances ah'll need tae start callin the hoor, goes. — It wis only whin Ally came back, n she smiles through hur tears, — thit eh telt me thit yir faither wis still in toon!

Ehs mates hud a whip-roond, aw the auld miners, n pit oan a rare spread; aw different sannies, sausage rolls n a karaoke wi tons ay booze. Ah cracks open a can ay lager, n Jenni does the same. — This is great, she sais, — my family would never do anything like this!

Ah dinnae think she kens her auld boy aw that well. Big Tam wis never shy aboot pittin ehs hand in ehs poakit, n eh's no bad company oan a night oot. That wis a guid yin at Starkers, ah'll gie the hoor that.

A nice buffet, but, ya hoor. As a swect-tooth, ah'm fair taken by the big Black Forest gateau, so ah cuts masel a piece ay thon action. Ah pick up a fork n lift a wee stodgy chunk ay nirvana intae ma gob. Jenni smiles at ays. — I need to pee, she says, risin and headin fir the bogs as ah clock that erse feelin like ah'm in Eden.

Jist then a viper enters paradise. That big cunt Monty comes in n looks aroond. The punters that notice him are a bit wary, but maist ur jist absorbed in ma auld man's mate Alec's rendition ay 'The Green Green Grass of Home'. Big Monty comes up tae me, n bends doon, stickin ehs face in ma ear. — Hear you've been makin insinuations aboot dugs, eh sais, ehs breath stinkin ay something. — Lit's step outside, the hoor threatens softly, — or I bring some ay the boys in. It wid be a shame tae see this happy occasion git ruined, eh smiles, lookin doon at perr Ambrose in disgust, whae's under the table, chowin oan some quiche.

Ah cannae really say that much, as ah've goat a bit ay gateau in ma mooth. Ah forces it doon n turns tae the Duke whae husnae heard what he said but whae looks awfay unhappy. — Jist sortin something oot, ah explain wi a wink. — it's aw cool, ah'll be back in a minute.

N ah gits up n the big cunt n me baith start walkin tae the door, mair like wi were best mates thin gunfighters.

The funny thing is thit ah realise that ah dinnae feel scared at aw. Ah'm jist ready tae take a slap, n that's aw it wid be here, wi aw they cunts around; mibbe a couple ay digs. Ah'll go doon, listen tae the hollow threats n thir honour will be restored n the perty willnae be disrupted.

Whin ah gits outside ah see that Pars cunt Klepto's thaire n aw. The hert's flutterin a wee bit now. A big cunt like Monty'll jist gie a wee cunt like me a couple ay wee digs. Eftir aw, honour will only be compromised by a sustained liberty-takin dwarf massacre. A vicious wee bastard like Klepto though, that hoor will go slutty oan ye. Ah actually feel masel shrinkin fae him, movin *taewards* Big Monty like eh wis ma protector, hopin eh unloads first tae pit ays oot ma misery. Eh susses muh game, steppin back, littin that Klepto cunt take ower. — Ye obviously didnae git the message, jockey, you n that Chinky mate ay yours, the hoor sneers, n eh pushes ays in the chist, workin up the boatil tae dae something mair. Ah takes a step back, jist as Richey the Assaultee comes oot the Welfare tae stand by ma side.

— Whae the fuck ur you? Monty asks incredulously.

Richey goes, — Look, this is a very good friend of mine, n ah hear Monty laugh behind ays.

Ah'm aboot tae tell the daft hoor that ah've everything worked oot and that ehs blowin it aw n eh should go inside, when Klepto says tae Richey, — What the fuck ur you sayin? Eh? Eh?

But the daft cunt stands ehs groond. — Ah'm jist sayin thit this is a good friend ay mines. I think we all need to calm doon here, eh sais, straight oot that ScotRail staff trainin manual, the chapter oan diffusin violence, written by so-called behavioural experts whae've never faced a radge doon in thir puff.

Of course, it disnae impress the Klepto fellay. — What . . . ? eh gasps in outrage, like Richey hud accused um ay shaggin ehs kid brother.

Daft hoor thit Richey is, eh's still puffed up, rooted tae the spot. — Look, mate –

— Ah'll fuckin mate ye! Klepto roars, n eh rams ehs nut intae that ginger puss. N as Richey faws tae the groond ah'm sure thir's a big smile playin acroas ehs lips.

— Whae's next? Klepto says in excited satisfaction, lookin right at me. — You want some then, ya cunt? Eh?

Ah glances roond at Big Monty, almost in appeal, then at perr Richey, lying spreadeagled. — Nup, ah goes.

This sort ay stops Klepto in ehs tracks. Eh disnae really ken what tae say fir a bit, so eh opts fir, — Shitein cunt!

— Sorry, mate, ah'm no much ay a fighter, ah explain, stickin ma mitts intae ma jaykit poakit, soas eh kin see ah'm no aboot tae swing. Ah feels something blunt and metallic in thaire. It's yon fork. Ah dinnae even mind ay slippin it in thaire. Probably no very sherp, but.

— Whaire's yir posh wee burd then? She no here tae look eftir ye? eh goes, pushin ays in the chest. — Wee hing-oot wis –

Blunt or no, eh shouldnae be giein it loads tae a tooled

man, n ah whip the fork oot n ram intae ehs puss. N fuck me, it's no *that* blunt, like a silver bullet oan a vampire, ya hoor! It's stickin oot the side ay ehs face, embedded in ehs imitation Fife cheek. Ah backs away, but ehs paralysed wi the shock. Whin the hoor finds ehs tongue, it's like a bairn greetin, — Eh chibbed ays! Eh fahkin chibbed ays!

— It wis jist a fork, ah protest, stepping back. Ah looks at Monty whae's jist standin thaire. — Ah telt um that ah cannae fight. What else am ah meant tae dae? ah appeal again.

Monty's aboot tae drop-kick ays when thir's a cry fae across the road n a healthy mob ay the local Young Team led by yon big Craig, wi some lassies in tow, aw come chargin ower. — That's the big cunt, Soakin Wi Rain points at Monty. — Gied ays a bairn n did a runner! The CSA's gittin tae ken you're in Dunfermline, son! she screeches.

Monty snarls something n slaps Soakin, whae owerdramatically faws tae the groond bawlin hur eyes oot. Craig fae the Young Team shouts, — That's ma fuckin bairn she's cairryin! n leathers Monty, whae gits intae him, but the Young Team swarm in, n the Dunfy boys are drowning in a sea ay Burberry. Ambrose steps oot the doors ay the Welfare wi Jenni, n ehs goat that 'dinnae look at me, ah might be maistly pit bull, but ma soul's pure retriever' expression. Ah'm wonderin if thir's some sort ay command wi kin use tae activate the boy, but the Young Team huv goat it aw in hand n Dunfy take a bit ay a splatterin, or the stragglers dae, cause the rest ay the cunts ur oan thir toes, heading back at speed taewards thir scabby toon. The Young Team gie chase but let it go, preferin tae panel the slowcoaches and the wounded. A mature mob thuv bested, quite a result fir thum, n fir me n aw! Monty's got away, but yon Klepto's taken a bad yin n ehs left groanin at the boatum ay the Welfare steps.

Jenni's now flanked by the Neebour n the Duke, whae

fair fly oot the doors ay the Welfare. — What's going on? she asks, then she sees Klepto takin a fair skelpin fae two young boys at the boatum ay the steps. Ah catch something skite through the air and ah realise that the fork's been punched *ootay* ehs puss! She's right doon, n she pushes past the boys n fair boots the buck-toothed cunt right in the chops! Ya cunt, muh erse fair tightens, nivir mind his. Mental note made: no tae mess. Standin ower um, she shouts, — Ma dad's Tam Cahill. We know where you live and you are fucking dead!

The boot goes in again. Ah gits doon n pills her oaf um. — Steady, Jen, ah goes, pickin up the bloodied fork fae the groond. Eh looks up at us, as if beggin fir mercy. The Young Team boys stand ower um, open-moothed, waitin fir the signal tae indulge in mair pavement opera. — Ye'd better git doon the fuckin road, pal, ah tells um, mercy bein an underrated quality in this world.

The cunt staggers tae ehs feet, wobbling doon the street like a new-born calf, tae the laughter n cheers ay every cunt. The mobile-phone cameras uv been trained oan um fir some time, documentin the proceedins wi cauld insect eyes; a global media democracy where nae cunt hus a private life n nae cunt escapes humiliation. The only bone ay contention is the size ay the audience tae witness it.

Big Craig shouts in triumph, — The Cowdenbeath Casual Firm came ay age the night! Dunfy pricks! Let's git this posted up for they Methil wankers tae think aboot next Saturday!

As they congratulate each other, Craig goes, — Kent you wir the man, Jase! eh sais, giein ays a big hug. — Stuck the cunt wi a fork! Right in ehs Dunfy chops!

— I saw the blood, it was spurting from his face like a fountain, Jenni says admiringly, n ah feel like the fuckin King ay Fife awright. Whaever said that violence was shite has never been in that satisfyin position ay vanquishin a bad cunt ay an adversary.

— This is the fuckin man! Craig shouts again, n some wee jailbait neds gie ays pats oan the back.

— Thanks, boys, ah say. — Aye, ah think ye cawed it right, big man, ah tells Craig. — Wi fair witnessed the birth ay a formidable wee mob the night.

— Whaire wir the auld team? Inside wi thir beer n sannies! Craig laughs, lookin at Neebour n the Duke, whae've goat the guid sense tae smile n take it aw in jest.

Aye, thir's cackles aw roond, so ah decide tae chance ma luck. — A wee question, ah whispers tae the wee big cunt. — Did youse buckle thon sign at the Perth Road? That 'REDUCE SPEED NOW' hoor?

Craig looks at ays wi ehs mooth open, thinking fir a bit, then ehs eyes come intae slow focus. — Aye. That wis us. How?

— Jist wondered, bro, ah say, slappin the big wee cunt oan the back. — Thanks again fir the backup, likes.

— Nae problem. We Beath boys huv tae stick thegither, Craig says, in a passionate address tae the rest ay the Young Team, then adds, — CCF!

— Fife Central, ya hoor, ah nods.

— That's right . . . Ah hear a semi-breathless groan n turn tae see thit perr Richey's goat tae ehs feet.

A fist tae the side ay ays coupon followed by a boot in the kidneys shuts him up. — Git fucked, ya tube, a hard-faced wee Young Team boy says.

Richey staggers oaf doon the road, groaning in agonised ecstasy. — See ye later . . . Jason . . . eh gasps.

— Is that your mate? Craig nods. — Cunt's eywis gittin wide wi us oan the fuckin train . . . Anyway, see ye, Jase, Craig says, gesturin tae ehs posse tae head oaf. We see a stunned Klepto still haudin ehs face as eh staggers doon the road. Ehs powerless as a wide wee cunt ay aboot twelve runs eftir um n boots um up the erse, tae the laughter ay the mob, whaire still filmin proceedins wi thir phones.

— Whaire ye gaun! Soakin Wi Rain shouts eftir the departin Craig.

— Ah'll phone ye! eh sais, hudin up ays mobile, then laughin as eh retreats, exchanging play kung fu kicks n a big laugh wi one ay ehs mates whae made some comment. Soakin Wi Rain turns tae these other two lassies, urgin thum tae follay the Young Team. Thir fair takin thir time respondin tae the lassie's request, but.

Ah well, that's young cunts fir ye. They dae what they dae; 80 per cent ay thum'll grow oot it, the other 20, well, that's why yuv goat prisons n cemeteries n drug overdoses. Ah wis thinking, anwey, thit Kravy wid huv bit the dust if eh'd hit the unbent sign, perhaps no quite as spectacularly, mind you.

So that night, n it's been an exhaustin yin, n it's good tae git tae kip eftir sayin goodbye tae ma Fife buddies. Thought the Neebour n the Duke wir pretty graceful aboot it aw, mair so thin Reg Comorton, whae skulked away doon the street. The auld man didnae seem too bothered, but ye could tell thit aw eh wis thinking aboot wis gittin Frances back hame n road-testin yon new placky hip ay hers. A win-win situ fir sure; if it doesnae stand the punishment, then it's surely grounds fir a big compo claim against the NHS. But eh's left us the hoose, n wi git in, too shagged oot fir any ridin, passin oot in the bed.

It's a murky dirty morning n wir oan the back ay the bike, ridin oot ay toon, hurtling doon a road, jist passin the spot where Kravy went oaf the bike. N ah feel free, cause the speed doesnae worry me, ah'm drivin us oot ay here n ay kin feel Jenni hudin oantae ma waist but as soon as ah appreciate the sensation wir no longer linked or even oan the bike cause wir fawin through blackness, hurtlin through space . . .

30.

TRIP

I elbow Jason in the side. He wakes up with a start. — We're in the motor, he gasps in a happy relief. How he can sleep through Marilyn Manson blasting out 'This is the New Shit' on the car stereo is beyond me.

I rub his head, tousling his hair. — You don't say. Where else did you think we were?

— I had a terrible dream . . . it wis awfay . . .

— I heard you mumbling in your sleep. C'mon, Jay, how do you expect me to stay awake and drive when you keep dropping off? I moan, looking quickly back to a drooling Ambrose. — Just as well I've got you here, isn't it, boy?

Poor dear doesn't know he's going to be banged up in quarantine for four months. Jason catches him sniffing at a 'Northern Soul – Keep the Faith' holdall on the back seat. He leans over and pulls it onto his lap. — Fuck off, Ambrose, ya cunt, he shakes his head, — yir no gittin that, ya hoor ye. He unzips it and looks again at Kravy's yellow-white skull.

— Keep that zipped up, I urge him, — it's a bad habit to get into, looking at it all the time.

He quickly complies, nodding and fixing me with those big, stary eyes. — Aye. Right enough, he stretches out and yawns. — Tell ye what but, ah'm gled thit Neebour Watson wanted tae buy yon bike.

— Yes, it was good to be able to offer your dad and Mrs Kravitz the money.

— Aye, n it wis even nicer ay thaime only tae take half!

— Maybe we should treat ourselves to a sleeping berth on that ferry, I squeeze his leg. — I think that we're due a wee bit of decadence.

I watch his eyes extend, almost to the point that you feel they're going to fall out of his head, like the robot in *Futurama*. — Aye, right enough, ya hoor ye. Adventures oan the high sea, goat tae be hud. Take turns tae play cabin boy n captain! Aye, oan yon Pompey tae Cherbourg ferry! He turns round to the dog. — Auld Ambrose here kin git intae the gender-bendin or species-bendin spirit ay things by playin the ship's cat, eh, auld felly, he says, rubbing a panting, excited Ambrose's scarred, slavering chops.

That crazy boy just cracks me up.

31.

SPANISH POSTSCRIPT

Ya hoor, Kravy wisnae half right aboot Spain. Ah fuckin well love it. Eh wis also right aboot the bird fae Setubal's prediliction fir threesomes n aw; first thing ah did wis insist tae Jenni thit wi looked her up. Unfortunately, she nivir shared the enthusiasm; so that yin wis snookered. Cannae moan but, life isnae sae bad.

Wi goat a joab in they stables. Jenni loves it and ah think ah might finally be gittin used tae hoarses. Nae bikes fir me, but, that's a definite non-starter. Spanish doaktirs'll amputate yir leg if yuv goat an itch oan it. Ah've kept Kravy's skull. Fir a while ah wis stuck as what tae dae wi it. Ah tried tae bury it in wur wee patio gairden but Ambrose kept diggin it up. It now sits in the bathroom. See um every morning; whin ah dae a crap, take a shower, or brush the choppers. It's only a piece ay auld bone, but ah sometimes think thit it smiles a bit mare broadly thin before. That's probably jist me, but.

Ah still think ay masel as the King ay Fife, but ah'm a king in exile, voluntary exile, n ah'm in nae hurry tae git back. Ye kin caw it the Kingdom ay Fife if ye like; ah prefer tae cry it the Fiefdom ay King, ya hoor, sor!

AFTERWORD

When you write about places such as Cowdenbeath, and you come from a physically wee (but spiritually vast) country like Scotland, you have the responsibility to emphasise that this is not meant to depict the 'real' place, but rather the 'Cowdenbeath' of my imagination at the particular time of writing. Any resemblance to 'real' persons is coincidental and purely unintentional. Obviously, the same goes for Arizona, Fuertaventura, Nevada, Montana, Montrose, Mars or wherever these stories are set.

Big thanks to Beth for her unfailing help, advice and love. Thanks to Robin, Katherine, Sue and Laura at Random House for their continued indulgence of me. Mark Cousins and Don De Grazia were kind enough to read some of these stories and give valued feedback. My screenwriting partner Dean Cavanagh was very generous in providing me with the space to complete these stories, at a period when demands on our time were particularly high. I'm fortunate in that if I listed my friends, family and colleagues who have provided me with all sorts of support, it would add considerably to the length of this book. I hope you know who you are and that I wish good things on you.